Self Healing

Self Healing

CP Arora

RUPA

First published in 2012 by
Rupa Publications India Pvt. Ltd.
7/16, Ansari Road, Daryaganj,
New Delhi 110 002

Sales Centres:

Allahabad Bengaluru Chennai
Hyderabad Jaipur Kathmandu
Kolkata Mumbai

10 9 8 7 6 5 4 3 2 1

Printed in India by
Repro Knowledgecast Limited, Thane

To All Those Who Have Resolved
To Be Full Of Life Energy,
Thankful For Health,
And For Long Life

He, who has health, has hope;
And he, who has hope, has everything.

Let us enjoy
The divinely ordained term of our life
With firm limbs and healthy body
A full satisfaction of mind
In the service of the Supreme Lord.

O Lord, the sustainer of the Universe,
Keep us away from disease.

– Rigveda

Contents

Preface

When meditating over a disease,
I never think of finding a remedy for it,
But instead, a means of preventing it.
— Louis Pasteur

Plato held that the most skillful physician, rather than being a model of good health, is one who has suffered from all sorts of illnesses.

I do not claim any authority on the subject, nor do I consider myself competent to write a book of this kind. The only claim to eligibility in undertaking such a venture has been the fact that I have had numerous health problems myself, right from birth.

Illnesses are divine messengers. They bring experiences and knowledge we could not have achieved otherwise. In the process of researching and trying out various remedies, sometimes in the course of helping others to heal, I discovered various important aspects of health and happiness for the body, mind and spirit.

I consider it my duty to bring this to every man and woman to enable them to live a long life, free of ailments and suffering. The readers are advised not to follow the recommendations blindly, but to practise discretion and draw their own self-healing plans.

It is a comprehensive book, and I have tried to cover all aspects related to food, nutrition, lifestyle and other areas which can affect our physical, mental and spiritual well-being. It is written in English, but Hindi/Indian names (of herbs, spices, etc.) have been used liberally with which the Indian reader is generally conversant.

I sincerely hope that the reader is able to benefit from this book.

CP ARORA

Section 1

FOOD

1
Right Choice

The art of self healing is the art of loving and cherishing one's own self, body, mind, and soul – all together. God, the Supreme Soul, pervades all through. You are a part of God. Consider this body as your temple, and the mind as its priest. True health aims at a harmonious state of your body, mind, and soul. That means providing nutrition for the body, mind, and the soul, by means of right food, right exercise, right thought, right profession and right resolve.

1.1 NUTRIENTS AND THEIR SOURCES

Food provides the necessary nutrients to nourish the body live a life of 100 years or more. According to the type of nutrition they provide, food items fall into different categories – proteins, carbohydrates, fats, vitamins, minerals, fibre and water. While proteins, carbohydrates and fats produce the necessary energy (calories) for the body, others are essential for maintaining good health. Food also provides other dietary compounds such as enzymes and antioxidants. Sources for these nutrients may be put in the categories of grains and cereals, legumes and pulses, vegetables, fruits, milk, nuts, seeds and oils, herbs and spices, sweeteners, beverages, and others.

1.2 WHAT YOU NEED TO KNOW ABOUT FOOD AND EATING HABITS

Free Radicals

Food is necessary for survival. But at the same time, the very food that we eat to survive may take us nearer to death as well. How?

The fact is that the process of metabolism produces a number of free radicals (FRs). FRs can also result from exhaust fumes, radiation, frying and barbecuing food, and even from harmful body processes.

Free radicals are radicals with free or unattached oxygen atoms. With unattached oxygen atoms, their molecules are incomplete. The free-oxygen in free radicals combines with radicals in neighbouring cells to complete itself. Thus, free radicals act as oxidants. They destroy cells by oxidising them. Free radicals are major players in the build-up of oxidised cholesterol plaque in arteries that leads to atherosclerosis, heart disease, and stroke, the nerve and blood vessel damage seen in diabetics, cloudy lenses, cataracts, joint pain, arthritis, and wheezing and tightening of airways in asthma, chronic cold and cough, and so on.

Antioxidants

Antioxidants are substances that make free radicals ineffective by chemically reacting with and neutralising the free oxygen atom in their molecule. Thus, they prevent free radicals from damaging body cells. Hence, they are anti-ageing.

Taking synthetic antioxidants, such as supplements of minerals and vitamins may no longer be a mantra for staying young and fit. New research shows that the body does not easily absorb these synthetic supplements. In fact, they may prove to be toxic. Therefore, nutritionists suggest that a balanced diet comprising natural antioxidants is the key to staying healthy.

Which Food Items Have the Most Antioxidants?

Fruits and vegetables, in addition to being rich sources of vitamins and minerals, are also the best source of natural antioxidants. Apples, grapes, red wine, cocoa, blueberries, broccoli, carrots, and tea contain the highest amounts of natural antioxidants.

It has now been found that cocoa beans, the source of all chocolate products, have the honour of being considered as the richest source of antioxidants. Look for cocoa content in chocolates. Higher the percentage of cocoa, the healthier they are.

Eat in Moderation

Moderation is essential in every aspect of life. Eat food that produces few or minimum free radicals and contains antioxidants, which neutralise the existing free radicals.

Oxygen Radical Absorbance Capacity (ORAC Value)

ORAC value is a measure of antioxidant capacity of any food item. Wide varieties of food stuffs have been tested. Certain spices, berries and legumes are rated very high in ORAC value. Barley, beans, cloves, cocoa, almonds, broccoli, cauliflower, kale, spinach, onions, beets, lettuce are rated among the highest ORAC value foods.

Some values, per 5 gram, in decreasing order, of their ORAC value are as follows:

Beans (small red and red kidney)	13,500
Blueberries, Cranberries	9,000
Other berries, Apples	7,700
Sweet cherries	5,000
Russet potato	4,700
Black beans	4,200

ORAC plays a great role in the free radical theory of ageing.

Tips for Healthy Eating

1. Eat a variety of foodstuffs so that the body receives all the nutrients, and it does not become deficient in any particular nutrient as that can lead to illness or physical disorders.
2. Eat correct amount of food. Both overeating and under-eating are harmful for health.

   Overeating is bad for two reasons. Firstly, one has to consume one's own energy in processing and digesting the food. Secondly, the excess food gets stored in the body as fat.

According to *Charak Samhita*, while eating, one third of stomach should be filled with solids (dal, chapatti, rice, and vegetables), one third by liquids (juices, soup, water), and the remaining one third be left empty. When you take your meal, the best time to stop eating is when you feel that you are still a little hungry.

3. Choose to eat the foodstuff that suits you. Remember that no food is perfect. There is no food which is good for everyone and remains so for ever. Individuals may have allergy for certain kinds of foods. For example, many people are allergic to wheat, corn, eggs, milk, peanuts, chocolate, etc.

   Some of the most commonly repeated pieces of advice are not meant for everyone. For example, everyone is diligent about consuming enough fibre. But that advice may practically kill someone who suffers from Celiac disease or irritable bowel syndrome. Some people may not be able to digest and absorb even fruits and vegetables like grapes, plums, tomatoes, capsicum, etc., with a thin film-like skin covering. Some get constipation even with an apple or a banana. And a few get diarrhoea after eating green leafy vegetables which are otherwise very rich in iron. You being the best judge of yourself should decide accordingly what you should eat and what you must avoid.

4. It is better to heal the body by consuming foodstuffs that do not aggravate the disease but support healing. Consuming supplements should be avoided.

   For example, calcium supplement is good for healthy bones. But it may also cause kidney stones. Aspirin, which is prescribed for thinning blood for heart patients, may cause damage to the lining in stomach and intestines.

5. Food supplements may, however, become necessary once the body becomes deficient in certain nutrients. Take your supplement/s along with food unless otherwise instructed. This ensures better absorption as digestive juices are released simultaneously.

6. Use a pressure cooker as far as possible for cooking. A pressure cooker will cook quickly and preserve nutrients. In a study,

pressure-cooked broccoli retained 88 per cent of vitamin C and 76-95 per cent of vitamin B.

Preferably use a stainless steel pressure cooker and avoid an aluminium one.

7. Food is not merely to nourish the body and the mind but is also meant for the soul. Whatever you will eat will affect your mind, body and soul.

Negative or Negligible Calorie Foods (NCFs)

Negative Calorie Foods or NCFs give less energy than that consumed by the body in chewing, digesting, and absorbing it. So when one consumes NCF, there is a net loss of calories in the body.

The list of NCFs in descending order is as follows: celery, asparagus, beet, broccoli, cabbage, carrots, cucumber, papaya, orange, apple, strawberries, etc. But at the same time these foods are rich in vitamins and minerals. They make the human body produce enzymes in greater quantities than are necessary to digest them. The surplus enzymes help breaking down other foods for digestion. There is at least one category of food whose NCF value is decidedly negative. That category is fibre.

1.3 VEGETARIAN VERSUS NON-VEGETARIAN FOOD

There is enough evidence now to prove that a diet rich in plant food products protects human beings against many diseases that are extremely common among non-vegetarians.

People are either vegetarian or non-vegetarian, at times not by choice, but just by birth and habit. Some non-vegetarians would most probably stop eating animal food if they had to kill the animals themselves.

There are several examples of people who were born non-vegetarian but changed to vegetarians: Pop star Prince, in his music album, noted Mahatma Gandhi's statement: 'To me the life of a lamb is no less precious than the life of a human being.'

American actress Kristen Bell, when only twenty-five, said this about turning into a vegetarian: 'I had a hard time dissociating the animals I cuddled with, dogs and cats for example, from the animals on my plate.'

Remember again, food is to nourish the soul as well. How can one hope to be loved after killing living beings merely for food? Health benefits associated with eating vegetarian food are indisputably clear.

Vegetarians consume higher levels of fibre, potassium, magnesium, folate, vitamins C and E, and natural antioxidants. Non-vegetarian food brings with it toxins and saturated fats in plenty. Vegetarians have been found to have lower risk of cancer and heart disease. An important reason is the absence of inflammation. Many major diseases begin with inflammation. Fruits and vegetables contain salicylic acid, an inflammation-fighting compound contained in aspirin.

Uric Acid

Uric acid is a breakdown product of purine compounds present largely in non-vegetarian foodstuffs and some vegetarian protein foods also like rajma, chana, lentils, peanuts, etc., and also in cabbage, brinjals and custard apple. Our bodies produce uric acid after eating sugars (fructose), and it sticks around longer. Uric acid is normally present in blood in a small amount. With normal water intake, the bulk is excreted through the kidney.

Problems that are caused by high uric acid levels are:

1. Propensity to develop kidney stones and kidney failure.
2. Gout, a kind of arthritis as a result of deposition of uric acid crystals in joints.
3. Predisposition to develop hypertension that can further inhibit kidney function.

The holistic treatment to bring uric acid levels to normal range requires the following:

1. Drink lots of water.
2. Exercise regularly.

3. Eliminate non-vegetarian food from the diet.
4. Cut down on proteins and sugars in general.

Vegansexuals

A new trend of vegansexuals has emerged in New Zealand. Vegansexuals are people who choose not to have sex with people who follow a non-vegetarian diet.

One vegan said: I believe we are what we consume.

Another said: I would not want to be intimate with someone whose body is literally made up from the bodies of animals who have died for his/her sustenance.

Likely Nutrient Deficiencies in Vegetarian Diet

Some nutrients may not be as easily obtained in vegetarian diet though. It is important that vegetarians consume adequate amounts of the following nutrients:

Proteins: Beans, legumes, soy products, milk, yoghurt, cheese, etc.

Iron: Beet-root, pomegranate, dark leafy vegetables, legumes, beans, nuts, etc.

Zinc: Whole grains, beans, legumes, rajma, cashews, other nuts, pumpkin, sesame and sunflower seeds.

Iodine: Iodised salt, strawberries, sea vegetables, etc. Those suffering from hyperthyroidism may need to avoid iodine.

Essential Fatty Acids: Broccoli, flaxseeds, walnuts, mustard, canola and hempseed oils.

Vitamin B12: Milk, yoghurt, cheese, fermented/sprouted foods, etc.

Calcium: Low oxalate green leafy vegetables like broccoli, kale, okra (*bhindi*), milk, yoghurt and cheese, oranges, almonds, legumes, figs, etc.

Vitamin D: It is best obtained by exposure of skin to the sun. It can also be obtained from milk.

1.4 THREE HUMOURS/TEMPERS OF THE BODY

Our body and even personality fall within three tempers or humours of *vaata*, *pitta* and *kapha*. *Vaata* means air/gas/space. *Pitta* is solid/fire/heat. *Kapha* implies water/fat/liquid. *Pitta* is for heat in the body, *kapha* is for flow, and *vaata* is for all movements inside the body. They respectively represent solid, liquid, and gas components primarily.

Compare the body to an engine receiving food as fuel. The function of all movement, bowels or thoughts, can be equated with *vaata*/gas. If the gas is in excess, the engine/body may blast off. If gas is less, it may not move at all.

Now when the engine starts moving, temperature increases. This is the function of *pitta*/heat. To exercise a control on temperature and make different parts of the engine body work without causing any friction, for which a lubricant is required. This function of lubricant is provided by *kapha*/liquid. A balance between the three is absolutely essential according to Ayurveda. An imbalance, excess or lack of one with respect to others is a *dosha/rog* or disease.

Vaata – It controls all movements.

Nature: *Vaata* people are particularly lean and restless. *Vaata-rog* or *vaata-dosha* is caused or manifested when the mind is disturbed and worried. But *vaata* people have an active mind. They make good artists, and enjoy travelling. Such type of people suffer from gas, stiff joints, rheumatic problems, and constipation.

Harmful Foods: They should not eat *rukha-sukha khaana*, that is, the food that is fat-free, dry, bitter, hot, and pungent. They should steer clear of cold foods and coffee and avoid foods like buffalo milk, sour things, okra (*bhindi*), *arabi*, urad dal (black eye beans), cauliflower, deep-fried foods, etc. These foods cause excess of gas. Arhar dal and peas should not be taken in large quantities. Eliminate caffeine from your diet. It makes the *vaata* type more anxious and restless.

Beneficial Foods: People with *vaata-dosha* should eat regularly but only wholesome food with healthy fats. Add some butter and raw olive oil to your diet. Carrots and gourds like *lauki, turai, parval, tinda*, etc., are recommended. Ashwagandha reduces gas. *Chhoti Pipal* and ginger (*saunth*) are also recommended.

Beneficial Activities: *Vaata* types are more prone to insomnia, restlessness and anxiety. Hence, corrective steps should be taken to correct the sleep disorder. Practise relaxation, Shavasana, pranayam, meditation, spinal bath, oil massage, etc. *Vaata's* sensitive nervous system needs to be calmed.

Pitta – It controls metabolism and digestion.

Nature: *Pitta* people have oily skin. They tend to have pimples/acne. They may develop acidity problem. Such people are hot-blooded, intense, argumentative, and sharp. The following suggestions will help to balance *pitta*:

Harmful Foods: They should not take fried/heavy foods and avoid alcohol, hot and sour foods with too much salt, hot pepper and spices.

Beneficial Foods: Fennel and mint will soothe the *pitta*. Light food stuffs and juices are beneficial. Consume vegetables like *lauki*, gourds and cucumber. Take lots of water.

Beneficial Activities: Rest in a cool place. Take long walks amidst natural surroundings. Greenery of nature cools the fire element. Exercise as often as you can. It dissipates *pittic* intensity and tension. Relax and laugh. Slow down.

Kapha – It controls fluids in the body.

Nature: *Kapha* types are often overweight and are endowed with a smooth complexion. They move slowly. They are usually cool, calm, emotionally secure, romantic and sentimental. But they may suffer from lethargy, cough, sinus problems, etc. Increased *kapha* also causes early greying of hair.

Harmful Foods: Cut down on milk products, sugar, and sour foods – they contribute to excess mucus. Dahi, particularly with sugar, is harmful.

Beneficial Foods: Spices such as black pepper, cloves, cardamom, and cinnamon will help improve metabolism. *Kapha* people should take warm foods, and small meals.

Ginger, turmeric, black pepper, tulsi leaves, honey with warm water, etc., taken separately or in combinations are recommended. Those who can tolerate milk can take it with chhoti pipal and turmeric.

Beneficial Activities: *Kapha* people need to exercise to keep off weight. Moong dal is the best. It is the only dal suitable for people of all the three humours.

1.5 FOODSTUFFS ACCORDING TO SEASON/WEATHER

Certain foodstuffs are good for summer, and some are good for winter. Some are not suitable in rainy weather. Some of the following recommendations are made month-wise:

Month	To Eat	Not To Eat
March-April	Neem leaves	Jaggery (*gur*)
April-May	*Bel* fruit	Oils, oily foods
May-June	Melons	Nuts, jaggery
June-July	Mangoes	*Bel* fruit
July-August	*Harad*	Green leafy vegetables and curd
August-September	Apples/Pears	Curd
September-October	Sweets	*Karela*
October-November	Radishes	*Mattha* (buttermilk)
November-December	Dry fruits	
December-January	Milk	Coriander, mint
January-February	*Ghee-khichri, Gur*	
February-March	Oranges/Grapes	

Some food items, at times, become dangerous for health if consumed out of season.

For example, green leafy vegetables become a breeding ground for worms in rainy season. Consuming dahi in the evening or in rainy weather is harmful. It affects tonsils/throat. Curd prepared in rainy weather does not set properly, and lacks in good quality probiotics.

Monsoon aggravates *vaata dosha* which leads to gas formation. Hence, avoid rajma/urad, *arabi*, and okra. Uncooked and raw food/ salads should be given a miss. Include small amounts of ghee or oil in diet. It pacifies the *vaata*, and acts as a lubricant in stomach/ intestines. Again, fats, jaggery *(gur)* and nuts are not suitable for summer. They generate heat/*pitta*.

Activities according to weather: We must also become involved in activities suitable to the weather. Exercise is good for winter. Intense physical activities are not recommended for summer. Afternoon nap is recommended in summer when the days are longer.

Foods of Opposite Nature (*Virudh-Ahaar*)

Foods of opposite nature such as hot and cold foods, salty items (*namkeen*) with milk, dahi along with milk, *kheer* (rice pudding) and raita together, milk and radishes (*muli*), milk and melon or milk and papaya should not be taken together.

1.6 ALKALINE VERSUS ACIDIC FOODS

It is a plain and simple fact of medicine that all diseases thrive in an acidic medium. Alkalinity or acidity is measured by the pH value of body fluids. The pH scale extends from 0 to 14:0 being the most acidic, and 14 the most alkaline.

The table below tells us about some foods as to what extent they are alkaline or acidic:

Alkaline and Acidic Content of Foods

Food Category	Most Alkaline	Alkaline	Lowest Alkaline	Lowest Acidic	Acidic	Most Acidic
Sweeteners/ Deserts		Maple Syrup	Raw honey, Cane juice	Molasses, Jaggery		White sugar, Equal (sugar free sweetener), Chocolates
Fruits	Lemons, Melons, Limes Grapes, Mangoes, Papaya	Apples, Pears, Berries Grapes, Figs, Dates	Bananas, Oranges, Cherries Pineapple, Peaches, Avocados, Blueberries	Plums, Processed fruit juices	Sour cherries	Blueberries, Cranberries, Prunes
Beans/ Vegetables/ Legumes	Asparagus, Onions, Garlic, Broccoli, Spinach, Fresh vegetable juices	Okra, Squash, Green Beans, Beets, Celery, Sweet Potatoes	Carrots, Tomatoes, Cabbage, Peas, Mushrooms, Corn, Olives	Cooked Spinach, Kidney Beans, Potato with skin	Potato without skin, Beans, Dals	

Nuts/Seeds		Almonds		Pumpkin seeds	Cashew	Peanuts, Walnuts
Grains/Cereals			Amaranth	Rice	Oats, Corn, Wheat	White flour, Pasta, Pastries
Non-Veg food						Meats
Egg/Dairy		Breast milk	Soy milk	Butter, Cheese	Milk, Eggs	Homogenised milk, Cream
Beverages	Lemon water	Green tea	Ginger tea	Tea with milk/sugar	Coffee	All alcohols, Soft drinks

Contrary to the commonly held belief that acidic foods are sour, the table shows lemons as alkaline, and white sugars as highly acidic, and so on.

This classification is based on the effect foods have after they have been digested, not on their intrinsic acidity or alkalinity. All fruits become alkaline in the body.

Lemons, oranges, and mangoes are thus alkaline in effect although tasting acidic. Sugars, sweets, and milk chocolates, though tasting sweet, have highly acidic effects. Another point to remember is that proteins, in general, are acidic including dals. Amaranth (*ramdana*) is the lightest protein grain, and it is the least acidic. Complex carbohydrates are not acidic. Refined carbohydrates and sugars are acidic. All non-vegetarian foods are acidic.

1.7 SPROUTS

Sprouts are germinated seeds. Introduction of sprouts in our daily diet may balance the ratio of acidic to alkaline food requirement. In principle, our food should be 80 per cent alkaline.

Moong dal, chana, soybeans, and *methi* (fenugreek) seeds are commonly sprouted. The amount of vitamin B and C in cereals increases after sprouting them. Starch present in the grains changes into glucose. The nutritive value of other nutrients also increases with sprouting. Sprouted foods are more easily digestible. Cooking reduces the nutritive value. However, if necessary, sprouts can be steamed for easy chewing and better digestion.

1.8 HIGH AND LOW GLYCEMIC INDEX FOODS

How rapidly a food increases sugar level in blood determines its glycemic index (GI).

High glycemic index foods include white sugars, white flour, polished rice, potatoes without skin, and so on. These foods have some nutrients though. But alcohol is a very high GI food. It has empty calories and no nutrients at all.

Such foods lead to sudden rise in sugar level in blood requiring an enormous amount of insulin to be produced by the pancreas to process these foods. It may lead to insulin resistance, and Type-2 diabetes.

Low glycemic index foods take time to be converted into glucose. They slowly raise the sugar level. The rate of production of sugar level, that is energy, is close to the rate of utilisation of energy. The system remains balanced and one remains in good health.

Low glycemic index foods primarily contain fibre, and little sugar and fat. Thus, whole grains, vegetables and fruits (excluding a few) are low glycemic index foods. The studies led by various researchers have found that a diet high in low glycemic index foods prevents the risk of diabetes and cardiovascular disorders.

1.9 UNSAFE FOODS AND COOKWARE

Junk foods have very less or no nutritional value. Junk and processed foods contain certain ingredients that are unsafe and unhealthy for all of us. Such unsafe ingredients are at times also present in natural or whole foodstuffs. Following are some of the examples of unsafe contents in foods:

Food Additives

Food additives are used to enhance the flavour of food and prevent its spoilage. They include preservatives, artificial colours, flavourings, acidifiers, salts and sugars. These are responsible for many chronic diseases such as asthma, allergies, arthritis, depression, hypertension, migraine headaches, learning disabilities, etc.

A yellow dye is added to almost every packaged food. It is known to induce asthma and allergies. In fact, those suffering from allergies must avoid all artificial colours.

- Saccharin and aspartame are the two commonly used artificial sweetners. It is worth noting that Saccharin is known to cause cancer in rats. Aspartame can significantly alter brain chemistry and effect mood and behaviour.

- Sodium benzoate, nitrates, nitrites and sulphites are some of the common preservatives. Nitrates and nitrites are known carcinogens. Benzoates and sulphites can produce allergic reactions. Sodium benzoate has been used as a preservative for decades in processed foods like jams, juices, squashes, salad dressings, carbonated drinks, etc.

Professor Peter Piper of Sheffield University has shown that this substance causes serious damage to DNA. It can result in degenerative diseases such as Parkinson's disease, and cirrhosis of liver. When mixed with vitamin C, it forms benzene. Benzene is highly carcinogenic in nature.

It is always best to consume freshly prepared foods.

Pesticides, Herbicides and Waxes

Pesticides have serious long-term health risks namely, birth defects, cancers, diarrhoea, nerve damage, and so on. Apples, cherries, grapes, peaches, nectarines, pears, red raspberries, strawberries, bell peppers, celery, potatoes, and spinach are often known as the 'dirty dozen foods' for the high content of pesticide residues in them.

There is strong evidence to prove that pesticides can cause Parkinson's disease. Parkinson's disease is marked by the death of brain cells that produce dopamine. Dopamine is a neurotransmitter associated with muscle movement.

The best way to avoid pesticides is to use organic foods that are produced without using synthetic chemicals, fertilisers, pesticides and herbicides.

Even though it is known that the skin of fruits and vegetables are rich in vitamins, it is always safe to peel off the skin before consumption.

Agriculturalists often use wax to prevent moisture loss from fruits and vegetables. Most of the wax cannot be washed off and gets deposited on the fruits and vegetables. These when consumed clog the arteries.

Chemicals in Fruits and Vegetables

Fruits and vegetables, though necessary for good health, may pose serious threat to health. Some farmers use hormone shots of oxytocin to help pumpkin, watermelon, brinjal, gourd, cucumber, etc. grow faster and larger in size. Oxytocin hormone is given to pregnant women to ease labour pain, and increase breast milk supply. You can imagine how much damage such fruits and vegetables can cause to children who eat them.

Calcium carbide that is used to ripen mangoes, papaya, etc., can harm eyes, lungs, and skin.

Chemical Bisphenol A (BPA) in Plastics

The chemical Bisphenol A used in plastic bottles and containers has been shown to affect the functioning of the intestines. In a study, National Institute of Agronomic Research in Toulouse, France found that the digestive tract of rats reacts negatively to even low doses of this chemical. BPA lowers the permeability of intestines, and the immune system's response to digestive inflammation in humans.

Cookware

Glass and ceramic cookwares are the best cookwares as they pose no danger of entry of chemicals and metals in your food. About plastics, we have already mentioned above. Some people use plastic wares to cook in microwave ovens. Microwaving may leach harmful compounds from plastics into food. Among metals, stainless steel is satisfactory, but aluminum is the worst. Using aluminum cooking wares over a long period of time can result in memory loss and also cause Alzheimer's disease.

2
Proteins

Proteins are the building blocks for much of the body including muscles, various organs, brain tissues, blood cells and hormones. They are synthesised from amino acids.

Lack of proteins weakens the body, damages the nervous system, results in the lack of lactation among nursing mothers, and so on. Excess of proteins produces toxins/acids. It may damage liver and kidney, and also impair digestive system.

There are nine essential amino acids. A complete protein is one that comprises of all nine. Eggs and milk are examples of complete proteins. Meat and fish are also complete proteins. However, eating meat is not only inhuman, but it also leads to many degenerative and incurable diseases.

Animal foods are difficult to digest. They are also highly acidic in nature and release uric acid and toxins that are very harmful for the body. Furthermore, animal proteins are always accompanied with extremely harmful saturated animal fats. In any case, a high protein intake that the body cannot process, and which is over and above the daily requirement of the body, is not to be recommended.

Legumes and soy products are rich sources of proteins. All legumes, beans, sprouted moong dal, most grains, soybeans, tofu, oatmeal, brown rice, milk, curd and paneer are excellent sources of quality vegetable proteins.

Amaranth (*ramdana*) is a protein punch. It has high quality easily digestible proteins.

Nuts such as almonds, walnuts, cashews, seeds of pumpkin/ sunflower/sesame, and vegetables particularly spinach, kale, broccoli/

cauliflower, mushrooms, lettuce, peas, beans, cucumber, etc., contain significant amounts of high quality proteins.

Plant foods individually do not contain all nine essential amino acids. But in combination, they provide all necessary proteins. Thus, by eating wheat and legumes (dal-roti) or rice and legumes (dal-chawal), one is assured of all amino acids.

A diet rich in grains, legumes, milk, eggs, and vegetables provides all the proteins. With age though, one should slowly cut down on proteins, including even legumes. Moong dal can, however, be taken most of the time.

Tyrosine

Tyrosine is an amino acid used by cells to synthesise protein. Tyrosine is a precursor to many hormones like dopamine that helps us relax. At the same time, it reduces stress hormone levels. Tyrosine is the starting material for neuro-transmitters. Cheese is high in tyrosine.

3
Carbohydrates

Carbohydrates primarily provide us with energy. Their deficiency leads to weakness, while their excess leads to build-up of fat. Carbohydrates from rice, fruits, etc., are easily digestible. They are alkaline in nature. Carbohydrates from wheat, coarse grains, etc., are slightly acidic in nature.

Carbohydrates fall into two categories: Simple and complex carbohydrates.

Simple carbohydrates are sugars, both refined and natural. Refined sugars are sucrose, glucose, lactose, maltose, fructose, corn syrup, etc. The problem with refined sugars is that they are 'empty calories' stripped off all nutrients. These are high glycemic index foods. They enter the bloodstream instantly raising the level of blood sugars to a very high point. This could be harmful, and dangerous to a diabetic.

Natural sugars can be obtained from fruits, honey, and some vegetables. They have the advantage of bringing with them a wide range of other nutrients such as vitamins, minerals, antioxidants and enzymes, in addition to fibre and pure water.

Complex carbohydrates or starches are formed by many different kinds of sugars joined by chemical bonds. Grains like wheat and rice, legumes, vegetables like potatoes and sweet potatoes, as well as nuts are excellent sources of complex carbohydrates.

The advantage with complex carbohydrates is that the body breaks them into sugars slowly. As such they are absorbed into the bloodstream gradually without raising the blood sugar level adversely. Even for a diabetic, it results in better sugar control.

Another advantage is that these complex carbohydrates contain some amounts of proteins, fats, and other nutrients as well. So this makes them a complete food.

New research recommends eating more of complex carbohydrates as compared to proteins and fats for better health and for meeting a greater percentage of energy needs of the body.

A high carbohydrate diet, contrary to belief, controls weight loss in addition to enhancing mood, and speeding up the thought process. But these complex carbohydrates are often refined. For example, white flour, white rice, etc., are produced by removing their outer bran and inner germ. In the process they are stripped of many nutrients and fibre. In refined form, they are absorbed into the bloodstream more rapidly. This leads to poor blood sugar control.

DIFFERENCE IN ENERGY FROM PROTEINS AND CARBOHYDRATES

The body breaks carbohydrates into glucose, which is used to produce energy for activity including the activity of the brain.

Proteins, on the other hand, break down into glycogen, which can also be used as fuel to produce energy for activity. However, glycogen cannot be used as efficiently as glucose.

People who go on a diet tend to eliminate carbohydrates from their diet. This might reduce the brain's source of energy. Hence, they are at risk of impairing brain function.

4
Fats

Like proteins and carbohydrates, fats also provide energy to the body. They occur in two forms – saturated and unsaturated.

Typical saturated fat is an animal fat which exists in a state of semi-solid to solid at room temperature. For example, butter and ghee are saturated fats. A diet high in saturated fat leads to plaque formation in arteries (atherosclerosis), heart disease, strokes and numerous types of cancers.

Unsaturated fats are of two types: mono-unsaturated fatty acids (MUFAs) and poly-unsaturated fatty acids (PUFAs). Plant oils, except coconut and palm oils, are high in unsaturated fats. They remain liquid at room temperature. They may, therefore, be simply referred to as oils.

Role of Fats

In addition to providing energy, there are some essential fats that function in our bodies as components of nerve cells in the brain and the heart, and for producing many hormonal substances. They are also essential for transporting vitamins, minerals and hormones through each cell in the body.

The idea of avoiding all fats because they make you fat or clog your arteries is a nutritional myth. Everyone needs a certain amount of fats to stay healthy. The human brain, for example, is about 60 per cent fat. It is, however, important to reduce saturated fats in our diet, and to increase unsaturated fats.

4.1 UNSATURATED FATS AS DIFFERENT FROM SATURATED FATS

EPA, DHA, ALA and GLA

When you have enough omega-3 in your diet, your body creates Eicosapentaenic Acid (EPA) and Docosahexaenoic Acid (DHA). Both EPA and DHA help protect and heal our bodies. DHA is found primarily in brain tissues, fish oil and mother's milk. EPA is anti-inflammatory. It lowers blood pressure, cholesterol and triglyceride levels.

Your body makes only small amounts of EPA. EPA originates in plants and algae, and as fish eat enough of these, it is available in fish oil.

Vegetarian sources of EPA include spirulina. Some soy oils contain EPA and DHA. Flaxseed/linseed oil increases the amount of EPA made in cells. It also increases the amount of Alpha-Linolenic Acid (ALA) and DHA in cells.

ALA is an omega-3 fat. It is richly found in canola oil, flaxseeds and walnuts. Mediterranean diet is rich in ALA.

GLA (Gamma-Linolenic Acid) regulates the body's hormonal balance, lowers hypertension caused by stress, and can also lower blood cholesterol and triglyceride levels. GLA may also treat skin problems. Evening primrose oil and black currant oil are the best sources of GLA.

GLA is an omega-6 fat, but unlike other omega-6 fats which promote inflammation, it reduces inflammation. Research suggests use of GLA to curb symptoms of arthritis, allergies, eczema, PMS etc.

4.2 ESSENTIAL FATTY ACIDS (EFAs)

The two PUFAs, omega-6 and omega-3, are referred to as essential fatty acids (EFAs). Our body does not synthesise these fats. Hence, they must be obtained from food sources.

There are two types of EFAs – omega-3 and omega-6. Both EFAs raise HDL, the good cholesterol. They lower LDL, the bad cholesterol, by escorting it to the liver where it is broken down and excreted.

Health Benefits of Omega-3 Fats

Among the many health benefits of omega-3 fats, the important ones are as follows:

1. Omega-3 fats are anti-inflammatory. They lower the risk of inflammations and inflammatory diseases like asthma, arthritis, eczema, skin diseases, etc.
2. Maintain healthy and supple skin. Prevent ageing.
3. Lower triglyceride levels.
4. Lower blood pressure.
5. Prevent blood clotting, heart disease, and stroke. They somehow trigger release of nitric oxide which causes arteries to relax and dilate thus influencing vascular function so that more blood can flow to protect the heart.
6. Calm nerves. EPA and DHA are omega-3 fats. They are key brain components. Higher levels of each can bolster serotonin and dopamine which are potent mood enhancers. They prevent depression, migraine, etc.
8. They reduce risk of prostate and other cancers.

Balance Between Omega-6 and Omega-3 Fats

High levels of omega-6 may increase the probability of every disease including depression, arthritis, asthma, colitis, irritable bowel syndrome (IBS), atherosclerosis, multiple sclerosis, psoriasis/eczema, PMS, high blood pressure, heart disease, and stroke.

Omega-6 produce inflammation as an immune response, while omega-3 help subside inflammation. The problem becomes serious when omega-6 are excessive, omega-3 are low, and the inflammation does not abate. Hence, it is important to balance them in your diet.

Foods which contain high amounts of omega-6 fats simultaneously with negligible or no omega-3 fats are not recommended.

Omega-3 and omega-6 help you only when you eat them in nearly equal amounts. The ratio of 1:1 is ideal. The ratio accepted by WHO is 4:1.

Flaxseed oil has this ratio equal to 2.4. Hempseed oil has 3.75. In contrast, the typical Western diet has a very harmful ratio of more than 10 to 1.

4.3 QUALITY FATS

One-third, or at least 25 per cent of our calorie requirement should come from quality fats. As seen above, we find that the quality fats for us are the following:

1. **Monounsaturated Fatty Acids (MUFAs)** like oleic acid (omega-9 oil) contain maximum antioxidant polyphenols also. Statistics show that MUFAs actually reduce belly fat. They raise good cholesterol and lower bad cholesterol. As such, risk of heart disease is lowered. Pick your MUFAs from olive oil, almonds, pumpkin seeds, avocados and cocoa.
2. **Polyunsaturated Fatty Acids (PUFAs)** like linolenic acid (omega-3 oil) are extremely beneficial. They lower cholesterol and have been shown to reduce inflammations, risk of heart attacks, and other problems. PUFAs like linoleic acid (omega-6 oil) that are present in vegetable oils also lower total cholesterol, but they can create prostaglandins of series 2 variety that can lead to inflammations and related diseases.

Plant Sterols

Plant or phytosterols are also quality fats from plants. They are a natural way to lower total and bad LDL cholesterol. They are powerful antioxidants. Pistachios are one of the best sources of plant sterols.

Fats are as much essential as proteins and carbohydrates. There are fats in membranes surrounding cells of brain and heart. Brain chemicals such as serotonin transmit messages properly when the consistency of these fats is fluid and flexible as present in quality fats rather than hard as in saturated and trans-fats.

Further studies show that 10 times more nutrients are absorbed from vegetables we eat if they are consumed together with healthy fats like olive oil.

Sources of Omega-3 Fats

Omega-3 fats are present in flaxseeds, cold pressed canola/rapeseed oil, mustard oil, soybean products, liquid soy oil, walnuts, pumpkin seeds, cloves, hempseed oil, wheat germ, broccoli, green leafy vegetables like kale and spinach, squash, eggs and fish.

Broccoli is one of the vegetables which contains a high amount of omega-3 fat.

Due to the similarities between flaxseed/linseed and fish oils, cooking with flaxseed/linseed oil smells much like frying fish. Note that all omega-3 fats including flaxseed oil go rancid quickly even in a refrigerator. Rancid oil is oxidised oil. Any rancid oil is as bad as consuming free radicals. Moreover, flaxseed oil should never be heated.

Sources of Omega-6 Fats

Omega-6 fats are found in vegetable oils. Corn oil contains 59 per cent, sunflower oil 65 per cent, and sesame (*til*) oil 45 per cent of omega-6 fats.

Most plant oils contain only omega-6 configuration and no omega-3. They tend to be pro-inflammatory. Some foods containing omega-3 also contain omega-6 though. These are canola oil, walnuts, pumpkin seeds, soy, and mustard oil.

4.4 TRANS-FATS OR HYDROGENATED FATS

The process of hydrogenation converts plant oils into semi-solid trans-unsaturated fats (Vanaspati Ghee) in a chemical process in the presence of toxic metals like nickel, etc., which act as catalysts. Such fats are referred to as trans-fats. Vegetable ghee, margarine, shortenings, etc., are typical examples of trans-fats. French fries, popular brands of cookies and crackers, cakes, pastries, doughnuts, etc., have highest content of trans-fats. Avoid processed foods as they all contain trans-fats.

Trans-fats are more harmful to the body than even the natural saturated fats, because they are not only saturated but they may also carry traces of highly toxic catalyst metals, and they lack trace minerals and antioxidants.

Such fats not only raise LDL, the bad cholesterol, but they also lower HDL, the protective good cholesterol. They may lead to coronary heart disease (CHD).

These trans-fats are suspected to be the cause of many cancers as they lack in antioxidants, and contain harmful toxic elements that the body is unable to eliminate.

The body can fight infection but not the toxic elements. Infection lasts for some time only. But the toxic elements stay forever in the body, and even get passed on to the progeny.

Ironically, hydrogenated trans-fats are even more plaque-forming than the natural saturated fats like butter. They are more harmful than the naturally occurring oils from which they are made, and are not easily digested.

5

Vitamins and Natural Antioxidants

Vitamins are necessary to prevent and fight diseases. They also assist in the biochemical reactions of the body. However, we need them only in very small quantities. Some vitamins are fat-soluble, while others are water-soluble. Water-soluble vitamins if taken in excess are excreted by the body. Fat-soluble ones if taken in excess get stored in the body. The fat-soluble vitamin A, if taken in excess as a supplement, could become toxic. It could cause diarrhoea and could also raise the risk of having brittle bones in old age. Vitamin supplements are not meant to replace healthy eating.

One big problem with supplements is that our body is not naturally designed to derive nutrients from supplements. Our digestive system is adept at absorbing nutrients from food only. So if you take supplements, most of them will be excreted without being absorbed. And if you take them in excess, you will end up with vitamin toxicity.

Moreover, with supplements you do not simultaneously get other nutrients that are needed to work in combination.

For example, iron is better absorbed when vitamin C is present. It is thus healthier to eat green leafy vegetables which contain both iron and vitamin C. Similarly, we need vitamin D to absorb calcium. It is therefore best to take milk and milk products for calcium. They have both calcium and vitamin D.

5.1 FAT-SOLUBLE VITAMINS

Vitamin A

Vitamin A was the first vitamin to be discovered in 1913 when it was found that animals fed on a diet deficient in vitamin A became ill frequently indicating poor immune system. Also, they showed an inability to grow.

Vitamin A is found in natural fats like breast milk, butter, etc.

Vitamin A is primarily known for the following health benefits:

1. **Anti-infection vitamin.** It protects us from infections and chronic diseases. It has been found that if you take foods rich in vitamin A (like carrots, mangoes, etc.) over a long period, you develop immunity against respiratory problems too.

2. **For healthy eyes.** Human retina has vitamin A containing compounds. Night blindness is an indication of vitamin A deficiency. A deficiency of vitamin A is the leading cause of blindness in developing countries/South Asia. UNICEF administers about 400 million vitamin A supplements annually.

3. **For maintaining healthy skin, hair, and mucous membranes.** Many skin disorders are treated with vitamin A.

4. **Growth vitamin.** Vitamin A is necessary for cell growth, and hence for overall development of the body.

5. **Important for reproductive system**, and for manufacture and activity of adrenal and thyroid hormones. Men, if extremely low in vitamin A, may lose their fertility.

6. **Necessary for nerve cell maintenance and function.** The most concentrated sources of vitamin A are mother's milk, butter, whole milk, and eggs.

Vitamin A can also be formed from beta-carotene and other carotenoids, the plant versions of vitamin A. They impart yellow and orange colour to carrots, sweet potatoes, pumpkin, apricots, cantaloupe, papaya, peaches, watermelon, and cherries, and green colour to vegetables like broccoli, cabbage, peas, kale, spinach, etc. The darker the colour, the more is the vitamin A content.

Vitamin D

Vitamin D is often referred to as the 'sunshine vitamin'. It is synthesised in the body under the effect of sunlight. Vitamin D helps the body to absorb calcium, thereby facilitating growth of bones and teeth.

Carsten Geisler of Copenhagen University found that the immune system's killer T-cells rely on vitamin D to become active. They remain dormant if this vitamin is lacking in blood.

Vitamin D is considered as the insurance against cancer and auto-immune diseases like multiple sclerosis. Vitamin D is considered as nature's antibiotic.

Just 20 minutes exposure to the morning sun is required to obtain our vitamin D requirement. An hour of sunshine can boost a man's testosterone hormone level by 69 per cent or so.

Food sources of vitamin D are butter, eggs, full-fat dairy products and fortified milk.

Vitamin E

Vitamin E was discovered in 1922 when it was found that rats fed on a diet lacking in vitamin E lost their ability to reproduce. Their fertility was restored when wheat germ was added to their diet. The scientific name for vitamin E, tocopherol, comes from the Greek word *tokos* meaning 'to give birth'. Vitamin E plays a major role in fertility. It is therefore referred to as the 'fertility, sex, or youth vitamin'.

It is essential for proper functioning of pituitary gland, the master gland that controls all other glands in the endocrine system. Its deficiency results in low sperm count in men, and in the disturbance of menstruation cycle and ovulation in women.

Following are the prominent properties of vitamin E:

1. Powerful antioxidant. It protects cell membranes from oxidative damage. It promotes cardiovascular health by preventing LDL cholesterol from oxidising.

2. Blood thinner. As an antioxidant as well as a blood thinner, it prevents clot formation, and hence protects against heart attack and stroke.
3. Anti-ageing. It promotes hormonal and sexual activity.
4. Promotes health of cartilage and reduces arthritic pain.
5. Good for skin, hair and nails.

Sunflower seeds, wheat germ oil and almonds have the maximum vitamin E. Other good sources are whole grains, sprouted cereals, moong dal, butter, milk, eggs, nuts and seeds, vegetable oils, asparagus, and green leafy vegetables.

Note that most commercial oils are heat processed. Heat destroys vitamin E. Simple cold processed oils are, therefore, to be preferred.

While whole wheat flour and unpolished rice have it in good amounts, white flour, polished white rice, etc., have no vitamin E.

Vitamin E deficiency may occur in people who cannot absorb dietary fat. Even otherwise, it is hard to get vitamin E from food alone. A supplement may become necessary.

In a study, those who took 400-800 IU of vitamin E daily reduced their risk of heart attack by as much as 77 per cent.

Vitamin K

Good bacteria, as in yoghurt, stimulate production of vitamin K in the intestines.

This vitamin helps to clot blood. After an injury, it helps to stop bleeding and prevent blood loss. It is responsible for holding calcium in bones. Hence it improves bone density by serving as biological glue for calcium in bones. Its deficiency leads to impaired bones, osteoporosis, severity of fractures in patients due to osteoporosis, and so on.

Rich sources of vitamin K are dark green leafy vegetables like spinach, milk, fermented/sprouted foods, and green tea. But if you are taking a blood thinner medication like aspirin, too much of vitamin K in your diet may upset your protection from blood clotting.

Higher dietary intake of vitamin K lowers the risk of cancer.

5.2 WATER-SOLUBLE VITAMINS

B-Vitamins

There are a range of B-vitamins that are very important for our digestive and nervous systems. People with an impaired digestive system are often deficient in vitamin B. We get B-vitamins primarily from whole grain cereals. Processing of foods may strip them off their B-vitamins.

Alcohol destroys B-vitamins. Regular drinkers of alcohol will have its deficiency.

Vitamin B1 or Thiamine

Thiamine or B1 is necessary for the production of energy by the enzymatic conversion of carbohydrates and fats into glucose.

B1 is also needed for neuro-transmitters. Thus, it protects against dementia. It is also a factor in maintaining body temperature, and proper muscle coordination.

Rich sources of vitamin B1 are wheat germ, whole wheat flour, brown rice, all beans, dal, rajma, sunflower seeds, and all nuts.

Vitamin B2 or Riboflavin

Vitamin B2 is referred to as the 'beauty vitamin'. It plays a crucial role in the development of healthy skin, hair, and nails. It helps in healing wounds, and making eyesight better. Its deficiency may lead to burning and itching in eyes, make eyes sensitive to light, trigger formation of cataract, etc. It helps to protect against build-up of homocysteine molecules that damage arteries. It also helps to break down and utilise carbohydrates, protein, and fats. Rich sources of Riboflavin are whole grains, rice bran, beans and legumes, nuts, green leafy vegetables, mushrooms, milk, cheese, yoghurt (dahi), and eggs.

Vitamin B3 or Niacin

Vitamin B3 is synthesised in the body by the conversion of the protein tryptophan. This vitamin plays a key role in the following chemical processes in the body:

1. Co-functions with enzymes to produce energy from foods.
2. Cholesterol metabolism. Its deficiency may result in high cholesterol levels. It lowers total cholesterol while simultaneously raising good HDL cholesterol.
3. Manufacture of adrenal and sex hormones.
4. Brain function. Its deficiency may cause dementia/ schizophrenia of brain.
5. Repair of mucous membrane of gastro-intestinal tract.

Supplements of niacin may cause liver disorders, ulcers, glucose intolerance, etc.

Rich sources of niacin are milk, eggs, whole grain wheat, brown rice, legumes, almonds, and other high quality protein foods and mustard seeds. Other sources are asparagus, mushrooms, lettuce, spinach, green peas, green beans, carrots and potatoes. A diet low in proteins can cause niacin deficiency.

Vitamin B5 or Pantothenic Acid

Vitamin B5 is referred to as 'anti-stress vitamin' as it takes care of adrenal function, and cellular metabolism. It lowers blood cholesterol and triglyceride levels. Rich sources of pantothenic acid are brewer's yeast, milk, yoghurt (dahi), oatmeal, whole grains, brown rice, beans and legumes, broccoli, cauliflower, oranges and strawberries.

Vitamin B6 or Pyridoxine

Vitamin B6 participates in formation of red blood cells and neuro-transmitters. Hence it helps the nervous system to function smoothly. It maintains hormonal balance and helps in PMS (Premenstrual syndrome). It plays an important role in reducing homocysteine level, thus lowering risk of damage to artery walls and heart disease.

We get enough vitamin B6 from the food we eat. But some of it is destroyed by modern lifestyle that involves food colours, certain drugs, antibiotics, oral contraceptives and alcohol.

Whole grains, beans, bananas, and broccoli are rich in B6. Other very good sources are bell peppers, spinach, garlic, soybeans, legumes, oatmeal, and potatoes.

Vitamin B7 or Biotin

Biotin, known as 'beauty vitamin', helps maintain healthy skin, hair, and nails. A Biotin deficiency results in dry scaly skin, dermatitis, premature greying and hair loss.

Many people find noticeable improvement in skin, hair and nails with biotin supplement. Biotin also supports healthy carbohydrate, protein and fat metabolism.

Vegetarian diet alters the intestinal flora to help production of biotin. The gut bacteria in healthy intestines manufacture biotin.

Good sources of biotin are whole wheat, unpolished rice, legumes, rice bran, oats, nuts, broccoli, cauliflower, spinach, whole wheat, unpolished rice, legumes, and egg yolk. White of eggs prevents absorption of biotin.

Folate or Folic Acid

Folate is a generic name of a B-vitamin found in foods. The form of folate available in supplements is known as folic acid. The body uses it to make new cells. Without it, cells will not divide properly. Thus, folic acid is very important for growth of foetus. Its deficiency during pregnancy may result in birth defects in the child. It is considered a must for mothers to take folic acid supplements during pregnancy. Folate is also necessary for the manufacture of healthy red blood cells. Just like women, men should also take a diet rich in folate. It boosts male fertility.

Folic acid is known to reduce inflammatory chemical homocysteine in blood. Homocysteine, if unconverted, damages the walls of blood vessels. Folic acid converts dangerous homocysteine molecules into benign amino acids.

Folate is easily destroyed by light, heat, alcohol and drugs. The word is derived from the word 'foliage', implying that it is found in large concentrations in dark green leafy vegetables like spinach, lettuce, kale, parsley, etc. Beans and asparagus are rich in folate. Folate is also found in fruits like papaya, apples, pomegranate, and oranges.

Vitamin B12 or Cobalamin

The molecule of vitamin B12 contains cobalt mineral and hence it is called cobalamin.

Vitamin B12 was first extracted from the liver in 1948. This is why it is considered as an important factor in liver health. Its deficiency causes severe anaemia. It has far-reaching implications in keeping red blood cells (RBCs) and nerve cells healthy. Without sufficient B12, RBCs (red blood cells) would fail to carry oxygen from lungs to the body, and nerve cells would fail to send messages throughout the body. Vitamin B12 helps in cell development, cell division and many cell processes together.

Further, vitamins B6 and B12 are involved in the formation of sheaths around nerve cells that contribute to communication between these cells. Without enough B12, the coating enclosing the nerves doesn't form, potentially causing nerve damage. Hence, vitamin B12 is necessary for maintaining a healthy nervous system.

Symptoms of B12 deficiency include anaemia, impaired nerve function, depression, mental confusion, dementia, Alzheimer's disease, etc.

Lack of vitamin B12 in diet can predispose a person to strokes much more than being prone to the usual risk factors like diabetes and high blood pressure. Since folic acid works in the body together with B12 to reduce homocysteine level, increased levels of homocysteine in blood at times may be the result of B12 deficiencies. B12 deficiency is very common among elderly people and vegetarians.

Vegetarians may supplement their diet with milk, cheese, yoghurt, eggs, and fermented plant foods. Sprouted soybeans, moong dal, legumes, etc., contain decent quantities of B12.

Vitamin C or Ascorbic Acid

Being water-soluble, it cannot be stored in the body. Hence, it has to be taken regularly. It is destroyed by heating, cooking, and by oxidation on drying and exposure to air.

Vitamin C has the following important functions:

1. **Synthesis of collagen.** Collagen is the fibrous protein constituent of skin, cartilage, tendons, bones and other connecting tissues. Collagen keeps the skin elastic. More than one-third of body's protein is collagen, and makes up 75 per cent of our skin. This vitamin also enhances wound and bone repair.

2. **Critical for immune function.** This means that it stimulates white blood cells to fight infection. Thus, it enhances body's ability to fight disease including cancer.

3. **Powerful antioxidant.** As a powerful antioxidant, vitamin C helps neutralise free radicals which damage the skin's healthy collagen and cause the skin to thin and wrinkle. As such, it is anti-ageing. It reduces risk of cancer, cataracts, heart disease, protects against pollution, and increases life expectancy.

4. **A liberal intake of vitamin C is necessary to facilitate absorption of iron.** In case of anaemia, at least 2-3 helpings of citrus fruits should be taken daily.

5. **Influences vascular function** of the heart by keeping arteries more relaxed and open so that more blood can flow to the heart.

Symptoms of vitamin C deficiency are bleeding gums, poor wound healing, and susceptibility to infections.

Most people think that only citrus fruits contain vitamin C. Of course, oranges and grapefruits have high amounts of vitamin C. And just by squeezing some lemon juice in a glass of water, you can boost your daily vitamin C intake.

But in fact, all fruits and vegetables contain high amounts of vitamin C. However, it is not found in dried fruits and grains.

One cup of guava has almost five times more vitamin C than a medium-sized orange. Maximum vitamin C is found in *amla* (Indian gooseberry). Radishes contain about half as much vitamin C as oranges. Other good sources are asparagus, berries, broccoli, cabbage, cantaloupes, cauliflower, celery (ajwain), mangoes, mustard greens, and tomatoes.

Note that vitamin C gets easily oxidised. So even if the fruits and vegetables are kept in the refrigerator after cutting, they lose up to 35 per cent of the vitamin in a day.

5.3 NATURAL ANTIOXIDANTS

Antioxidants are vitamin-like substances. Some consider them as future vitamins. They are present in fruits and vegetables, whole grains, and in tea, cocoa and wine.

Preparation of bread and pizza crust with whole wheat flour by baking it longer releases up to 80 per cent more antioxidants. Baking changes amino-acid lysine contained in wheat flour into an antioxidant compound. Thus, dark brown crunchy edges of a toast contain the maximum antioxidant.

Alpha Lipoic Acid

Alpha lipoic acid is found naturally in every cell of the body. It converts glucose into energy. It is an antioxidant miracle as it is both fat and water soluble as distinct from vitamins E and C. Thus it can access all parts of the cell. It can be found in very small amounts in foods such as spinach, broccoli, peas, and rice bran. Supplements are available in combination with vitamins B6, B12 and folic acid. It treats chronic liver problems, diabetes, atherosclerosis, psychiatric diseases, antimony and mercury poisoning, age-related degenerative diseases, heart disease and stroke, cataracts, cancer, Alzheimer's disease, Parkinson's disease, HIV, AIDS, etc.

Choline

Choline is converted in the brain into neuro-transmitters that form an important chemical bridge between nerve cells. Choline deficiency is experienced in Alzheimer's disease.

An array of choline precursors are found in breast milk. It provides an infant as much choline as an adult would need. This emphasises the importance of breast feeding.

It has been found that getting enough of choline in your diet reduces risk of breast cancer. Foods containing choline are egg yolk, soybeans, whole grains, legumes, fats and lecithin.

Enzymes

The entire digestion process depends on enzymes. Enzymes work to break down larger molecules into smaller ones. They work along with vitamins to speed up biochemical reactions, and metabolism.

The body produces its own enzymes. After forty years of age, the body loses one-third of its enzymes and so it is wise to take digestive enzymes supplement thereafter.

Fresh fruits and sprouted grains are natural sources of active enzymes. Bromelain, found in pineapples, is the best plant enzyme and is an antioxidant. It assists in digestion, reduces inflammation in arthritis, prevents swellings, inhibits blood platelet aggregation, relieves sinusitis, enhances wound healing, and so on.

Phytochemicals

Phytochemicals are natural antioxidants obtained from plants of more than 900 diverse varieties such as the following:

Allicin containing sulphides in allium family vegetables like garlic, onions, etc. Sulforaphane in cruciferous vegetables like broccoli, cauliflower, cabbage, etc. reduces risk of cancers. Phytoestrogens are found in soy.

Capsaicin that is found in chili peppers is a home remedy for pain. Lignans or Isoflavones are contained in beans, legumes, grains, seeds, etc.

Some other phytochemicals are categorised as following:

Bioflavonoids

There are some 500 bioflavonoids, recognised by the colour of the pigment for example, curcumin, deep yellow, is present in haldi.

Anthocyanins are red/purple/blue pigments in blueberries, strawberries, cranberries, beets, brinjals, red peppers, plums, grapes, etc.

Lycopene is red as in tomatoes, sweet peppers, water melon, guava, etc. It lowers prostate cancer risk and reduces oxidation damage from bad LDL cholesterol. It keeps the heart healthy.

Lutein and zeaxanthin are found in form of yellow/green colour as in eggs, corn, spinach, bell peppers, and carrots. They protect the eyes and prevent cataract formation.

Betacyanin, in purple/crimsom colour, is a powerful cancer fighting antioxidant.

Carotenes

There are a number of carotenes including beta-carotene (vitamin A), which is found in carrots, mangoes, squash, etc. Note that the excess of vitamin A is stored in the liver.

On the other hand, excess of carotenes are stored in cells of skin, lungs, respiratory tract, gastrointestinal tract, genitourinary tract, adrenals, testes, ovaries, etc. Accordingly, high consumption of carotenes is able to enhance the health and immunity of all these parts and organs in the body.

The best sources of carotenes are carrots, sweet potatoes, squash/pumpkin, apricots, mangoes, papaya, peaches, berries and all other yellow-orange coloured fruits and vegetables. Green leafy vegetables such as lettuce and spinach also provide significant amounts of carotene.

Orange carotenoid beta-cryptoxanthin, found in high amounts in mangoes, pumpkin, papaya, red bell peppers, oranges, peaches, and corn, etc., reduces the risk of lung cancer by 27 per cent.

Polyphenols

Polyphenols act more strongly as antioxidants as compared to vitamins C and E.

Red grapes and red wine are great sources of polyphenols like resveratrol. Other types of polyphenols are contained in cantaloupes, berries, melons, pomegranates, whole grains, legumes, honey, cocoa and tea.

Polyphenols keep gastrointestinal systems intact. The phenols present in tea reduce the risk of cancer. Cancer rates are low in Japan possibly since the Japanese, on an average, drink three cups of green tea everyday.

Polyphenols are also found abundantly in walnuts, pomegranates, apples, cocoa, dark chocolate, extra virgin olive oil, beans, legumes, and brinjals. Blueberries and olive oil are high in polyphenol antioxidants. Apples have the highest total flavonoid and polyphenol content. Cocoa and tea have remarkably high and most active kind of polyphenol epicatechin.

Plant Sterols

Plant sterols are antioxidants present in plant foods with healthy fats such as almonds, pistachios, beans, olive oil and avocados. They lower cholesterol level.

Quercetin

Quercetin, contained in tea, is a flavonoid which bolsters your immune system. Mayo Clinic research has revealed that quercetin may prevent or stop the growth of prostate cancer. Quercetin inhibits the release of histamines which trigger allergies.

In addition to tea, quercetin is present in concentrated amounts in apples, strawberries, onions, red wine, broccoli, spinach and kale.

Coenzyme Q10

Coenzyme Q10 is an essential component of our cells. It is an amazing heart energiser and a miracle treatment for damaged heart. The body uses amino acids, vitamins E and B12 to produce coenzyme Q10. But as you age, the body produces less and less of it.

Milk fat, wheat germ and whole grains contain coenzyme Q10, but in small quantities. Its deficiency is best met by supplements. It is known that heart muscles, once damaged after a massive heart attack, cannot be repaired. This impairs the blood pumping capacity of the heart referred to as ejection fraction (EF). Coenzyme Q10 is the only antioxidant that helps to regenerate heart muscles after a heart attack, and to improve the ejection fraction.

Depending on the severity of the condition, a minimum dose of 100mg to 300mg daily is usually recommended.

Coenzyme Q10 also lowers blood pressure, total cholesterol and triglyceride levels, while raising good cholesterol.

5.4 PIGMENT/COLOUR OF FRUITS AND VEGETABLES

Two recent books, *What Color is your Diet?* by David Heber and Susan Bowerman, and *The Color Code* by James A Joseph, emphasise the importance of pigment/colours present in fruits and vegetables. The darker the pigment, the more is its nutritive value.

Red

Tomatoes, watermelon, grapefruit, etc., are rich in antioxidant lycopene that protects against prostate cancer as well as against heart and lung diseases.

Red/Purple/Blue

Grapes, blueberries, strawberries, beets, brinjal, sweet red peppers, plums, etc., are full of antioxidants such as anthocyanins. They prevent formation of blood clots.

Orange

Carrots, mangoes, squash, and sweet potatoes are rich in cancer fighting alpha and beta carotenes that protect the lungs and skin against free radical damage.

Orange/Yellow

Oranges, peaches, and papaya provide beta cryptothanxin which supports intracellular communication, and may help prevent heart disease.

Yellow/Green

Spinach, corn, green peas, and honey dew melons are sources of lutein and zeaxanthin. They reduce the risk of cataract and age related macular degeneration.

Green

Broccoli, cabbage, sprouts, cauliflower, etc., are rich in sulforaphane, isocynate and indoles which inhibit the action of carcinogens.

White/Green

Garlic, onions, celery, etc., contain allicin which has anti-tumour properties.

5.5 VITAMIN/MINERAL ROBBERS

Chemicals in food, water, polluted air, common medicines, drugs, laxatives, refined sugar, alcohol, tobacco and stress act as vitamin robbers. Some vitamins are destroyed by heat and some when exposed to air, i.e. when they undergo oxidation.

Air Pollutants – Pollutants in air destroy vitamin A. Remedy: Take plenty of milk, yellow-orange fruits and vegetables, green leafy vegetables, nuts and seeds.

Fried Foods – Frying destroys EFAs as well as vitamins A and E. Remedy: Stick to a two-minute stir frying. Add olive oil only after cooking is done.

Refined Foods – Refining of whole grains, raw sugar, etc., robs them of zinc, chromium, antioxidants.

Alcohol – Alcohol destroys all B-vitamins. It also depletes the body of vitamins A, C, D and E, and minerals calcium, magnesium, potassium, zinc and selenium. Remedy: Minimise your alcohol intake. Stick to red wine.

Antibiotics – These infection fighters also destroy healthy gut bacteria which produce B-vitamins. Remedy: Take B-Complex and a probiotic food like curd while on antibiotics.

Smoking – To detoxify the effect, smokers need to take four times as much vitamin C as non-smokers.

Filtered Water – Filtering often robs the naturally occurring calcium and magnesium in water. Remedy: Choose a filter which does not remove minerals from water.

Artificial Additives/Colours – Orange squash contains tartrazine colourings. They make the body excrete far more zinc than required. Remedy: Take fresh juices only.

6
Minerals

Minerals are needed as constituents of bones, blood, etc. in the body. They are also needed for maintenance of cell functions. There are at least twenty minerals required by the body. Eating a wide variety of foods helps us in attaining all the necessary minerals required for proper growth. Some minerals are required in large quantities, while some are required in small traces by the body.

6.1 MINERALS REQUIRED IN LARGE QUANTITIES

Of all the minerals, our body requires calcium in maximum amount. Calcium is followed by phosphorous, potassium, sodium, chloride, sulphur, and magnesium in decreasing order.

Calcium

Calcium is the constituent mineral of bones and teeth. Bones contain 99.5 per cent of the body's total calcium content. In addition to this, calcium is also important for muscle function. It keeps muscles toned and is crucial for healthy muscular action of heart.

Calcium is essential for the release of neurotransmitters, nerve signal transmission and heartbeat regulation. It regulates clotting of blood and blood pressure. It also helps in the absorption of vitamin B12.

On an average, the daily requirement of calcium is about 800-1000mg. During pregnancy and lactation, women are advised to take more than the normal intake of calcium.

Women who workout, to the extent of sweating, lose almost 100mg of calcium through sweat. Because of the additional need of calcium for child-bearing, women are advised to eat more calcium-rich foods. As age advances, it may become necessary for them to take calcium supplements also, to prevent brittle bones or osteoporosis.

The best way to get calcium is to drink milk and to consume yoghurt (dahi), cheese, tofu, almonds, sesame seeds, oats, oranges, and leafy greens like spinach. Broccoli, cauliflower, root vegetables, figs (anjeer), etc., are also important sources of calcium.

Note: It is not enough to increase calcium intake but also important to ensure absorption of calcium. Calcium absorption is improved with vitamin C and D.

Hence, it is best to get your calcium from milk, which contains both calcium and vitamin D, and oranges which contain calcium and vitamin C together. Exposure to, preferably 15-30 minutes of morning sun is the best source of vitamin D.

It is a myth that eating meat can improve calcium reserve. In fact, too much protein can prevent calcium absorption. Further, meat brings with it a lot of unhealthy fat and toxins.

It is also important to prevent calcium loss from the body. Lack of calcium intake and its absorption could lead to osteoporosis. Note that smoking and caffeine can lead to loss of calcium, and bone mass. One must cut down on caffeine and soft drinks.

Boron reduces urinary calcium excretion. Hence, it prevents arthritis and osteoporosis. Fruits and vegetables, particularly cauliflower and broccoli, are main sources of boron.

However, there is a possible downside to high intakes of calcium. Excessive calcium may cause diarrhoea, and may also result in stone formation in kidneys.

Calcium may also lead to clotting of blood. Hence, people prone to blood clot formation, heart disease and stroke should not take calcium supplements. Calcium works only in partnership with magnesium. It is, therefore, advised to consume foods rich in both calcium and magnesium.

Phosphorous

Phosphorous ranks only second to calcium in regard to content by mass in the body. About 80 per cent of it goes into bones and teeth.

Phosphorous is essential in metabolism, and in calcium absorption and utilisation.

Maintaining a proper ratio of calcium to phosphorous is important. A diet having too little calcium but too much phosphorous can result in osteoporosis. Animal foods have high amounts of phosphorous, but very less calcium. This is the reason why many non-vegetarians develop osteoporosis in old age. Phosphorous is easily available, especially from high protein foods.

Pomegranate contains good amounts of phosphorous.

Magnesium

Magnesium activates around 300 enzymes. It is an additional constituent of our bones, muscles, body tissues, cells and fluids.

Next to potassium, it is the most common mineral present in our cells. Like potassium, it is involved in maintaining the electric charge of cells, particularly of nerve cells. It helps in maintaining stable levels of calcium and phosphorous in the bones.

Its deficiency produces symptoms similar to potassium deficiency, viz., mental confusion, heart disturbance, high blood pressure, muscle cramps, kidney stones, cancer, insomnia, pre-disposition towards stress, premenstrual syndrome, etc.

Magnesium may prevent the onset of metabolic syndrome, a bundle of risk factors for diabetes and heart disease. This is partly due to magnesium's ability to regulate blood sugar by influencing the amount of insulin secreted.

Magnesium deficiency may cause heart attack due to inflammation caused by C-reactive protein (CRP) in blood. Inflammations produce a spasm of coronary artery and heart muscles reducing flow of blood and oxygen. Magnesium-rich foods reduce blood inflammations. It also increases solubility of calcium in urine, thus preventing the formation of kidney stones.

Magnesium is abundant in seeds of all types, particularly sunflower and pumpkin seeds. Grains have high amounts of magnesium and tryptophan in combination.

Other rich sources of magnesium are honey, whole grains, brown rice, legumes, celery, radishes, dark green leafy vegetables like spinach, almonds, cashews, pistachios, mustard and sesame seeds, cloves, all fruits particularly bananas, pomegranate, and pineapples, soymilk, milk and yoghurt.

A ratio of 2:2:1 (between calcium, phosphorous and magnesium) is necessary for a healthy body.

Potassium, Sodium and Chloride

Potassium, sodium and chloride are electrolytes or ions of salts that can conduct electricity when dissolved in water. Electrolytes maintain water and acid-alkali balance. They are involved in muscle contraction, nerve transmission, heart, kidney and adrenal functions.

Potassium is an important mineral that helps regulate and lower blood pressure.

Ill Effects of Potassium Deficiency

Most important function of potassium is to keep blood pressure under control, and help in intercellular nutrients transfer. Its deficiency may cause high blood pressure, weak memory, heart problem, insomnia, depression, acne and skin related problems, allergies, kidney stones, etc.

Studies have shown that mere restriction of salt/sodium in diet does not control high BP. It is also necessary to increase potassium intake. A diet rich in fruits and vegetables can maintain high potassium-sodium ratio since most fruits and vegetables have this ratio in excess of 50 as shown below:

Fruit/Vegetable	Potassium: Sodium Ratio
Lima beans	580
Bananas	440
Oranges	260
Asparagus	165
Potatoes	130
Apples	90
Tomatoes	89
Carrots	6

The same for non-vegetarian food is only 5:1.

Bananas, guavas, oranges, apples, papaya, prunes, radishes and avocados are very rich in potassium. Consuming them can significantly help in lowering the blood pressure.

One medium-sized guava can provide 63 per cent more potassium than one gets from a banana. Radishes contain as much potassium as bananas.

Almonds, cashews, pistachios, pomegranates, watercress, celery, fennel, lettuce, ripe tomatoes, asparagus, beets, broccoli, carrots, egg plant, green beans, kale, mustard greens, spinach, squash, turnip, are also very good sources of potassium.

What About Too Much Potassium?

Most people can handle excess potassium except those having kidney problems. They need to take medical advice to restrict their diet so as to avoid potassium toxicity.

Magnesium and potassium together in a food synergistically lower blood pressure.

Go Easy on Salt

Add only a little salt to food. Enough natural salt is present in all foods. A diet rich in sodium increases risk of HBP, heart attack and stroke. A study published in the British Medical Journal in April 2007 states that keeping diet low on salt not only lowers blood pressure, but also reduces risk of heart attack and stroke by 25 per cent, and subsequent death by 20 per cent. Reason: Sodium may make blood vessels less capable of expansion and contraction. People who are fond of consuming a lot of salty snacks (*namkeens*) should take a special note of this.

American Medical Association has urged the US Government to take action to reduce excess salt in food. It believes that reducing the salt in diet by 50 per cent over the next 10 years could save at least 150,000 lives a year just in US alone.

Ill Effects of Sodium Deficiency

Sodium deficiency happens very rarely. But it can occur due to sodium loss by excessive sweating, chronic diarrhoea, or use of diuretics, kidneys and adrenal gland dysfunction, and malnutrition. Together with potassium, sodium is important for functioning of nerves and muscles, maintaining balance of fluids, and electrical function. Its deficiency can lead to dehydration, low blood pressure, muscle cramps, confusion, slurred speech, seizure, coma or even death in extreme cases.

Sulphur

Sulphur is a component of many amino acids (proteins). It is present in high amounts in the proteins of joints, skin, hair, and nails, and in insulin hormone produced by pancreas. Sulphur deficiency may result in diabetes and arthritis.

Apart from legumes and whole grains, garlic, onions and cabbage/cauliflower/broccoli contain rich amounts of sulphur.

6.2 MINERALS REQUIRED IN SMALL AMOUNTS/TRACES

Some minerals are required by the body in small amounts. This is not to under estimate their importance for they carry out certain vital functions in the body, despite being present only in small traces. These minerals include boron, chromium, cobalt, copper, fluoride, iodine, iron, manganese, molybdenum, selenium, silicon, vanadium and zinc.

Iron

Iron is the main component of haemoglobin molecule of red blood cells (RBCs) that carry oxygen from lungs to body tissues, and bring carbon dioxide back from body tissues to lungs.

Iron is also involved in energy production. Iron requirement increases during pregnancy, lactation, infancy and adolescence and after blood loss during menstruation and injury. Iron deficiency causes anaemia, low energy, pale skin, cold hands and feet, brittle nails, and impaired immune function.

The deficiency may result not only from decreased intake of iron, but also from decreased absorption of iron in old age, or due to chronic illness, or blood loss.

Use of iron supplements usually causes diarrhoea. It is better to take iron in its natural organic form through foods.

Beetroot and pomegranate juice boost iron content in blood. Apples contain iron in its easily digestible form. Pistachios, dates, leafy greens, and mustard oil also have high iron content.

It is beneficial to cook in cast-iron vessels to increase the iron content in your diet.

Note: To increase the absorption of iron, consume foods and liquids rich in vitamin C.

Copper

Copper is essential for the utilisation of iron in the manufacture of haemoglobin. It also helps stimulate the absorption of iron.

It is an important part of enzymes. It is involved in manufacture of collagen, and in energy production.

Copper deficiency results in anaemia, fatigue, and elevated cholesterol levels. Cashews, walnuts, and sesame seeds, which are also rich in zinc are good sources of copper.

Drinking water left overnight in a copper jug can help augment copper intake.

Zinc

Zinc is essential for cell growth, cell function, synthesis and secretion of hormones, prostate function, and fertility. It improves sperm count. During puberty, zinc supplementation helps to cure skin acne which is the result of hormonal imbalance.

Best sources of zinc are nuts, mustard oil, and seeds of pumpkin, sunflower and sesame. Other good sources are ginger, mushrooms, peas, legumes, beans, rajma, whole grains, root vegetables like potatoes, cocoa, orange juice and grape juice. With age, the body becomes deficient in zinc. To slow ageing, one must increase the intake of zinc-containing foods.

Consuming a diet rich in zinc and magnesium increases hormone level in the body. This, in turn, results in maintaining or restoring the libido. Zinc is known to lower the levels of good HDL cholesterol.

However, it is advised not to take zinc supplements indiscriminately. Cooking in gun metal (*kaskut*) vessels increases the zinc content in the food.

Iodine

Iodine is the principal component of hormones produced by the thyroid gland. These hormones control overall body metabolism. The function of thyroid gland is to add iodine to an amino acid to produce thyroid hormones (thyroxin).

When thyroid gland is under-active, it does not produce enough thyroxin. One develops hypothyroidism, which results in making a person lethargic and overweight.

Over-active thyroid gland produces excess of thyroxin and one develops hyperthyroidism, which results in weight loss. One reason of hypothyroidism is iodine deficiency.

Use of iodised salt prevents iodine deficiency. Vegetables grown near the sea contain plenty of iodine.

On the other hand, if you have hyperthyroidism, you should avoid iodine. Iodised salt is not a very good choice in such a case as it plays havoc with the hormones. You need to consult a specialist immediately.

Chromium

Chromium works in conjunction with insulin to maintain sugar levels within the narrow permissible range. By metabolising sugar, chromium decreases cholesterol and triglyceride levels. Chromium is, thus, an important mineral that prevents diabetes, atherosclerosis and high blood pressure. Its deficiency causes insulin insensitivity and hence, diabetes.

Chromium can be easily obtained from whole grains, unpolished brown rice, legumes, rajma, beans, peas, grapes, fresh cane juice (without white sugar), and black pepper.

Grape juice/wine has the highest amount of chromium. Refined foods are stripped off their chromium content. All whites – white flour, white rice, and white sugar have no chromium.

Note: Foods rich in zinc are generally rich in chromium also.

Boron

Boron is found to activate female hormone oestrogen. It also reduces urinary calcium excretion, thereby preventing arthritis and osteoporosis.

Fruits and vegetables are major dietary sources of boron. Cauliflower and broccoli are the richest sources of boron.

Manganese

Manganese helps in inflammations and reduces symptoms of arthritis. Adequate levels of manganese are necessary for a healthy central nervous system.

It has been found that deficiency of manganese leads to low HDL levels. Manganese deficiency can also cause epilepsy.

Consume mustard oil, oats, whole wheat and grains, brown rice, almonds, walnuts, sesame seeds, beans and legumes, tea, ginger, cinnamon, cloves, garlic, onions, beets, green vegetables, etc., to meet the requirement of manganese.

Silicon

Silicon plays a major role in bone formation. It is silicon which helps strengthen bones and prevents osteoporosis. Silicon is required in connective tissues, muscles, tendons, ligaments, cartilage, bones and nails.

Referred to as a 'beauty mineral', it is essential for healthy skin, hair, nails and teeth. Cucumbers, beets and oats are rich sources of silica.

Beer made from barley is considered to be one of the most important source of silicon.

Molybdenum

Molybdenum is a component of several important chemical processes that contribute to detoxification of liver. It is concentrated primarily in the liver, kidney, bones, and skin.

Carrots, cucumbers, celery, dark green leafy vegetables, peas, beans and legumes, and cereal grains are very good sources of molybdenum.

Selenium

Selenium is a trace mineral that particularly suppresses prostate cancer cell growth.

Selenium mineral with vitamin E prevents damage to cells from free radicals. One of the reasons for many degenerative diseases could be low levels of selenium.

Garlic contains both selenium and vitamin E. Brazil nuts (*Bertholletia ke beej*) have maximum selenium content. One or two Brazil nuts a day are enough for your daily needs. If you take more, it may lead to selenium toxicity. Sunflower seeds are the next best source of selenium. Other very good sources of selenium are oats, brown rice, turnips, and nuts.

Intake of selenium through supplements may cause toxicity. It may cause loss of hair and nails, and skin rashes.

Germanium

Germanium helps to improve tissue oxygenation at cell level. Foods high in germanium are garlic and onions.

Nitrate

Nitrates are not metals, but they are radicals in the same way as chlorides. Nitrates expand arteries. In this manner, they lower blood pressure, and increase blood flow to all organs including brain, genitals, kidneys, etc. Foods rich in nitrate include ajwain, beetroots, cabbage and spinach. Arginine herb is nitrate-rich.

IMPORTANT NOTE

Do not overdo vitamins and minerals. Do not believe that if little doses of vitamins and minerals are good, large doses would be better.

- The recommended dose of vitamin E for adults is only 15mg daily. High doses raise blood pressure.
- Taking too many fat-soluble vitamins (like A, D, E and K) is dangerous because it is difficult for the body to get rid of any excess through the urine.

- Thus, vitamin D, iron, zinc, and selenium can become toxic in overdoses. Note that energy/calories come from the food you eat. Vitamins and minerals do not provide calories.

7

Fibre and Water

7.1 FIBRE

Fibre, often referred to as roughage, though not a nutrient, is very essential. Beneficial effects of dietary fibre are many. They may be listed as follows:

1. Food moves faster through intestines. Hence, residence period of toxic residue in the body is reduced.
2. Food is released gradually in the intestines. Hence, no sudden increase occurs in blood sugar levels.
3. Increased satisfaction and satiety from food due to feeling of filling.
4. Increased secretions from pancreas.
5. Increased bulk of stool. It has a cleansing effect, and prevents constipation.
6. Increased removal of cholesterol along with the bulk during excretion.
7. Good bacterial flora in intestines as compared to bad bacterial flora with animal foods. Animal foods have no fibre.

Most plant foods have fibre. The fibre can be of two kinds: insoluble fibre and soluble fibre.

The soluble fibre, like the flesh of apples, dissolves in water and plays an important role in lowering cholesterol and triglyceride levels by scavenging them out. It is almost totally digested.

The insoluble fibre does not dissolve in water. It adds bulk to stool, and helps to stimulate intestinal contractions. It is found in the stalks, stems, peels, skin and bran of produce. It passes undigested. The insoluble fibre is mainly cellulose. Wheat bran is rich in insoluble cellulose. Cellulose is easily digested by animals, but not by humans.

The traditional advice about fibre in general is wrong – the insoluble fibre foods not only fail to soothe irritable bowels but may actually make things worse.

Fruits, vegetables, barley, lentils, legumes, oats, unpolished rice, etc., have plenty of fibre that is soft on the lining of the stomach and intestines. An example of a highly soluble fibre food is oat bran.

Scientists at Sydney's Garvan Institute of Medical Research have found out that fibre boosts the immune system to combat diseases like asthma, diabetes and arthritis.

In addition to eliminating toxins, cholesterol, etc., when foods high in fibre reach the gut, bacteria convert them to compounds known as short-chain fatty acids that are known to alleviate inflammatory diseases.

Psyllium husk (isabgul) is one single item that contains 100 per cent soluble fibre. It, therefore, is one single item of food with no nutrients or calories but with tremendous benefits. It prevents and cures many diseases, especially those related to the digestive system, including heart disease, diabetes, asthma, arthritis, Alzheimer's disease, etc.

7.2 WATER

According to *Atharvaveda,* water is the elixir of life. It is vital to our health as it forms more than 66 percent of our body weight.

Effect of Dehydration

If one loses just 5-6 per cent of body water, one may develop headache, and feel nauseated. At 8 per cent loss, renal failure may begin to develop. At 10 per cent loss, muscle spasms occur and eyes become dim and one might become delirious. And 15 per cent loss is life-threatening.

To replace the water that we lose daily through urination, defecation, perspiration and evaporation from skin, our body needs a minimum of 2 litres or 8 glasses of water everyday. Some water comes from the food we take; certain foods such as leafy greens, cucumber and fruits that are water-dense also provide necessary water to the body.

There are conflicting opinions whether caffeinated drinks like colas, coffee, etc., account for any water intake. Some believe they cause more dehydration than hydration.

Drinking coconut water and juices of fresh fruits and vegetables is the best way of consuming water in its pure and natural form.

What are the health benefits of drinking eight or more glasses of water per day?

You know that it is through water that nutrients are carried throughout the body cells, and toxins and waste are eliminated from the body.

Water helps in prevention of urinary tract infections, kidney stones, bladder cancer, colon cancer, constipation, and obesity. It rejuvenates skin and other tissues. Water is the best cleanser nature has provided us. In case of illness, one should drink enough water as it would help in flushing out toxins from the body.

One can give hundred reasons in support of drinking plenty of water. By not drinking enough water, the kidney function will be affected, stones may form, bowels will become hard, and blood can thicken leading to clot formation eventually causing heart attack or stroke. Due to sluggish blood circulation and not receiving enough nutrients skin will become dull.

You should drink some cold water about 15 minutes before your meals. Cold water before meals enhances metabolism and thus, increases the appetite.

How does one know whether one is taking enough water?

The best way is to note the colour of your urine. If you are adequately hydrated, it is the colour of lemonade. But if it is amber or a deeper colour, you need to drink more water.

Do not drink cold water after meals

It will solidify the oily stuff. The sludge reacting with acid will break down and will stick to the intestine linings. Soon it will turn into fats that may lead to cancer.

Note: Water should be taken not only in adequate quantity, but it should also be pure. It should be free from harmful bacteria and toxic elements. Chlorine and fluoride are routinely added in city water supply to kill the harmful effect of pesticide, nitrates, and heavy metals (such as mercury, lead and cadmium, etc.) that percolate into water through the ground and polluted air.

Have your own water purifier, preferably of the reverse osmosis (RO) variety, rather than suffer from serious water-borne diseases. Also use copper vessels for storing water.

8
Grains and Cereals

Grains and cereals are essentially carbohydrates. Till sometime back, health experts advised against eating food with high fat content. But now it is known that apart from saturated and trans-fats, MUFA and PUFA like omega-3 fats in canola oil, mustard oil, flaxseeds, walnuts, etc., are also essential.

In the same vein, we are often advised by some to shun carbohydrates, and to consume proteins instead.

Neither piece of advice is correct. Just as some types of fats are actually healthy for the body, similarly complex carbohydrates as in whole grains are healthy for the body. It is only the refined ones like white flour, white rice, etc., that are not very healthy.

To maintain a sound metabolism, one needs to take a balanced diet comprising all nutrients – proteins, carbohydrates and fats. Roughly one-third of the total calorie requirement of the body should come from each of these, with minor modifications. For example, those who have heart problem should cut back on fats. Whatever fats they take should be in the form of olive, mustard and canola oils, and from nuts like almonds, walnuts and pistachios.

Every grain contains the following four anatomical parts: the bran (the fibre), the aleurone layer, the endosperm (the compartment that primarily stores complex carbohydrates and some protein), the germ (the embryo or the sprouting section of grain).

In the production of white flour, white rice, etc., the bran, the aleurone layer, and the germ are removed. Removing these results in the loss of essential nutrients, that is, 97 per cent of thiamine, 94 per cent of vitamin B6, 88 per cent of niacin, 87 per cent of chromium, 80 per cent of magnesium, 77 per cent of potassium, 72 per cent of zinc, 70 per cent of essential fatty acids, 68 per cent of riboflavin, 60 per cent of calcium, 57 per cent of panteothenic acid, and 25 per cent of protein.

This is quite a tremendous loss. Hence, it is advisable to consume only whole grains. The amount of phytochemicals in grains is equal to or at an even higher level than in vegetables and fruits.

All grains provide tryptophan and magnesium in addition to carbohydrates and fibre. Tryptophan is the natural sleep inducer, while magnesium calms the nerves. No wonder, after having a regular meal that involves foods that are made from wheat, rice and other grains, one naturally feels sleepy. Wholesome food is the best tranquiliser.

The two most important grains are rice and wheat. In some cultures, wheat is the staple food, and in some others it is rice.

Amaranth (*Ramdana*)

Amaranth or *Ramdana*, also called *chaulai*, is the least allergenic of all grains. In some cultures, it was even considered as the symbol of immortality. It is, at present, a forgotten food except in India. 'Amaranth' is the Greek word for 'never-fading flower'. It is one of the most nutritious grains on earth.

Amaranth is high in protein (15-18 per cent) as it includes amino acids lysine and methionine, which are not frequently found in other grains. No doubt, it is considered a protein punch.

It is also considered a brain food for being high in fibre, minerals like calcium, iron, magnesium, potassium, zinc, copper, manganese, and phosphorous, and vitamins A, E, B2, B6, folate and C.

It is five times rich in iron content as compared to wheat and has more calcium than milk. It contains a form of vitamin E that helps in lowering cholesterol levels.

Being easily digestible, it is frequently given to people convalescing from illness.

Amaranth contains 6-10 per cent oil in its germ. This oil is predominantly linoleic acid, an EFA omega-6 fat linked to cholesterol lowering activity.

However, it has moderately high content of oxalic acid. Hence, people with kidney disorders/stones, gout, and rheumatoid arthritis should avoid it.

Rice (chawal)

Unmilled unpolished brown rice (chawal) is very nutritious. It is a very good source of manganese, selenium, magnesium and tryptophan.

Note that wheat contains more protein than rice, but the quality of rice protein is better. As a result, rice is the most easily digestible food. Even infants and patients suffering from diarrhoea can be fed with rice or just with rice water.

Milling and polishing of rice destroys 67 per cent of its B-vitamins, chromium and zinc, all of its fibre and EFAs.

Manganese in rice produces energy from protein and carbohydrate. And it is involved in the production of fatty acids essential for a healthy nervous system, and of cholesterol used in the body to produce hormones. Whole brown rice helps in maintaining lower cholesterol levels.

Selenium in brown rice, with fibre, prevents cancer.

Magnesium is plentiful in rice. It reduces severity of asthma and migraine attacks, calms nerves, lowers blood pressure, and reduces risk of heart disease and stroke.

Rice is free of allergy-causing gluten that is present in wheat.

Black Rice

Black rice is grown in China as some kind of a super food. Food scientist Zhimin Xu at Louisiana State University analysed samples of black rice grown in the US and found that it contained more anthocyanin antioxidants than blueberries, and at the same time had less sugar, more fibre and more vitamin E. Anthocyanins mop up free radicals, help protect arteries, and prevent DNA damage that leads to cancer.

Sama ke Chawal

Sama ke Chawal is classified as a fruit but it looks and tastes like rice. It is consumed in India during festive fasting since it is not a cereal and is more easily digestible as compared to normal rice.

Wheat (*Gehun*)

Wheat is better suited to make bread because of its gluten content, which enables the bread to rise because of its elasticity.

But some people are either allergic to gluten or they lack the ability to digest it. Gluten is found in many other grains like rye, oats and barley.

Apart from complex carbohydrates, fibre and tryptophan, whole wheat is a very good source of manganese, magnesium, and potassium. Potassium plays a key role in maintaining optimum blood pressure. White flour, and white bread prepared from it contain less than half the potassium of whole wheat. Wheat bran is a bulk laxative. It provides the fibre, B-vitamins, and about 20 per cent of protein content of whole wheat.

Whole grain wheat and wheat germ are good sources of the antioxidant vitamin E.

Whole grain wheat is a true anti-cancer food. Among all grains, only wheat bran reduces colon-cancer-causing bacterial enzymes in stool.

Women who eat more whole wheat have their oestrogen level in control. Otherwise, excess of this hormone can produce fibroids and breast cancer.

Lignans are present in whole wheat, brown rice and oats. They maintain friendly flora in intestines, and protect against many degenerative diseases including cancer.

Pasta is made from refined white flour. But one should prefer new varieties, made from whole grain, being marketed now. Lentil, chickpeas, flaxseeds, and pastas blended with seeds and legumes are also available in the market these days.

Sprouted wheat bread contains 28 per cent more B1, 315 per cent more B2, 66 per cent more B3, 65 per cent more B5, 111 per cent more biotin, 278 per cent more folate, and 300 per cent more vitamin C than plain bread.

Note: The crusty dark brown portion of the bread has 8 times more antioxidants than the inside of the loaf. That is because baking changes the amino acid lysine contained in flour into a compound that destroys cancer-causing free radicals.

Corn (*makka*)

Corn is a rich source of vitamins B1, B5, folate, and C, and phosphorous and manganese. It has high amounts of lutein and zeaxanthin antioxidants which strengthen vision.

Corn contains folate which helps lower levels of homocysteine which damages arteries. Fibre and folate rich diet is also associated with reduced risk of colon cancer.

Beta-cryptoxanthin, an orange-coloured carotenoid found in corn, as also in pumpkin, papaya, red bell peppers, oranges, peaches, etc., reduces the risk of lung cancer by almost 27 per cent.

With vitamin B1, needed for neuro-transmitters, there is less risk of dementia and Alzheimer's disease.

Corn, however, is an allergenic food.

Barley (*jau*)

Barley is a coarse grain. It is a good source of fibre and selenium. But as barley contains an insoluble type of fibre, some people find it difficult to digest. However, many bacteria in intestines multiply on feeding on this fibre.

Barely lowers cholesterol and triglyceride levels. Because of presence of fibre in barley, it has a very low glycemic index and hence is recommended to those suffering from diabetes.

It is a good source of tryptophan, copper, manganese, phosphorous, selenium and silica. Barley is known to prevent gallstones since the fibre not only reduces intestinal transit-time, it also decreases secretion of bile acids which contribute to the formation of gallstones. Selenium in barley is good for prostate glands. Silica in barley strengthens bones.

Millet (*bajra*)

Millet, a coarse grain, was once a staple of Indian diet, but gradually lost popularity when the focus shifted to rice and wheat. Wheat farming demands lots of chemicals and plenty of water. As a result, the soil turns sterile. And rice fields with their stagnant water produce methane, which is a greenhouse gas. Millet crop, on the other hand, requires minimum water and least protection.

Bajra Khichdi and *Bajra* Roti are the two preparations in which it is popularly consumed.

Buckwheat (*kotu*)

Buckwheat flour is considered as a non-cereal food and is consumed during festivities. An important thing to note is that it contains no allergy-causing gluten.

Oats (*vilayati jau*)

Oats are an excellent source of manganese, of selenium, and reasonably rich source of tryptophan, phosphorous, vitamin B1, fibre, magnesium, and protein.

Oats, when simply boiled in water, taste as if boiled in milk.

The wonderful thing about oats is that they have a specific water-soluble fibre called beta-glucan. Consuming a bowl of oatmeal lowers cholesterol by 8-23 per cent. Note that with each 1 per cent drop in serum cholesterol, there is a 2 per cent decrease in the risk of developing heart disease.

Beta-glucan fibre helps immune cells to migrate to the site of infection to fight it.

Oats contain a unique antioxidant, an avena-compound, which slows progression of atherosclerosis i.e. the build-up of plaque that narrows blood vessels. Thus, it helps reduce risk of cardiovascular diseases.

Beta-glucan fibre helps in lowering blood sugar levels as well, thus lessening the amount of insulin needed. Soluble fibre prevents constipation, piles, colon cancer, and gastro-intestinal disorders.

Oats are a remedy for insomnia, because of the avena-compound and also because of their high tryptophan and magnesium content.

Avena Sativa mother tincture, concentrate of oat extracts, is a homoeopathic treatment for both sexual debility and insomnia.

Sabudana (sago), Tapioca and Arrowroot

Sabudana pearls, tapioca and arrowroot – all three are extracted from the roots of the three different plants/trees. They do not contain any protein, vitamins or minerals. However, they are easy to digest.

9
Legumes/Beans/Dal/Rajma

Legumes, dried beans, rajma and pulses (dals) of various kinds are essentially proteins. They provide 2-4 times more protein than grains.

The common Indian meal comprising grains and legumes, dal-roti or dal-chawal or rajma-chawal is a wholesome food. It provides all the necessary high quality proteins and carbohydrates. Legumes, in addition to milk and dairy, are the only item of food which provides vitamin B12 to vegetarians.

A diet rich in legumes lowers cholesterol levels, improves blood sugar control, and reduces risk of many kinds of cancers.

Legumes, particularly red kidney beans, rajma and urad dal, may increase intestinal flatulence/gas. The gas produced can be significantly reduced by properly soaking legumes overnight, draining the water, and then cooking them well enough for 1-3 hours. Moong dal may require only half hour or even less.

Sprouted Legumes

Sprouted legumes are not only easy to digest, but also higher in nutritional value. Sprouted moong dal is an excellent source of vitamin B12.

Dried Beans

Beans are classified as a super food. They are loaded with protein (15 gram per cup) and dozens of key nutrients including calcium, magnesium and potassium, in addition to trace minerals like molybdenum, manganese, iron, and vitamins B1 and folate.

A recent study analysing the antioxidant content of 100 foods showed that red, kidney, and black beans are the highest vegetable sources of antioxidants providing benefits similar to grapes, apples, blueberries and cranberries. They contain 10 times more antioxidants than oranges.

The darker the seed coat of dried bean/rajma, the higher is its antioxidant content. Yellow and white varieties have lower content.

Iron in beans synthesises haemoglobin. Iron is synonymous with energy.

The combined effect of antioxidant flavonoids and polyphenols, fibre, folate, and magnesium result in lower heart disease risk and protection against cancer. Soluble fibre helps lowering cholesterol. Folate helps lowering homocysteine level, an independent risk factor in heart disease.

About 100 per cent daily value (DV) of folate can reduce the risk of heart attack by 10 per cent. One cup of cooked black beans (urad) provides 64 per cent of DV of folate. Magnesium is an essential mineral that keeps veins, arteries and heart in good condition. Lack of magnesium makes the heart vulnerable to free radical damage.

Even the proteins in beans and legumes are protective against coronary heart disease.

Pulses

Black urad dal, brown masoor, yellow arhar dal or chick peas, chana *or* gram dal, and moong dal are the commonly available pulses.

As stated earlier, moong dal is the easiest to digest. Sprouted moong dal is a health food containing large amounts of nutrients particularly vitamins B12 and C.

Gram or Chana

Chana is a highly nutritious legume and plays an important role in dissolving *kapha*.

It is available in many varieties. The one known as Bengal gram is taken in roasted as well as sprouted form. Sprouting makes it richer in vitamin C content.

The other popular variety is the *kabuli* chana. It is best taken in boiled form.

Soybean or Soy

Soybean is a species of legume with high nutritional value. In fact, soybean is an oilseed rather than a pulse. Studies show that soya foods lower bad LDL cholesterol, and maintain good HDL cholesterol.

Soy is a complete protein food, as it contains all essential amino acids. Soya milk offers the same protein content as dairy milk, minus the fat and cholesterol. Similar to legumes, soybeans provide ample vitamin B12 to vegetarians. They are a good source of B-vitamins thiamine, niacin, folate, and riboflavin.

Cold pressed unrefined soybean oil is rich in omega-3 and omega-6 fats, which prevent heart disease and maintain healthy blood cholesterol levels.

Soya milk can be prepared by first soaking beans in water overnight before blending them and filtering, and then boiling the liquid portion.

And highly nutritious tofu, equivalent of paneer (extracted from milk), is prepared from soya milk. Tofu is also a good source of calcium.

Soybeans contain natural chemicals that mimic the effect of female sex hormone oestrogen. Hence, menopausal women who get depleted of the hormone are advised to eat soybeans.

Soy contains genistein, known to interact like oestrogen. But a new study by Ren-Shan of Wenzhou Medical College in China found that genistein could interfere with the production of enzymes involved in the production of sperms in men.

10
Vegetables

Vegetables, like fruits, are the greatest source of minerals, vitamins and antioxidants. The more vegetables you eat, the lower would be your risk of heart disease, stroke, cancer and other illnesses.

Studies show that eating 5-6 servings of fruits and vegetables daily curtail the risk of cancer by 30 per cent.

Vegetables are completely alkaline foods. They are low in calories. Some vegetables like asparagus, carrots, celery, gourds, lettuce, etc., are negative-calorie foods (NCFs).

Asparagus (*Shatavari*)

Green stalks of the plant are used as vegetable. Asparagus is very rich in vitamins A, C, K, riboflavin, folate, minerals and protein.

Powder of its dried stalks is used as a health tonic in Ayurveda under the name *Shatavari*. The plant, both in its vegetable form and as *Shatavari* powder is considered very important for curing ailments specific to women.

Avocados

Ripe avocado pulp can be eaten raw in some form of preparation like guacamole.

Avocados are high in fat content (22 per cent). But the fat is heart-healthy MUFA. MUFA and vitamin E present in avocado make it good for heart, skin and hair. There is no cholesterol and sodium in avocados.

Avocados are rich in potassium, vitamins and antioxidants lutein and beta-carotene.

A study showed that those who ate avocados with their salad had 5 times more lutein in their body that helps in improving the vision and 15 times more beta-carotene that increases the haemoglobin, than those who did not consume avocados.

Arabi

It is a root vegetable. It may cause gas.

Bathua

It is a very healthy green leafy vegetable available only during winters in northern part of India. It can be used as a dry vegetable after boiling, mincing, and sautéing. As it has a warming effect, it can be made into *raita* by churning it with curd.

Beans (Green)

Green beans, especially dried ones, are high in antioxidants, beta-carotene, vitamins B1, B2, B3, C, K and folate, minerals like potassium, magnesium, manganese, copper, calcium, and phosphorous, and protein, and omega-3 fats. They are termed as 'super foods'.

Vitamin K in beans anchors calcium in bones. Potassium, magnesium, folate, and vitamin B2 individually and synergistically reduce risk of atherosclerosis, heart disease and stroke. Magnesium and potassium together lower blood pressure.

Vitamin B2 serves to protect against build-up of homocysteine. It also reduces the frequency and intensity of migraine attacks.

Vitamin B1 protects against dementia and Alzheimer's disease.

Beta-carotene and omega-3 have anti-inflammatory effects in heart disease, asthma and arthritis.

Copper with manganese reduces symptoms of arthritis by neutralising free radicals.

Fat soluble vitamins A (beta-carotene) and water soluble vitamin C together as antioxidants take care of all areas of damage from free radicals.

Beetroot

Beetroots are best sources of folate and betaine. These two help in lowering homocysteine levels in blood.

The purple crimson natural pigment betacyanin in beets helps in fighting cancer. Beetroots are also very good sources of iron, manganese, potassium and silicon.

Beetroots are high in iron. They quickly increase haemoglobin in anaemic patients. Beets contain silica, vital for skin, hair, nails, ligaments, tendons, and bones.

They also purify blood and enhance the activity of natural antioxidants to detoxify organs such as kidney, gall bladder and liver. Beetroots have long been used for liver disorders.

Nitrate in beetroots expands arteries. They are as effective as nitrate capsules that lower BP, prevent dementia, and reduce risk of heart disease and stroke.

Bell Peppers/Capsicum

These are available in green, yellow, orange, red, and other varieties.

Peppers are rich sources of antioxidants vitamins C and A that help in neutralising free radicals in water-soluble and fat-soluble areas. They prevent clot formation.

Red bell peppers additionally contain lycopene and are rich in orange-red carotene that provides protection against lung inflammation and lung disease.

Vitamin C and beta-carotene in bell peppers have protective effect against cataracts. Sweet red peppers also supply lutein and zeaxanthin that have been found to protect against macular degeneration (damage to the eyes due to ageing). These can reduce the need for cataract operations.

Vitamin C-rich foods such as bell peppers provide protection against inflammatory rheumatoid arthritis. Persons consuming negligible amounts of vitamin C are three times more likely to develop arthritis than those who consume high amounts.

Capsicum and chilli peppers are rich in capsaicin – an antioxidant. It is used as an ingredient in several pain-relieving creams. It also leads to a rise in the production of nitric oxide which relaxes blood vessels, and may help in lowering the blood pressure.

Bitter Gourd or Bitter Melon (Karela)

Bitter gourd is best characterised by its typical bitter taste. It is full of essential minerals like calcium, phosphorous, iron, copper, and potassium, and vitamins A, B1, B2, and C.

It is majorly known for containing the substance insulin. It is highly effective in lowering sugar levels in diabetic patients.

Scientists from Saint Louis University, USA, have found that an extract from karela not only destroys breast cancer cells but also prevents them from multiplying.

Bottle Gourd (*Lauki/Ghiya/Doodhi*)

This vegetable is high in fibre and thereby, cleanses the digestive system. Taking 200 ml of its juice in the morning cures acidity/*pitta*, sugar (diabetes) and gastric troubles.

Some fresh apple and pomegranate juice can also be mixed with it. The combination would help in increasing haemoglobin. Adding some amount of mint and tulsi would enhance the effect.

Lauki juice is diuretic and helps in lowering blood pressure. It prevents blood urea from increasing, and thus aids in removing kidney stones.

Warning: Do not take the juice if the vegetable is bitter. If a vegetable belonging to the cucumber family – bottle gourd, pumpkin, eggplant, and cucumber – tastes bitter, do not eat or drink its juice. It contains a toxin called cucurbitacins that may cause vomiting of blood, severe diarrhoea and ulcers, and even death.

Broccoli/Cauliflower/Cabbage/*Gobhi*

These cruciferous family vegetables are high in sulforaphane and isothiocyanates. Sulforaphane is the most powerful plant chemical that destroys cancer cells. Recent researches show that it may even help stop the growth of cancer cells in ovaries. The healing power of these vegetables works at the cellular level.

Broccoli is rich in vitamins A, C, K, carotenoids, folate, niacin, thiamine, phosphorous, protein and omega-3 fats. These compounds in broccoli increase excretion of oestrogen linked to breast cancer.

Cabbage too contains sulforaphane. Cabbage juice is very effective in treating peptic ulcers. It increases urine flow and sperm production.

Cabbages are rich in nitrate which expands arteries to allow more blood to flow to heart, lungs, brain, genitals, etc., preventing high BP, dementia, heart disease and stroke.

Cauliflower also contains the same anti-cancer phyto-chemicals and sulphoraphane.

Broccoli and cauliflower contain boron which reduces urinary calcium excretion, and thus prevents the risk of arthritis and osteoporosis.

Carrots

Carrot, often considered as the king of vegetables, is the richest source of beta-carotene. One serving of carrot or pumpkin squash everyday provides high beta-carotene in diet and curtails the risk of heart disease by 60 per cent.

Beta-carotene helps to sharpen vision. After being converted to vitamin A in the liver, it travels to the retina where it is transformed into a purple pigment named rhodopsin necessary for night vision. The antioxidant action of beta-carotene provides protection against macular degeneration, and against development of cataracts in the elderly.

Carotenoids provide cancer protection. Consuming one cup of carrots everyday may result in 20 per cent decrease in menopausal breast cancer, and 50 per cent decrease in cancers of bladder, cervix, prostate, colon, larynx and oesophagus.

One cup of carrot juice has as much beta-carotene and vitamin C as three medium-sized carrots but, of course, less fibre than one carrot.

Carotenoids also provide protection against lung inflammation/ asthma. They enhance the quality of breast milk, improve skin, hair and nails, and regulate blood sugar levels.

Celery (*Ajwain* green)

Celery is a vegetable rich in both potassium and sodium. Celery juice makes a very good electrolyte replacement drink after sweating.

Celery contains pthalides that help in lowering blood pressure. These compounds lower stress hormones, and allow muscles around arteries to relax and dilate.

Potassium, calcium, and magnesium present in celery together work to relax nerves and muscles, and reduce blood pressure.

Celery contains coumarins. They enhance the activity of white blood cells and thus bolster immune system. It also contains apigenin, a phytochemical linked to cancer protection. Another set of compounds in celery called acetylenics stop the growth of tumour cells.

Chilly (Green)

Green chillies have vitamins C and E in abundance. They improve blood circulation and are good for the heart. Those with digestive problems cannot tolerate chillies.

Cucumbers

Fresh cucumbers are primarily composed of water. Eating cucumbers is the easiest way to increase consumption of both water and fibre. But it is important to remove the bitter part of cucumber first.

Silicon in cucumbers provides nourishment to connective tissues, muscles, tendons, skin, ligaments, cartilages and bones. Silicon is important for strong bones. It prevents osteoporosis.

Cucumber largely benefits the skin. It contains vitamin C and caffeic acid. Both of them help soothe skin irritations and reduce swelling. Cucumber juice rejuvenates the skin and makes it radiant. Cucumber paste is used in face packs.

Cucumber is the most alkaline among all vegetables. People who have acidity should consume it in plenty.

Potassium, magnesium and fibre in cucumbers help in lowering the blood pressure. Mixed juice of bitter gourd, cucumbers, and tomatoes is recommended for diabetics.

Egg Plant/Brinjal

Brinjal contains an antioxidant called nasunin. It protects lipids present in the membranes of brain cells. It is regarded as a good brain food as it enables the nutrients to enter brain cells, and helps in extracting the waste out of them.

Nasunin is not only a free radical scavenger but also an iron chelator. By chelating iron, nasunin protects blood cholesterol from oxidation. Menstruating women who lose blood every month are not at risk. But for post-menopausal women excess iron can be harmful. Anti-LDL cholesterol activity of nasunin reduces plaque formation.

Eggplants should be fresh, firm, and heavy. Their skin should be free from damage. Eating fried brinjals should be avoided as they soak up oil like a sponge, even more than french fries.

Garlic

Garlic belongs to allium or lily family of vegetables that also includes onions. It is a natural antibiotic. Consuming three cloves per day is considered healthy. Allicin present in garlic is anti-inflammatory, anti-bacterial, and anti-viral in nature.

Garlic is rich in a variety of sulphur-containing compounds responsible for several health benefits. When garlic is cut or crushed, hydrogen sulphide is formed. Sulphur compounds activate vascular nerve endings that induce vasodilatation, relaxation and enlargement of blood vessels in the same manner as nitric oxide, thus lowering blood pressure and improving blood flow to heart and in the body.

Selenium and vitamin E together in garlic work as strong antioxidants. Germanium in garlic helps to improve oxygenation of tissues at cell level.

Garlic rejuvenates the respiratory organs, strengthens the functions of the heart, and lowers blood pressure.

Ginger (*Adrak*)

Ginger contains calcium, phosphorous, iron, electrolytes sodium and potassium, and magnesium. It contains a number of volatile oils that improve circulation, warm the body and help it sweat and thus, eliminate toxins through perspiration.

It stimulates the expelling of mucous, thus decongesting lungs and airways. It soothes sore throat and is an expectorant and an antiseptic. Consuming ginger with honey helps in the treatment of cold and cough at the onset. Ginger and tulsi juice taken with honey is the best expectorant for alleviating asthmatic symptoms.

It stimulates the production of saliva helping in digestion and boosting appetite. It is a carminative agent, and expels gas from intestines.

Chinese women drink ginger tea to alleviate PMS. Taking ginger daily also relieves arthritic pain in knees. It is very effective in treating nausea.

Kakari

Kakari is one of the most alkaline vegetables, like cucumber. It treats acidity.

Kale (*Karam Kalla*)

Kale belongs to cabbage family and is a rich source of calcium. It is also very high in sulforaphane, beta-carotene, vitamins A, K and C and zeaxanthin.

Lemon

Lemon is a storehouse of vitamin C. It also contains copper, phosphorous and potassium.

To cure common cold, nausea, etc., roast a lemon on slow fire and suck its juice after sprinkling some salt, black pepper, and roasted cumin seed powder on it.

Drinking a glass of warm water with lemon juice and honey empty stomach in the morning burns fat, and thereby helps in treating obesity. Eating 3-5 years old dried lemon pickle provides relief in stomach ache.

In winter, a mixture of lemon juice, glycerin and rose water is recommended for application on dry skin. Application of lemon juice on scalp also helps in arresting hair fall and getting rid of dandruff. One can also add curd to it.

Although sour in taste, lemon is not acidic in nature. Its pH value keeps it on the alkaline side. Drinking lemon with water after meals calms down *pitta* in the body.

Shikanji prepared with lemon juice and glucose or sugar in water is a very refreshing drink, and is considered many times better than aerated drinks. Some salt can also be added to it for taste. But people who have high blood pressure should avoid taking salt in *shikanji*.

Lettuce

Salads are the best way to get your daily requirement of vitamins and minerals. Lettuce not only gives you a mega dose of vitamins and minerals together with antioxidants but also increases the satiety value of your meal.

It is rich in vitamins A, C and E, and potassium, calcium and other minerals.

Mixing lettuce with tomatoes, cucumber, onions, garlic, cheeses, mint, salt, pepper and lemon multiplies health benefits.

Romaine lettuce has more folate, lutein and vitamins A and C than Iceberg lettuce. It has 7 times more vitamin C, 18 times more vitamin A, and more calcium and potassium.

Methi (Fenugreek)

Methi leaves are available during winters. They make a very good combination with potatoes and help in generating body heat. Methi is also beneficial for arthritis patients.

For more therapeutic benefits, see under Herbs.

Mushrooms, White Button

Mushrooms are a high protein food. They are also high in antioxidants, and protect against cancer.

Mustard Green (*Sarson-Ka-Saag*)

Sarson-ka-saag is usually savoured with *Makke-ki*-Roti (corn bread) during winters in North India. It contains sulforaphane that protects against cancers. Mustard and mustard greens have anti-inflammatory omega-3 fats.

Onions

Onions are similar to garlic in many respects. While garlic is suitable for consumption in winter, onions are predominantly suitable for summer. They protect you from heatstroke.

Like garlic, onions also contain germanium, a mineral that improves oxygenation of tissues at cell level. Vitamin B6 in onions lowers levels of homocysteine, a strong marker of heart disease.

Onions offer powerful protection from cancer. People who ate two onions a week were found to have 38 per cent lower colorectal cancer risk, 43 per cent lower ovarian, and 56 per cent lower throat cancer risk.

About 3 oz onion juice when taken daily in the morning for 40 days helps in controlling epileptic attacks.

Onions prevent and cure flu by absorbing virus if kept near a person. Thereby, it is advised not to consume previously cut onions for they may be laden with virus.

Parwal

Parwal is a form of little gourd. The vegetable being light in nature is highly recommended in sickness.

Peas (Green)

Green peas have abundance of nutrients such as vitamin K, A, B1, B2, B3, B6, C, folate, and minerals like manganese, phosphorous, magnesium, copper, iron, zinc and potassium.

Potatoes

Researchers have discovered some 60 different vitamins, minerals, and antioxidants in potatoes. These include good amounts of vitamins

B6 and C, minerals like copper, potassium and manganese, and antioxidant phenols, quercetin, and chlorogenic acid.

Potatoes have kuko-amines, which are newly identified blood pressure lowering compounds. This surprise discovery has identified potatoes as a very good food source for lowering blood pressure.

B6 is responsible for the formation of new cells, and for the production of the neurotransmitters in the brain like serotonin that lead one to relax and get sleep. Its deficiency leads to insomnia and depression.

Other hormones that are helped by B6 are melatonin that helps inducing sleep, and GABA that is needed for normal brain function. B6 can convert dangerous homocysteine molecule into benign substances.

Thus, potatoes provide protection from cancer and heart attack, and aid one to sleep.

Potato is an amazing neutral vegetable that causes neither *vaata,* nor *pitta* nor *kapha*. It is a carbohydrate comfort food that soothes our taste and digestive system. Potato contains vitamins that help prevent rheumatism.

One must eat boiled or baked potatoes and avoid its fried from. Eating baked potato along with the skin is beneficial as potato skin has far more fibre, iron, potassium and B-vitamins. A single potato skin may contain as much as 2mg of iron. Potato peels are often used for treating skin wounds and burns, and for toning facial skin.

Avoid potatoes that have turned green. They contain toxic compounds.

Potato Chips Taste-Alikes

Preheat oven to 400 F (200 degree celsius). Wash one large potato and cut it into thin slices. Lightly coat a baking sheet with olive oil. Arrange slices on sheet. Brush or spray lightly with olive oil. Sprinkle with herbs. Bake for 30 minutes turning once until crisp.

Pumpkin (*Kasiphal/Sitaphal/Kaddu*)/Pumpkin Seeds

Pumpkin, particularly the orange variety, is a very rich source of beta-carotene.

Thanks to its rich content of beta-carotene, vitamin C, and its pH value that helps in keeping one's skin slightly on the acidic side to keep the bacteria at bay, pumpkin helps in smoothening the skin and prevents it from becoming dry, rough, and scaly.

Beta-carotene and vitamin C in pumpkin also help in treating sore throats, coughs and colds. This vegetable is favoured by singers and speakers.

Pumpkin seeds are very rich in lutein and zeaxanthin, beta-carotene, and zinc. Lutein, zeaxanthin and vitamin A together are very good for eyesight. Beta-carotene and zinc are good for treating skin and hormonal disorders. Zinc helps reduce prostate gland enlargement.

Radishes (*Muli*)

Though radishes are 90 per cent water, they contain as much potassium as is present in bananas, and about half the vitamin C of an orange. They are a good source of magnesium too. Because of the presence of potassium, magnesium, and vitamin C, radish helps in lowering blood pressure.

Radishes dissolve fat and also help in the detoxification of liver and gall bladder, and facilitate removal of kidney and bladder stones. Radishes, sautéed with leaves, make for a delicious food item.

Spinach (*Palak*)

Spinach (*palak*) is a certified super food as it contains the broadest spectrum of nutrients among all green leafy vegetables.

It is high in folate, vitamins A, C, E and K, antioxidants lutein and zeaxanthin, and minerals like iron, potassium and calcium. It contains nitrate that expands arteries.

The healthy amounts of potassium, calcium and nitrate help in regulating blood pressure. Lutein in spinach increases the pigment on the macula in the eye. Zeaxanthin arrests macular degeneration.

Sweet Potatoes/Yam (*Shakar-kandi*)

Nutrition profile of sweet potatoes is similar to that of potatoes. Additionally, they are loaded with vitamins A (beta-carotene), C and B6.

About 100 grams of sweet potatoes have four times the recommended daily allowance (RDA) of beta-carotene which is important for healthy vision, skin and hair.

Inspite of being sweet, they are good for diabetics. They contain carotenoids that stabilise blood sugar levels, and lower insulin resistance. Sweet potatoes have recently been classified as an anti-diabetic food.

Tindas

Tindas are the most easily digestible and neutral vegetable of little gourd variety.

Tomatoes, Tomato Juice and Tomato Ketchup

Tomatoes, tomato juice and ketchup contain high amounts of lycopene. But beware of processed tomato juice. It contains artery-unfriendly sodium salt. One should also go easy on ketchup. A tablespoon of ketchup contains about 180mg of sodium.

Lycopene reduces risks of heart disease and cancer. It is beneficial for prostate problems. Niacin in tomatoes provides a safe way to raise HDL in cholesterol.

Researchers at the Biomedical Science Department of University of Portsmouth found that during two weeks of consumption of 400 grams of tomato soup, the levels of lycopene in the men's semen rose significantly by 7-12 per cent. The study suggests that higher levels of lycopene are associated with increased fertility.

Note: Watermelons have more lycopene.

Turnip

Turnips contain vitamins A and C, zinc, magnesium, potassium, and phosphorous. They are the liver's best friend and help in increasing appetite, libido, vision, etc.

Watercress (*Singhara*)

Watercress is an aquatic vegetable. It is regarded as a fruit as it can be eaten raw after peeling.

Nutritionally, watercress is a good source of potassium, and is low in sodium. Flour of dried watercress is often used to make sweet pudding (*halwa*) during festivals.

Researchers at the University of Southampton have found out that watercress can prevent breast cancer by increasing the number of cancer fighting molecules.

It is quite digestible and is recommended for healthy libido.

Top Six Nutrition Stars Among Vegetables.

- Broccoli
- Carrots
- Potatoes
- Pumpkin
- Red bell peppers, and
- Spinach

Are Fresh Raw Vegetables Always the Best?
No. Beware of toxins like tetracyclic triterpenoid cucurbitacin (bitter) in *lauki*, solanine and chaconine in potatoes with green patches and sprouting, toxins in bitter almonds, goitrogenic substances in cabbage and broccoli, laden with sewage water and chemicals from irrigation, and pesticides. Carefully wash them with potassium permaganate solution before consumption.

Some vegetables that are frozen immediately after harvest often have the same nutritional value. Do not cut vegetables in advance lest they lose nutrients due to oxidation with air.

Boiling of cruciferous vegetables robs them off of their anti-cancer properties by 75 per cent. Bring water to a boil before adding vegetables. It destroys fewer nutrients.

Eat vegetables with healthy fats like olive oil, avocados or healthy fat dressings. Absorption of nutrients from vegetables is enhanced when eaten with a little fat.

In case of kidney stones, avoid tomatoes and spinach as they contain oxalic acid.

11
Fruits

All fruits are ample sources of minerals, vitamins and antioxidants. They contain twice as many antioxidant phenols as vegetables.

Fruits when eaten on an empty stomach, play a major role in detoxifying the system. But when fruits are eaten after meals, they mix with the decomposed food to produce gas and bloating.

There is no such thing as acidic fruit, including orange and lemon, because all fruits become alkaline in the body.

Always prefer to eat the whole fruit rather than drinking its juice. The pulp contains the maximum nutrients and fibre. If you take only the juice, you will lose on the major portion of nutrients. Often, juice causes diarrhoea because it is gulped without saliva.

Always cut the fruits only at the time of consumption. Fruits cut earlier lose vitamins like C, Thiamine, B6, Biotin, and A, and minerals like iron by oxidation.

Apple

Apple is a recognised super food packed with some 200 trace minerals.

Apples have plenty of soluble pectin fibre that helps in reducing blood cholesterol. Pectin also has binding effect on stools, which is why some people find apple constipating.

An apple is packed with 150mg of potassium, 4 mcg of folate, and about 10mg of calcium, 6-8mg of vitamin C, with trace amounts of B-vitamins, magnesium and zinc.

Folate in apples reduces homocysteine level to protect arteries from damage. Apples contain quercetin in concentrated amounts that enhances the immune system.

The antioxidant activity in one apple is equivalent to 1500mg of vitamin C.

Apricots (*Khubani*)

Apricots are full of beta-carotene (vitamin A) which, apart from protecting the heart, also provides good vision and prevents cataract by quenching free radicals that cause injury to eye lens.

Bael

Ripe *bael* fruit cleans and tones the intestines, and cures diarrhoea and dysentery. Taken in excess, it may lead to bloating. The fruit is available only during summer months.

Banana

A single banana can contribute to your daily needs up to 36 per cent of vitamin B6, 15 per cent of vitamin C, 20 per cent of potassium, 9 per cent of carbohydrates, and 7 per cent of fibre, and magnesium.

Bananas are rich in potassium (450mg in a banana) that aids in maintaining electrolyte balance, and magnesium that relaxes nerves. Due to their low sodium and high potassium content, they help lowering blood pressure, and prevents risks of heart attacks and strokes.

According to a study at Kasturba Medical College in Manipur, eating just two bananas a day can lower your blood pressure by 10 per cent in one week.

High potassium levels in this fruit also aid in toning up the muscles to maintain their functions.

Bananas help in maintaining a healthy nerve system for they contain good amounts of tryptophan, which the body converts into serotonin to aid peaceful sleep.

Bananas, like apples, have soluble fibre pectin, which has binding effect on stools. Ripe bananas are recommended for people suffering from digestion problems. Banana-yoghurt mixture produces synergetic effect, thus giving richer dividends. Bananas, eaten about half an hour before meals, help in combating acidity and diarrhoea.

According to Japanese research, ripe bananas contain TNF, a substance having immune enhancing and anti-cancer qualities. Yellow skinned, ripe bananas with dark spots (*Chittis*) are eight times more effective in enhancing the properties of WBCs than green ones. BanLec (banana lectin) in bananas is found to be as potent as anti-HIV drugs.

Blueberries

Blueberries are considered to be the storehouse of powerful antioxidant phenols.

The anthocyanins in blueberries protect against high blood pressure (HBP) and some types of cancers. A research by Harvard University has shown that eating blueberries reduces the risk of developing HBP by at least 10 per cent.

Cantaloupes

They are the most alkaline among fruits. They are full of nutrients, having high water content and few calories especially suited for summer consumption. Eat before meals to lose weight.

Cheeku

This fruit grows in the Western Ghats of India. It has a typical flavour and is rich in iron.

As it is very sweet, it is not recommended for diabetics.

Cherries

Cherries have high content of melatonin hormone that supports sleep. Drinking a glass of unsweetened cherry juice twice daily helps people suffering from insomnia.

Apart from possessing many nutrients, cherries have been found to control gout. In an article in Texas Reports on Biology and Medicine 1950, Ludwig Blau described how he had cured his crippling gout by eating 6-8 cherries every day.

Cranberries (*Karonda*)

Karondas, are available in India during the monsoon season. They are equivalent of cranberries and are powerful antioxidants. They prevent urinary tract infections. Cranberry juice is also helpful for bladder and kidney problems.

Drinking cranberry juice is a natural way to raise your good HDL cholesterol level.

Dates

Dates are rich in calories and iron.

Figs

Figs are very high in calcium, iron, potassium, beta-carotene, and anti-carcinogenic benzaldehyde, flavonoids, and a digestive enzyme called ficin. Three figs have the same amount of potassium as a large banana. Figs have 83 per cent natural sugar. Dried ones have 5 times more calories than fresh ones, and hence are not recommended for diabetics.

Gooji Berry

Most experts believe that Gooji Berry grown in mineral-rich million-year old soil in the Himalayas is a very nutritious food.

Grapes and Red Wine

Grapes, particularly red/purple, contain poly-phenol resveratrol, a powerful antioxidant referred to as the longevity molecule. Poly-phenols not only fight free radicals, but also block the production of a protein linked to cardiovascular disease.

Resveratrol appears to activate a gene called SIRT-1. Activation of this gene appears to slow down the ageing process, and postpone or eliminate diseases of old age.

Poly-phenols in grapes help to prevent bad LDL cholesterol from oxidising and blood from clotting, and hence protect the heart, and prevent cancer.

People in a study experienced better blood flow in their arteries just 3 hours after eating 1 ¼ cups of grapes. Maximum resveratrol is to be found in the skin and seeds of grapes.

Red grape seeds contain proantho-cyanidin, which is also a powerful heart medicine.

There is compelling evidence that natural chemicals in grapes help in preventing, and even curing certain types of tumours. In her book *The Grape Cure* (1928), Johanna Brandt claims to have conquered her stomach cancer with the power of purple grapes.

Just 4 oz of red wine prepared from red grapes cuts down the risk of prostate cancer to half. On the other hand, Rachel Thompson of World Cancer Research Fund warns that just 2 units of alcohol a day increases the risk of bowel cancer by 18 per cent and the risk of liver cancer by 20 per cent. Hence, drinking wine only in moderation can be healthy.

A glass of fresh grape juice in the morning is believed to provide relief from migraine. Dried grapes (*kishmish*) strengthen the lungs, and also relieve constipation.

Guava

Guava has as much antioxidant benefits as blueberries and broccoli.

Pink guava has the highest lycopene content. Lycopene fights heart disease and cancer, and is beneficial for prostate health.

In addition, one medium sized guava provides 688mg of potassium, which is 63 percent more than what you get from a banana. Moreover, one cup of guava has five times more vitamin C than an orange.

Jamun (Jamboo)

Jamun is believed to be the perfect fruit for diabetics. It contains the enzyme jamboline, which helps control blood sugar level.

The powder of dried seeds of *jamun* is also used in Ayurvedic medicine to cure diabetes and digestive ailments.

Kiwi

Kiwi fruit contains more vision-saving lutein than any other food except corn.

Lime (*Musammi*)

Lime or *musammi* juice is an extremely good source of the powerful vitamin C.

Melon or Musk-Melon (*Kharbooza*)

Melon has all the health benefits of cantaloupe. Also, *hakeems*, practitioners of *Unani* Medicine in India, have been using melon extract to cure leukoderma.

Water Melon (*Tarbooz*)

Melons have very high water content. Almost 92 per cent of watermelon is water. However, the remaining 8 per cent is packed with lycopene, carotenes, and glutathione.

Contrary to popular belief, watermelon has 40 per cent more lycopene than raw tomatoes. Lycopene may help reduce risk of heart disease, cancer, and other diseases.

Bhimangouda Patil at Texas A&M Fruit and Vegetable Improvement Center at College Station has found citrulline, an important phyto-nutrient, in water melon.

Citrulline is converted to arginine, an amino acid that helps the heart and circulation system, and maintains a good immune system. Arginine further boosts nitric oxide in the blood. Nitric oxide relaxes blood vessels in a way similar to the effect of Viagra, the drug that cures Erectile Dysfunction (ED).

Mango

Mango's yellow/orange pulp is a very rich source of beta-carotene. It is good for eyes, skin, hair, immune system, and for protection against infections like cold/cough.

It also contains high amount of antioxidant beta-cryptoxanthin, and helps reduce the risk of colon and cervical cancer.

As the body best absorbs beta-cryptoxanthin when eaten with fat, it is desirable to eat mangoes as dessert with cream or ice-cream.

Mulberry (*Shahtoot*)

Mulberries contain protein, linoleic, stearic and oleic acids, calcium, phosphorous, potassium and magnesium. They strengthen eyesight, increase appetite, promote healthy growth of hair, lower BP, cholesterol and blood sugar levels, and prevent cancer of liver.

Oranges and Grape Fruits

Oranges contain vitamin C, folate, potassium and calcium in abundance. They lower BP. A plant chemical called hesperidin found in oranges helps in making the heart strong.

Citrus fruits contain flavonoids that may reduce blood cholesterol levels by 20-25 per cent. Researchers at Hebrew University, Jerusalem, reported that flavonoids not only reduced levels of bad LDL cholesterol but also increased the ratio of good HDL to bad LDL cholesterol. Those with high cholesterol may try eating citrus fruits as first alternative to statin drugs. Grape fruit lowers cholesterol by changing the way the liver functions.

A glass of orange juice (OJ) daily can reduce the incidence of painful kidney stones.

Papaya

Papaya is a good source of folate that converts homocysteine into benign molecules. Hence, it protects the heart, and fights inflammations in arthritis and asthma.

Papaya has high amount of beta-carotene (vitamin A), which is an important nutrient for cells. Vitamin A is very beneficial for eyes, skin and hair. Ripe papaya cures chronic constipation and piles, and is good for liver.

Peaches

Peaches are rich sources of vitamins A, C, and E and phytochemicals which are beneficial for healthy skin, and provide protection from exposure to UV radiation from sun's rays.

Pears

Pears contain small amount of vitamins A and C, and some potassium, and riboflavin. They offer a natural quick source of energy through their fructose, glucose, and laevulose. Laevulose, the sweetest of known natural sugars, is found in fresh ripe pears.

Pineapple

Pineapple contains bromelain, an effective anti-inflammatory enzyme/antioxidant. This explains its ability to curb painful inflammations making it exceptionally good for problems of joints. Rich in vitamin C and bromelain, pineapple supports the immune system and defends against free radical damage.

Pomegranate (*Anaar*)

Pomegranate juice can curb genetically-transmitted heart disease. In a study, it was found that the blood flow to the heart increased by 17 per cent in heart patients who drank 250 ml of pomegranate juice daily for three months.

Pomegranate is a great source of vitamin C, niacin, folate, calcium, magnesium, phosphorous and potassium, and has a high content of polyphenols.

It contains almost three times the antioxidants as present in the same quantity of green tea, red wine, orange or cranberry juice. It lowers BP. It was observed that men who consumed 2 oz of its juice daily for a year experienced a decrease in systolic blood pressure by 21 per cent, and a significantly improved blood flow to the heart.

It also has anti-inflammatory actions. Researchers at Case Western University suggest that consumption of pomegranate may help reduce inflammation in arthritis and asthma.

Pomegranate is a cure for diarrhoea and dysentery.

It reduces LDL, prevents dementia and Alzeihmer's disease risk by retarding brain degeneration. Researchers at Edinburg University found that it may lower the storage of abdominal fat.

Pomegranate helps in increasing the levels of oestrogen, the female sex hormone.

Prunes/Plums (*Aloo-Bukhara/Alucha*)

Prunes are high in iron and potassium. Dried prunes have higher antioxidant capacity than green tea. In the regions where this fruit is grown and consumed, the longevity of people has been found to be greater.

Sea Buckthorn

Sea buckthorn is a rare and wild fruit found in Leh, Laddakh. The fruit is supposed to be a storehouse of nutrients. Russian astronauts used it as a health food and medicine during space flights. Its juice is now available in processed form.

Custard Apple (*Sharifa*)

Sharifa contains vitamin B2, referred to as the beauty vitamin. It imparts vigour to skin, hair and nails.

Strawberries

Strawberries are an excellent source of vitamin C, manganese, and iodine, and good source of potassium, folate, vitamins B1, B5, K, omega-3 fats, potassium, magnesium, copper, and antioxidant phenols. They have the highest antioxidant power than any other fruit. They protect against macular degeneration, rheumatoid arthritis, etc.

Watercress

See under 'Vegetables'.

Fruits Splashed with Alcohol

Chanjirakul and his team from University of Thailand and US Department of Agriculture found that adding a splash of ethyl alcohol in strawberries and blackberries boosted the fruit's antioxidant effect and scavenging capacity with regard to free radicals.

Smoothies

Take frozen yoghurt or milk and churn it with frozen fruits like strawberries, blueberries, bananas in a mixer. Add some honey. This makes for a healthy and refreshing drink.

Fruits and Vegetables Have Inflammation-fighting Salicylic Acid

Many diseases begin with inflammation. Fruits and vegetables contain salicylic acid, an inflammation-fighting compound similar to aspirin in its effects. A study found that the blood of vegetarians contained 12 times more salicylic acid than the blood of non-vegetarians.

Top Seven Nutrition Stars Among Fruits

In alphabetical order they are:

- Apples
- Bananas
- Grapes
- Mangoes
- Oranges
- Pomegranates
- Strawberries

12
Nuts, Seeds and Oils

Nuts and seeds have long been used not only as sources of nutrient dense foods, but also as sources of oils for culinary and medicinal purposes.

Boost your intake of nuts and seeds, as they are high in good quality proteins, EFAs and plant sterols.

12.1 SEEDS AND OILS

Most recommended oils are mustard, olive, canola and soy oils. There are also vegetable oils like sesame (*til*), corn and sunflower oils. Mustard, *til* and canola oils are preferred for cooking which requires heating.

Table 2.1 gives the type and proportion of fat content of many oils.

Flaxseed oil has very high (58 per cent) omega-3 content. Soy oil is high in omega-3. Both walnuts and soy oil have nearly 50 per cent of omega-6, but soy oil has higher proportion of omega-3, 9 per cent as against 5 per cent of walnuts.

Coconut oil primarily contains saturated fat. However, it is good for the digestive system.

Table 2.1 Fat Content and Types of Fats in Oils

Nut/Seed	Total Fat Content	PUFA omega-3 per cent of total	PUFA omega-6 per cent of total	MUFA omega-9 per cent of total	Saturated Fat per cent of total
Almond	54		17	78	5
Canola	30	7	30	56	7
Cashew	42		6	70	18
Corn	4		59	24	17
Coconut	35		3	6	91
Flaxseed/ Linseed	35	58	14	19	9
Mustard		7	15	60	12
Olive	20		8	76	16
Peanut	48		29	47	18
Pistachio	54		19	65	9
Pumpkin Seed	47	15	42	34	9
Sesame (*Til*)	49		45	42	13
Soy	18	9	50	26	15
Sunflower	47		65	23	12
Walnut	60	5	51	28	16

Values given in the table are averages. Note that flaxseeds, pumpkin seeds, soy, canola, mustard, and walnuts have high content of omega-3 fats.

Olives/Olive Oil

Olive oil can be added to foods, salad dressings, dips, etc directly, even without heating.

Black olives are the ones that are fully ripe. The oil content of olive oil is overwhelmingly heart healthy 75 per cent oleic acid (MUFA). And olive oil has very little omega-6.

The health benefits of olive oil are due to both its high content of MUFA and antioxidant substances, particularly vitamin E and polyphenols.

Olive oil lowers blood pressure. Researchers at Stanford Medical School found that three table spoons of olive oil a day could lower systolic pressure by 9 points and diastolic pressure by 6 points. A University of Kentucky study found that just 2/3rd of a table spoon of olive oil daily reduced systolic pressure by about 5 points and diastolic pressure by 4 points. Adding olive oil to your diet may prove to be an easy way to control your blood pressure.

What Makes MUFA Better For the Heart?

MUFA lowers a person's total cholesterol. It lowers bad LDL cholesterol without lowering the good HDL cholesterol, thereby keeping the arteries clear of plaque.

The amazing proof of olive oil's effectiveness against heart disease is evident from the robust health of the people living on Mediterranean diet, the main components of which are olive oil and red wine apart from a generous helping of whole grains, fruits and vegetables.

In spite of the animal foods they take, they have the world's lowest mortality rates from cardiovascular diseases, and have beautiful and supple skin.

Polyphenols in olive oil are an added advantage. Olive oil is more than just MUFA. Virgin olive oil is much richer in polyphenols which have antioxidant, anti-inflammatory, and anti-coagulant properties. They are known to reduce cancer risk and decrease oxidised LDL, and lead to increase in HDL and HDL/LDL ratio.

Olive oil phenols prevent bone loss that causes osteoporosis. Potent anti-inflammatory compounds have been discovered in olive oil. Anti-inflammatory benefits include curbing severity of asthma and arthritis.

Olive oil phenols support gastro-intestinal health while preventing obesity as well. Olive oil is anti-ageing. The anti-ageing properties are because of high amounts of vitamin E and MUFA, and also because olive oil has properties of easy digestibility and absorption.

Extra virgin olive oil is the least processed and the healthiest. It is obtained from first pressing of olives. Virgin comes from second pressing. Extra-virgin and virgin olive oils are rich sources of polyphenols. Pure olive oil is a blend of refined olive oil and extra virgin or virgin olive oil.

Mustard Oil

Dr SC Manchanda, a well known cardiologist, says that mustard oil is 20 times better for heart than olive oil as it increases good HDL cholesterol since it contains 7 per cent of anti-inflammatory omega-3 fats. About 5 grams of mustard seeds contain 0.2g of omega-3. Presence of 7 per cent omega-3 and 60 per cent MUFA makes it highly anti-inflammatory. It combines the benefits of both canola and olive oils.

Mustard oil is also a very good source of zinc, selenium, manganese, magnesium, calcium, iron, vitamin B3 (niacin), and tryptophan.

The presence of magnesium helps lowering the blood pressure. Phyto-nutrient compounds in mustard oil are protective against gastro-intestinal cancer. Niacin and omega-3 in mustard oil raise HDL level.

Dr K Srinath Reddy from AIIMS, Delhi, in a study with others found that those who use mustard oil for frying foods lower their risk of heart attack by 71 per cent.

People with thyroid problem should avoid mustard and mustard oil as it contains goitrogens that interfere negatively with thyroid gland.

Canola Oil

Canola oil is made from rapeseeds. It is primarily a produce of Canada. It contains a high percentage, about 7 per cent, of omega-3 oils, which help in increasing HDL cholesterol.

In addition, it is lowest in saturated fat, even in comparison with olive oil, and second highest in MUFA, coming next only to olive oil. It has the highest content of vitamin E.

Another reason is that it can be used in cooking/frying without much destruction of nutrients while olive oil is best taken as raw. Cooking destroys the quality of olive oil.

Liquid Soy Oil

Liquid soybean oil is high in PUFA and MUFA. It is also a principal source of omega-3 fats and vitamin E. And it contains EPA and DHA, more potent than common fish oils.

Flaxseed/Linseed/*Alsi*

Flaxseeds contain high percentage of lignans. These are hormone-like substances that produce a number of protective effects against breast cancer.

Flaxseed oil is richest in omega-3, and has the lowest omega-6 to omega-3 ratio of 1:4. About 1-2 tablespoons of ground seeds or 1-2 tsp of oil per day provides sufficient omega-3.

Which is Preferable, Flaxseed Oil or Fish Oil?

Flaxseed oil is safer. It doesn't contain lipid peroxide contaminants found in fish oil.

Long-chain omega-3 fats EPA and DHA found in fish oil are considered to be good for heart because they are more easily absorbed than shorter-chain fats in flaxseeds. But fish oil bring along with it the dangers of contaminations, mercury poisoning, etc.

Hempseed Oil

A non-cannabis variety of hemp grown in Canada offers a rich source of omega-3. Hempseed oil is obtained from hempseeds harvested from this hemp and is highly anti-inflammatory.

Its EFA profile is close to that of fish oil. Its medicinal property is due to its GLA content, and its low ratio of omega-6 to omega-3.

Note: A combination of mustard and olive oils is better than either one of them alone. Mustard oil has high concentrations of omega-3 that increases HDL, while olive oil has heart-healthy MUFA that decreases LDL.

Sesame Seeds/Sesame Oil (*Til*)

Sesame seeds have 50 per cent oil and 25 per cent protein on an average. About 87 per cent of oil is omega-6 and omega-9. There is no omega-3 in *til* oil.

Sesame has copper, manganese, calcium, magnesium, zinc and vitamin B1.

Copper provides relief in rheumatoid arthritis. Magnesium supports cardiovascular/respiratory health by relaxing muscles, preventing spasm in air passages in asthma, lowering blood pressure, and promoting normal sleep. Calcium is vital for the health of bones, teeth, nails and hair, and provides relief in PMS.

Women usually suffer from calcium deficiency. They are advised to take 2 spoons of white *til* with a glass of milk or tea every day to meet their calcium requirement.

Zinc promotes prostate and male sexual and bone health. Sesame like pistachios and sunflower seeds have the maximum amount of phytosterols. Sesame is also shown to inhibit absorption of cholesterol from diet and manufacture of cholesterol in liver. Thus, sesame seeds and oil may be able to lower cholesterol levels.

Sunflower Seeds

Sunflower seeds are an excellent source of vitamin E, phytosterols and omega-6 fats. After Brazil nuts, sunflower seeds come next as a major source of the mineral selenium which, as mentioned before, works to prevent cancers.

Pumpkin Seeds

Pumpkin seeds are high in magnesium and zinc, MUFA and EFAs, and phytosterols. Eating pumpkin seeds is the easiest way to consume magnesium.

Due to their high content of zinc and EFAs, they have been used for treating prostate enlargement. Their components are instrumental in interrupting prostate cell multiplication.

Phytosterols in pumpkin seeds lower cholesterol, enhance immune response, and decrease rates of certain cancers.

Peanuts/Peanut Butter/Refined Peanut Oil

Peanuts are a good source of manganese, vitamin B3, folate, copper, and protein.

Around 76 per cent of oil is omega-6 and MUFA. It has no omega-3 to balance omega-6. Peanuts have traces of vitamin E and resveratrol phenol antioxidants.

However, peanuts are susceptible to moulds and fungi. Fungus produces alfatoxin, a poison that is 20 times more carcinogenic than DDT. It is linked to mental retardation even if consumed in trace amounts. Roasting peanuts offers protection against this toxin. Lectins in peanut & are sticky. They attach to the arteries' walls and contribute to plaque build-up. Peanuts are an allergenic food for some.

Vegetable Oils

Vegetable oils such as corn, safflower, sesame, sunflower and peanut contain high amounts of omega-6 with negligible or no omega-3. In spite of their many benefits, they tend to be inflammatory. Such oils are not recommended because of the inflammatory effects on people suffering from asthma, arthritis, rheumatic heart, irritable bowel syndrome, psoriasis, etc.

Coconut Oil

Fresh mature coconut contains 50 per cent water, 35 per cent oil, some carbohydrates and protein.

Around 90 per cent of coconut oil is saturated fat. It is one of the easiest fats to process, absorb and digest. The concern about high saturated fat is misplaced. Fifty per cent of this fat is lauric acid which has anti-inflammatory, anti-microbial and anti-bacterial properties. It also helps in preventing high cholesterol and high blood pressure. It boosts growth of good bacteria in intestines, and thus, helps in proper functioning of the digestive system. It gives smooth texture to hair, making it glossy and preventing hair from greying.

A diet rich in coconut oil protects against insulin resistance, a major factor in diabetes.

12.2 NUTS/DRY FRUITS

Nuts provide protein, EFAs, and phytosterols. The most popular nuts are almonds, cashews, pistachios and walnuts. Peanuts are nuts, that also belong to the pea family.

Almonds

Almond is the king of nuts. They are an excellent source of vitamins E, B2 and B3, MUFA, minerals such as manganese, magnesium, potassium, calcium, copper, iron, etc.

They are also cholesterol free. About 95 per cent of fat in almonds is unsaturated. Like olives, they are rich in MUFA. Hence, they are associated with reduced risk of coronary heart disease. Eating almonds helps lowering total and bad LDL cholesterol and triglyceride levels, and increasing good HDL cholesterol.

Magnesium present in almonds helps in the relaxation of veins and arteries. Potassium is necessary for contraction of heart muscles. Almonds make our heart healthy by providing 257mg of potassium as against only 0.3mg of sodium in a cup. This provides protection against blood pressure, atherosclerosis, and heart attack.

Almond oil is applied on scalp for it helps in strengthening brain and nerves.

Vitamin E, a powerful antioxidant, gives almonds the reputation of being an anti-cancer food. Known for its emollient properties, vitamin E maintains beautiful and soft skin.

The good fat in almonds prevents gallstones. Eating 25 grams of almonds daily helps in preventing Type-2 diabetes and heart disease.

Almonds soaked in water have cooling energy. They reduce *pitta,* especially in summer.

Researchers from Institute of Food Research Norwich UK and Italy's Policlinico Universitario have found that chemicals in the skin of almonds boost the immune system by improving the ability of white blood cells to fight viral infections.

Cashews

Cashews contain good amounts of magnesium, potassium, copper and zinc. About 65 per cent of fat in cashews is unsaturated, of which 70 per cent is oleic acid, the MUFA, the same heart healthy fat found in olive oil, and 6 per cent is linoleic acid, an omega-6 fat.

Cashews are considered to raise cholesterol level as they contain 18 per cent of saturated fats.

Copper is vital for iron metabolism, and development of bones and connective tissues. It is involved in the production of skin and hair pigment, melanin.

Deficiency of copper results in anaemia, ruptured blood vessels, osteoporosis, joint problems, rheumatoid arthritis, elevated LDL, reduced HDL, and irregular heartbeats. Magnesium balances calcium in cashews. By balancing calcium, it helps to regulate and relax nerves, and tone muscles.

Magnesium deficiency can lead to high blood pressure, disturbance in sleep, muscle spasms, migraine headaches, and fatigue.

Pistachios

Pistachios are an excellent source of B-vitamins, iron, magnesium and potassium.

They have the maximum amounts of antioxidant plant sterols that lower cholesterol levels, enhance immune response, and decrease cancer rates.

Pistachios are rich in antioxidant lutein, which is necessary for healthy eyes. Lutein also blocks the absorption of cholesterol in the bloodstream, thus helping lower cholesterol levels.

A study by researchers at Pennsylvania State University found that eating 85 grams of pistachios a day cuts total cholesterol by 8.4 per cent, and bad LDL cholesterol by 11.6 per cent.

Pistachios contain antioxidant vitamin E that helps combat cancer, particularly the cancers of prostate and lung.

Walnuts

Around 5 per cent of oil in walnuts is omega-3, and 51 per cent is omega-6, which is not a very healthy ratio.

But walnuts have more omega-3 fat than any other nut. Seven walnuts provide 2.6 grams of omega-3, which is more than the recommended daily amount. Omega-3 fats lower total cholesterol and LDL cholesterol.

A recent study showed that those eating 8 to 13 walnuts a day had 64 per cent stronger artery-pumping action and 20 per cent less sticky plaque molecules after just four weeks. Omega-3 in walnuts also lowers C-Reactive Protein (CRP), indicating an anti-inflammatory effect.

Besides, walnuts are rich in vitamin E, calcium, iron and zinc.

A handful of walnuts has more polyphenols than a glass of apple juice or red wine.

Fox Nut (*Makhana*)

It is the most easily digestible nut and has a warming effect. It is used as a snack, and in religious festivities in the form of pudding (*kheer*).

12.3 DRESSINGS

Dressings usually have saturated fats. Mayonnaise is entirely composed of saturated fat.

A combination of yoghurt, apple sauce and vinegar is recommended for dressing. Dressings containing olive and canola oils are a good choice.

Nutrients from fruits and vegetables are absorbed better if taken with some fat. An Ohio State University study found that when salad was eaten with fat-rich avocados or full-fat dressings, the subjects absorbed 4 times more lycopene, 7 times more lutein, and 18 times more beta-carotene than those who ate plain vegetables without fat.

Hence, it is always beneficial to eat your vegetables with some good natural fats. Take fruits with cream or ice cream.

13
Eggs, Milk, Soy and Products

Eggs

Eggs are a good source of protein and iron. The protein is present in an easily absorbable form.

Eggs contain the maximum amounts of carotenoids lutein and zeaxanthin, essential for good eyesight. They also contain vitamin B12, not generally available in plant foods.

Milk

Milk is an important source of calcium and vitamin D. Milk and its products are the main source of vitamin B12 for vegetarians. But remember that most of it is destroyed by pasteurisation and boiling. For your vitamin B12, you may need to take a course of B12 supplement.

Following are some points in connection to milk's effect on our health.

1. Heart disease: If full-cream milk and its products are consumed in large amounts, then they may raise cholesterol level in blood, and may contribute to heart disease. After a certain age one should switch to low fat or cow's milk.
2. Cancer: A study found that women who developed ovarian cancer actually drank less milk than those who did not have cancer.
3. Osteoporosis: Milk and other dairy products are the leading source of bone-building nutrients, primarily calcium and vitamin D together.

4. Milk also contains protein, but the ratio of calcium to protein is high enough to favour bone and teeth development.

   In addition, the calcium and other components in milk may help prevent high blood pressure (HBP), and thus prevent heart disease and stroke.

But many people give up milk because they are lactose intolerant. This happens because they lack the lactase enzyme, which plays a crucial role in digesting lactose.

Such people should derive their calcium from orange juice, sesame seeds, yoghurt, cheese, etc.

Children have natural lactase content in their body. This is why they can easily digest milk. But as one grows in age, the body produces less of this enzyme, and one loses ability to digest milk. The condition is called lactose intolerance. However, some people are also genetically lactose intolerant.

Yoghurt (*dahi*)

Yoghurt can be given to infants at an early stage. Lactose intolerant people should especially eat yoghurt (dahi) to get their requirement of calcium.

Yoghurt/Dahi contains probiotics, the opposite of antibiotics, which help maintain friendly flora in intestines. Lactose in yoghurt is already digested by these probiotics.

Commercial ones always contain the good bacteria S. Thermophilus and L. Bulgaris. Most contain Lactobacilus Acidophilus. But look for a brand which adds Bifidobacterium to the above mentioned list of bacteria.

Do not discard the whey, for it contains B-vitamins and minerals, and almost no fat.

Cheese and Paneer

Cheese is high in cholesterol, but it contains conjugated linoleic acid, a good fat that may reduce risk of heart disease, cancer and diabetes.

It is an important source of calcium. It also has good amounts of tyrosine, an amino-acid used by cells to synthesise protein – the starting material of many hormones and neuro-transmitters.

Although dairy products are widely perceived as fatty, but researchers from Curtin University of Technology in Perth Australia have found that those who increased their daily servings of dairy products including cheese from 3 to 5 lost weight the maximum.

Paneer is Indian cheese made by separating solids from milk and yoghurt by boiling them together, or by adding lemon juice to boiling milk. This has all the benefits of milk. It does not cause lactose intolerance. It can be used as a snack, or in vegetables, or to make sweets.

Buttermilk (*Chhaach/Matha*)

Buttermilk is diluted yoghurt/dahi from which butter has been removed. It has very little fat, but all the benefits of milk and digestibility of yoghurt. It causes no lactose intolerance.

Soy Milk, Soy Yoghurt and Tofu

Soy yoghurt/curd and tofu can also be made from soy milk. All these are rich sources of calcium. However, some people are allergic to soybeans.

Tofu, a high protein food, is paneer made from soymilk. It is easy to digest as the soya bean's fibre gets removed. Consuming tofu brings down cholesterol levels.

A single serving of tofu provides about 10 per cent of our daily requirement of calcium.

Almond Milk

If you have lactose intolerance, and are also allergic to soymilk, the best alternative is almond milk, which you may take with porridge during your breakfast. Almond milk can be extracted by soaking a few almonds overnight and then blending them to get instant milk.

14

Sweetners/Beverages

14.1 SWEETENERS

Cane Juice, Jaggery or *Gur*, Sugar, Molasses

Fresh and pure cane juice is a very healthy drink. It is rich in chromium and helps in increasing the sperm count.

Jaggery is made by concentrating cane juice. It has 50 times more mineral content than refined sugar. One tsp of *gur* has 3-5mg calcium, 3-5mg phosphorous, 6mg magnesium, and 45mg potassium. It is also rich in copper, iron, chromium, and zinc. It helps reverse anaemia, regulate liver function, and prevent rheumatic problems. *Gur* is also eaten as a sweet after meals in winter.

Refined white sugar made from cane juice gets depleted of nutrients such as chromium and zinc. Sugar adversely affects our metabolism. It contributes to obesity, diabetes, etc. Our bodies produce uric acid on eating sugars, sweets or fructose. Uric acid causes gout.

Molasses and brown sugar, on the contrary, are very nutritious. They contain B-vitamins, calcium, iron, magnesium, potassium, chromium and zinc.

Researchers from University of New South Wales and Queensland University found that sweetened drinks had a calming effect on people, thus making them less aggressive as sugar rush provides the brain with the energy it needs to keep impulses under control.

Honey

Honey contains honeybee pollen which has thousands of immunity boosting enzymes and antioxidants.

Enzymes in honey protect against premature ageing. The darker the hue of honey, the higher is its antioxidant level. Studies claim that it cures throat better than cough syrup. Buckwheat honey works better at easing coughing and promoting sleep.

In asthma, honey provides the necessary warmth to the body and dissolves the phlegm. By drinking warm water with honey (mixed with black pepper, and tulsi leaves) one can delay the onset of the asthmatic attack. If done on a regular basis, it can completely rid one of the ailment.

Warm water taken with honey and lemon every morning is an effective way to reduce your weight. Remember that honey should never be heated as it produces toxins when heated.

Study showed that burns treated with honey healed four days faster than those without it.

Aspartame

Aspartame is an artificial sweetener used in diet drinks. It is found to increase the frequency and duration of migraine attacks.

14.2 BEVERAGES

Alcohol

All alcoholic drinks contain ethyl alcohol. There are two categories of alcoholic drinks: In the first category come hard liquors like whisky and brandy, which have high alcohol content. In the second category fall beer and wine, the mild liquors with less alcohol.

Hard liquors are made by fermenting and distilling grains, starches, molasses, etc. The product is pure alcohol with water and flavours. Hard liquors have no nutrients whatsoever. Excessive drinking of hard liquors may cause cirrhosis of liver. Researchers at Milan University, Italy found that alcohol damages telomere, part of the DNA in cells. It accelerates the process of ageing and increases the risk of cancer.

Mild liquors like beer and wine are made by fermenting ingredients and then filtering. There is no distilling which is why they retain most of the vitamins, minerals and antioxidants of the ingredients.

Beer

Beer is made by the fermentation of barley. Beer retains vitamins, antioxidants, and minerals like silicon contained in barley.

Beer is diuretic, and cleanses the urinary system. It has been claimed to be one of the most important sources of silicon, the mineral that plays an important role in bone formation.

Beer is also rich in phyto-oestrogens, plant versions of female hormone oestrogen, which helps keep bones healthy for women. Immediately after menopause, women's bones start weakening because of reduced levels of oestrogen. Hence, a moderate consumption of beer may help in fighting osteoporosis.

Swapping other alcohols with beer may help avoid weight gain as it has less calories.

Wine

Wines are made by fermentation of grapes. White wine is made from white grapes and red wine is made from red/purple grapes. Wines retain the nutrients of grapes.

Red wines are a better option among all varieties of alcohols since, like red/purple grapes, they contain antioxidant poly-phenols such as resveratrol.

Apple cider is a kind of wine made from apple juice.

Harmful Effects of Alcohol

According to British Independent Scientific Community on Drugs (ISCD) and European Monitoring Center for Drugs and Drug Addiction (EMCDDA), alcohol is almost three times as harmful as cocaine or tobacco.

It has been shown that drinking too much wine can lead to various types of cancers particularly of mouth, oesophagus, stomach, liver, lung, breast and prostate.

There is increased risk of obesity with alcohol because it is high in calorie content. While drinking alcohol, one also tends to consume excessive food, particularly junk food.

Uric acid production increases in the body due to alcohol. It invariably raises the blood pressure and is thus considered harmful for those who already suffer from high blood pressure. Body's levels of magnesium and vitamin B Complex declines after consumption of alcohol. Drinking alcohol regularly increases C-Reactive Protein (CRP), a strong marker of inflammation causing heart attack and stroke.

Vinegar

Any wine if exposed to air at temperatures above 26-27 Celsius turns into vinegar. Apple cider vinegar is like any other vinegar but made from apple juice.

Vinegar is considered good in small amounts. If taken in small amounts, it can increase the acid level and make it easier for the stomach to absorb nutrients such as calcium and magnesium.

It can be harmful if consumed in large amounts because of its highly acidic nature. Taking too much vinegar can cause damage to our stomach and intestines.

A typically healthy amount is about two tablespoons daily. The acid will clear your internal system to some degree by killing bacteria. But we also need some good bacteria to remain in the gut in order to stay healthy.

Vinegar helps control blood sugar and insulin levels if taken with meals. Daily dose of apple cider vinegar in water keeps high blood pressure under control. Vinegar is a fat buster. Apple cider vinegar helps in losing weight and brings a healthy and rosy glow to the skin.

Carbonated/Soft Drinks

Research done by Professor Peter Piper of Sheffield University has shown that sodium benzoate found in soft drinks sold by leading cola makers can switch off vital parts of DNA, causing serious damage to cells, thus leading to degenerative diseases.

When mixed with vitamin C, it forms benzene, a carcinogenic substance. Many people consider soft drinks to be harmless, or just worry about their sugar content, and the potential for putting on weight. But the erosive potential of soft drinks is very high and often ignored. A study showed that any type of soft drink corrodes teeth due to the citric acid and/or phosphoric acid present in it. It is very detrimental to tooth enamel.

These drinks create acidity. They may cause ulcers and gastric problems, irregular heart beats, high blood pressure, risk of cancer, restlessness, nervousness, irritability and sleeplessness.

Phosphoric acid in colas causes the excretion of calcium. Scientists found that women who consumed more cola had weaker bones.

Coconut Water

In addition to natural sugar, fresh coconut water contains saline and albumen, an array of vitamins, potassium, chloride, calcium and magnesium. It kills intestinal worms. It dissolves kidney stones. And it protects eyes from glaucoma and cataract.

Energy Drinks

A study published in the journal *Drug and Alcohol Dependence*, authored by Roland Griffiths of John Hopkins Medical Institutions warns about the possibility of caffeine addiction by energy drinks. It says that the caffeine content of energy drinks varies, with some containing the equivalent of 14 cans of Coca-Cola.

Cocoa and Chocolates

Both cocoa and tea contain polyphenols, the chemicals present in fruits and vegetables. But they have a more active form of polyphenol, that is, epicatechin or simply catechin. Professor Norman Hollenberg of Harvard Medical School says that the health benefits of epicatechin could be enormous. He found that people of Kuna tribe, living close to Panama, rarely suffer from high blood pressure, and have much lower rates of cancer, heart disease, and strokes. Kunas start drinking cocoa from the moment they are weaned away from milk.

Cocoa also has high amounts of blood-pressure-lowering magnesium in addition.

A study published by The Archives of Internal Medicine 2006 showed that individuals who ate even 10g of dark chocolate per day had lower blood pressure.

Cocoa is considered one of the most concentrated sources of flavonoids. About 100g of wine contains about 63mg of flavonoids. The same amount of dark chocolate contains about 510mg of flavonoids.

Cocoa is the primary ingredient of chocolate. The other ingredients of chocolate are milk and sugar. To get the health benefits of cocoa, and to avoid milk and sugar, one should opt for dark chocolate. Better still, one can take cocoa powder in milk and cereal as well.

Chocolate is a good source of arginine, an amino acid which is a component of most proteins. Arginine is crucial in boosting the body's immunity besides being beneficial for the liver, and for blood circulation that may even improve one's libido.

As regards caffeine, a typical dark chocolate bar contains only 1-11mg of caffeine. An 8 oz cup of coffee contains 137mg of caffeine.

Chocolates appear to improve serotonin in the brain. Patients taking dark chocolates reported significantly less fatigue because of the effect on the level of serotonin.

Dark chocolate can prevent clotting of blood. Researchers at Johns Hopkins University showed that chemicals in cocoa beans have an effect similar to aspirin in reducing platelet clumping.

Cocoa and dark chocolate could be best medicine for liver. Those who ate dark chocolate after meals had smaller rise in blood pressure, which may otherwise reach dangerous levels in liver patients and may cause rupture of blood vessels.

Cocoa also contains good amounts of theobromine. It has been found to cause headaches like migraine in some people.

Coffee

Coffee has high content of caffeine. It is a stimulant and can disturb sleep. However, some people experience a sound sleep after a hot cup of coffee. Ultimately, it depends from person to person. It stimulates the flow of gastric juices, but in the long run it weakens the ability of the system to secrete juices. Caffeine in coffee is responsible for lowering our calcium levels.

Data gathered by researchers at University of Minnesota revealed that consuming 4-6 cups of coffee per day lowers the risk of diabetes by 22 per cent. Drinking coffee with daytime meal helps in fighting against diabetes.

Coffee, being acidic in nature, aggravates arthritis.

Tea

Tea is high in antioxidants like quercetin, catechin, polyphenols, thianine and EGCG.

Studies show that regular tea drinkers are at lower risk of heart disease, stroke, dementia, osteoporosis, cancer, and bacterial and viral infections.

Could drinking tea help reduce cholesterol?

Yes. People who drank 5 cups of black tea daily saw their LDL cholesterol drop by 11 per cent.

Quercetin in black tea helps prevent blood clotting that triggers heart attack. Those who had already suffered heart attacks were found to reduce their risk of having a second attack by 44 per cent if they drank a cup or more of black tea daily.

Tea strengthens the immune system. Harvard researchers found that people who drank five cups of tea per day for two weeks, experienced a rise in the strength of their immune system.

Drinking tea can, therefore, lower the risk of cancer. A Swedish study conducted over a period of 15 years found that women who took just a cup of tea everyday saw a 24 per cent drop, and those who took 2 cups a day saw an amazing 46 per cent drop in their ovarian cancer risk. A reverse relationship exists between consumption of tea and risk of ovarian cancer. Polyphenols present in green tea help prevent prostate cancer.

Further, drinking tea builds bone density, and reduces risk of osteoporosis. It is reported that women who drink tea have higher bone-mineral density.

Drinking tea helps one to lose weight. People who drink 5 cups of tea every day burn 12 per cent more fat as compared to non-tea drinkers.

Black tea also has its own set of benefits. A cup of black tea contains 286mg of flavonoids, whereas green tea has 316mg of them.

Tea has much less caffeine as compared to coffee. Tea contains thianine, a protein, which actually counters the side effects of caffeine such as rise in BP. Thianine relieves stress, boosts concentration, and supports immunity.

Recent studies suggest that tea has fluoride which can help strengthen teeth, reduce plaque and bacteria in mouth, and protect the heart and brain from plaque and infection.

Super Green Tea

By adding 2-3 tablespoons of citrus juice, like that of orange or lemon, to a cup of tea (green or black) one could increase the antioxidant benefits of tea up to five times.

However, anaemic people should not take too much tea as it causes loss of iron. Those who suffer from hyperthyroid and are already losing weight due to higher metabolism caused by excess secretion of thyroxine, are advised to avoid tea.

It is recommended that you always take tea with some snack. This will reduce the effect of acidity caused by drinking tea. Biscuits or toasts with butter or cheese make a very good combination with tea.

Pregnant women should limit their consumption of caffeine lest there is a risk of miscarriage or of their baby being underweight.

Epicatechin in cocoa, tea, grapes, and blueberries, is beneficial for cardiovascular health. A recent study published in the American Journal of Neuroscience shows that the compound may also boost memory by improving blood flow to the brain.

A Japanese study on people aged over 70 revealed that those who drank 2-3 cups of green tea daily scored better in cognitive tests.

Soy Milk

Soy milk is cholesterol and lactose-free, and rich in proteins like soybeans. For those with lactose intolerance, soy milk is an excellent alternative. It has no saturated fat and contains naturally occurring omega-3 fats.

Thandai

Thandai is a healthy drink, particularly for summer season.

It is prepared by blending together almonds, watermelon seeds, poppy seeds, aniseed, cardamom, cayenne or white pepper, petals of desi rose, milk (if desired), sugar and water. Cashews, pistachios, and saffron may also be added for taste.

Almonds in *thandai* are packed with nutrients, MUFA, Vitamin E, magnesium, potassium, copper, iron, etc.

Rose petals are excellent for decreasing *pitta* (fire element) in the body which, under the effect of immense heat in summer, becomes in excess.

Cashew nuts are rich in protein, MUFA/oleic acid, magnesium balancing with calcium, phosphorous, and vitamin B which is good for nervous system.

Poppy seeds are effective in quenching thirst, and are also good for curing fever, irritation, and inflammation of the stomach.

Green cardamoms reduce *vaata* (air element) and *kapha*. They also increase appetite and soothe mucous membranes.

In the ancient texts, saffron is mentioned as a tonic for liver disorders.

Thandai with Hemp (Bhang)

Bhang paste is prepared by grinding the buds and leaves of cannabis plant. The preferred way of taking bhang is in the form of a refreshing drink, i.e. by adding it to *thandai.*

Jal-Jeera

It is made by adding *bhuna-jeera* (roasted and powdered cumin seeds), *podina* (mint), lemon juice, *kala namak* (black salt), and *chhoti pipal* to pure water. It makes for a healthy digestive drink to be taken before a meal, or for filling into *batashas/puris* in Indian chaat.

15

Ayurvedic Medicines, Herbs and Spices

The aim of Ayurvedic medicines is to achieve a state of balance between the three humours/tempers of the body: *vaata*, *pitta* and *kapha*.

Homoeopathic mother tinctures are essentially extracts of Ayurvedic medicines dissolved in alcohol.

According to Ayurveda, the most important thing is to remove toxins from the body. *Triphala,* described in this chapter, is excellent for removing waste.

Spices are used as condiments in cooking. Herbs have medicinal use. The terms 'herbs' and 'spices' can be used interchangeably. Some spices have profound medical use, while some herbs can be used as condiments.

All herbs and spices are loaded with minerals and antioxidants. They are usually strong stimulants.

Ajwain (Thyme/Celery Seed)

Ajwain/thyme improves digestion by increasing the flow of enzymes in the stomach. It is an antacid and chewing it along with some hot water is a useful remedy for upset stomach. This herb is anti-spasmodic, anti-bacterial, and carminative. It helps in treating gout and rheumatism. Pthalide compound present in it lowers stress hormone levels and muscle tension, even inducing one to sleep.

Alfa-alfa

It is a health builder as it boosts appetite and provides nourishment to the body. It provides relief in arthritis.

Aloe Vera

Aloe Vera is widely used as an ingredient for skincare products such as creams and soaps. Aloe Vera pulp or juice is a traditional remedy for joint pains, as in arthritis.

Alum (*Phitkari*)

Majorly used for purifying drinking water, alum also treats swollen throat and mucous membrane of respiratory system. Powdered alum placed on tongue is said to arrest an attack of asthma.

Amla (Indian Gooseberry)

This Indian berry is a storehouse of vitamin C and iron. The vitamin C content is not destroyed even by heating and processing *amla*. *Amla* hair oil is considered very effective for maintaining healthy and dark hair.

Anise/Aniseed/Fennel (*Saunf*)

Anise is a herb belonging to the *saunf* family. It helps to expel gas, and relax intestinal spasms. It is a rich source of coumarin compound that helps to regulate blood sugar level.

Arjun

The bark of *Arjun* tree has been found to be extremely helpful in treating high blood pressure and coronary artery disease. It is considered as a great cardiac tonic as it stimulates the heart muscles to draw in nutrients from the blood.

Asafoetida (*Heeng*)

Asafoetida has a typical flavour, and is warming and aphrodisiacal in its effects. It helps in increasing appetite. It is primarily used for frying (*chhonk*) in dals. Its use in dals/legumes curbs gas formation.

Ashoka (Jonasia Ashoka Mother Tincture)

The bark, leaf and fruit of *Ashoka* tree are used extensively in the treatment of excessive uterine bleeding, dysmenorrhoea, and menstrual disorders.

Ashwagandha (Withania Somnifera as Mother Tincture)

Ashwagandha, the most revered herb of Ayurveda, has antioxidant properties. It is often referred to as India's Ginseng minus the blood-pressure-enhancing disadvantage of Ginseng. Researchers at All India Institute of Medical Sciences, Delhi, have demonstrated how *Ashwagandha* strengthens heart muscles.

Ashwagandha has been shown to reduce anxiety-induced stress by relaxing nerves.

Aspidosperma Mother Tincture

It is a tonic for lungs for it stimulates respiratory centres, decreases carbon dioxide and increases oxygen in the blood. It also induces sleep simultaneously.

Avena Sativa and its Mother Tincture

Avena Sativa is oat straw. Oats is a nutritious cereal that contains silica. It restores nervous system, and is a definite cure for sleeplessness.

Rich in saponins, flavonoids, minerals, and alkaloids necessary for healthy hormonal system, it acts as a uterine tonic, and stimulates both male and female sexual systems.

Its steroidal saponins nourish pancreas, liver, adrenals, and help stabilise sugar levels.

Basil (tulsi)

Tulsi is a tonic for the respiratory system. It helps in asthma, bronchitis, fever, coughs, arthritis, rheumatic pains, and bladder, urinary and kidney infections. It enhances immunity and keeps flu at bay.

Bay Leaf (*Tej pata*)

A regular intake of bay leaves along with its oil cures cold, urinary infections, skin diseases, dandruff, etc. It can be used with other spices in *pilau* and tea, especially in winter.

Berberis Aquifolium-Mahonia Mother tincture

It is an effective remedy for acne, eczema and psoriasis. It stimulates all glands and improves nutrition.

Betel (*Paan*) Leaves

Betel leaves rid you of cough. Topical application can reduce inflammations in arthritis.

Bilwa

Bilwa, an Ayurvedic herb, treats diarrhoea and dysentery.

Black Cohosh

It has oestrogenic effects as it balances the levels of female hormones. It provides relief in menopause discomfort, delayed periods, ovarian cramps, pain in uterus, menstrual pain, etc.

Black Pepper

Black pepper increases breakdown of fat cells. It increases stomach acid secretions, thereby improving digestion. It forms an ingredient of the combination Trikuta which supports the digestive system. Add 1/8 tsp of black pepper to each meal as a digestive aid.

It provides relief in cold, cough, asthma and arthritis. Black pepper contains piperine, an antioxidant and anti-bacterial. It can also be added to tea.

Blessed Thistle

It boosts the production of breast milk in nursing mothers. But it should not be taken during pregnancy.

Brahmi

Brahmi improves memory. Students can greatly benefit from it.

Central Drug Research Institute, Lucknow, recently launched a *Brahmi* extract, which is very effective for strengthening hair, and providing relief in headaches. *Brahmi* together with *amla* boiled in *til* oil is the well-known formulation for *Brahmi-Amla* hair oil in India.

Capsicum (*Shimla Mirch*)

It reduces cholesterol, lowers blood pressure, and improves blood circulation.

Cardamom (*Elaichi*)

Both varieties of cardamom – large black and small green – are used as digestives. The small green variety is a stimulant and has a warming effect. Dark large ones soothe the throat.

For relief in cough/asthma, ¼ tsp cardamom powder mixed with honey should be eaten. Chewing cardamom checks bad breath and controls hiccups.

Cayenne Peppers/White Pepper (*Dakkhini Mirch*)

It strengthens immune system, and improves blood circulation. It is useful in rheumatic pains, asthma, bronchitis, fevers, sore throat, and other such infections of respiratory tract. Cayenne ointment reduces joint pains.

Moreover, it stimulates the body to dissolve blood clots. Hence, it reduces risk of heart attack.

It produces endorphins which not only reduce pain but also produce a sense of pleasure. Cayenne also helps the body to burn abdominal fat and control blood sugar.

Cayenne is of hot potency and is, therefore, preferred in items of cool energy such as *thandai*.

Chammomile

Chammomile tea alleviates stress, promotes sleep, and soothes the digestive system.

It is neutral, neither warm nor cool. It can even be given to a mother right after childbirth. Chamomile oil steam inhalation/forehead massage is used for soothing the nerves and calming the mind.

Chhoti Pipal

This Ayurvedic herb allows even cow's milk to be digested by infants.

Chicory (Kasni)

It is good for both liver and kidney. It regulates heartbeat, lowers high blood pressure and fever, stops diarrhoea, increases menstrual flow, and reduces high blood sugar.

Chiraita

It is an Ayurvedic blood purifier.

Chyavan-Prash

This anti-ageing Ayurvedic formulation is composed of *amla* and a host of herbs. It boosts immunity.

Cinnamon (Dalchini)

Cinnamon comes next only to cloves in their composition. It contains 18 per cent of antioxidant phenols. Coumarin, a powerful phenol in cinnamon, has been shown to increase glucose metabolism by as much as 20 times. Cinnamon should form a part of a diabetic's diet.

Cinnamon is loaded with chromium, zinc, manganese, iron, calcium, and blood sugar regulating proteins.

It contains compounds that help insulin bring glucose to cells. In a study, 60 adults with Type-2 diabetes who added 1-6 grams of cinnamon to their diet daily had their glucose levels dropped by 18-29 per cent in 40 days. Their triglyceride and LDL cholesterol levels also dipped significantly.

Studies show that just ½ tsp of cinnamon per day can lower bad LDL cholesterol. Cinnamon acts as blood thinner as it has anti-clotting effect on blood.

Cinnamon is used for enhancing taste and giving health benefits along with black peppers, cardamoms, cloves, etc in rice *pulao*, vegetable curries, and tea. It is highly effective in colds, bronchitis and asthma.

Calcium and fibre in cinnamon bind bile salts, thereby reducing the risk of colon cancer. A recent study done by the US Department of Agriculture said that cinnamon reduced the proliferation of leukemia, and lymphoma cancer cells.

In a study at Copenhagen University, patients given ½ tsp of cinnamon with honey before breakfast every morning experienced significant relief from arthritic pain after one week.

Cinnamon is, thus, useful in treatment and prevention of arthritis, cancer, diabetes, diarrhoea, fever, *kapha,* heart problems, insomnia, PMS, ulcers, psoriasis, and muscular spasms.

It has proven effects as sedative, antibiotic, anti-ulcerative. Added to food, it inhibits bacterial growth and spoilage, making it a natural preservative.

Cloves (*Laung*)

Cloves have the most number of antioxidant phenols among all spices. The phenol content is 30 per cent of their dried weight.

The anaesthetic action of its oil relieves toothache. Eugenol, an anti-inflammatory, is the main ingredient in clove oil. Keep a clove in your mouth every night to counter toothache, heal sore throat, and to maintain teeth in good health. Clove makes the breath pleasant and thus, acts as a mouth freshener.

Sauté one clove in a tsp of sesame oil and put 3-5 drops in the ear to cure ear pain.

It is an excellent source of manganese, omega-3 fats, calcium, and magnesium. High in EFAs and flavonoids, cloves help in flu, cold, bronchitis, etc., and can cure first stage rheumatism and relieve arthritic pain.

Cloves promote enzymatic flow, and boost digestion. They prevent the formation of gas in intestines and provide relief from flatulence. Some cloves should be added in tea to regulate gas.

Coriander/Cilantro (*Dhaniya*)

Coriander is aromatic like mint, cardamom, cinnamon, ginger, etc.

Its leaves are added in vegetables for flavour. Its seeds are used as spice and added in vegetables to enhance taste and provide health benefits.

It is carminative and digestive. It helps in curing piles, worms, and acidity.

Crataegus Mother Tincture

The homoeopathic mother tincture of crataegus is said to have a solvent power upon deposits in arteries. Thus, it prevents arteriosclerosis, reduces blood pressure and increases flow of blood to the heart. It, thus helps in controlling chronic heart disease.

Cumin Seeds (*Jeera*)

Cumin seeds are an essential ingredient in our kitchen. They alleviate abdominal bloating and distension. Cumin improves liver function and is a cure for stomach disorders.

Roasted or *bhuna jeera* is extremely good for digestion. It is the favoured ingredient in curds, *chhole*, Indian chaat, etc. Drinking buttermilk with roasted *jeera* after meals helps to get rid of piles.

Cumin has powerful anti-cancer properties. It can block chromosome damage caused by cancer-causing chemicals.

Cranberry (*Karonda*)

Cranberries are particularly recommended for curing urinary tract infections (UTI). A recent study revealed that cranberries contain even more antioxidants than blueberries and red wine.

Damiana

It is used for treating hormonal imbalance, infertility, frigidity, etc. It increases testosterone level.

Echinacea

It is a treatment for frequent nasal discharges, usually caused by allergy.

Elderberry/Sambucus Nigra

The fruit prevents flu virus from latching on to cells. Take 3 tsp of its extract four times a day at the first appearance of flu symptoms. Sambucus Nigra 30 is used as a homoeopathic medicine in potency when nose gets choked due to cold.

Evening Primrose Oil

It is omega-3 oil, and is useful in PMS. The oil treats menstrual pain, hormonal disorders and produces female hormone progesterone.

Eucalyptus

It has a warming effect. Eucalyptus oil, being antiseptic in nature, cures colds, coughs, lung and sinus congestion, and rheumatic pains.

Fennel (*Saunf*)

Saunf is an old remedy for colic, and irritable bowel syndrome.

Colic (in infants) results from an immature nervous system, and not from indigestion. Medicines that are prescribed usually sedate brain by inhibiting neurotransmitters.

Fennel seeds contain essential oils that dilate the vessels of gut increasing blood flow and speeding metabolic rate of digestive system.

Fenugreek (*Methi*)

Both the vegetable and the seeds of fenugreek (*methi*) have similar effect. *Methi*'s therapeutic properties include providing relief in sinus and asthmatic conditions.

Methi seeds promote lactation in nursing mothers. It prevents inflammations and is highly beneficial for joint and arthritic pains. In Himachal Pradesh, people prepare chutney of *methi* and garlic in order to relieve joint pains.

Methi is the best therapeutic herb for diabetes. Similar to cauliflower and broccoli, *methi* is a powerful cancer-preventing plant.

Garam Masala

It is a combination of a number of spices, mostly suited for consumption during winter and rainy season. Its composition varies, but the common formulation is achieved by mixing 2 tsp of roasted cumin seeds, 2 tsp large black cardamom seeds, 1 tbsp cinnamon, bay leaves, 1 tsp ground black pepper, ½ tsp nutmeg, and ¼ tsp mace and some cloves.

It can be added to tea, to channa/gram, curry, vegetables and dals. For adding to tea, cumin seeds are not included in garam masala.

Garlic

Garlic reduces high blood pressure, blood sugar, asthma, bronchitis, arthritis, rheumatism, etc. It controls blood clotting and prevents heart attack and stroke. See under 'Vegetables'.

Giloi/Amrita (Tinospora cordifoli)

Giloi, an Ayurvedic remedy, enhances the immune function. Giloi with tulsi is a suitable remedy for curing all kinds of flu.

Ginger (*Adrak*)

Dried ginger powder is called *saunth*. Ginger promotes elimination of intestinal gas, treats nausea and vomiting, improves liver function, provides digestive comfort, decreases swelling and gives pain relief in arthritis.

If taken over a long period, it is very potent in inhibiting formation of inflammatory prostaglandins.

It has antioxidant abilities credited with cancer-fighting properties. Like garlic, it reduces cholesterol, dilates blood vessels and increases blood flow. See under 'Vegetables'.

Gingko Biloba

Gingko Biloba is used to enhance memory in elderly people. It improves blood flow in general, specifically to the optic nerve. It is recommended in glaucoma.

Glucosamine

It is preferred in the treatment for arthritis as it repairs joints.

Gokshara

This Ayurvedic herb provides comfort in case of urinary incontinence.

Golden Seal/Hydrastis Mother Tincture

It promotes the production of biles and is an effective remedy for liver and for increasing appetite.

Gotu Kola

It is an Ayurvedic herb for enhancing memory, and is produced by Himalaya Herbal Care.

Grape Seed Extract

Grape seed extract is a powerful antioxidant. It prevents stickiness in blood platelets that can lead to blood clots, thereby reducing the risk of heart attack and stroke.

Guduchi

It improves resistance to infections.

Guggul

Guggul is a shrub that exudes gummy resin from its bark once every 10-12 years. The shrub dies after the gum is extracted. The resin, which is very effective in reducing high cholesterol, is used in over 100 Ayurvedic formulations. Dr David Moore from the Baylor College of Medicine, Houston, has reported that this traditional 2500-years-old Indian medication for lowering cholesterol really works wonders.

Gymnea

This Ayurvedic herb lowers blood sugar levels.

Harar (Terminalia Chebula Mother Tincture)

It helps in digestion, and is a suitable cure for constipation.

Hibiscus (*Adhul/Gulhar/Jawakusum*)

It is a tropical flower high in antioxidants. Studies show that it may lower blood pressure by as much as 65 per cent by acting as diuretic, removing salt from body that helps relax blood vessels. It is a tonic for heart and may also prevent damage from bad LDL cholesterol.

It is available in supplement form. Experts recommend drinking tea made from its flowers.

Hops

Hops flower, used in the brewing of beer, is a well-known sedative often recommended to treat insomnia. The bitter components in hops stimulate and strengthen digestion.

It contains some oestrogen-like substances. As such it is found to alter menstrual cycle.

Kachnar

The pink and white flowers of this tree and its bark are known to prevent cancer, cure leucorrhoea, and dissolve uterine fibroids. Drinking the water in which the bark has been boiled is useful.

Kala Namak (Black Salt)

Kala Namak is a taste-enhancing salt. Unlike MSG in Chinese food, it is not a chemical. MSG raises BP. *Kala Namak* is commonly used in Indian snacks and is beneficial for the digestive system.

Kalmegh

Kalmegh, an Ayurvedic herb, is a blood purifier. It helps in the proper functioning of the liver.

Kari-Pata (Indian Curry Leaves)

Kari-Pata has a very desirable aroma and provides a great taste to Indian curries and snacks. It slows down the action of a digestive enzyme in the breakdown of dietary starch to glucose. This leads to even more trickle of glucose into the bloodstream from the intestine. It is considered as India's traditional diabetic remedy.

Kattha

An astringent vegetable extract, it is eaten in betel leaf. Ayurvedic pills of *kattha,* along with some other ingredients, are available as Khadiradi in the market. Allow the pill to be dissolved in the mouth. It is useful in curing khansi/cough, sour throat, etc.

Kudzu

This Chinese herb is useful in reducing the craving for alcohol.

Kudzu has oestrogen-like elements. Kudzu root was found to reduce blood pressure, blood sugar levels, and the fat hormone leptin. It brings relief in problems related to menopause, works against lack of sexual interest, frigidity, and so on.

Lavender

Lavender oil promotes sleep and is helpful in curing migraine and depression.

Lemon Grass

Lemon grass tea is useful in treating colds. It is used to banish anxiety, boost memory, and aid sleep and digestion. It has the potential to relieve headaches and migraines.

It also works to calm an overactive thyroid gland.

Licorice (*Mulhethi*)

Mulhethi soothes the throat and strengthens the mucous membranes of the respiratory system. It is not recommended for people with high blood pressure and heart ailments.

Mace (*Javitri*)

It has a warming effect and is used as an ingredient of garam masala.

Magrail

These are tiny black onion seeds. They impart a typical flavour to wheat snacks like *mathari*.

Manduk Parni

Regular use of *Manduk Parni* enhances blood circulation, and improves digestion.

Marijuana (*Ganja*)

One wonders why alcohol is freely allowed, while a mild drug like marijuana is banned. An active ingredient called tetrahydrocannabinol (THC) in marijuana may help fight lung cancer, the most lethal of all cancers, says Anju Preet, a Harvard University researcher in Boston.

Earlier studies suggest that THC could help fight brain, prostate, and skin cancers as well. Marijuana provides a legal treatment for nausea in patients undergoing chemotherapy.

The cannabinoid helps to control pain, inflammation, anxiety, depression, stimulates appetite and settles the stomach. It also provides relief from PMS and glaucoma.

A new study at Ohio State University has revealed that a daily puff of marijuana can help reduce memory loss in old age and fight Alzheimer's. But one must also be cautious of the many side-effects of using a drug like this.

Marshmallow

It has a cooling tendency and works best in treating urinary infections and stomach ulcers.

Milk Thistle

It is widely accepted as the herb that supports liver health. The antioxidant silymarin in it not only counteracts toxins and pollutants, but also regenerates liver cells.

Mint (*Podina*)

Podina promotes digestion. Peppermint oil made from mint plant relieves gastro-intestinal tract spasms, and gas. *Podin-Hara*, an

Ayurvedic extract, treats disorders of the digestive system, flatulence, nausea and vomiting.

Mushroom, Sacred (Psilocybin)

Psilocybin is a compound extracted from a mushroom variety called sacred mushrooms. Roland Griffiths at John Hopkins University found that psilocybin could induce heightened mystical and spiritual experiences with lasting positive effects for many of the subjects. However, due to its potency of affecting the nervous system, its use is prohibited in money countries.

Mustard Seeds

Mustard seeds have all the benefits of mustard oil including those of the omega-3 fats. Their paste is used as an alternative to tomato ketchup.

Mustard seeds speed up our metabolism rate and help in weight loss. In addition, it has anti-bacterial, antiseptic and anti-inflammatory properties.

Neem

Its leaves, bark, oil, etc., are all useful. Neem has anti-fungal properties and helps in the purification of blood. Like many other bitter plants such as *karela* and *jamun*, it treats diabetes.

Nutmeg (*Jaiphal*)

It is considered as a digestive stimulant. It is added to desserts and cakes.

Onions (See: Vegetables)

Onions stimulate digestive system and lower blood sugar levels.

In the Middle Eastern traditional medicine, onions were prescribed for diabetes. Theosulfinates (sulphur compounds in onions responsible for their smell) reduce diabetes symptoms and protect against cardiovascular diseases. They lower cholesterol and increase good HDL cholesterol.

In *Materia Medica*, William Boericke recommends onions for respiratory and digestive problems. Onions destroy E. Coli bacteria in intestines and prevent cancer of digestive system.

Quercetin in onions prevents inflammations, and protects against allergies, stomach ulcers, and cancers. Your body absorbs quercetin from onions three times faster than it does from apples and tea.

Opium

Opium is cannabis. It works on mucus membranes of the digestive tract and respiratory system. It helps in reducing anxiety and is considered to give relief to cancer patients. But as with marijuana, it should only be taken on the advice of a doctor.

Oregano (*Karpuravalli*)

It is a herb belonging to the mint family native to Italy and Europe. It is also nicknamed as Pizza herb.

It is high in antioxidant phenolic compounds and flavonoids. It is used in South India where it is called Karpuravalli. It relieves headaches, sore throat, and cough.

Parsley (*Ajmod*)

It increases urine output, lowers BP, and provides relief in urinary tract infections.

It increases the count of white blood cells in the body, thereby increasing immunity. It also prevents cancer.

Passion Flower (Passiflora Incarnata Mother Tincture)

Passion flower reduces nervous tension. It is a tranquilliser, and is helpful in depression.

Passion Flower or Passiflora mother tincture lowers blood pressure. It is used in the treatment of throat, asthma, cold, cough, and diarrhoea. It is very helpful in asthma in which sleep is disturbed by early morning aggravation.

For menstrual pain and headaches caused by stress, passion flower plus chamomile can be used.

Peppermint

The leaves and flowers of mint plant contain menthol, a volatile oil.

It inhibits muscle spasms, and is effective in reducing headaches. It relaxes the muscles of the GI tract reducing cramping and helping expel gas. It is a highly recommended age-old remedy for stomach aches and gas.

It reduces water retention, hence is a fine remedy for menstrual pain due to water retention.

Pippali/Chhoti Pipal

An age-old remedy for rejuvenating the lungs is to take grounded powder of seven *pippalis* with honey and cow's ghee along with warm water for a year.

Pippali is a herb useful for digestion. It forms an ingredient of the combination *trikuta*.

Red Yeast Rice

It is used in Chinese medicine as a remedy for lowering cholesterol as well as for indigestion and diarrhoea. It is prepared from bright purple rice that is fermented with mould *Monascus purpureus* until it turns red. It is used in whole or powdered form as a food colouring, preservative, and spice.

Rosemary

Both fresh and dried leaves of this bush-like plant are used extensively in Italian cuisine.

Caffeic acid and rosemarinic acid are the two important ingredients in rosemary. These are antioxidant and anti-inflammatory agents and are effective in reducing inflammation which may contribute to asthma, liver disease, heart disease, etc.

Antioxidants in rosemary are known for their ability to slow down production of free radicals. Accordingly, rosemary is proving to be an important defence against cancer.

It has been used to treat stomach upsets, digestive disorders and headaches. French scientists from the National Institute of Agronomic

Research in Dijon found that rosemary extract encouraged detoxifying enzymes to flush harmful toxins from the liver.

Dr Zhu and colleagues from State University of New Jersey found that rosemary extract, by significantly inactivating excess oestrogen in women, helps prevent breast cancer.

Rosemary acts as a mild diuretic. It helps combat the effects of water retention, improves kidney function, and reduces swelling, inflammations, bloating, etc.

Pregnant women should not take rosemary extract.

Rose Petals and Rose Hips

Rose petals when boiled, strained, and mixed with unrefined sugar, and taken as a *sherbet*, strengthen the immune system. Rose hips are a blood purifier and are also good for the digestive system. Rose water is highly recommended for soothing the eyes.

Rose oil when massaged around the forehead helps in easing tension.

Sada-Bahar (Periwinkle)

This plant blossoms round the year. Its pink and white-coloured flowers are believed to be a cure for cancer. American scientists extracted several chemical compounds from the plant, some of which are similar to cancer drugs.

Saffron (*Kesar*)

Saffron contains the only water-soluble carotene named crocetin which is a potent antioxidant. It lowers LDL and triglycerides and increases HDL. It has memory-enhancing properties and is used in Ayurveda to treat cancerous tumours and depression.

Saffron reverses age related macular degeneration and improves blood circulation.

Sage

It stimulates hair growth, and improves skin.

Sandalwood (*Chandan*), and Sandalwood Oil

Sandalwood oil, apart from being beneficial in anxiety and tension, is also an aphrodisiac. It helps in chronic bronchitis, urinary problems, bladder infections and inflammations. Its use in steam inhalation or for massage has a soothing effect on the body.

Try sandalwood oil diluted with sweet almond oil and massage it to reduce stress-related headaches.

Sarpa-Gandha (Rauwolfia Serpentina Mother Tincture)

Sarpa Gandha is an Ayurvedic herb that lowers blood pressure. Rauwolfia Serpentina is available in the form of mother tincture from homoeopathic stores.

Saw Palmetto

Saw Palmetto is commonly used in enlarged prostate problem. It has no side effects and has the added advantage of improving libido.

Seetophala

An Ayurvedic herb, it suppresses production of cough and cures *khansi*.

Shallaki

This herb is used for joint pains.

Shankhpushpi

This well known herb is especially good for memory, nervous system, and relieving stress. It is highly recommended for students.

Shatavari (Asparagus)

Shatavari word translates to 'she who possesses hundred husbands'. It has a profound effect on female sexual system. It improves the quality of breast milk, brings balance in female hormonal system and cervical pH, decreases PMS pain, relieves inflammatory conditions, and aids digestion.

Western asparagus root has similar properties as *shatavari*, but is more diuretic.

Skullcap

It is recommended in the treatment of insomnia.

Spirulina

There are 42 trace elements in spirulina that are not easily found in fruits and vegetables. It is also a high source of protein.

St. John's Wort

It is a well known herb for treating stress depression.

Tobacco

According to Indian Journal of Community Medicine, nearly half the cancer cases in India are tobacco-related. Exposure to cigarette smoke induces rapid changes in blood chemistry making it more prone to clotting that causes heart attack or stroke.

Trikuta

Trikuta, a mixture of *chhoti pipal, saunth* and black pepper, supports the gastric system.

Triphala (*Harar, Bahera, Amla*)

Triphala is a common Indian Ayurvedic antioxidant which is made by a combination of three potent herbs *harar*, *bahera*, and *amla* in equal quantities. *Bahera* cleanses the system. *Harar* relieves constipation, and improves digestion. It is also available in the form of homeopathic mother tincture *Terminalia Chebula*. *Amla* is an excellent source of natural vitamin C.

Scientists at the University of Pittsburg Cancer Institute have shown that Triphala has the potential to slow down pancreatic tumours without damaging normal pancreatic cells.

Tulsi (Basil)

Tulsi tea is used for curing mild fever, headache, etc. It treats menstrual pains.

Tulsi leaves have a warming effect. When boiled in water, they relieve cough, cold and flu, and bring down fevers. It lowers blood sugar levels. Besides, tulsi has anti-bacterial, anti-fungal, and anti-viral properties.

Tulsi together with *Giloi*, is a treatment for flu. Taking ginger and tulsi juice with honey twice daily provides relief in cough, asthma and fever related problems.

Turmeric (Haldi)

Turmeric (Haldi) is the wonder spice of India. Curcumin in haldi has anti-inflammatory, antioxidant, anti-cancer, and multiple disease fighting properties.

Indians eat 100-200mg of curcumin through turmeric everyday. Recent clinical studies indicate that curry, as it contains the powerful spice turmeric, is effective in preventing arthritis, heart disease, and Alzheimer's disease.

It has clinical use in prevention of arthritis and osteoporosis. It lowers cholesterol levels, helps treat cold, sore throats, fevers, acne, arthritis, kidney, and liver problems.

It is commonly used to treat pain, bruises, flatulence, PMS, etc. Turmeric is a great antiseptic and has skin and wound healing properties.

According to researchers at Ohio State University, synthetic molecules derived from curcumin can help kill cancer cells and stop them from spreading. Curcumin interacts with certain proteins to generate anti-cancer activity inside the body, says James Fuchs Assistant Professor at Ohio State University.

Use turmeric and ginger liberally in food. They are anti-inflammatory, and anti-cancer. They also help in treating uterine fibroids.

Wheat Grass

Wheat grass cleanses blood and gastrointestinal tract. It increases red blood cells (RBCs), and dilates blood vessels, thus reducing blood pressure.

It is highly recommended as an anti-cancer remedy by naturopaths.

Section 2

Body

16

Digestive System

A disease happens as a result of improper food that our body and mind consume.

16.1 GASTROINTESTINAL (GI) TRACT

The digestive system comprises the gastrointestinal (GI) tract. If the digestive system is not working properly, then other systems will also be affected. Even medicines will not help because they have to be absorbed through this system.

The digestive system is concerned with the intake, digestion, and absorption of the nutrients from the food we eat. An overview of the digestion process will help you understand better the ailments associated with them

16.2 PHYSIOLOGY OF DIGESTION

The process of digestion actually begins with the smell, sight, and taste of the food. The sensory perception results in the brain sending impulses through nerves to glands to start producing digestive juices.

What Are Digestive Juices?

Digestive juices are produced by the salivary glands, the stomach, the pancreas, and the liver. About 10 litres of these juices pour into your digestive tract.

The process of digestion begins with salivary glands being initiated to produce saliva.

The mechanical process of breaking down food starts with chewing. As we chew, saliva moistens the food, and enzymes in the saliva help break the starches down to simpler sugars.

Peristalsis of the stomach churns the food, mixing it with mucous and gastric juices containing enzymes and hydrochloric acid. Additional load will come on the stomach if the food is not chewed properly in the mouth.

Very small amount of absorption takes place in the stomach. However, water, glucose and alcohol are directly absorbed from the stomach. That is why alcohol taken on empty stomach produces an enhanced effect.

Food leaving the stomach and entering small intestine is in the form of a highly acidic thick liquid called chyme.

Digestion takes place in the small intestine with the help of pancreatic juice and bile. Bile breaks down fats and helps in their absorption. Enzymes in pancreatic juice help break down carbohydrates into sugars, proteins into amino acids, and fats, with the help of bile, into fatty acids and glycerol.

These products along with vitamins and minerals are then absorbed directly into the bloodstream from the walls of the small intestine.

Sodium bicarbonate in pancreatic juice neutralises acidity of the chyme. If this process fails, the highly acidic chyme may corrode the walls of duodenum and one may develop ulcers in duodenum.

The main function of the large intestine is to absorb water. At the same time, bacteria in the colon aid digestion of the remaining products.

Liver, apart from producing bile, acts as a detoxifier. It absorbs all toxic substances such as nicotine, various drugs, and poisons. As a result it swells. But it allows only blood, without any poisonous substances, to go to the heart. Note that liver has great regenerative capacity. Occasionally, bile goes into the bloodstream and causes jaundice-like effects.

After meals, lie down on your left side to enhance digestion, and prevent gas formation.

16.3 METABOLISM

Metabolism is the set of chemical reactions that take place in the body. Metabolic processes are the very basis of life, allowing living cells to grow and reproduce, and maintain their structure. There are two categories of reactions:

1. Catabolic reactions that break down food to yield energy.
2. Anabolic reactions that use energy to construct components of cells such as proteins and fats.

Metabolism involves how each cell receives its nutrients and oxygen. Metabolism of an individual determines which substance he or she will find nutritious, and which substance poisonous. White sugar/sweets are far more dangerous for our health. They not only damage our teeth and add to our body weight, they can devastatingly alter our metabolism, says Richard Johnson, one of the authors of *The Sugar Fix: The High Fructose Fall Out That Is Making You Fat and Sick.*

Metabolic Rate

The speed of metabolism is the metabolic rate. It is the calorie burning rate or the rate at which an organism burns food. In turn, it determines how much food your body requires. With age, metabolic rate may slow down. It may then become necessary to take enzyme supplements to improve the metabolic rate. Healthy diet with moderate exercise is necessary to maintain a satisfactory metabolic rate.

Mustard seeds and vinegar increase your metabolic rate. Drinking cold water before meals too has the same effect.

Research shows that within 10 minutes of drinking a large glass of cold water, your metabolism begins to speed up. It can increase your calorie burning rate by as much as 30 per cent for an hour. Water lowers down the temperature in the gut. It sends nerve signals indicating that the body requires more food for heat.

In this respect, a hormone called thyroxin secreted by thyroid gland plays a key role. If too much thyroxin is secreted, then metabolism becomes above normal. The person becomes hyper/over-active, and starts losing weight very fast. But if less hormone is secreted, then the person becomes hypo/under-active, sluggish and depressed, and starts gaining weight.

Digestion

Cells cannot absorb food macromolecules such as starch, cellulose, protein, etc. in their complex form. They need to be broken down into smaller units before they can be used in cell metabolism. Biochemical substances convenient for cell metabolism are continuously produced, consumed, and then recycled. Several sets of enzymes digest these macromolecules from food. In these reactions, enzymes are produced and recycled too.

After a meal you should take rest and avoid any activity, physical or mental. This is to let the blood flow to the digestive system, and to allow it to do its work.

Keep colon clean. Ayurveda says that death begins in the colon. That shows how important it is to keep the colon clean. Seven black pepper corns ground into a fine powder and one tsp of a year-old honey taken first thing in the morning with a glass of warm water is an effective tonic for rejuvenation, for keeping the colon clean, and for reducing fat.

Metabolic Syndrome

A cluster of health problems arising out of disorders in metabolism is collectively known as metabolic syndrome. These include abdominal obesity, diabetes, hypertension/high blood pressure, high cholesterol and triglyceride levels, etc.

16.4 FOOD ALLERGIES

Body's immune system has to fight any infection by first identifying the foreign invaders, and then activating its armies – white blood cells – to fight them.

In some cases, the immune system wrongly identifies a harmless substance as a foreign invader and WBCs overreact. In the process, they inflict damage on the body itself rather than on the invader. Such allergic response of the body becomes a disease in itself.

The substances that provoke allergy are called allergens. Ingestion of the offending food may trigger the release of chemicals like histamine resulting in symptoms of an allergic reaction. Histamines are simple chemicals that your immune system cells or some cells in hypothalamus produce when reacting to foreign invaders like bacteria/germs. Histamines increase the permeability of capillaries to white blood cells in order to allow them to engage foreign invaders. They may cause inflammation. Anti-histamines can deactivate the histamines.

The symptoms of allergy may be mild rashes, itching, swelling, etc., or more severe like trouble in breathing, gastric upset, diarrhoea, nausea, inflammations, and so on.

Some allergic reactions can be life-threatening.

Most Allergenic Foods

One could be allergic to any food. But eight foods accounting for 90 per cent of all allergic reactions are meat, eggs, milk/cheese, corn, peanuts, fish/sea food, soy and wheat.

The other foods that cause allergic reactions in some are chocolates, processed and canned foods, saturated fats and soft drinks. Tomatoes may also cause allergy.

Least Allergenic Foods

Rice, apples, carrots, potatoes, lettuce, and olive oil are the least allergenic foods.

Gluten Allergy

Some common foods like wheat, barley, rye and oats contain gluten. Gluten cannot be digested by many people. For some people, it may affect the GI tract itself. People with gluten intolerance feel better by eliminating gluten in any form from diet.

Remember that wheat-free products may not be gluten-free. Gluten may be present in many different types of products, especially seasonings, salad dressings, sauces and soups, canned foods, and even in beer (made from barley), and ice creams.

Rice, gram-flour (besan) and buckwheat are gluten-free. Fruits and vegetables, dried fruits, milk, cheese, butter, legumes, rice, arrowroot, potatoes, etc, are also gluten-free.

Dealing with Allergies

First, identify the allergenic food by the method of elimination. The only way to get rid of the allergy is to avoid the food causing the allergy.

The food must be avoided not only in its identifiable state such as eggs in omelets, or wheat in chapatti, but also in its hidden state such as eggs in cakes and wheat in biscuits.

In general, rotate your edible items. No food should be taken too often.

Celiac Disease

Celiac disease is a disorder caused by intolerance to the gluten protein. When a person with celiac disease eats gluten foods, the mucous membrane lining of the small intestine gets gradually damaged. This, in turn, leads to failure to absorb nutrients.

Olive Oil

No one has ever complained of any problem with olive oil. Olive oil phenols, through their antioxidant action, support gastro-intestinal health by reducing production of carcinogenic compounds.

Recent studies show that olive oil has beneficial effect on the lining of the stomach. Researchers believe that olive oil reduces stomach acids and thus, prevents and cures stomach ulcers.

When animal fats were replaced with olive oil in the diets of ulcer patients, the result was a reduction in lesions in 33 per cent of cases.

For centuries, olive oil has been prescribed for gall bladder problems. It protects against the formation of gallstones because it stimulates gall bladder to empty its bile completely.

Quercetin

Quercetin inhibits the release of histamines which trigger allergies. Foods high in quercetin like apples, strawberries and other berries, red grapes and red wine, tea, onions, broccoli, spinach and kale can help in allergies.

16.5 PROBIOTICS VERSUS ANTIBIOTICS

There are close to 100 trillion bacteria of 500-1000 varieties (some good and some harmful) that inhabit the GI tract. The good bacteria help in digestion and also fight the harmful bacteria.

Our body has 10,000 times more bacteria than cells. It takes two years or more for our flora to get established. In between, if you take antibiotics, it wipes them out, but the bacteria keep coming back.

With bacteria being involved in our health, is there a way to manipulate them? Probiotics are the step in that direction. They are the opposite of antibiotics. Probiotics means 'for life' or 'the good friendly bacteria'. Antibiotics destroy all bacteria, good as well as bad. Probiotics supplement good bacteria. They produce enzymes that help us digest our food. They even manufacture B-vitamins in the process of metabolism. Antibiotics, on the other hand, destroy B-vitamins.

If you have suffered from diarrhoea or if you have had a course of antibiotics, chances are that you are depleted of good bacteria and vitamin B. Inflammation in the mouth is an indication of the same. A dose of probiotics and B-Complex may then be necessary.

Natural sources of probiotics are fermented foods, most importantly yoghurt/dahi.

Gregor Reid at Lawson Health Research Institute, Canada, says that at least 50 per cent of the population suffers from one or the other form of irritable bowel syndrome which can be pain, constipation, bloating or even diarrhoea (*The Times of India*, 25 December, 2009). There are a number of studies suggesting that probiotics can provide relief in these problems.

When you get diarrhoea or even when you are stressed, there is a breakdown in the wall of the gut, so toxins can pass through the gut. Probiotics seal off the gut. They have a barrier effect. Isabgul also acts as a barrier. Dahi with isabgul is even more effective.

Eat only freshly prepared dahi. As much as 91 per cent of yoghurt is digested within an hour of consumption.

Probiotics are being considered the new age supplements. They boost immunity. Institute of Cholera and Enteric Diseases, Kolkata, and ICMR found that diarrhoeal episodes dipped by 14 per cent in children who consumed probiotics for three months.

Probiotics must be kept refrigerated to increase the length of time the bacteria survive. Look for supplements that contain lactobacillus and bifidus bacteria. Nutrifit, yoghurt-based drink developed by Mother Dairy, containing these bacteria, can be tried.

16.6 OBESITY

Obesity is simply excess body weight. Some stored fat is necessary in the body to provide cushion effect and to take care of emergency when one falls sick and cannot eat anything. Then the body can derive energy from stored fat.

Further, women's bodies are meant to carry higher proportion of fat tissues. This ensures enough energy during pregnancy and nursing.

The most common measure of obesity is the Body Mass Index (BMI) expressed as:

BMI = W/HxH, where W is the weight in kg and H is the height in meters.

BMI of 18.5 to 24.9 is normal. Below 18.5 is underweight, and above 24.9 is overweight. BMI of 30 and greater implies obesity.

Common causes of obesity are poor eating habits, lack of exercise/ physical activity, glandular malfunctions, diabetes, emotional stress, boredom, and simply love of food.

A men's health magazine has referred to this phenomenon as the plague of plenty.

The illustration of this 'plague of plenty' can best be seen in rich private schools where obesity is extremely common among students. The reason is that their dietary intake is almost four times the recommended quantity. Moreover, their consumption of junk foods like burgers, pizzas and colas is too high, while their physical activity is less.

The effect of obesity leads to accumulation of fat in two forms:

1. As visceral/abdominal fat, inside gut surrounding and invading the vital organs.
2. As subcutaneous fat, that lies just under the skin, on top of muscles.

While subcutaneous fat might be annoying, the visceral fat is far deadlier, raising risks of developing hypertension, heart disease, and diabetes.

Why Visceral Fat is So Bad?

There are two reasons:

1. It surrounds and inhibits the functions of vital organs, especially the liver. Excess weight can damage your liver more fatally than alcohol.
2. Since the liver is slow to respond, pancreas is forced to produce more insulin to activate the liver. As the fats and carbohydrates remain un-metabolised in the absence of bile, this causes a viscous chain reaction leading to rising triglyceride and cholesterol levels, and high blood pressure. If the situation continues, the pancreas stops the production of insulin, which results in Type-2 diabetes.

A modest loss of 5-10 per cent of body weight dramatically reduces the risk of Type-2 diabetes.

While a majority of people understand that obesity could cause diabetes, high blood pressure and infertility, few know its link to certain cancers and cirrhosis of liver.

A correct weight loss program has to include fibre, nutritious but low-in-calories diet, physical and mental exercise, positive attitude, and drinking of water in plenty.

A low calorie diet also slows down the process of ageing.

However, a crash dieting program is a strict no-no. A study by California University San Francisco and Minnesota University revealed that dieting increases stress and levels of cortisol hormone. Chronic stress, in addition to causing weight gain, is linked to heart disease, high blood pressure, diabetes and cancer.

Obesity and Fertility, Lung Function and Cancer

Obesity could be the biggest threat to fertility and libido for both males and females. It affects production of sex hormones by the body. More than half of the women who attend fertility clinics are found to be obese.

Carrying excess weight around your abdomen can impair lung function. Greg Martin, Science and Research Manager of World Cancer Research Fund, says excess fat around the stomach increases the production of the hormone oestrogen, which is potentially carcinogenic. Obesity could, therefore, trigger hormone-sensitive cancers of breasts and womb lining. It is also linked to oesophagus and bowel cancer.

Recommendations for Diet

Calorie intake must be less than calories burnt. One should take plenty of water to cleanse the system and increase metabolism.

Some amount of cold water must be taken just before meals. This will also increase satiety factor. Eat large quantities of fresh fruits and vegetables.

Cooking can destroy 97 per cent of water-soluble and 40 per cent of fat-soluble vitamins. Uncooked foods contain more nutrients, induce satiety, reduce intake, and improve weight loss.

Low Calorie and High Protein Diet

Those eating a high protein diet (25 per cent of calories from protein) feel fuller throughout the day. They do not feel the need to eat often, and are less preoccupied with the thought of food.

MUFA (Olive Oil)

Studies show that a diet high in MUFA actually prevents accumulation of fat. MUFA could boost calorie burning for five hours after the meal.

Using olive oil may also help you lose weight. Even olive oil extract can help fight obesity.

Country star Wynonna lost 45 pounds in 4 weeks after following a garlic and olive oil diet.

Fibre

Importance of including fibre in diet can be seen from the following benefits:

1. It slows down the eating process.
2. It improves intestinal bulking action, increasing excretion of calories in faeces.
3. Soluble fibre slows the entry of fats and glucose into the bloodstream.

Calcium and Vitamin D

Recent researches have shown that women over 50 who regularly take calcium and Vitamin D rich foods are less likely to gain weight. This is due to an improved breakdown of fat cells, and an increase in the production of leptin that curbs appetite.

A two-year study on 300 overweight men and women published in the *American Journal of Clinical Nutrition* states that those who drank two glasses of milk a day lost an average of 5.5 kg.

Asparagus (*Shatavari*) and Garlic

They help fight obesity by suppressing hunger and keeping the sugar level under check.

Pomegranate

Experts at University of Edinburgh found that pomegranate juice reduces abdominal fat.

Eating Slowly

It takes 20 minutes for the brain to register that you are full. Eating rapidly may lead to overconsumption. Research by Alexander of Athens University found that when men ate slowly, they showed higher levels of hormones for 3 hours after meal. These hormones are released as fullness signals to brain, thereby curbing appetite.

Tips On What to Avoid

Do not eat white refined cereals. Always include only whole grains in your diet.

Avoid eating dinner late at night. Calories consumed then are not burnt. They get stored.

Avoid sugar. Richard Johnson in his book *The Sugar Fix* emphasises on 'The high fructose fallout that is making you fat and sick'. Proteins and complex carbohydrates, through metabolism, get converted to glucose sugar anyway. And, while they provide energy, they also provide other nutrients as well. No soft drinks, not even processed juices as they contain added sugars.

Avoid unnecessary calories of alcoholic drinks. They do not provide any other nutrients. On the other hand, they raise the sugar level to dangerously high levels. If energy is not required, it is converted to fat and stored in the body.

Salt intake should be kept to minimum. You cannot leave out salt altogether. The body requires sodium-potassium electrolyte balance for cell function and to generate current to run the heart-pump also. However, excess of sodium is harmful for cell functioning. Sodium increases water retention and tendency of weight gain. It increases blood pressure too.

All natural foods contain salt in varying proportions adequate for our body's needs. Avoid eating high-salt snacks, and fast foods.

The mistake people make is that they choose fat-free foods, which often leads to a high intake of sugars and salt.

High Carbohydrate Diet Not Harmful

Researchers at University of Virginia in USA found that people who consume diets rich in carbohydrates tend to be slimmer. Carbohydrates are not fattening. They are necessary to process and break down fat. The enemy is the fatty food.

Carbohydrates play an important role in a balanced diet providing highly important fibre, vitamins, minerals, and antioxidants. One should prefer complex carbohydrates over refined ones.

Naturopathic Remedies to Increase Fat Burning Rate

The following is found very effective in achieving weight loss:

1. Warm water with lemon and a little honey taken first thing in the morning burns your fat slowly. It will help your body balance the pH value too.
2. Take cold water before meals. Brenda Davy, Virginia Tech Institute, USA, found that dieters who drank water before meals 3 times a day lost, in 12 weeks, about 2.25 kg more than those who did not increase their water intake.
3. *Trikuta* powder, dried ginger, black pepper, and *pippali* or *chhoti pipal*, taken with water twice daily supports digestion. Good digestion is the key to weight loss.
4. Vinegar and Mustard are fat burners. Acetic acid in vinegar breaks down fat.
5. Bitter and pungent herbs like cayenne, black pepper, cumin seeds, fenugreek seeds and vegetable, basil, etc., burn up the fatty tissues and dry up the excess weight. Spices with meals could boost up the metabolic rate by as much as 25 per cent.
6. EGCG in green tea boosts metabolism, and increases fat burning by 33 per cent. Green tea stops fat cells from releasing inflammatory chemicals which attract more fat. A *Daily Mail* report stated that sipping three cups of green tea a day could help one stay trim. You can also add lemon to your black tea.

Importance of Physical Exercise

Exercise is a must to reduce visceral fat. Exercise suppresses unnecessary hunger or hunger for unhealthy food. Even a light 30-minute walk, 6 days a week and a little sweat can prevent fat formation. 24-year-old Chris Thomas, weighing 120 kg at one point, shed 27 kg in six months by merely walking (*The Times of India*, 16 December 2009) two hours daily.

The importance of exercise can be seen from the following:

1. When weight loss is achieved only by dieting without exercise, it comes primarily as water loss from lean tissues. It is not conducive to a healthy body.
2. When weight loss is achieved by exercise along with a prudent diet, it is accompanied with increase in muscle mass along with decrease in body weight. It is healthier.
3. Exercise helps to counter the reduction in basal metabolic rate (BMR) that follows a low calorie diet. Without exercise, body's metabolism slows down, and energy levels drop.

Physical Benefits of Exercise

The whole body benefits from exercise due to improved cardiovascular and respiratory functions. Exercise enhances transfer of oxygen and nutrients into the bloodstream, cells and tissues, and simultaneously enhances the removal of carbon dioxide and waste products from cells and tissues into bloodstream, and ultimately from the body through eliminative organs.

As a whole, exercise lowers cholesterol levels, increases good HDL cholesterol, improves supply of blood carrying oxygen and nutrients to heart, thus increasing its pumping capacity, reducing blood pressure, and exerting a favourable effect on blood clotting.

Psychological and Social Benefits of Exercise

Anxiety, worries, tension, insomnia, depression, low self-esteem, etc., are greatly diminished with regular exercise.

Keep Stress Away

A lot of stomach fat is the result of stress in life. Some people deal with it by overeating. Make sure you have a healthier solution. Go for a walk or join an aerobic/Yoga group.

Importance of Mental or Intellectual Activity

Reading encourages the production of adrenaline hormone. Researches commissioned by the bookstore Borders found that adrenaline causes the basic metabolic rate to rise up to 1.75 calories per minute. So if you read a novel of 600 pages, you can burn 1050 calories.

Importance of Laughter

An hour of laughter can burn up to 100-120 calories. It gets the heart beating faster and increases blood flow and oxygen. Also the abdominal muscles get a good work-out.

Importance of Pranayam

Kapalbhati pranayam is found most effective in reducing flab.

16.7 FOR GAINING WEIGHT

Poor digestion/absorption of nutrients is usually the reason why people can't gain weight.

Food should be properly chewed. Do not let stomach and intestines be burdened with the work which you can do in the mouth.

Probiotics and digestive enzymes can often help. Eat high fat and high carbohydrate foods such as avocados, potatoes, nuts, etc. The two foods that are found very helpful are the following:

1. Fully ripe *chitti-dar* bananas with cream.
2. Baked or mashed potatoes with cream.

If you are too thin, do not avoid workout. Weight training builds muscle bulk, but simply stuffing calories may make you puffy without keeping you in good shape. Besides, you can end up with high cholesterol and triglycerides problems due to a high fat diet.

16.8 CONSTIPATION/PILES/HAEMORRHOIDS

It is a well established face that a low fibre diet, high in refined foods, low fluid intake, and lack of exercise causes constipation. Dietary fibre increases the frequency and quantity of bowel movements. Some recommendations are as follows:

- Eat high fibre diet with plenty of fruits, vegetables, salads and whole grain cereals.
- Take papaya and also iron-rich green leafy vegetables. Iron makes the bowels move.
- Drink 8-12 glasses of water everyday.
- Take warm water in the morning before bowel movement. Never repress the urge to defecate. Make a rule to visit the toilet at a fixed time, preferably after doing some exercise and after breakfast, irrespective of urge.
- Stop using laxatives and enemas. If necessary, use glycerin suppository once in a while.
- You may take *Harar* or *Terminalia Chebula* mother tincture at bedtime.
- Isabgul greatly helps in elimination process.
- Raisins (*kishmish*) are the best way to ease your constipation. They speed up the time taken by food to pass through your GI tract.
- Exercise relieves constipation by increasing intestinal contractions.

Piles and Haemorrhoids

Individuals with chronic constipation, sedentary lifestyle, junk food habits, stress and smoking tend to strain their muscles during bowel movements. Hard stools make the condition worse. This may cause piles and haemorrhoids to develop.

Prevention and treatment follows the same regimen as for constipation. Fibre in diet attracts water and makes a gelatinous mass producing bulky and soft faeces easy to pass, resulting in less straining of muscles. Drinking buttermilk with *bhuna jeera* (roasted cumin) helps to get rid of piles. Avoid caffeine and spicy foods.

16.9 DIARRHOEA/DYSENTERY

Diarrhoea is usually self-limiting. It implies that if you control your diet, or stop eating solids, and take only electrolytes to ward off the risk of dehydration, it will cure itself. The rule is: Just fast and hydrate.

But if it lasts longer than a few days, its cause must be found and treated appropriately.

Causes of diarrhoea can be:

1. Overeating, and/or dietary indiscretions.
2. Food allergies. Identify allergenic foods, and avoid them.
3. Food poisoning. Try Arsenic Album, a homoeopathic medicine.
4. Gastrointestinal infections. In this case, it may be necessary to be treated properly with antibiotics. Even in acute infections, fasting restores the body to normal health.
5. Deficiency of enzymes. Foods like yoghurt and cheese are predigested probiotics.

Isabgul with yoghurt (dahi) or water is a common remedy for diarrhoea/dysentery. Curd-rice is an effective remedy, as well as a full meal in itself.

Bel fruit is also a very good remedy in summer and can be taken in its dried powder form in winter.

BART diet, meaning banana, apple, rice and toast, is always recommended. You may also add tea to this diet.

Dysentery

One should eat light foods, low in spices and fat. Non-vegetarian food, eggs, and milk are strictly prohibited. One may also avoid certain fruits like mango, and green and raw vegetables.

Isabgul, *bel* fruit and curd-rice, help in dysentery as well. Consuming dahi regularly is recommended to increase healthy bacteria in the gut.

To help bind stools, pectin-rich fruits and vegetables such as pears, apples, bananas, carrots, potatoes, etc., are recommended. Fresh blueberries have a long history of counteracting diarrhoea/ dysentery.

Pomegranate is best for diarrhoea and dysentery.

Chamomile tea helps in treating spasmodic diarrhoea.

Merc Sol 200, homoeopathic drug, may help in diarrhoea/ abdominal cramps/dysentery. Merc Cor 30 may be taken, 5 pills twice daily for curing dysentery with blood.

16.10 IRRITABLE BOWEL SYNDROME (IBS)

In irritable bowel syndrome (IBS), also referred to as nervous diarrhoea, the intestines fail to function properly. The muscle movement in intestines is either faster or slower than normal. As a result, one suffers from diarrhoea or constipation. If the movement of intestinal wall muscles is faster, the food also reaches the intestinal tract faster causing diarrhoea. People get cramps and feel the sudden urge to empty their bowel.

If the movement of muscles is slower, people experience pain due to accumulation of gas, and have the feeling of incomplete evacuation.

Causes of IBS

Allergies from certain foods may trigger IBS. It is often seen that IBS starts after an intestinal infection.

People with high levels of stress, anxiety and depression are prone to develop IBS. Stress affects the transmission of nervous signals to the intestine. It worsens the IBS condition.

The cause of IBS has psychological and behavioral factors, in addition to stress and anxiety, particularly a tendency to push oneself against one's capacity to keep going and then collapse, and encounter IBS. If this process continues, IBS may become chronic.

Soluble Fibre versus Insoluble Fibre

The traditional advice about fibre is wrong: Wheat bran, coarse grains, and other insoluble fibre foods not only fail to soothe irritable bowels but may actually make things worse. Sometimes roughage, hard and heavy items of food, fruits and vegetables with tough skin like grapes, plums, tomatoes, capsicum, etc., trigger IBS diarrhoea.

But, water-soluble fibres as in some fruits and vegetables, lentils, legumes, oats, unpolished rice, etc., have all the benefits of insoluble fibre. In addition, they are soft on the lining of the stomach and intestines. Oats have very high water-soluble fibre content.

Psyllium husk (isabgul) is one single item that has 100 per cent water-soluble fibre. It is a preventive as well as a cure for IBS. The best way to consume isabgul is with water or with yoghurt or dahi.

If the problem becomes very acute; it can be taken twice daily, once between breakfast and lunch, and second time between lunch and dinner.

Probiotics Relieve IBS

In one study, 75 per cent of IBS patients reported significant improvement with probiotics. Yoghurt is the best probiotic.

Whatever helps in common diarrhoea, also helps in nervous diarrhoea. A diet low in proteins and rich in complex carbohydrates is effective. Find ways to relax the body and the mind. Anxiety is the main cause of IBS. One should refrain from worries. Pranayam, breathing exercises, regular walks, etc., are of immense help.

Other Recommendations

Eat slowly and chew thoroughly to encourage gastric juice secretions.

Opt for a bland diet. Avoid red pepper and *khatais* (sour foods) including mango and tamarind. No refined sugars. Sugars have a serious effect on IBS patients.

Low salt diet is recommended. Salt increases BP, anxiety and stress levels. Hard and heavy foods are not tolerated by mucous membrane. Baked potato with olive oil makes the best food as well as medicine.

Eliminate allergenic foods. Avoid animal fats, eggs, milk, caffeine especially coffee, carbonated drinks, sugars, sweeteners, pastries, all fried and junk foods, margarine, all processed foods and juices, spicy foods, wheat bran, etc. They encourage secretion of mucus by the membrane and prevent absorption of nutrients. Avoid alcohol, tobacco, etc. They irritate the lining of stomach and colon.

Practise deep breathing. Shallow breathing reduces oxygen available for bowel function. Wear loose fitting clothes. Do not wear anything that is tight around the waist.

Gut Brain

Every single cell has its own brain which connects it to other cells so that they all work together towards a purpose. 'Why do I get a stomach ache when I am nervous, or why do I get diarrhoea when I have an examination or when in a hurry for something'.

The fact is that 60 per cent of the neurotransmitters are in the stomach and the intestines. A total of 72,000 nerves pass through the navel moving below and up the spine to the brain. They cross again at the *ajna cakra*, the eyebrows centre.

That is why IBS is often linked to stress, anger, fear, anxiety, and other negative emotions that get stored and expressed in the gut.

When you skip a lunch, the gut remains silent. As soon as you eat something, gut starts working. Contractions all along the line start. Small intestine starts mixing the food with enzymes, and so on.

But if the food is rotten, reverse contractions will force everything in the gut back through oesophagus at a high speed to throw out.

In each situation, the gut brain must assess, decide on course, and initiate reflex action.

Abdominal Wet Pack

Wrap a bandage of thick wet towel/cloth around the abdomen for 15-30 minutes. It soothes the gut brain, brings out the heat, and helps in all cases of digestive disorders.

Natural Remedies

Bilwa
This Ayurvedic herb helps in treating diarrhoea and dysentery as encountered in IBS.

Ayurvedic Formulation for IBS, Diarrhoea, Dysentery

Take half teaspoon of this formulation with water before meals: Prawal Panchamrit 5-10g, Swarna Basant 1-2g, Shankha Bhasma

10g, Kapardaka 10-20g, Mukta Shakti 10-20g, Kamadhudha 10g, Bilwa 100g.

Mint (*Podina*) and Peppermint Oil

Mint and peppermint relieve symptoms of IBS. In a study, 79 per cent of those taking peppermint oil reported feeling less abdominal pain. It relaxes the muscles of the GI tract. Peppermint is a highly recommended age-old remedy for stomach ache and gas.

Coconut oil has been used to treat IBS. Include plenty of fruits like apples and bananas, and drink plenty of water.

Herbs such as caraway, chamomile, dill, cinnamon, fennel seeds (*saunf*), lavender, lemon balm, rosemary, and thyme are recommended.

Gentle massage of abdomen, before a meal, with a blend of black pepper/rosemary or ginger/tulsi or caraway/peppermint or *saunf* in olive oil treats digestive disorders.

Fennel (*Saunf*) seeds or fennel tea helps to soothe the stomach.

Homoeopathic Medicines

Nux Vomica for anxiety, sleeplessness, and constipation, Gelsemium for people who suffer from apprehension and nervousness, and Arsenic Album may help people who are anxious and sensitive by nature.

Diverticulitis

It is an inflammation of diverticula, sac or bulging pockets due to pressure, in the GI tract especially the colon causing stagnation of faeces, pain, constipation or diarrhoea.

It is caused by heavy and high-residue diet. Take low-residue diet. That means less of fibre, white flour, white rice, potatoes, olive oil etc. Avoid raw vegetables, nuts at all costs, whole grains etc.

16.11 ACIDITY

Glands in the stomach secrete acids that help dissolve and digest the food we eat. Normally, the mucous membrane of the stomach is protected from the harmful effects of the acids with the help of its own structure and intrinsic mechanism. In cases where the person is under stress, or indulges in overeating, or is taking too much of certain food items such as spices, fatty foods, tea, coffee, alcohol, sweets, etc., and medications like Aspirin, Brufen, etc., the level of acid in the stomach increases.

Acidity is the precursor to formation of ulcers.

Drink plenty of water to keep the juices flowing while at the same time to keep the acidity under control. One must realise that while acid is necessary for digestion, excess of it is harmful for the stomach.

It is important for the person first to recognise and remove the cause of acidity. It is then necessary to relax and keep free from stress.

People should avoid heavy meals, and rather take small frequent meals. It is important not to go on fasting, or be on empty stomach for a long time. Instead of three big meals, one should take 4-5 small meals. But avoid overeating.

Avoid all acidic foods. That means spices, pickles, chutneys, vinegar, sweets, animal foods, tea, coffee, alcohol, smoking, chocolates, refined sugar, aerated drinks, etc.

Make sure that you take more alkaline foods. That includes most vegetables. Cucumber, *kakari, lauki* and *tinda* are the most alkaline.

Lauki/Bottle Gourd, high in fibre, cleanses the digestive system. Take 200 ml of its juice in the morning. It cures acidity, gastric troubles, indigestion, etc.

The most alkaline of all fruits are banana and watermelon. Coconut water is great for treating acidity. Avoid proteins, including pulses, for some time. Fats like olive oil, mustard oil, ghee, butter will not do any harm if taken in moderation.

Natrum Phos (phosphate) and Biochemical Combination 32 are found to reduce acidity.

16.12 ULCER

Ulcer is the result of damage done by stomach acids to the lining of stomach or duodenum. People going through a life of hurry, worry, and curry are at high risk of developing stomach ulcers.

Yoghurt can help in ulcers too. The bacteria H. Pylori causes most stomach ulcers. In a study, H. Pylori disappeared in 91 per cent of ulcer patients who ate 300 grams of yoghurt for four weeks, and then took a course of antibiotics.

For treating ulcers, the causative factor must be identified, controlled and eliminated.

Common causative factors are food allergy, low-fibre diet, acidic, heavy, fried and spicy foods, smoking and drugs like aspirin and analgesics. Stress and worry cause more acids to be formed. Alcohol, carbonated drinks, coffee and tea are all acidic.

Alkaline and light foods must be taken. Considering cold milk as alkaline, people often consume lot of cold milk without realising that milk itself could be an allergen.

Note that vegetables are more alkaline than fruits. Juices of fresh cabbage, lauki, celery, etc., are extremely effective in treating ulcers. Among fruits, bananas are recommended because they are the most alkaline. Soft water-soluble fibre such as in isabgul is strongly recommended.

16.13 ULCERATIVE COLITIS

Ulcerative colitis is a chronic inflammatory disorder of the bowels. A Canadian study showed that taking daily probiotics, like yoghurt (dahi) with live cultures, provided complete relief to 56 per cent people after 6 weeks.

Most common offending foods/allergens are wheat, milk, eggs, corn, peanuts, chocolate, sweets, tomatoes, etc., and acidic foods. After elimination of allergens from diet, introduce soft foods such as cheese that are easy to handle.

Use of psyllium husk (isabgul) twice daily in between meals is a must. Consumption of olive oil and omega-3 fats is recommended. Olive oil contains powerful anti-inflammatory compounds.

Easily tolerated by the stomach, olive oil is a boon for those suffering from ulcers and gastritis. It activates the secretion of bile and pancreatic hormones/juices.

Research reveals that olive oil killed eight different strains of H. Pylori, the bug that causes most peptic ulcers, and some types of stomach cancers.

16.14 GAS/COLIC PAIN

Colic pain means pain due to constipation and gas. Gas may also cause headache. About 20 per cent of the gas in the gut comes just from swallowing of air while eating.

The remaining 80 per cent comes from the odiferous gas produced by bacteria in the small intestines during the process of digestion of foods. The foods that trigger most gas include eggs, meat, milk, beer, beans, *urad dal*, cabbage, cauliflower, broccoli, okra, and *arabi*. Fried foods, sugars and sodas also cause gas. Avoid foods that trigger gas for you. It will also be helpful to take foods like beans, cauliflower, etc., in well-cooked form. Throw out the water in which beans had been soaked overnight. Add fresh water instead. Breast feeding mothers should avoid these foods lest the baby develops colic pain.

Podin Hara, *saunf*, cloves, ginger, chamomile, lemon balm, provide the best treatment. Cloves promote enzymatic flow, boost digestion and prevent the formation of gas. *Rukha-Sukha Khana*, food without fats also causes gas. Hence, it is necessary to consume some butter, olive oil, etc., to reduce gas. Treating constipation reduces gas as well. A pinch of baking soda in a glass of water relieves flatulence/gas.

16.15 LIVER HEALTH AND DETOXIFICATION

Liver is the most remarkable organ in the sense that it can regenerate itself. It is responsible not only for the production of bile for digesting food, but like the lungs and the kidneys, it also extracts and neutralises all toxic chemicals and foods you take in.

Apart from the unhealthy foods you consume, your liver is burdened by environmental chemicals, air pollutants, pesticides, auto-exhausts, preservatives and colourants used in foods, and often by alcohol, cholesterol-lowering medications, anti-depressants, and other drugs.

Detoxify

Detoxification is the body's natural process of neutralising and eliminating toxins. Liver transforms many toxic substances into harmless substances, though we also clear toxins through exercise and sweating. Anything that supports this elimination can help us in detoxification.

Help your body to detoxify by the following ways:

- Abjure tobacco and smoking.
- Avoid alcohol for a fixed time. Avoid tea, coffee, colas, etc.
- Have wholesome short meals. Leave your stomach a little empty.
- Exercise daily or walk for 45 minutes as your health permits.
- After exercise, take fresh lime juice and breakfast with ample protein.
- Lots of vegetables and fruits should form a major component of your meals and snacks.
- Take plenty of water throughout the day.
- Before going to bed, meditate for a while or say a little prayer.

Fasting

Water fast, viz., abstinence from food and drinks except water for a specific period for therapeutic or religious purposes is the age-old method of detoxifying the liver. As no new food goes into the body during fasting, no new toxins are produced, and the liver works full time to eliminate the existing toxins.

Benefits of fasting in treating obesity, food and chemical poisoning, allergies, arthritis, psoriasis, eczema, diarrhoea, dysentery, IBS, asthma, depression, neurosis, and various other disorders are well known. The blood becomes purer and the skin begins to glow.

Fresh juice fast is a better idea instead of water fast in some cases. Break the fast with melon or orange. Then resume a normal healthy diet, but gradually.

However, never fast during pregnancy, or if you suffer from tuberculosis, diabetes, hyperthyroid, any form of cancer, diseases of kidney, etc.

Liver-healthy foods

Molybdenum is the trace mineral that takes part in several important interactions that lead to detoxification of liver. Carrots, cucumbers, celery, dark green leafy vegetables, peas, beans, legumes, and whole grains are good sources of molybdenum.

Artichoke, beets, carrots, papaya, fresh fruits, vegetables, nuts and seeds, and herbs like turmeric, cinnamon, etc., also promote healthy liver function.

Beets, used for liver disorders since long, enhance the activity of natural antioxidants in liver cells. Papaya is also considered a good fruit for liver health.

Cocoa/Dark Chocolate

At a meeting of European Association for the Study of Liver in Vienna Spanish researchers presented, the results of a study of end stage liver disease patients. It shows that those given 85 per cent cocoa dark chocolate had a markedly smaller rise in blood pressure, which can otherwise reach dangerous levels in cirrhotic patients, and lead to blood vessel rupture.

Cirrhosis of Liver

Cirrhosis is chronic injury of the liver often caused by excessive alcohol consumption.

So, it is important to abstain from alcohol. Reduce the intake of fats and oils, and restrict salt in diet. Avoid refined, processed and canned foods, sugars, condiments, tea and coffee.

One is advised to take three meals daily comprising only fresh fruits like apple, pear, lemon, papaya, oranges, pineapple and peach, and milk, and easily digestible proteins such as homemade cheese, sprouted grains, and fibre-rich foods.

A tablespoonful juice of papaya seeds with lime juice can be taken twice daily. Vegetables like bitter gourd (*karela*), brinjal, beetroot, etc., help in strengthening the liver. Juice of bitter gourd (*karela*) is antidote to alcohol damage.

Camel or goat milk is also considered beneficial.

Herbs

Silymarin in milk thistle prevents damage to healthy liver cells and stimulates regeneration of damaged liver cells.

Kalmegh and Hydrastis, Ayurvedic powder and mother tincture respectively, support the liver.

16.16 GALL BLADDER DISORDERS, INFLAMMATION, AND GALLSTONES

Gall bladder stores bile, produced by the liver. Bile is used to digest fats. Bile contains cholesterol, bile salts, lecithin, and other substances.

When gall bladder becomes inflamed, it causes severe pain in the upper abdomen on the right side near the liver and gall bladder region. It may be accompanied with fever, and nausea. It has to be treated immediately; otherwise it may become life threatening.

Gallstones are stones formed in the gall bladder as a result of taking too much cholesterol in diet and not having enough bile acid to dissolve it.

As a result, cholesterol crystallises, and combines with bile to form gallstones. Then if stones block the passage of bile to duodenum, it will result in pain, nausea, vomiting, etc.

Animal foods and even dairy products promote formation of gallstones because of their fats content. Vegetarian diet, which is high in fibre and low in cholesterol and fats, protects against gallstone formation.

Obesity results in increased synthesis of cholesterol, and reduction in bile acid output. Obese people often develop gallstones.

Recommendations

Take remedies to improve liver function by increasing the solubility of cholesterol in bile. Alfalfa is good for cleansing liver. It supplies the necessary minerals and vitamins as well.

Peppermint oil is used to cleanse the gall bladder.

While suffering from pain, nausea, vomiting, etc., follow a fasting programme. Follow a detoxification program for liver and colon.

In case of inflammation, avoid all solid food. Drink only distilled water. Slowly come to juices of pears, beets, and apples. Then take a soft diet, like one comprising freshly-made applesauce.

For gallstones, take three tablespoons of olive oil preferably with lemon or grapefruit juice before going to bed, and after waking up. Stones often get passed in stool by this method.

To relieve pain, use hot castor oil packs on gall bladder areas.

To cleanse the system, drink fresh apple, pear and beet juice for five days. After improvement, take freshly prepared applesauce, yoghurt (dahi), cottage cheese and 75 per cent raw foods consisting of fresh apples, beets, etc. The good fat in almonds also prevents gallstones.

Avoid sugars, animal food, milk, fried and spicy food, soft drinks, refined oils, coffee, chocolate, refined carbohydrates, etc. Do not overeat under any circumstance. Obesity and gall bladder disorders are related.

Surgical removal of gall bladder can be avoided if the above measures are followed.

16.17 JAUNDICE

Jaundice results when bile produced by the liver does not get processed. It starts circulating in blood causing yellowness in urine, and a yellow pigment surfacing off from the body. One may also get fever. The liver gets damaged.

Presently, there is no treatment for jaundice. But you can bring the body to heal itself.

Take the load off the liver. The best way to do this is to consume very light food, without fats and salt. Instead, take plenty of juices like cane juice, lime juice, lemon in warm water with honey, juice of green leaves of radish, coconut water, barley water, curd and buttermilk sweetened with honey, etc.

17

Circulatory System

17.1 ANATOMY OF CIRCULATORY SYSTEM

Circulatory or cardiovascular system comprises heart, blood vessels, and capillaries. Heart is the organ that pumps blood. Blood vessels are a network of tubes for collecting and distributing blood in the body. Capillaries from the blood vessels are the channels through which interaction between the cardiovascular system and body tissues occurs.

The function of the circulatory system is:

1. To supply oxygen, nutrients, and other essential substances to the tissues.
2. To remove metabolic waste products from the tissues.

Blood

There are three components of blood:

1. Red blood cells (RBCs) – The red colour of blood is due to an iron pigment called haemoglobin present in RBCs. The average haemoglobin content of blood for an adult male is 15, and for female 14.5 gm per litre.

    Low haemoglobin level means anaemia. It may result from nutritional deficiency of iron, loss of blood from accidents, ulcers, and impairment of haemoglobin production or RBC destruction due to some disease.

2. White blood cells (WBCs) – White blood cells are colourless elements of blood, containing enzymes and antibodies. They play

an important role in defence and are an integral part of the immune system of the body. They help in fighting and protecting the body from foreign microorganisms, infections, etc. The total WBC count should be 4,000-11,000 cells/cubic mm of blood. A low WBC count makes one susceptible to frequent infections, fevers, etc.

3. Platelets – Platelets are other colourless cell fragments of the blood, smaller than RBCs and WBCs, having the property of sticking together. They help in the formation of clots, and thus, prevent blood loss from injury. Platelets release a number of growth factors.

The normal platelet count for a healthy adult is 150,000-450,000 per micro litre. If count is too low, it may lead to prolonged and perhaps, fatal bleeding. If the count is too high, it may lead to clot formation in blood vessels leading to heart attack, stroke, pulmonary embolism, or blockage in other parts of the body. Platelet count may be low due to their destruction or decreased production by infections, drugs, chemotherapy, leukaemia, anaemia, etc. No particular diet can increase the platelet count. Best thing you can do is to remain well-hydrated, and eat a variety of foods, and enough protein-foods such as yoghurt. One should not, at any cost, take the risk of travelling if platelet count is below 50,000. Platelet transfusion is recommended for controlling severe haemorrhage.

For higher platelet counts, blood thinners like aspirin must be taken.

Anaemia

In anaemia, the blood becomes deficient in haemoglobin which is the iron-containing portion of RBCs.

Primary function of RBCs is to transport oxygen to tissues, exchange it there for carbon dioxide, and bring the carbon dioxide laden blood back.

The most common deficiencies causing anaemia are that of iron, and vitamin B12.

Iron deficiency is either due to increased iron requirement or decreased intake from diet, or due to diminished iron absorption/ utilisation, or blood loss.

Vitamin B12 deficiency usually occurs because if diet is lacking in B12 or if there are disorders in its absorption. Vitamin B12 affects liver health. That, in turn, affects haemoglobin production.

Beets and pomegranate juice prominently increases haemoglobin level. Mixed juice of *lauki,* apple and pomegranate too raises haemoglobin level.

Dates have very high iron content. Green leafy vegetables contain chlorophyll, as well as iron and folic acid. The chlorophyll molecule in green leafy vegetables is very similar to haemoglobin molecule. Also, vitamin C is the most important enhancer of iron absorption.

Foods that inhibit iron absorption are tea, coffee, eggs, etc. Antacids and calcium supplements also decrease iron absorption.

Blood Vessels

There are three types of blood vessels:

1. Arteries – They carry oxygen and nutrient-rich blood from heart to tissues.
2. Veins – They bring back oxygen and nutrient-depleted carbon dioxide laden blood back from tissues to heart.
3. Capillaries – They are the communicating links between tissues and arteries and veins.

17.2 PHYSIOLOGY OF HEART/CIRCULATION OF BLOOD

When we say the heart beats, it means it contracts and expands. It beats about 72 times per minute.

It means that in the average lifespan of a person, it beats more than 2.5 million times. The number of beats per minute is known as the pulse rate.

The dynamics of blood flow are governed by the contraction and expansion of the heart muscles which enable the flow of blood.

The heart muscles themselves are fed with blood through their own arteries referred to as the left and right coronary arteries.

The primary responsibility of initiating the heartbeats rests on a nodal region in a special muscle in the right atrium. This node may be referred to as the natural pacemaker of the heart. The electricity generated by this pacemaker causes the wall of the atriums to contract and force the blood into the ventricles.

Coronary Artery Disease (CAD)

CAD is a common and a serious effect of blockage in the coronary artery. If the coronary arteries become blocked, the cardiac muscle begins to fail, causing blood circulation to decrease, which includes the circulation to the heart muscle itself.

Blood Pressure (BP)

The contraction of the heart muscles is called systole while their relaxation is called diastole. The pressure exerted by blood on the arterial walls is called blood pressure.

Blood pressure has two components – systolic and diastolic.

The higher systolic pressure is exerted when the heart contracts to discharge blood while the lower diastolic pressure is exerted when the heart relaxes to get filled with returning blood.

For a normal healthy person, the systolic blood pressure is 120 mm Hg while and diastolic blood pressure is 80 mm Hg.

17.3 ATHEROSCLEROSIS/ARTERIOSCLEROSIS

Atherosclerosis or arteriosclerosis refers to the narrowing and hardening of arteries due to formation of plaque as a result of deposition of fat on the inner wall, and also due to some other causes including stress, uncontrolled negative emotions, smoking, being overweight, air pollution, etc.

As the arteries narrow, the resistance to blood flow increases. As a result, the blood pressure and the workload on the pumping system of the heart increase.

There are chances of blood clot formation within the arteries when plaque gets detached from the wall of the blood vessel, often as a result of high blood pressure, and goes into the bloodstream and blocks flow in some artery.

If it blocks coronary arteries, it deprives the heart of blood supply. It may, thereby, cause a heart attack.

If it blocks one of the two cerebral arteries, one side of brain gets deprived of blood supply, and there may be a stroke and paralysis of that side of the body.

There is also a link between pollution and clogging of arteries. Findings show how fats work together with air pollution particles. Environmental and medical engineering groups at University of California investigated the relationship between oxidised LDL cholesterol and the diesel exhaust particles. Heart patients should avoid prolonged exposure to pollution.

Taking garlic daily may arrest or even reverse atherosclerosis. Exercise makes the blood rush through arteries, thus cleansing their walls of deposits.

Smoking constricts the arteries, encourages the growth of plaque, and makes blood more likely to clot. The theory is that a diet high in saturated fats is responsible for high cholesterol that causes atherosclerosis.

Chromium Deficiency and Atherosclerosis

Another significant cause of atherosclerosis is chromium deficiency. The problem is caused by the modern food-refining processes. For example, raw sugar has 24 mcg/100g of chromium in it while processed white sugar contains just one-third, that is, 8 mcg/100g.

In a study it was found that animals had elevated blood cholesterol and sugar levels when they were fed on a diet low in chromium.

The same thing can be said about carbohydrates. Whole wheat contains 175 mcg/100g, but refined white flour contains only 23 mcg/100g of chromium.

Hence, to protect ourselves from atherosclerosis, we must avoid the following in our diet:

1. Refined white sugar, and all foods containing it. Use raw sugar, honey, etc.
2. White flour. Substituting it with whole wheat and other whole grains like unpolished rice, oats, etc. is recommended.
3. Saturated fats. Substitute them with canola, mustard, and olive oils.

Grape juice/wine has a high amount of chromium, 47 mcg/100g. It forms an important item of the Mediterranean diet, and that is why atherosclerosis is uncommon in Mediterranean countries.

17.4 CHOLESTEROL

Minimum levels of cholesterol are essential for sustenance of life. It is required to build cell membranes, for cell formation, and production of various hormones in the body. It also aids in the manufacture of bile in liver. Cholesterol is important for the metabolism of fat-soluble vitamins A, E, D and K.

• Cholesterol is more abundant in tissues of liver, spinal cord and brain.
• However, excess cholesterol can contribute to atherosclerosis.
• Cholesterol in your body does not come from food alone. Liver itself manufactures cholesterol to fulfil the purpose of building the body.

Lipoproteins

Cholesterol is insoluble in blood. It is transported in the circulatory system by a kind of protein molecule called lipoprotein.

There is a large range of lipoproteins, such as very-low-density lipoproteins (VLDL), low-density lipoproteins (LDL), high-density lipoproteins (HDL), and so on.

Cholesterol is transported towards cells in peripheral tissues by VLDL and LDL. Cholesterol attached to and carried by LDL is called LDL cholesterol or simply LDL.

Any excess cholesterol is carried back to the liver to be disposed of by HDL. Cholesterol attached to and carried by HDL is called HDL cholesterol or just HDL.

Bad Cholesterol

As cholesterol, carried by LDL, builds up in arteries, it causes atherosclerosis/formation of plaque, which hardens and blocks the arteries.

When plaque cracks or gets detached from the arteries, a blood clot may form that in turn can block the artery to the heart or to the brain, thereby causing heart attack or stroke. LDL particles are, therefore, strongly associated with atherosclerosis. For this reason, LDL is referred to as bad cholesterol.

Good Cholesterol

HDL particles transport cholesterol back to the liver for excretion. Having a large number of HDL particles in the bloodstream is, therefore, considered good because it helps to rid the body of excess cholesterol. On the other hand, having a small number of HDL particles will lead to atherosclerosis. Hence, HDL is referred to as good cholesterol.

Though named bad or good, cholesterol in both LDL and HDL is, however, the same/identical.

Dietary Sources of Cholesterol

Most of the dietary cholesterol comes from animal foods. All foods containing animal fats contain cholesterol. Cheese, egg yolk, beef, pork, poultry and shrimp are major sources of cholesterol.

Human breast milk contains significant amounts of cholesterol needed for the baby.

Trans- and saturated fats, and also stress significantly raise LDL levels in blood. The more the trans- and saturated fats you eat, and the more stressed you are, the more the LDL and less the HDL produced by the liver, setting the stage for clogged arteries, heart attack and stroke.

Recommended Levels of Lipids

We need to keep our LDL levels low, and HDL levels high, and thus a high HDL/LDL ratio.

HDL/LDL ratio largely determines whether cholesterol is being used for benefiting the body, or is getting deposited into tissues and arteries. HDL level should be above 40. Recommended levels of lipids for a normal healthy person in mg per 100 mL of blood are given in Table 17.1.

Table 17.1 Desirable, Borderline and High-risk Lipid and Sugar Levels

	Desirable	Borderline	High Risk
Total Cholesterol	Below 160	Between 160-200	Above 200
LDL	Below 70	70-160	Above 160
VLDL	10-30		
HDL	Above 60	Between 35-60	Below 35
Triglycerides	Below 150	150-200	Above 200
Blood Sugar Fasting	80-100	100-120	Above 120
Blood Sugar PP	140-150	150-200	Above 200

Triglycerides are the fats circulating in the bloodstream. They are used by the muscles for energy and are stored as fat for later use. They eventually get converted to cholesterol. High levels of triglycerides are associated with risk of heart disease.

17.4.1 BEST WAY TO LOWER CHOLESTEROL

Cholesterol-lowering statin drugs have adverse impact on the ability of muscles to regenerate. Researchers at University of Alabama,

Birmingham, have stated that these drugs carry the risk of muscle damage.

A study at University of California, San Diego, found that drugs deplete the body of Coenzyme Q10, an antioxidant compound, which is highly important for the health of the heart. There are many alternatives to drugs. Some recommendations are as follows:

1. **Eliminate trans-fats and saturated fats from diet**
   Eliminate from diet those foods that are high in cholesterol. Meat, eggs, tropical oils such as palm and coconut which contain saturated fats, whole-fat dairy products, and processed and fast foods, which contain trans-fats should be avoided.

   When you reduce saturated and trans-fats in your diet, the cholesterol level gets reduced automatically, and there is a simultaneous reduction in the production of cholesterol by the liver.

2. **Increase intake of:**
   • **Plant sterols**
     Eat more fruits, vegetables, and whole grains that provide plant sterols. Plant sterols are proven natural remedies for lowering cholesterol.

     Pistachios are a great source of plant sterols. In one study, subjects who ate pistachios could lower their total cholesterol by an average of 6.7 per cent and bad LDL cholesterol by 11.6 per cent.

     In another study carried out at Pennsylvania State University, it was found that eating 10 grams of pistachios daily cut cholesterol levels by 8.4 per cent, with LDL dropping by a higher 11.6 per cent. Pistachios are rich in antioxidant lutein, which helps prevent cholesterol from clogging up the arteries. It also prevents eye damage.

     Beans and dals, olive oil, almonds, nuts and seeds, apples, and avocados contain significant amounts of plant sterols. About ¼ cup of sesame seeds has 144mg of phytosterols; ¼ cup of wheat germ has 119mg; ¼ cup of sunflower seeds has 104mg and ¼ cup of pistachios has 83mg of plant sterols.

Cocoa/Chocolate and tea also contain phytosterols. In a study, chocolate lovers were found to have lower levels of LDL. Drinking black or green tea is an easy way to lower your total and LDL cholesterols and triglyceride levels.

- **Apples for Arteries**

  According to Tanaka Keiichi of National Institute of Fruit Tree Science, Japan, eating about 400 grams of apple a day reduces the cholesterol content of blood.

- **MUFA**

  It has been established that MUFAs lower cholesterol. Olive oil, avocados and almonds are the best sources of MUFA.

- **Omega-3 fats**

  Omega-3 reduces hardening of arteries. Walnuts are rich in omega-3 fat alpha-linolenic acid (ALA) and have been proven to lower cholesterol.

  Remember that walnuts contain omega-6 fats which can induce inflammation.

  Nuts reduce cholesterol. Joan Sabate of Loma Linda University in California found that people who ate 67 grams of nuts a day saw a fall of 5.1 per cent in total cholesterol level and 7.4 per cent in LDL cholesterol.

  Flaxseed, mustard and canola oils, and broccoli are rich vegetarian sources of omega-3 fats.

- **Fibre/Isabgul**

  Fibre promises to lower your cholesterol level dramatically. It works by creating an ultra-thin layer with water in the intestinal tract hindering absorption of cholesterol and helps in its removal with stool bulk.

  It also suppresses the production of cholesterol by liver. Chemicals in grapefruit fibre might also interact with plaque to dissolve it and thus open up arteries. The grapefruit fibre is also water-soluble like isabgul.

  Oats, containing high amount of soluble fibre, lower cholesterol.

- **Chromium-rich foods** such as whole grains, onions, tomatoes etc., as stated earlier, help in lowering cholesterol.

That means avoiding all refined foods, white sugar, white flour, and white rice.

• **Cinnamon**

Studies have shown that just ½ tsp of cinnamon per day can lower LDL cholesterol.

• **Lycopene in Tomatoes/Watermelon**

Researchers found that those who consumed a small quantity of tomatoes everyday just for three weeks saw their LDL levels drop significantly.

• *Lauki* (**Bottle Gourd**)

This vegetable is high in fibre. Juice of *lauki* taken everyday greatly reduces cholesterol.

It lowers blood pressure as well. You may add an apple and pomegranate to it.

• **Guggul**

An Ayurvedic herb recognised for lowering cholesterol.

• **Red Yeast Rice**

This Chinese fermented rice powder can lower cholesterol almost with the same effect as that of statin drugs.

17.4.2 HOW TO RAISE HDL, THE GOOD CHOLESTEROL

HDL serves the body by producing hormones, building cell walls, digesting dietary fats, and most importantly by carrying excess cholesterol to the liver for modification and elimination.

HDL must be higher than 60, and in any case not less than 40. Ways to raise HDL are quite similar to the recommendations for lowering cholesterol.

HDL level can be raised as follows:

1. Exercise, aerobic or any that raises your heart rate, for 20-30 minutes at a time, not only lowers bad LDL but also increases good HDL. Duration of exercise rather than intensity is the most important factor. It is the best and most accepted method of increasing HDL level.
2. Weight loss in overweight people will, in most cases, improve HDL. This is especially important if your excess weight is

stored in the abdomen. Take a low fat, high fibre diet. But weight loss from dieting alone can cause the desirable HDL to drop along with a drop in LDL. Hence, doing exercise, simultaneously with the diet programme, is necessary.

3. MUFAs increase your HDL simultaneously reducing LDL and triglycerides. Olive oil, avocados and almonds are the best sources of MUFA.

4. Omega-3 fats raise HDL. Take ground flaxseeds, canola oil, mustard oil, hempseed oil, walnuts, pumpkin seeds, broccoli and green leafy vegetables.

5. Red grapes juice (resveratrol) significantly raises HDL. You may take a glass of red wine a day, provided it does not raise your blood pressure.

6. Cranberries (*karonda*) are powerful antioxidants. They are a natural way to raise your HDL. It was found that drinking three 225 ml glasses of cranberry juice a day raised HDL by 10 per cent.

7. Beans, legumes and nuts have been shown to increase HDL level. Curcumin in turmeric, phytoestrogens in soybean and soy products, raw onions, and oranges are also recommended.

8. Modify the factors that suppress HDL. Eliminate refined sugars, white rice, white flour (*maida*), cookies, refined foods, cheese, trans-fats, etc. Trans-fats lower HDL. Substitute them with healthy fats. Quit smoking.

9. Vitamin B3 or niacin boosts HDL levels. Rich sources of niacin are milk/yoghurt, whole wheat, brown rice, legumes, almonds, and other high quality protein foods. Diet low in protein runs the risk of causing niacin deficiency.

10. Vitamin D also raises HDL. A walk in the morning sun daily for 20-30 minutes also helps.

11 Vitamin C intake could raise your HDL up to 11 per cent. Take more of vitamin C-rich fruits.

Note: Do not take high dose zinc supplements. Though zinc is very important for many body functions, its excess can lower the heart-protecting HDL.

17.5 WHAT ARE TRIGLYCERIDES?

Triglycerides are needed by muscles for energy. They come from the fats you eat as well as from other sources like carbohydrates (sugars, rice, and potatoes) which get converted to fats if in excess.

When more calories are consumed than are burnt by the body, they become triglycerides stored in fat cells. They eventually get converted to cholesterol. Experts recommend keeping triglyceride levels in the range 50-150, viz., lower than 150.

The best remedy for high triglyceride levels is to reduce intake of foods like potatoes, biscuits, chocolates, sweets, desserts, etc., and to do brisk walking.

According to a study by Duke University, adults who walked for 50 minutes, 4 times in a week decreased their triglyceride levels by 22 per cent – nearly twice as much as those who ran for the same amount of time.

Lower intensity work-outs may control triglyceride levels better because they use fat as their primary fuel while high intensity exercises utilise glucose for energy.

For optimal health and longevity, do not cut off all the fat from your diet. Fats have to form a key component of everyone's daily diet.

Children essentially need all the EFAs, and also sufficient amount of high quality saturated fats such as butter and ghee for optimal brain development.

Women who follow a low-fat diet may not be getting essential nutrients. This places them at greater risk of developing osteoporosis, certain types of cancers, and other health problems.

The moderate fat diet in which half the fat is MUFA produced a 14 per cent reduction in heart disease risk.

Note that saturated fat is not the same thing as cholesterol. The real culprit is trans-fats; it should not be consumed at all.

17.6 WHAT IS HOMOCYSTEINE?

Although most people consider cholesterol as the main factor responsible for heart disease, homocysteine is increasingly being recognised as another major risk factor.

Homocysteine is an amino acid (protein) produced in human body by the chemical conversion of methionine, a compound regularly consumed in the diet in the form of foods like meats, cheese, and fish which are methionine-rich.

While cholesterol leads to blockage of blood vessels, homocysteine damages the artery walls. The irritated lining of walls becomes a dumpsite for deposits, becoming prone to cholesterol build-up. With time, the artery becomes so clogged that blood flow to the heart and the brain is suddenly and totally cut off. The result is heart attack or stroke.

Elevated levels of homocysteine are also associated with many degenerative diseases such as high blood pressure, dementia and Alzheimer's disease, diabetes, osteoporosis, etc.

Methionine can, however, get converted to S-alenosyl methionine (SAMe) – which helps you produce feel-good chemicals – in the presence of B6, B12 and folate. But if there are not adequate amounts of B6, B12 and folate, methionine will convert into homocysteine. SAMe itself, helped by vitamin C, will convert homocysteine to glutathione.

Glutathione is the body's best anti-ageing agent. It also works as a detoxifier. It is a major antioxidant, highly active in lungs, and other organs and tissues.

The key to a long healthy life is to keep homocysteine levels down and glutathione levels up. For this, take folate to produce SAMe since the former is crucial for the conversion of homocysteine into benign substance glutathione. Vitamins B6 and B12 also help lower homocysteine levels and increase SAMe and glutathione.

Foods rich in folate are beets, beans, peas, nuts, spinach, asparagus, papaya, apples, carrots, etc. Beets are the best source of folate and betaine. The two work together to lower homocysteine levels in blood.

Alpha Lipoic Acid supplement causes increased levels of glutathione. Vitamin B2 also serves to protect against build-up of homocysteine.

DASH Diet for Lowering BP and Homocysteine Levels

DASH (Dietary Approaches to Stopping Hypertension) diet is a vegetarian diet. It includes lots of fruits, vegetables, grains, nuts, and low-fat dairy foods. It lowers BP and protects against heart disease by reducing artery-damaging homocysteine. In a study at John Hopkins University, Baltimore, the DASH diet (explained in detail later) was found to markedly lower homocysteine levels in the body.

17.7 C-REACTIVE PROTEIN (CRP)

CRP is an amino acid, a protein, produced by the liver, and found in the bloodstream. It plays an important role in immunity by functioning as an early defence system against infections.

It is now considered a strong marker for heart disease. High levels of CRP are linked to inflammation, which can lead to heart disease, cancer and Alzheimer's disease. CRP levels rise dramatically during inflammatory processes.

Inflammation caused by CRP contributes to damage to arteries. CRP can, thus, be a heart-hazard.

CRP Levels for Heart

Low risk   <1mg/litre
High risk   >3mg/litre

Studies at Brigham and Women's Hospital in Boston, and Cleveland Clinic showed that people with lowest levels of CRP had lowest risk of having a second heart attack, as their clogged arteries had opened up.

How to lower CRP levels, and reduce blood vessel inflammation?

- Do not smoke.
- Do exercise. Exercise not only keeps LDL and homocysteine levels low and HDL levels high but it also keeps the CRP levels low. Just 30 minutes of walking, five days a week, has been shown to lower CRP levels.

- Minimise infections. Keep your teeth clean to prevent infections. Niacin not only keeps the HDL high, it also keeps the CRP levels low.
- Minimise inflammations. Take anti-inflammatory foods like beans, seeds, whole grains, bananas, apricots and dark green leafy vegetables.

Magnesium-rich foods and vitamin C cut inflammations and lower CRP levels. Hence, if you eat plenty of fruits and vegetables, your CRP levels will naturally remain under control.

Omega-3 fats like canola and mustard oil, walnuts, and flaxseeds, MUFA as in olive oil, almonds, avocados, and ginger, broccoli, red grapes, pineapple and green tea are also beneficial. You may call these foods as inflammation or CRP quenchers.

18
High Blood Pressure/Hypertension

The heart contracts and expands as it beats. When it contracts, the blood pressure rises to maximum or systolic one. And when it expands (or relaxes), the blood pressure reduces to minimum or diastolic one.

Systolic pressure higher than 120 mm Hg means heart has to contract harder to pump blood against greater resistance such as blockage or narrowing in the arteries. Diastolic pressure higher than 80 mm Hg implies the heart is not able to relax to let blood flow into it. Blood pressure measuring higher than 120/80 means ill health.

For a healthy BP, you need unclogged arteries, and a relaxed mind. If the mind is tensed, arteries tend to shrink. As a result, the BP rises to meet the strained situation.

18.1 PREHYPERTENSION AND HYPERTENSION

Prehypertension

Prehypertension is a blood pressure reading between 130/85 and 139/89. Indications of impending hypertension are seen even before it becomes chronic. Systolic pressure less than 130, and diastolic pressure less than 85 can be considered normal with advancing age. Above this figure, the BP must be watched.

Diastolic pressure up to 89 can be easily brought under control by change in diet and living style.

With proper care, this problem can be treated without medicines. But if diastolic pressure is above 89, medication is necessary.

Hypertension/High Blood Pressure (HBP)

A blood pressure reading of 160/95 or greater is a serious threat to health.

High diastolic pressure usually affects the heart, and high systolic pressure may lead to clot formation in the arteries resulting in heart attack or stroke. Chronic stress, work pressure, long working hours, being overweight, exposure to noise above 60 decibel, watching television for long hours, etc., cause blood pressure to rise.

Hypertension remains undetected, as most people do not become alert until it gets aggravated and causes serious health problems. Hence, it is called a silent killer.

In HBP, blood pushes harder against the walls of the arteries. In due course, the walls of the arteries become thicker to adapt to HBP, and to prevent the vessels from bursting. That means, further progression of atherosclerosis and hardening of arteries. As walls become thicker, the passage left for flow of blood decreases. Narrowing of arteries leads to further increase in BP. This causes excessive load on the heart to pump the amount of blood necessary for the body and organs. With time, the heart becomes enlarged due to excessive load on it.

HBP impacts all organs. Heart, kidney, and brain are the first to get affected. Filtering units in the kidneys get damaged, thereby, impairing the filtration process. In the long run, this results in chronic kidney disease (CKD).

If not treated, HBP can lead to stroke and the damage in the brain can be irreversible. It can also affect eyesight. In the case of pregnant women, HBP could prove fatal for the foetus.

Extreme Weather Conditions Play Havoc with Blood Pressure

For those who have hypertension, hot summer nights disturb sleep and result in higher BP. Do not be misled from low readings in summer. This may be due to loss of sodium from sweating.

Exposure to chill in cold weather is much more dangerous, as it causes constriction of arteries while at the same time thickening of the blood, raising its viscosity and BP, thereby overstraining the heart.

Do not go for early morning walks in winter. Do not step outside in the open immediately after coming from a heated room. The sudden change in temperature could prove fatal and may result in cardiac arrest.

18.2 DRUG THERAPY

The first step in medicated treatment is to take a diuretic. Such a drug lowers BP by getting rid of excess fluid and salt (sodium) from the body. But it may also lower potassium level as potassium is also excreted along with sodium through urine. Diuretics may, therefore, cause muscle weakness.

The second step medicine is a beta-blocker which calms the sympathetic nervous system and eases the pressure. But beta-blockers hinder sleep, and lack of sleep increases BP. Thus, a vicious circle starts, and the disease is never cured permanently with medicine.

Good restful sleep is a must for reducing BP.

Step three is a vasodilator. It is a drug that dilates narrow blood vessels. Vasodilators may step up heart rate, and may have some other side-effects.

Hence, to bring BP under control, a change in diet and lifestyle is very important along with medication.

18.3 DIETARY CONSIDERATIONS FOR MAINTAINING HEALTHY BP

Following are the two important dietary cares one must take to lower blood pressure:

1. Do away with extra salt.
2. Do away with fried foods, hydrogenated or trans-fats, etc.

Go Easy on Salt

A study published in the *British Medical Journal*, April 2007, states that keeping diet low on salt does not only lower BP, but reduces risk of heart attack and stroke by 25 per cent and of death by 20 per cent.

Reason: Sodium may decrease the flexibility of blood vessels and may toughen heart cells. Sodium may also cause cells to burst because of water retention.

Also look out for hidden sources of sodium in your diet. The simplest way of lowering your blood pressure is by refraining from eating food that has high salt content.

For some, it may also prove to be a cure for insomnia since sodium hinders sleep. The less sodium you take the better sleep you get. The vicious cycle of sleeplessness and HBP can, thus, be broken.

American Medical Association believes that reducing salt in the diet by 50 per cent over the next 10 years could save at least 150,000 lives a year just in USA.

Consume Potassium-rich Foods

A lot has been said about lowering sodium intake to lower BP, but not enough on increasing potassium intake. Potassium works by replacing sodium in cells. Its deficiency can also cause BP to rise. Susan Hedayati from University of Texas found that potassium intake was strongly related to managing BP. Increasing potassium intake while reducing sodium intake simultaneously is one single change some people have made to get themselves off BP medication.

Sodium (salt) restriction must be accompanied with high potassium/sodium ratio which is present in fruits and vegetables.

Fruits, vegetables and legumes contain a high amount of potassium. Bananas, figs, guavas, oranges, and radishes have the most blood-pressure-lowering potassium. One medium-sized guava provides 63 per cent more potassium than one can get from a banana. Radishes contain as much potassium as bananas.

Consuming orange juice that is high in calcium, magnesium and potassium helps in relaxation of the nervous system, and lowering of BP.

Include potatoes, tomatoes, bananas, figs, dried apricots, oranges, nuts, beans, peas, etc. in diet. Beans are rich in potassium and magnesium that helps keep BP under control.

You can reduce your BP by obtaining calcium from low-fat dairy products. In a study conducted at Arizona State University, men who ate a high calcium diet for 6 weeks saw their BP readings drop dramatically.

A quick and effective way to help lower BP is to consume banana with yoghurt. This will give a boost to your daily need of calcium plus potassium to counter HBP.

High Cadmium and Low Zinc in Foods Raises BP

Studies have shown that the presence of high amounts of cadmium with low levels of zinc in kidneys is a contributing cause of HBP.

Cadmium has more affinity for kidney tissues than zinc has. Foods containing more than usual amounts of cadmium and less than usual amounts of zinc might slowly lead to accumulation of the former. An excess of zinc could prevent and a slight deficiency could allow accumulation of cadmium.

It is recommended to take foods rich in zinc but low in cadmium, having high zinc to cadmium ratio. Such foods are nuts, legumes, whole grains, cocoa, orange juice, root vegetables, and grape juice in that order.

Refining of foods removes beneficial zinc but does not remove harmful cadmium.

Negative foods in this respect are refined sugars, processed foods, coffee, whisky, gin, soft drinks, etc.

Another source of cadmium is the atmosphere or the air we breathe which contains the metal coming from industrial smoke, the by-products released during burning of coal and petroleum products. Cigarette smoke also has a sizeable amount of cadmium.

Chromium Deficiency Leads to Atherosclerosis and HBP

Chromium deficiency leads to atherosclerosis which in turn leads to high blood pressure. Refined foods like white sugar, white flour, and white rice should be avoided since they are totally stripped off chromium and zinc.

Lauki Juice and Pomegranate Juice

Lauki juice is diuretic. It lowers BP. But bitter lauki should not be consumed since it is poisonous.

Experts at University of Edinburgh found that pomegranate juice significantly lowers blood pressure.

Beetroot Juice/Nitrate Lowers BP

Beets contain nitrate which dilates blood vessels. Amrita Ahluwalia and researchers at Queen Mary University of London found that blood pressure came down within 24 hours among patients who took nitrate tablets or drank beetroot juice. Cabbage, celery/ajwain, spinach, and nuts are also rich in nitrate.

Garlic, Onion and Celery (*ajwain*) Reduce BP

Dipak Das, professor and director of the Cardiovascular Research Center at University of Connecticut found that crushed garlic relaxes blood vessels, thereby, lowering BP. Onions have a similar effect. They also hinder clot formation and raise HDL level.

Celery/ajwain contains pthalides/nitrate proven to lower stress hormones. They relax and dilate arteries allowing blood to flow at lower pressure. Potassium, calcium and magnesium present in celery further relax nerves and muscles to help reduce BP.

Vinegar

A daily dose of apple cider vinegar in water (one tablespoon in the morning and one in the evening) with meals brings high BP under control within two weeks.

Olive Oil (MUFA)

Olive oil provides an easy way to lower BP. According to a recent Harvard study, those with healthy blood pressure in the study were found to be consuming 100 ml of olive oil daily.

The Mediterranean diet is rich in olive oil in addition to whole grains, fresh produce, and grapes. According to an Italian study published in Archives of Internal Medicine, it was found that consuming olive oil reduced the systolic and diastolic BP of the participants by about 7 points.

Studies have also shown that consuming omega-3 fats like flaxseeds, mustard, canola and hempseed oils, soybeans/soy-milk, broccoli, walnuts, etc. lowers LDL, triglycerides, and BP.

Pistachios have been shown to significantly lower BP and reduce cardiac response to stress.

Vitamin C and Other Antioxidants

Vitamin C also helps to eliminate polluting heavy metals like lead and cadmium from blood. These are strongly linked to HBP. Obtain vitamin C and natural antioxidants from flavonoids in fruits and vegetables.

In general, eat foods that are packed with antioxidant poly-phenols such as apples, red/purple grapes, cranberries, strawberries, pomegranates, cocoa/dark chocolates, and tea.

Vitamin D

According to findings from Third National Health and Nutrition Survey in US, blood pressure increases as levels of vitamin D drop in blood. Vitamin D levels can be easily restored by a modest increase in exposure to sun.

High Fibre Diet

Extra fibre, regular intake of fruits and vegetables help in reducing blood pressure by 4-6 points in those already suffering from high BP. Take Isabgul. Complex carbohydrates and high fibre lower BP.

DASH (Vegetarian) Diet for Lowering BP

Most of the above listed requirements are met with an intake of a vegetarian diet.

The DASH Menu (for a single day):

1. Whole grain products for getting energy and fibre.
2. Vegetables (4-5 servings) such as broccoli, spinach, etc., to provide potassium, magnesium, and fibre.

3. Fruits (4-5 servings) such as orange, apple, cantaloupe, etc., to provide the same as above.
4. Low-fat dairy food like ¼ litre milk and 1 cup yoghurt to provide calcium and protein.
5. Nuts, seeds and dry beans (4-5 servings weekly) to provide energy, magnesium, potassium, protein and fibre. One-third cup almonds, ½ cup cooked beans is the amount sufficient for a day.
6. Omega-3 and MUFA to provide energy, to minimise inflammations, and to lower cholesterol.

Thomas Moore, author of the book *The DASH Diet for Hypertension,* says that researchers have known for decades that vegetarian people usually have lower BP than their non-vegetarian counterparts.

In the first 2 weeks of the trial, participants following a DASH diet registered a drop of 11.4 points in systolic BP, and 5.5 points in diastolic BP.

Cocoa/Dark Chocolate Lowers Blood Pressure

A study published in *The Archives of Internal Medicine*, 2006, showed that people who ate just 10g of dark chocolate per day had lower BP than those with low chocolate intake.

In a Swiss study, participants were found to have 59 per cent greater artery flexibility and 36 per cent less clot-forming activity just two hours after eating 40 grams of dark chocolate. The reason is believed to be the extremely high polyphenol content of cocoa/dark chocolate.

The added sugar and fat in chocolates would, however, cancel out any good they might do. Take cocoa powder or dark chocolate to ensure beneficial effects without any negative effects. Improving artery flexibility is a key factor in promoting healthy blood pressure and heart condition.

Water Therapy

Hypertension can be treated by increasing the daily water intake. Place a big jug of water near your desk so that you are constantly reminded to drink from it. Drink a litre of water early in the morning in 2-4 installments. On the whole, drink 10-12 glasses of water during the day.

Herbs/Supplements

- Dandelion, Rauwolfia Serpentina (*Sarpa-Gandha*) and Hawthorn; ½ to 2 tsp of the herbs with water on empty stomach 2-3 times daily helps in controlling BP.
- Passiflora Incarnata mother tincture – a homoeopathic extract of passion flowers – treats asthma, hypertension, sleeplessness and diarrhoea simultaneously.
- Hibiscus, a tropical flower, high in antioxidants, may lower BP by as much as 65 per cent.
- According to Diane L. Mckay, PhD, Tuft University, flavonoids in hibiscus may work by dilating blood vessels. Scientists at Tuft University found that drinking 3 cups of hibiscus tea a day can lower BP.
- Theanine in tea has a calming effect on stress hormone level. Melatonin is used to induce sleep. Good sleep will lower blood pressure.
- *Kari patta* (curry leaf), used to give a typical flavour to curries and other food preparations, lowers BP.
- Lavender or Rosemary: Sniffing the oils for 5 minutes caused the levels of the stress hormone, cortisol, to drop by as much as 24 per cent, as per one study. Cortisol raises the BP and weakens the immune system.

Preventive Measures

- Say no to smoking and tobacco. High concentration of lead and cadmium in cigarettes is strongly linked to HBP.
- Caffeine and alcohol should be eliminated. Sugar intake may be reduced. Remember that alcohol, caffeinated drinks, coffee, and sugar increase the amount of potassium excretion by the kidneys.

18.4 LIFESTYLE CHANGES TO LOWER BP

Patients can be helped to better their health by learning to control certain workings of the internal body and mind processes such as thoughts that normally occur involuntarily.

Scientists have found that the very genes that are activated by stress can be de-activated by yoga, meditation, and prayer. To an extent, the mind can actively control genes. It's a mind-body game, and so you must attend to the mind before you attend to the body.

Reduce weight: The more overweight you are, the more susceptible you are to HBP. Obesity puts extra load on the heart.

Reduce stress: Chronic stress increases cortisol stress hormone level in blood which, in turn, increases the blood pressure.

Be Tolerant and Equanimous

It is observed that people who are intolerant often develop hypertension. So, learn to accept things as they are. Do not always expect to have things your way. Be a balanced person. It is better not to have strong likes and dislikes. Make sure that you respond to situations appropriately without affecting your peace of mind.

Om Chanting

Om the primordial word (*shabda*) pronounced as 'Aum' is the cosmic vibration. This universal mantra unfurls the closed inner world. Chanting calms the mind, dissolves worries, lightens the heart and brings you in harmony with the Creator and the Creation.

Pranayam

Research has shown that just by making breathing slower and deeper, more oxygen is taken into the lungs and the muscles surrounding blood vessels. If enough oxygen does not reach these muscles, they constrict causing HBP. But once the muscles relax, the blood pressure gets reduced.

Take a slow deep breath. Then exhale just as slowly.

Breath is the link between the body and the mind. By working on one's breath, one can bring one's mind-body system to wellness. Doing 15 minutes of pranayam daily acts like a drug-free method of lowering BP.

Anulom-Vilom and Bhramri Pranayams are a great way to reduce BP.

Meditation

There are various types of meditating exercises from which you can choose according to your liking, capacity and necessity:

1. Aan-Apaan Meditation – This is the basic form of meditation involving awareness of the breath. It involves just sitting and observing the breath. Bring the mind back to the breath persuasively in case it wanders away, without, in any way, reacting to it.

   Meditation calms the mind. Thus, it helps reduce the level of stress hormones and keeps blood pressure low. Meditation can raise you to a high spiritual level, and establish you in equanimity, a state of balance or state of harmony with no rigid likes or dislikes.

2. So-Ham Meditation – This is a very powerful type of meditation to help reduce blood pressure.

   Sit in a comfortable meditative posture and keep your eyes closed. Begin to practise slow deep breathing. Now co-ordinate your breath with the chanting of mantra *so-ham* as follows:

   - Inhale taking your head backwards mentally uttering '*so—*'.
   - Then exhale simultaneously saying '*ha—m*', bringing your head forward till it touches the chest.
   - Inhale from the nostrils, and exhale from the mouth.
   - As you inhale, let the breath completely fill your lungs.
   - As you exhale, feel the stress leave your body.

Do this 14 times or more in three rhythms – slow, medium and fast. In the end just relax, be aware of the stillness, and let go.

Yoga Asanas

The simplest and the best Yoga asana is Shavasana or Yoga-Nidra (i.e. Yoga induced sleep-like state). You just lie down on your back on a flat hard surface with your hands a few inches away from the body, and your feet spread out a foot from each other. Then close your eyes, instruct the mind to relax each part of the body, from head to toe, and from toe to head. Meditate on your breath observing the rise and fall of the abdomen.

Cardiovascular Exercises

Researchers in Indiana University found that both short walks and long walks decreased the blood pressure by the same amount. However, the effect lasted for 11 hours after the short walks, compared to 7 hours after the long walk. To keep your BP low you need to keep exercising regularly.

But excessive exercise may worsen BP. On the other hand, sedentary activity like watching television raises BP as evident from the giddiness caused, in case you are already on medication.

Rest and Sleep

Blood pressure automatically comes down when you take proper rest and sleep.

There is a link between sleep and lifespan. In a study, it was found that those who slept 6 hours or less had a 70 per cent higher mortality rate than those who slept 7 or 8 hours. In HBP and heart disease, it is very necessary to get adequate amount of sleep. Waking up early in the morning may be bad for your heart, and for BP.

A study conducted by Japanese physician, Mayuko Kadono, presented at the World Federation of Sleep Research and Sleep Medicine Societies in Cairns, Australia in 2007 announced that subjects who woke up before 5 a.m. were 1.7 times more prone to suffering from HBP/hypertension, and 2 times more prone to developing hardening of the arteries.

Laughter Therapy

A hearty laugh elevates the mind, body, and the nervous system. It is immaterial whether laughter is natural or even contrived. Laughter is a complex, physiological exercise involving biochemical, endocrine and circulatory systems, which work together to protect the body against HBP and heart disease.

BP Readings Show How Happy You Are

Doctors have known for a long time that BP is one measure of an individual's health and happiness.

Loneliness and Chronic Stress

Psychologists Louise Hawkley and John Cacioppo at the University of Chicago reached the conclusion that the lonelier the people, the more helpless/threatened they felt when faced with stressful life events. They found that lonely people had higher levels of stress hormones in their body. This indicates that lonely people remain in a heightened state of arousal. Continued high levels of stress hormones in the body make the immune system weak and incapable of fighting inflammations and infections. This then contributes to wear and tear, HBP and ageing.

Loneliness is a matter of perception. Why not consider it as an opportunity for peace?

18.5 LOW BLOOD PRESSURE (LBP)

Chronic low blood pressure is a non-existent scientific entity. The Joint National Committee of the US National Heart, Lung, and Blood Institute has stressed that when it comes to low blood pressure, lower the reading, the better it is, and fitter is the heart provided there has not been a sudden drop, and the individual is able to go about his/her daily routine normally. In fact, studies have hinted at a correlation between better longevity and a blood pressure that could be as low as 90/60.

But too large a gap between two readings may be a cause for worry. Low BP becomes a problem when there are symptoms like dizziness or fainting.

To help raise your BP, just increase the amount of salt you have been normally taking. Also, drink plenty of water to keep you from becoming dehydrated. Often, dehydration can also cause BP to fluctuate to low levels. Drinking coffee would help increasing the blood pressure. Camphor also helps to raise blood pressure.

Primary causes of low blood pressure are faulty nutrition, and inadequate supply of oxygen, perhaps due to lack of physical activity. Deep breathing, in particular, is a good exercise for the respiratory system, blood circulation, cardiovascular, nervous, and other systems. In any case, an individual with very low BP should take a good diet.

19
Coronary Heart Disease (CHD) and Stroke

Heart, a muscle organ, is the most essential muscle in our body that is expected to work continuously for a lifetime, without rest. In coronary heart disease (CHD), the blood flow to the heart gets restricted or even completely blocked due to hardening of arteries and building-up of plaque. This results in narrowing and blockage of arteries.

The blockage is not only from cholesterol but can also be from calcium deposits or calcification of the arteries. This calcification is very common in people prone to chronic stress and sleeplessness.

Heart Attack

The heart receives blood for itself through a system of three main coronary arteries. If the artery becomes too narrow due to atherosclerosis, it cannot supply enough blood to the heart muscle enhancing the chances of heart attack. A blood clot in the coronary artery may also block the flow of blood to the heart. Chances of clot formation are increased with high blood pressure. Other risk factors are heredity, smoking, diabetes, high cholesterol, and high homocysteine levels.

Heart attack may cause severe damage to the heart muscles, or even death. Some tissues of the heart die due to lack of oxygen. Once dead, these tissues are lost for ever. Unlike the other body tissues, heart tissues generally do not regenerate.

Co-enzyme Q10 is the only supplement that has been found to improve the condition. Though the heart remains crippled after heart attack, the remaining tissues should be strengthened to prevent further problems.

Angina Pectoris

This refers to pain in the heart caused by insufficient supply of blood. The literal meaning of angina is 'I cry'. There is excruciating pain in the heart, chest, jaw, left arm, and sides of the face.

Silent Heart Attack

A silent heart attack is the same as any heart attack but the person does not feel it, possibly due to nerve damage around the heart. It can often be diagnosed by a regular timely check-up.

Dental Surgery Triggers Risk of Heart Attack and Stroke

Francesco D'Aiuto of University College London Dental Institute says that heart attack and stroke occur more often in the first four weeks after dental surgery, maybe due to infection, inflammation and clot formation. I myself had a massive heart attack four days after a tooth extraction.

19.1 RISK FACTORS FOR CHD AND STROKE

The risk factors for CHD can be put in two categories: Non-modifiable and modifiable.

Non-modifiable Risk Factors: That Can't Be Controlled

These are age, gender, and heredity.

Older people in their sixties are more prone to heart disease. Men are at greater risk of developing CHD than women. Female hormone oestrogen helps protect women against heart disease but male hormone testosterone has no such ability. This is because oestrogen decreases LDL and total cholesterol levels, whereas testosterone has an opposite effect. Younger women are less likely to suffer heart disease because their body has a high oestrogen level. Researchers found that men and post-menopausal women between 40 and 45, both short of oestrogen hormone, are more likely to have damaged arteries.

CHD, tendency to clot formation and stroke can also be inherited. Family history doubles the chances.

Modifiable Risk Factors: That Can Be Controlled

Science has identified metabolic syndrome, a group of seven major risk factors, as the cause for CHD and stroke. It includes physical inactivity, high blood pressure, unhealthy cholesterol (triglyceride, homocysteine and CRP) levels, diabetes, unhealthy diet, smoking/alcohol, and stress.

- Inactivity: It kills 2 million people worldwide every year. Just 30 minutes of moderate exercise daily can greatly reduce the risk. Regular exercise keeps obesity, diabetes, cholesterol and BP under control.
- High Blood Pressure: It increases load on heart and leads to plaque rupture. Maintain below 130/80.
- High Cholesterol: For those who have already had a heart attack or stroke, LDL should be less than 70. The acceptable range of ratio of LDL/HDL is 2.5-3.5, and Total Cholesterol/HDL is 3.5-5.0.
- High Triglycerides: Maintain triglyceride levels lower than 150. Reduce consumption of sugars.
- Homocysteine level: Avoid non-vegetarian food. Take foods rich in folate and vitamin C.
- High Blood Sugar/Diabetes: Sugar damages blood vessels.
- Obesity: A large waistline is an indicator of an unfit heart and puts one at risk of developing heart disease and stroke. A BMI of 23 or less is healthy.
- Smoking: A smoker stands double the chances of developing heart attack.
- Alcohol: Excessive consumption of alcohol causes HBP, weight gain, and irregular heartbeats.

- Stress, Behavioural Factors, and Negative Emotions: Stress, anxiety, sleeplessness, Type A personality (aggressive, impatient, competitive), unforgiving nature, people with strong likes and dislikes, negative emotions such as anger, hatred, greed, jealousy, selfishness, etc., promote internal production of LDL by the liver itself. It also triggers deposition of calcium and narrowing of arteries.

Chronic Inflammation: High levels of C-Reactive Protein (CRP) are caused by chronic inflammations. Vitamin C, niacin, magnesium foods, omega-3 fats and MUFA reduce CRP levels and inflammations.

Inflammation is an expression of the body responding to injury, stress or shocks, when WBCs and antibodies rush to tackle the invading bacteria. This is good when you have been affected by them. But when it becomes chronic, a constant battle against such inflammations is harmful and weighs heavily on your health.

Infections and Viruses

Lesions that cause heart attacks and strokes result as much from infections and viruses as from cholesterol. And infection starts with the teeth. Thrombosis Research Institute, London, has found that there is 70 per cent likelihood of reduction in heart attacks/strokes if you brush your teeth twice a day as opposed to just once.

19.2 HOW TO PREVENT AND REVERSE HEART DISEASE WITH A PRUDENT DIET?

First and foremost, maintain healthy BP, cholesterol, sugar, homocysteine and CRP levels.

If your weight is above normal, it may put more pressure on your heart. Lose weight if in excess. It is important to burn the calories we eat. Remember that an increasing waistline means decreasing lifeline.

Foods high in MUFA, omega-3 fats, antioxidants and fibre are best choices for maintaining heart health. Fruits and vegetables should fill more than half of your plate at every meal. People who eat a diet high in fruits, leafy green and other raw and cooked vegetables have 30 per cent lower risk of having heart attacks.

Note that yellow, orange and red coloured ones like carrots have beta-carotene. Tomatoes and melons and other red/pink fruits have heart-strengthening lycopene. Apples, pomegranates, grapes, blueberries, etc., have powerful polyphenols like resveratrol.

If you are diabetic, then, do not take very sweet fruits such as mangoes, banana, *chiku* (sapodilla), and grapes.

Eat anti-inflammatory foods only; omega-3 fats and MUFA are anti-inflammatory. Vegetarian sources for omega-3 fats include flaxseeds, pistachios, walnuts, pumpkin seeds, other nuts and seeds, hemp seed oil, mustard oil, canola oil, broccoli, dark green leafy vegetables, etc. Remember to balance omega-6 with omega-3.

Oils

Mustard Oil contains the least amount of saturated fats, and a high amount of omega-3. It is highly beneficial because it also has 30 per cent protein, and calcium, phenols and natural antioxidants. The pungent substance in mustard oil has anti-bacterial, anti-fungal and anti-carcinogenic properties.

Olive Oil and MUFAs – Oleic acid, a MUFA, in olive oil helps reduce the blood platelet clotting that can lead to heart failure. Olive oil protects good HDL cholesterol, and reduces the level of bad LDL cholesterol. Just this one simple change in diet is enough to prevent heart attack and cure heart disease.

Canola Oil is as rich in omega-3 as mustard. Use mustard/canola oils for cooking, and olive oil as raw.

Flaxseeds – Flaxseed oil is one of the most abundant plant-based sources of omega-3. You can add ground flaxseeds to your cereal or to your wheat flour.

Almonds

Almond fat is 78 per cent MUFA, the same percentage as in olive oil. Volunteers in a study ate about 48 almonds per day for six weeks.

During the period, their total cholesterol levels dropped by 4 per cent, LDL cholesterol levels dropped by 6 per cent, and triglyceride levels dropped by an impressive 14 per cent, while simultaneously raising HDL levels by 6 per cent.

Ample amount of magnesium present in almonds allows veins and arteries to relax. Potassium in almonds, necessary for nerve transmission/contraction of muscles, also helps the heart.

A single cup of almonds provides 257mg of potassium and only 0.3mg of sodium, thus, promoting heart health. This provides protection against BP, atherosclerosis, and heart attack.

Almonds also contain 20 per cent protein. They are a powerhouse of good proteins and nutrients.

Magnesium-rich Foods

Risk of heart disease increases when inflammatory chemical, CRP, is present in the blood. Magnesium-rich foods reduce blood inflammation and hence, lower CRP levels.

Magnesium-rich foods include whole grains, brown rice, legumes, almonds, cashews, pistachios, mustard, sesame and sunflower seeds/oils, all fruits, leafy greens, milk, yoghurt, cheese.

Whole Grains

Fibre and other nutrients in whole grains help in lowering cholesterol and blood sugar levels. The amount of phyto-chemicals in whole grains is even more than that in vegetables and fruits.

Highly processed grains like white flour and white rice are stripped off the bran, germ, zinc and chromium. In contrast, whole grains retain more of the nutrient-dense bran and germ.

Beans and Legumes/Soybean

These increase HDL and decrease LDL levels in addition to decreasing blood sugar levels.

Oats and Barley

Oatmeal cereal with its soluble fibre beta-glucan keeps your LDL levels low. Oatmeal is recognised by the FDA to lower cholesterol and subsequently, the risk of heart disease. Like oats, barley too has water soluble glucan fibre which seems to retard fat and cholesterol absorption by the intestine.

Bengal gram (*Bhuna* chana)

Eating 30 grams of *bhuna* chana a day may reduce the risk of heart disease by 24 per cent.

Amaranth/*Chaulai/Ramdana*

This fibre-rich easily digestible protein cereal lowers cholesterol. It is found to be extremely heart healthy.

Diet Rich in vitamins and Other Antioxidants

Vitamins C, E and antioxidants not only act as preventive but also as therapeutic heart medicines.

- **Vitamin E**
  Since one may not be able to fulfil all the daily need of vitamin E from food alone, it becomes necessary to take 400 IU of this vitamin through a supplement, particularly after the age of forty.

  Vitamin E improves blood circulation. It is a blood thinner and prevents clot formation. As antioxidant, it efficiently prevents artery clogging from cholesterol and build-up of plaque.
- **Vitamin C**
  Vitamin C enhances the dilation of arteries and keeps them and the heart relaxed so as to allow more blood to flow, thereby, reducing the chances of a heart attack to occur. Vitamin C also reduces CRP levels in bloodstream.

  Vitamin C from two *amlas* (gooseberries) a day can reduce risk of heart attack by 24 per cent.
- **Natural Antioxidants**
  Ageing, unhealthy foods, stress, pollution and synthetic chemicals, all create a higher need for antioxidants in the body. The higher the amount of antioxidants provided to the body, the lesser is the damage caused by free radicals.

Beta-carotene (present in yellow, orange, red, green fruits and vegetables like carrots), poly-phenols (found in tea, cocoa, grapes, etc.), lutein (in dark green leafy vegetables) and lycopene (in tomatoes, water melon, guava, etc., pomegranate, etc.), cut the risk of heart disease by 60 per cent.

- **Vitamin B3 (Niacin)**
HDL carries/diverts dangerous LDL and VLDL from artery walls to the liver for excretion. The process is called reverse cholesterol transport. It is considered crucial to the prevention of clogged arteries. Vitamin B3 or niacin is an HDL booster. It can increase HDL by as much as 35 per cent. Niacin also keeps down CRP levels.

    A low-protein diet is deficient in niacin. Get your niacin from proteins in milk, yoghurt, cheese, almonds, seeds, grains, brown rice and legumes.

- **Vitamin B5**
It is an anti-stress vitamin. It lowers cholesterol and triglyceride levels. Milk, yoghurt, cheese, whole grains, brown rice, beans and legumes, broccoli, cauliflower, cabbage and strawberries are rich sources of vitamin B5.

- **Folic Acid**
New research shows that most heart attacks are not caused by narrowing of arteries but by sudden bursting of plaque in arteries leading to clot formation, thereby, blocking the blood flow abruptly.

    Folic acid improves the health of arteries by reducing homocysteine levels. Folate is found in most fruits and vegetables.

    Oranges, spinach, lettuce, beans and legumes contain folate in abundance. It is also found in asparagus, beets, bell peppers, peas, papaya, apples and pomegranate.

    Vitamin B6 and folic acid work together with vitamin B12 to lower your homocysteine levels.

Fruits and Vegetables

How many fruits and veggies does one need to take to lower risk of heart disease?

The answer is that one probably needs to completely remodel one's eating plan to include at least 8 daily servings of fruits and veggies in order to lower the CRP level. In a study, those who ate 8 or more fruits and veggies a day lowered their risk of heart disease by 40 per cent.

- **Red Purple Grapes/Juice**

  Purple grape juice has the highest concentration of antioxidants like resveratrol. One study showed that drinking one 150 ml of purple grape juice twice a day reduced the tendency for blood clotting by 60 per cent. That is 50 per cent better than aspirin in blood thinning ability. Apple and cranberry come next in order.

- **Garlic/Onion**

  Two cloves of garlic a day are believed to reduce the risk of heart attack by about 24 per cent.

  With the help of garlic, a study group was able to slow down plaque build-up in arteries by up to 60 per cent over a year.

  Its health benefits are believed to be due to an antioxidant named allicin present in it. But most of its heart healthy effects seem to result from hydrogen sulphide, a chemical that is produced as soon as garlic is cut or crushed. That is why garlic is most beneficial when it is eaten fresh. Hydrogen sulphide relaxes blood vessels. Onions too contain an antioxidant named quercetin.

- **Tomatoes/Water Melon/Lycopene**

  Lycopene, in tomatoes, water melons, etc., protects the heart. In an experiment done on 14,000 people, it was found that those who consumed lycopene-containing foods, lowered their risk of heart attack by half. In addition, lycopene prevents growth of excess fat, and many cancers.

- **Capsaicin in Bell Peppers/Capsicum/Chilli/Spices**

  Researchers observed 85 per cent reduction in cardiac cell death when capsaicin, the main component of bell/chilli peppers and capsicum, was used. Capsaicin/spices relax blood vessels and lower BP.

- *Lauki* (Bottle Gourd)
  Lauki juice reduces cholesterol to a great extent. But never consume bitter juice as it is highly toxic.
- Quercetin
  Anti-inflammatory quercetin is present in concentrated amounts in apples, onions and tea. Quercetin has the remarkable ability to prevent formation of blood clots.
- Cocoa/Dark Chocolates
  Chocolates contain flavonoids and nitric oxide. These help in widening arteries leading to a drop in blood pressure and increased blood flow to heart and brain, thereby, cutting the risk of heart attack and stroke by 40 per cent.

  Polyphenols in cocoa/chocolate destroy free radicals. Their action is similar to that of a low dose of aspirin.
- Cinnamon
  Cinnamon is known to lower blood sugar, cholesterol, and triglyceride levels simultaneously.

  Dr. Joanna Hlebowicz and her team of researchers at Malmo University Hospital in Sweden found that when people with Type-2 diabetes added cinnamon to their diets for 40 days, they experienced a dip in their blood sugar and cholesterol level.
- Turmeric/Drumsticks
  Both are anti-inflammatory in nature. Drumsticks also reduce blood pressure.
- Black/Green Tea
  Tea is good for the heart. But adding milk to tea could destroy its health benefits. Tests showed that while thianine in tea helped improve blood flow by increasing the ability of arteries to relax and expand by producing nitric oxide, milk completely counteracted this effect.

  Additionally, black tea is full of antioxidants like quercetin, catechin, polyphenols, and folic acid.

  While catechin and thianine inhibit oxidation of LDL cholesterol, folic acid reduces homocysteine levels.

- **Isabgul**

  Isabgul, the soluble fibre, when taken 15 grams a day, can reduce heart disease risk by 30 per cent. It cleanses your gastrointestinal tract of toxins, and significantly lowers cholesterol and triglyceride levels.

- **Drink Water**

  Drinking 8-10 glasses of water daily not only helps in bringing down blood pressure (by excretion of excess sodium) but also makes the blood thinner and prevents clot formation. Drinking sufficient water helps to reduce high cholesterol, blood pressure, and even stress. Water flushes out toxins, transports nutrients, regulates temperature and aids digestion.

Vegetarian Foods

Animal foods contain highly saturated fats and cholesterol. Our body can handle plant proteins better than animal proteins since plant foods have almost zero cholesterol.

A vegetarian diet is necessary not only to eliminate risk factors, but also because it is rich in protective factors like providing fibre, antioxidants, flavonoids, EFAs, vitamins, and minerals such as potassium and magnesium for better blood pressure management and cell structure.

A regimen of two carrots daily, taken over three weeks showed a reduction of 11 per cent in cholesterol, increase of 50 per cent in faecal bile and fat excretion, and 25 per cent increase in stool weight.

Dr Dean Ornish showed how changes in eating habits could dramatically reduce and actually reverse arterial blockages.

The cholesterol found in meat, chicken, and fish accumulates inside the heart and sticks to the walls like chewing gum.

If you think being a vegetarian is a safe solution, then think again. If your cooking medium is butter, or hydrogenated oil, then you are hardly better off than a meat eater.

Prohibited Diet

- Diets high in fried foods, salt, sugars, eggs and meat increase the risk of heart disease by 35 per cent.

- Avoid consumption of animal foods, hydrogenated/trans fats, margarine, saturated fats, fried foods, all types of processed foods/canned foods.
- Taking tobacco in any form (cigarettes, *bidis*, *paan masala*, *gutka*) is a strict no-no. Arteries shrink and get damaged due to smoking. Exposure to cigarette smoke induces rapid changes in blood chemistry making it prone to clotting. Stella Daskalopoulou at McGill University Health Center, Canada, found that smoking just one cigarette increases the stiffness of the arteries in 18 to 30 years olds by a whopping 25 per cent. Arteries that are stiff increase resistance, making the heart work harder. The stiffer the artery, the greater is the risk. In Europe, after a public ban on smoking, rate of heart attacks dipped by 10 per cent in a single year.
- Alcoholic drinks and intoxicants raise blood pressure.

Eat Wisely

- **Reduce salt.** All sodium containing compounds cause HBP, and cell damage.

  Researchers in Adelaide, Australia, found that a single high-salt meal could restrict blood flow in your main arteries in just 30 minutes after eating. It indicates a rapid effect of salt on the stiffening of blood vessels.
- **Sugar is bad for your heart.** Sugar, on metabolising/oxidising glycates, creates inflammation in the arteries leading to scarring. The scars act as sites for plaque accumulation, and thus, set the stage for heart disease. Sugar increases urinary loss of potassium. Hence, cut back on sugar even if you are not diabetic. Avoid sugar-sweetened beverages and fructose.

Be Moderate on Coffee

Caffeine tends to block a chemical which helps in the relaxation and expansion of blood vessels. Coffee also raises BP.

Italian researchers at University of Palermo found that drinking a single cup of espresso coffee cuts blood flow to the heart by as much as 22 per cent within an hour.

In one study, coffee raised homocysteine level by 11 per cent. One can add cocoa instead of coffee.

However, experts at University of Athens say that a cup every day improves the elasticity of arteries. It was found that one third of subjects (belonging to Greek Island of Ikaria) who drink a cup or two of coffee daily reach the age of 90.

The best bet is to keep your coffee intake moderate.

Fasting

Researchers of Intermountain Medical Center and the University of Utah in Salt Lake City found that people who skipped meals once a month were about 40 per cent less likely to be diagnosed with clogged arteries and heart disease. Break from food helps the body to eliminate accumulated toxins and 'reset' its metabolism, thus, making it work more efficiently.

The best bet is to keep your coffee intake moderate.

Special Instructions

It is not enough to know what to eat. It is also very important to know when and how to eat.

- Always take fresh food.
- One must observe silence while eating. Do not watch television, or read newspaper. It hinders digestion, and raises blood pressure.
- Must feel gratefulness, and follow mindfulness while eating.
- Always eat a little less than your appetite. It is a good policy to feel a little hungry all the time.
- After meals, you must take rest. The heart has to work for digesting the food by pumping blood to stomach. Do not walk or exercise right after a meal. The heart will not be able to stand additional load. If you have had a heart attack in the past, it could prove all the more dangerous.

Herbs/Natural Remedies for Heart

Coenzyme Q10

Coenzyme Q10 is an antioxidant enzyme that supports healthy

cholesterol levels, muscle contraction, and supply of oxygen to heart cells while simultaneously helping cells to produce energy.

Heart muscle cells are highly demanding. For those who have had a heart attack in the past and whose heart tissues have been damaged already, Coenzyme Q10 supplement is the only way to revive their damaged heart muscles. Coenzyme Q10 could be the most important supplement for heart patients.

Aspirin

A small daily dose of 75mg of aspirin, a blood thinning medicine, is widely accepted as a strategy to keep away the formation of blood clots. But taking aspirin when you are absolutely healthy cannot be supported.

Apart from the side effects like bleeding, stomach ulcers and allergic reactions; risks of pancreatic cancer and cataracts, ringing in the ears and hearing loss caused by aspirin may outweigh the benefits.

Hawthorn

It is commonly prescribed in Europe for irregular heart beats and congestive heart failure.

Crataegus (Homoeopathic Mother Tincture)

It lowers BP, and acts directly on heart muscles. It is said to have solvent power upon deposits in arteries.

Digitalis (Homoeopathic Mother Tincture)

Digitalis stimulates the heart muscles and helps in difficult breathing. Gold drops with both tinctures will help to strengthen the heart damaged as a result of a heart attack.

19.3 HOW TO PREVENT AND REVERSE HEART DISEASE WITH LIFESTYLE?

Rest and Sleep

With adequate rest and sleep, the blood pressure and levels of stress hormone cortisol come down.

A study led by Diane Lauderdale of the University of Chicago Medical Center found that people, who on an average slept longer, were at reduced risk of developing new coronary artery calcifications. Calcium deposits in coronary arteries are considered a precursor to heart disease.

Among those who slept less than 5 hours a night, 27 per cent had developed artery calcification. Among those who slept for 5 to 7 hours, the number who suffered calcification dropped to 11 per cent. And only 6 per cent suffered calcification among those who slept more than 7 hours a night.

Sleep helps to repair all physical and mental systems. It is a great natural restorative process. A study found that those who slept 6 hours or less had a 70 per cent higher mortality rate than others.

Rising very early in the morning can actually be bad for your heart and BP. According to Japanese physician Mayuko Kadono, people who woke up before 5 a.m. were 1.7 times more prone to suffering from HBP, and twice more prone to developing hardening of arteries.

Afternoon Nap Benefits the Heart

First of all, even a healthy person should not do any work of exertion after having a meal. After a meal, the body itself demands rest because the blood needs to be directed towards stomach for digestion.

Midday naps after lunch may boost heart health. Researchers measured pulse and BP during the first ten minutes of people dosing off to sleep and found the readings dropped by a small amount.

Exercise and Active Life

Exercise reduces stress, eases anxiety and boosts happiness and energy levels. It also improves HDL/LDL ratio. According to American Heart Association, any activity which raises your heart rate for 30 minutes 5 days a week is healthy for your heart. Exercise should be just the right amount, according to your capacity, not to exhaustion. It should also be regular, not in fits and starts. A person I knew used to play tennis, squash, and badminton for hours daily during college days. Then, he left playing altogether. By the age of 50, he had to undergo triple bypass surgery.

Stay Happy

If you are not naturally happy, just try acting like one. Even faking happiness could help. Karina Davidson of Columbia University has found that there is a relationship between positive emotions and absence of heart disease.

De-stress Your Life

Each day, the average heart beats (contracts and expands) about one lakh times. The heart never gets a vacation. Experts say that stress could be considered as the heart's chief enemy.

Practise relaxation. Get involved in music, deep breathing or pranayam, meditation, Yoga asanas, exercises and walks.

Yoga Asanas, Daily Pranayam and Meditation

The most beneficial are Shavasana and Yog-Nidra. Others are Tadasana, Naukasana and Hasyasana. Hasyasana involves laughter therapy. Pranayam is very effective in scavenging of respiratory, circulatory, and nervous systems.

After Pranayam, do meditation. All forms of meditations are good. The simplest and best type is meditation on breath.

(Refer to section on Yoga and meditation).

Music Helps Arteries and Heart

Michael Miller, director of preventive cardiology at the University of Maryland Medical Center at Baltimore, along with other researchers found that when people listened to their favourite music, their blood vessels dilated in much the same way as with laughing, exercising or taking medications.

Miller found that the diameter of blood vessels in the upper arm expanded by 26 per cent in those who listened to music. He says that the effect of favourite music triggers release of nitric oxide into the bloodstream throughout the body. This helps blood vessels to expand and thus prevent the build-up of harmful LDL cholesterol blood clots.

Ragas for Heart

Listening to soft music set to less than 72 beats a minute can induce deep breathing, and a lower heart rate, consistent with deep relaxation.

Ragas that help in reducing stress on heart: Ahir, Nat Bhairava, Todi (day), Sohni, Pooriya Kalyan (night).

Noise builds stress and increases risk of heart attack. Michael Miller also warned that listening to stressful music can shrink blood vessels by 6 per cent, having the same effect as by eating a large hamburger as found in earlier studies.

A survey by scientists at Swedish Medical University Karolinska Institute showed that people who live with a back-drop of 50 decibel road noise are 40 per cent more likely to have a heart attack.

Live in a quiet, peaceful surrounding, and also practice silence.

Brush and Floss Teeth, and Wash Hands

Studies have shown that people with dental diseases are at an increased risk. There is preliminary evidence that bacterial infections in the mouth are linked to higher levels of inflammation in the body.

Bacteria can directly cause human blood and plasma to clot. Hence brush twice a day once in the morning after breakfast and next at bed time. It is also necessary to floss your teeth.

Tender Love and Care

Rabbits on a high cholesterol diet were found to develop atherosclerosis at a much slower rate when given tender love and care. If love and care can work for animals, then it can do miracles for humans.

But you receive love only when you give love. So learn to give.

Moral and Ethical Values

It is the divine truth: Whatever goes out from me shall come back to me.

- The first principle to learn is: *Giving is receiving.*

  Know that if you cause suffering or loss to any other soul by body, mind, and speech, it will come back to you. Hence, if you want happiness, and good health, start giving the same to others.

- The second vital principle is: *Best strategy to live this life is to live in equanimity/balance.*

  Hence, avoid having strong likes and dislikes, lest you might hurt yourself, and end up putting serious pressure on your heart and nervous system. You cannot change anyone or anything. It is difficult to change even your own self.

  The rule of the game of life is to keep balance. It applies to every activity, whether physical, mental, or spiritual. It means to eat in moderation, to exercise in moderation, to sleep in moderation, and to speak in moderation.

19.4 BEWARE OF THESE FACTORS

Extreme Winter Conditions

In the morning when you wake up, the blood pressure and the pulse rate are slightly higher due to the hormonal surge governed by the biological clock as the body gets ready to prepare for the day's work. The adrenaline level is highest in the morning. Because the body has to stay warm, it pumps glucose and adrenaline more rapidly, which increases the workload on heart. So do not dismiss early morning breathlessness or discomfort. Those susceptible to heart attacks are, therefore, more at risk of getting an attack in the morning all through the year. But the risk goes up as the chill sets in.

The cold weather causes the blood vessels to constrict, and blood to thicken and become stickier and more likely to clot.

Cholesterol levels also tend to be higher during winter. And an increase in respiratory infections may lead to inflammation that contributes to rupture of plaques. Harsh winters are bad news for heart patients.

Cardiologists say that patients who go for early morning walks in winter may suffer from accidental hypothermia which means the body temperature falls below normal. It occurs when the body cannot produce enough energy to keep the internal body temperature warm enough. Heart failure causes most deaths in hypothermia.

Wear layers of clothing in winter. The air trapped between layers forms a protective insulation. Wear a hat or head cover. Much of the body's heat can be lost through the head. Keep your hands and feet warm, as they tend to lose heat rapidly. Postpone your morning walk till the sun is out and the outside temperature is warm enough.

And never forget taking your medicines while going on a walk.

Important: The first thing to do after you realise that you are having a heart attack is to chew a 300mg aspirin tablet. Aspirin is a blood thinner and it reduces the risk of sudden death by 25 per cent.

Always carry a sorbitrate tablet with you, and put it under your tongue.

Extreme Hot Weather Conditions

It is well known that some people have more heart problems when it is hot. During the heat wave in Europe in 2003, there were an estimated 35,000 deaths above expected levels in the first two weeks of August. In France alone 15,000 people died. Even in Delhi, during hot months when temperatures soar to 45 degrees and above, it is very risky for heart patients to come out of the house.

In higher temperatures, we sweat more to get rid of the heat. The blood flows towards the skin where temperatures are lower. Accordingly, the blood flow to the heart gets reduced. In turn the heart rate rises, and blood pressure drops.

The combination is dangerous for older people, and for those with weak cardiovascular system.

Long Distance Flights

Non-stop long distance flights can be very risky for heart patients.

According to a WHO Research into Global Hazards of Travel (WRIGHT), travellers sitting immobile for more than four hours in a cramped seat are at great risk of developing a blood clot in a vein in the calves. When the clot migrates to the lungs, it causes pulmonary embolism (PE).

It may migrate to the heart or brain causing heart attack or stroke. The symptoms include pain or cramps in calves and swelling of legs and feet.

The risk of clot formation is greater in people who are shorter than 5-feet-4 inches, or taller than 6-feet-4. This is because taller people get cramped for space, while shorter people cannot reach the floor.

While in flight, it is advisable to frequently get up from the seat and stroll around in the aisle, and even do some exercises to keep the blood circulation normal.

It is interesting to know that a new study at the Leiden University Medical Center in Netherlands, published in the British Journal of Hematology, found that sitting by the window in a plane can double the risk of potential blood clot formation.

Drink more fluids like water and juices in the flight.

Doing Vigorous Exercise

Although regular exercise is recommended for all, it is not advisable for heart patients to do vigorous exercise. One should do exercise according to one's age, capacity, and health condition.

Calcium Supplementation

Investigations conducted by Bone Research Group at Auckland University, and a number of others have shown that elderly people who take calcium supplements to keep their bones strong are more prone to heart attacks. Apart from calcification of arteries accelerated by generation of stress hormones and lack of sleep, calcium supplements may further increase the possibility of calcium deposits.

Air Pollution

A new study conducted by Dr Andrew Lucking of University of Edinburgh has revealed that air pollution caused by car exhaust fumes (that is laden with toxic metals like lead and cadmium) makes the blood stickier, increasing the chances of heart attack or stroke. The study shows that if a person is exposed particularly to diesel exhaust even for a short time, the blood is more likely to clot.

Pressure of Deadlines

According to a study, those who toil under intense deadline pressure have six times greater risk of suffering from a heart attack. Hence, it is a better policy to be punctual in your regular work. Avoid delaying the work as that would then pressurise you to hurry up to finish the same to meet a sudden deadline.

Viagara

Viagra/sildenafil citrate for erectile dysfunction was originally developed by Pfizer as a heart drug.

The drug works by increasing the effect of nitric oxide which expands the blood vessels. That may also improve heart function by allowing more blood to flow to the heart. It also allows blood to flow to the lungs more efficiently, and thus to receive more oxygen.

19.5 RESULTS OF ABU HEALTHY HEART TRIAL

A 9-year long study conducted jointly by Defense Research and Development Organisation and Global Hospital Research Center, Mount Abu, has concluded that a low fat, high fibre vegetarian diet, and an hour-long daily walk, accompanied by stress management through Yoga and meditation had the following beneficial effects:

1. Regression of atherosclerosis in arteries by 11.82 per cent.
2. Increase in left ventricular Ejection Fraction or EF (pumping of pure blood by heart) by 30 per cent.
3. Reduction of cholesterol by 24 per cent.
4. Significant reduction in the production of stress hormones epinephrine, norepinephrine, and cortisol.
5. Increase of tranquility molecules such as serotonin, and beta endorphins in the body.
6. Reduction in LDL by 31 per cent.

7. Increase in HDL by 16 per cent.
8. Reduction in triglycerides by 32 per cent.

19.6 STROKE

A stroke occurs when a blood vessel in the brain bursts, or gets blocked by a clot. Blood clotting decreases blood supply to the brain causing a stroke.

Paralysis or weakness in one side of the body usually takes place depending on whether the artery of the left or the right brain is blocked.

In order to protect yourself from stroke, beware of HBP, diabetes, high homocysteine level, and high platelet count. HBP is the most common cause of stroke.

Large Waist to Hip Ratio Indicator of Stroke

Tobias Back at Saxon Hospital Arnsdorf Germany in a study found that individuals with highest waist to hip ratio had greater than 7-fold increased risk of stroke compared with those with lowest ratio.

What is the best way to minimise stroke risk?

Stroke is preventable. Exercise and morning walks help in bringing down the risk of stroke. Even mild to moderate exercise 30 minutes a day helps.

- Diet and lifestyle considerations as for HBP and CHD play a strong role in preventing stroke.
- Do not smoke. Nicotine in cigarettes causes blood vessels to constrict. Note that smoking doubles your risk of getting a stroke.
- Eat fresh fruits and vegetables daily.
- Take a low dose aspirin daily.
- Maintain your lipids and blood sugar levels within limits.
- Rich flavonoids in cocoa and dark chocolates lower stroke risk. A study found that eating 50 grams of chocolate once a week cut the risk of death after a stroke by as much as 46 per cent.

- There is higher risk of stroke with deficiency of vitamins B6, B12, and Folate.

Vitamins B12 and B6, in addition to folate, have a role in reducing homocysteine levels.

Rich sources of B6 are bananas, bell peppers, spinach, soybeans, legumes, oatmeal, and potatoes. Vitamin B12 is mainly found in milk, and some in legumes, soybeans, sprouted moong dal, etc. Folate is found in fruits and vegetables. Its deficiency is rare among Indians.

Chances of Brain Strokes Increase During Winter

Doctors find an alarming 15-20 per cent rise in brain strokes during winters. In an attempt to reduce the heat loss by the body, the arteries get constricted. This in turn leads to high BP, which may end up bursting a blood vessel. One may have a splitting headache.

Chances of Stroke Increase From Pollution

Japanese researchers found that high air pollution levels as caused by particulates of soot from car exhaust, burning coal and ground level ozone strain your lungs and blood vessels. It doubles the risk of getting a stroke.

Folate-rich foods like beans are recommended as a protection against pollution.

Recognising Stroke

A bystander can recognise a stroke by asking the victim to smile, or to speak a simple sentence, or to raise both hands, or to stick out his/her tongue. A person suffering from a stroke would not be able to perform these simple activities.

Most people do not even realise that they have suffered a stroke. Neurologists say that if they can get to a stroke victim within three hours, they can totally reverse the effects of the stroke.

20

Immune System

True health can be achieved only if the body is able to prevent and fight diseases on its own.

Weakening of the immune system makes one frequently ill. One may virtually be attacked by all kinds of diseases, from catching common cold to fever and various kinds of infections to even cancer and AIDS.

Why is that of all the people infected by the same bacteria or virus, only 20 per cent develop the disease? Those whose immune system is very strong do not succumb to the disease, while those who have a weak immune system fall sick easily.

20.1 WHAT COMPRISES IMMUNE SYSTEM?

It is the most complex system in the sense that it is not made up of one single organ. It is a collection of cells and organs in the body that defend us against foreign invaders such as dangerous viruses, bacteria, toxic materials, or some of the less harmful trespassers.

20.1.1 IMPORTANT ELEMENTS COMPRISING THE IMMUNE SYSTEM

Following are important elements of the immune system in the body:

Bone Marrow, Thymus and Spleen

Bone marrow is the soft red portion inside every bone where blood cells are produced. There, stem cells are constantly dividing themselves and producing red blood cells (RBCs) and white blood cells (WBCs). Our bone marrow is an extremely fast and efficient cell producing factory.

Thymus is located in front of the wind pipe. It is in the thymus where WBCs, also called leukocytes, collect, exchange information, learn about threats and ways to handle them.

Spleen is located on the left hand side below the rib. It is in the spleen where blood cells are taken out of circulation once they are rendered useless. The waste products of these dead cells are recycled. Thus, spleen is important for maintaining good health.

Lymphatic System

Lymphatic system is the body's drainage system. It comprises of a network of lymphatic vessels, lymph nodes and lymph capillaries in the same way as the blood circulation system comprises of arteries, veins and capillaries.

The main difference between the blood and lymph circulatory systems is that the lymph system does not have a pump, like heart, to circulate the lymph. Lymph flow is achieved by muscle contractions and by gravity. Thus, it is not a closed system. Lymph vessels have one-way valves, and muscle motion pumps the lymph.

Lymph

Lymph is a fluid that travels throughout the body cleansing tissues and keeping them nourished. Our entire body is soaked in lymph.

The cells receive their nutrients from the lymph, which in turn takes away harmful elements from cells.

Lymph Node

Lymph in the lymph vessels eventually reaches a lymph node. There are about 100 lymph nodes scattered around the human body.

Lymph nodes filter the lymph. Nodes contain a large number of WBCs which remove foreign cells and debris from the lymph. When we get any infection, lymph nodes swell with billions of WBCs acting to clear invading infection-causing cells. Thus lymphatic system forms an important part of the immune system.

Lymphocyte

Lymphocyte is a more scientific name for the general name of leukocyte or WBC. Lymphocytes are the specialised WBCs that are present in the lymph nodes. There are three types of lymphocytes – natural killer or NK-cells, Thymus or T-cells, and bone or B-cells.

NK-cells and T-cells coordinate the response of the immune system. They play a major role in defending you from tumours and virally infected cells.

The B-cells produce antibodies that fight against a specific invader. Harmful organisms are trapped and destroyed by these specialised WBCs.

The body develops disease-specific B-cells by immunisation technique. One is protected throughout one's life by these cells against that particular disease.

The lymph supplies nutrients such as glucose to different parts of the body where the bloodstream is not able to reach.

These lymph nodes exist almost everywhere in the body. Important locations are in the neck, chest, sinuses, abdomen, etc.

Swollen glands are an indication of a combat between our cells and foreign intruders.

Healthful Serum Factors

Obese individuals usually have elevated cholesterol levels, and a weak immune system.

High levels of cholesterol, triglycerides, free fats, bile acids, etc., inhibit immune functions and reduce the ability of the WBCs to produce antibodies, and to reach the areas of infections to overpower and destroy the organisms of infections.

The health of the immune system is also determined by the state of mind of an individual. A relaxed and stress-free mind boosts immunity.

20.2 NUTRIENTS CRITICAL TO IMMUNE SYSTEM

Sometimes, a single nutrient deficiency could drastically affect the immune system.

Vitamins

Vitamin A (beta-carotene) is anti-infection vitamin. It was found that animals fed on a diet deficient in vitamin A became ill frequently thus indicating poor immune system. They also showed inability to grow.

Vitamin C is the single most potent antioxidant and most important vitamin for immune system function. It is responsible for the production of lymphocytes/B-cells. It enhances WBC functions, antibody levels, and secretion of thymus hormones.

Vitamin C is present in excellent amounts in celery. Celery, in addition, contains coumarins. These compounds enhance the activity of WBCs and thus boost immunity.

Vitamin D

Carsten Geisler of Copenhagen University found that immune system's T-cells rely on vitamin D to become active. They remain dormant if vitamin D is lacking in blood.

Carotenes and Thymus Gland

Carotenes and all natural antioxidants have immune enhancing effects. They protect the thymus gland from damage. Thymus gland is the major gland of our immune system. Apart from producing a type of WBCs, it releases hormones that regulate many immune functions. But this gland is extremely susceptible to damage by free radicals, and also by stress, drugs, infections, and illnesses.

Thymus hormone levels are typically low in elderly and in individuals prone to infections, exposed to undue stress, or those suffering from cancer, AIDS, etc.

Almonds

Almonds, particularly the substance present in their skin, improve the ability of WBCs to fight viral infections.

Cruciferous Vegetables

Cabbage, cauliflower and broccoli have sulphur-containing compounds, in addition to vitamin C and carotenes. They detox cancer-causing compounds, and inhibit the progress of many types of cancers and tumours.

Garlic and Onions

Garlic and onions with allicin fight bad bacteria. Allicin stimulates production of WBCs. Garlic also contains germanium, a trace element for immune function.

Beets

The purple crimson natural pigment betacyanin in beets is a proven cancer fighter.

Probiotics/Acidophilus and Bifidus

These good bacteria found in dairy products like yoghurt suppress the growth of harmful bacteria, and improve immune function.

Cow's First Milk

Cow's 'first milk' provides immunity to the new-born calf just as the first milk from mother's breasts helps the baby to build its immune system.

Yoghurt

Yoghurt and probiotics keep the gut free of disease-causing bacteria/germs.

Tea

Tea contains powerful antioxidants theanine, catechin, and EGCG. Thiamine in tea produces virus fighting interferon in blood. Harvard researchers found that drinking 5 cups of tea for 2 weeks raised the strength of the immune system by four times.

Water and Fibre

Plenty of water, fresh fruit juices, and fibre should be included in diet.

Oats and barley contain beta-glucan, a soluble fibre, with anti-microbial and antioxidant capabilities. It boosts immunity and speeds wound-healing.

Herbs

Basil (tulsi) and Thyme (ajwain) leaves and seeds are immunity boosters. St. Johns Wort is a natural blood purifier. It fights AIDS virus. Astralagus protects liver and boosts the immune system. It generates anti-cancer cells.

According to Ayurveda, improperly digested foods accumulate in the body as *ama* (toxins). The toxins are the foundation for infections by pathogens. Toxins weaken the immune system. *Trikatu, pipali* herbs help in eliminating *ama*, increasing *oj* (vital energy).

20.3 HOW THE IMMUNE SYSTEM CAN GO WRONG

Immune Response

The action of WBCs and antibodies to invading organisms is called immune response. In most cases once the antibodies have been produced to fight a certain organism, it no longer poses a great threat.

The immune system can go wrong in two ways:

1. It may be overpowered by the invader when the immune system is too weak to tackle a powerful invader.
2. Or it may become overactive due to frequent infections and stimulations by emotions, stress, etc., and falsely sense a danger.

Overpowered Immune System

The immune system is overpowered by the enemy invader. This is commonly seen in developing countries where the nutrition and health standards are poor and the immune system is weak. Diseases like malaria, cholera, tuberculosis, etc., are very common.

Overactive Immune System

This is common in developed countries where the health standards are high and immune system of the people is otherwise strong, but people suffer from diseases like heart disease, stroke, diabetes, Alzheimer's disease, etc., which are caused by the overactive immune system.

Paul Ridker of Harvard Medical School found high levels of C-Reactive Protein (CRP) in the blood of those who had had a heart attack. Many degenerative diseases are preceded by high CRP levels.

Scientists are now beginning to believe the involvement of the overactive immune system in causing the disease.

For example, in one case of a person constantly suffering from H Pylori infection, it was found that immune system kept on producing antibodies to fight the bacteria. But, the disease was not cured. Instead the immune system, fighting the bacteria, also started affecting the eyes to the extent of leading the person to blindness.

It shows that, in the process of protecting us from a specific infection, the immune system is not able to coordinate its forces to precisely attack the infection only but instead starts affecting the other parts of the body.

Overactive Immune System Linked To Faster Ageing

Mark Liponis in his book *Ultra-Longevity* stipulates that the older you are the more likely you suffer from diseases caused by overactive immune system.

As we age, more and more antibodies are found in our bodies. The immune system has a large database of memories of invaders.

Ultimately, constantly fighting, the immune system becomes confused as to what forms part of your body, and what forms the invader in the body.

One of the important aspects of living to be hundred or more is the absence of antibodies. Centenarians have lived their lives in such a way that they have not suffered from many physical or mental ailments, and have fewer antibodies.

A healthy immune system is one which is strong but that which is not overacting. According to Liponis, the quieter your immune system the healthier you are.

20.4 INFLAMMATION

Inflammation is immune system's way of protecting the body from foreign invaders.

If you have injury, the resulting inflammation and swelling is part of the healing process. Of course, it is short lived. But, it becomes disastrous when it does not subside on its own.

Thus, inflammation is a double-edged weapon.

If the body does not turn off the inflammation response, the inflammatory chemicals stay in the system for a long time, and destroy the very organs and tissues the inflammation was meant to protect.

Such a damaging inflammatory response is the cause of every chronic disease whether asthma, arthritis, cancer, heart disease, HBP, diabetes, macular degeneration, Alzheimer's disease or obesity or illness of digestive tract.

Chronic inflammation may be caused by an infection as in low grade fever, or a wound or a mechanical irritant such as a kidney stone or a chemical irritant such as stomach acid or toxic metals, and so on.

Chronic inflammation can eat away a cartilage causing arthritis. Asthma is inflammation of airways and lungs in respiratory system. Kidney inflammation triggers HBP or damages the kidney itself.

Chronic inflammation destroys nerve cells in brain causing Alzheimer's disease.

Research shows that all types of inflammations can cause cancer.

What gives stimulus to the body not to turn off the inflammatory response?

First reason is bad diet which releases enormous amounts of free radicals. The constant introduction of free radicals overwhelms our antioxidant defense.

There are other foods that cause inflammatory homocysteine levels to rise in our body. People think wheat stands for energy. But many people have allergy to wheat gluten which inflames the gut. Most processed foods are high in inflammatory omega-6 fats.

The second reason is heavy metals, pesticides and chemicals.

The third reason is chronic stress producing hormones that trigger inflammation.

Fat cells in obese people produce large amounts of inflammatory chemicals. That is why overweight people suffer from so many illnesses.

Stress, pollution, smoking and obesity, all cause inflammations.

20.5 ALLERGIES

An allergic response is an overactive response of the immune system. It is triggered by mast cells that release inflammation-causing histamines and other chemicals.

Nasal discharges simultaneously with digestive disorders are an example of allergy. When your body is over-acidic, the response to allergic triggers is amplified.

The following are the secrets of dealing with allergies:

1. **Alkaline System**: Maintain your system as alkaline as possible by living on fruits and vegetables. You may take ¼ to 1 tsp of sodium bicarbonate (baking soda) with water.
2. **Bromelain**: This digestive enzyme available in pineapples reduces allergic inflammation. Take plenty of pineapples.
3. **MSM (methyl sulfonyl methane)**: This anti-inflammatory substance is known to reduce food allergies. It is contained in fruits, vegetables and whole grains. But in processed and refined foods, MSM is destroyed.
4. **Quercetin**: Found abundantly in tea and apples, this flavonoid inhibits histamine release and reduces sensitivity to allergens.
5. **Air Quality**: People who have allergies are particularly sensitive to air quality. They should beware of pollutants.

They must remain in clean environment. They must also keep their house and linen clean.

20.6 ANTI-INFLAMMATORY FOODS

Anti-inflammatory foods as follows boost the immune system:

MUFAs

MUFAs in olive oil, avocados, almonds, pumpkin seeds and other nuts contain maximum antioxidant polyphenols.

Olive oil has amazing power to fight inflammation, lubricate swollen red joints, and keep pain-causing prostaglandin chemicals at bay.

A study in England revealed that arthritis patients who consumed olive oil as a regular part of their diet experienced dramatic improvement.

Omega-3 Fats

Mustard, canola and hempseed oils, flaxseeds, walnuts, cloves, broccoli, squash/pumpkin, and spinach contain anti-inflammatory omega-3 fats.

Prostaglandins of series 2, in contrast, are inflammatory chemicals produced when we have too much of omega-6, animal fats, trans-fats, saturated fats and alcohol.

All vegetable oils contain high amounts of omega-6 with negligible or no omega-3.

Coconut Oil

A surprising fact is that coconut oil which is a saturated fat has anti-inflammatory, anti-microbial and anti-bacterial properties.

Folate

Most fruits and vegetables like spinach contain folate. Beans are very rich in folate. Folic acid converts inflammatory homocysteine into benign amino-acids.

Fruits and Vegetables

They contain salicylic acid, an inflammation-fighting compound contained in aspirin. In a study, it was found that the blood of vegetarians contained 12 times more salicylic acid than the blood of non-vegetarians.

Natural Antioxidants

Some of the natural antioxidants are given in the table below:

Table 20.1 Natural Antioxidants in Foods

Allicin	Garlic, onions.
Sulforaphane	Broccoli, cauliflower, cabbage.
Lycopene	Tomatoes, watermelon, sweet peppers.
Carotenes/Carotenoids	Carrots, celery, fruits (papaya) and eggs.
Polyphenols/Resveratrol	Grapes, red wine, apples, pomegranates, cocoa, olive oil, whole grains, tea.
Lignans	Beans, legumes, grains, seeds.
Flavonoids	Curcumin in Haldi, Citrulline/Arginine in water melon.
Phytoestrogens	Soy
Capsaicin	Peppers
Quercetin	Tea
Phytosterols	Pumpkin seeds
Bromelain	Pineapples

According to Susan Land of Stanford Medical School the following are anti-inflammatory.

Cocoa beans have the honour of being considered as the richest in antioxidants. Apples, grapes, red wine, blueberries, broccoli, carrots, and teas contain the highest amounts of natural antioxidants.

Beta-carotene enhances immune system, and gives freedom from infections of cold/cough, and protection from lung inflammation and asthma.

Allicin in garlic has anti-inflammatory, anti-bacterial, and anti-viral activity.

Bromelain, a digestive enzyme found in pineapples, reduces inflammation.

Quercetin, a bioflavonoid in tea and apples is highly effective in lessening inflammatory substances and inhibiting release of histamines which trigger allergies.

Polyphenols as in olive oil, grapes, etc., have extraordinary anti-inflammatory, antioxidant, and anti-coagulant properties.

Phytosterols in pumpkin seeds lower cholesterol, enhance immune response, and decrease rates of certain cancers.

Magnesium-rich foods reduce inflammations. Those with high levels of magnesium in blood have 40 per cent lower risk of early death. Grains have high amounts of magnesium and tryptophan in combination.

Selenium, together with vitamin E, prevents damage to cells from free radicals. One of the reasons for many inflammatory diseases could be low levels of selenium. Selenium is a trace mineral that, particularly, suppresses cancer cell growth.

Water is the most anti-inflammatory. It is through water that nutrients are carried throughout the body cells, and toxins and waste are eliminated from the body.

Herbs

Methi is anti-inflammatory to the extent that it is used to relieve arthritic pains.

Haldi is anti-inflammatory, antioxidant, and anti-cancer.

Ginger is very potent in inhibiting formation of inflammatory prostaglandins.

Rosemary has caffeic acid and rosemarinic acid. They are potent antioxidant and anti-inflammatory agents. The two are effective in reducing inflammation.

Mustard has anti-inflammatory omega-3.

Inflammatory Foods

All diseases thrive in the acidic system. It is the plain and simple fact of medicine.

White sugars, sweets, and milk chocolates, though tasting sweet, have acidic effects. Remember that proteins, in general, are acidic in nature. All non-vegetarian foods are acidic and meat is the most acidic. Complex carbohydrates are not acidic. Refined carbohydrates are acidic to some extent.

White sugar is inflammatory. Researchers in Denmark found that when patients with arteriosclerosis consumed drinks/soda with sugar, their markers of inflammation increased. But when they drank fruit juice, the markers were reduced although both liquids contained similar amounts of sugar. The difference is attributed to the fact that juice also has antioxidants that counter inflammation.

Food additives, pesticides, and herbicides have serious long-term health risks. Saturated and trans-fats, processed and refined foods should be avoided. Smoking, consuming alcohol, or beverages containing excessive caffeine are strict no-no.

20.7 HEALTHFUL LIFESTYLE FOR STRONG IMMUNE SYSTEM

Immunity can be strengthened by following the precepts of exercise, yogasanas and pranayama, drugs, herbs, diet and conduct.

Daily exercise may include just 30 minutes of aerobics, walking, or swimming depending upon an individual's age and health. Include 5-10 minutes of stretching exercises.

Lymphocyte production gets stimulated with exercise. It strengthens immune system.

Deep-breathing and pranayam, Shavasana, sleep, relaxation methods, meditation and prayer make the immune system strong and calm.

Stress-Free Mind and Required Nutrients

Stress impairs immunity. Study shows that stress makes cancer cells stronger, and less likely to die. Morbidity is much lower in cancer patients who have low stress and depression levels.

Eat the right comfort foods such as nuts, apples, bananas, oranges, asparagus, cocoa or dark chocolates, and chamomile, lemon balm and peppermint teas to beat the stress.

Stress depletes you of your B vitamins. Zinc is drained by high anxiety. Walnuts and other nuts can replenish these vitamins and zinc.

Almonds provide vitamin E that fights cellular damage linked to chronic stress.

Asparagus is a great source of folate, a natural mood lightener. Chocolate is the best comfort food. It is a good source of arginine, an amino acid, crucial in boosting body's immune function.

Sleep

Sleep gives rest to the body and mind, and time to repair. Prior research has suggested that sleep boosts the immune system at the cellular level.

Ethical and Moral Values

Positive thinking strengthens the immune system.

Stay away from negative emotions and thoughts. Anger, greed, hostility, and stress have been associated with heart disease, asthma, and other ailments. Negative emotions could change biological processes, and may weaken the immune system. It was observed that people had significantly poorer lung function after nurturing a level of long standing anger.

Giving is receiving. If you want money, distribute whatever you have to the needy. It will come back to you manifold times. If you want love, start giving love unconditionally to anyone who is a willing recipient.

Live a life of service. The greatest service is to consider everybody good, wish everybody well, and have the intention of doing well.

Detachment

Insecurity, fear of being abandoned by loved ones suppresses your natural killer immune cells. A study found that insecurity and skin diseases are related to immune dysfunction.

Laughter Therapy helps people improve their immune systems, prevent and even cure illnesses, according to Kazue Takayanagi of Nihon Medical School, Japan.

20.8 FEVERS

Fever occurs in response to inflammation which can accompany bacterial or viral infections, and even some non-infectious diseases like arthritis.

As the body's temperature rises by a few degrees, WBCs become more active. They then fight the infection harder. Also, most bacteria do not grow further at higher temperature. Thus fever helps the body to quash bacterial infection.

Even loss of appetite denies the bacteria necessary glucose to survive and multiply. The aches and pains force a person to lie down and conserve energy to fight the infection.

Fever, aches and pains, loss of appetite, and desire to lie down are part of an adaptive response coordinated by the hypothalamus to help you survive an infection.

In simple fevers, it may be enough to take rest, go on a fast, and drink lots of water to wash away the toxins and bacteria.

21

Cancer and Aids

What Is Cancer?

Consider that you have an injury. Then the cells around the injury divide, and reproduce to replace the cells damaged by the injury. Once new cells fill the injury, the cells stop to reproduce. This is the normal case.

But sometimes they do not stop, and continue reproducing which develops into a lump or tumour. This uncontrollable growth of cells is called cancer.

Often, such abnormal cells travel to other part/s of the body through blood, and begin reproducing there. The earlier the cancer is detected, the better are the chances of cure.

21.1 CANCER AND IMMUNE SYSTEM

No one can predict the actual causes of cancer. Some people get it, and some do not. It is believed that cancer develops because the body's immune system is overpowered. But if your immune system is strong, your body can keep cancers dormant for years.

You may also say that cancer is an overactive response of the immune system. Thus cancer attacks you in both ways, that is, when your immune system gets too weak and also when it becomes overactive.

Hence to prevent and cure cancer, you have to have an immune system that is strong, and that which is calm or not overactive.

Risk Factors for Cancer

Cancer is a man-made disease triggered due to pollution, unhealthy diet and stress in living style. There has been huge increase in cancer cases since the Industrial Revolution.

High-fat low-fibre diet is associated with colon and rectal cancer. Such a diet coupled with hormonal imbalance is linked to breast and prostate cancer. Breast-feeding reduces the chance of developing breast cancer.

Irritation in any part of the body over a long period can develop into cancer.

Smoking is a well established cause of irritations and cancers of oesophagus, pharynx, mouth, and lymph nodes. But through blood, cancer can spread to distant parts of body. Even those who do not smoke but are exposed to cigarette smoke have higher rates of lung cancer. Those who chew tobacco have higher rates of mouth cancer. Consumption of alcohol along with tobacco increases cancer risk.

All these factors have two things in common:

1. They increase the formation of and exposure of the body to free radicals.
2. They weaken the immune system.

21.2 DR BLOCK'S CANCER THERAPY

Dr Block's therapy includes macrobiotic diet, antioxidants and positive attitude.

Macrobiotic diet includes whole grains, brown rice, oats, beans, legumes, vegetables, low fat curd with plenty of omega-3, omega-9, soy, nuts, seeds, and some fish.

It is strictly meat-less. There is evidence that chemicals in meat promote cancer. The diet excludes alcohol and refined sugar, and prohibits table salt, yeast, dairy foods, eggs, tomatoes, most fats, processed foods and beverages.

High doses of vitamins A, D, E, C and B6, Coenzyme Q10 and bioflavonoids, foods like broccoli, garlic, mineral as organic selenium, and soybeans are given.

Nutrients like vitamin B6 and Coenzyme Q10 may help body avoid damage caused by cancer treatments such as that due to chemotherapy.

High beta-carotene foods like carrots, bell-peppers, etc., also provide cancer protection.

Foods high in germanium – garlic and onions – are effective in preventing cancers.

Emotional Intervention

Dr Block shows how meditation, prayer and positive imaging support immune system. Help the patient to develop positive attitude, zest for life, feeling of well-being and love.

Some diets may become restrictive so much as to result in malnourishment. Do not treat the diet with dogma. It is more important for the patient to remain happy.

21.4 IMPORTANT DIETARY RECOMMENDATIONS

In addition to the diet recommended in Chapter 20 for nutrients and anti-inflammatory foods for a strong immune system, particular mention may be made of the following:

Lemon

Lemon kills cancer cells. It is as effective, if not more, as chemotherapy.

Vitamin C, as in *amla*, celery, lemon, fruits and vegetables, helps in preventing cancer.

Linus Pauling who was awarded Nobel Prize for Chemistry in 1954 advanced the idea that vitamin C could be even used to treat cancer. It is selectively toxic to cancer cells.

Peels of lemon, orange and grapefruits kill enzymes that spur the growth of cancer cells.

Apples and Grapes

Finnish researchers found that those who ate apples were 58 per cent less likely to develop lung cancer.

Polyphenols in grapes can prevent and cure tumours. In her book *The Grape Cure* (1928), Johanna Brandt wrote that she cured her stomach cancer with the power of purple grapes.

Cumin, Turmeric, Ginger and Neem

Cumin has the most powerful anti-cancer properties. It blocks chromosome damage by cancer-causing chemicals.

By consuming anti-inflammatory foods like turmeric, ginger and neem liberally we can reduce the risk of cancer. According to James Fuchs at Ohio State University, curcumin interacts with certain proteins to generate anti-cancer activity in the body. It can help kill cancer cells and stop them from spreading.

Cloves, Cinnamon and Saffron

Eugenol in cloves acts against cancer cells.

Cinnamon is an anti-microbial food. It stops the growth of bacteria as well as fungi. A recent study conducted by the US Department of Agriculture said that cinnamon reduced the proliferation of leukemia, and lymphoma cancer cells.

Saffron is used in Ayurveda to treat cancerous tumours.

Carotenes

Carotenes and all natural antioxidants have immune enhancing effects. Higher the intake of carotenes, the lower is the incidence of cancer.

Consume yellow/deep orange vegetables/fruits like carrots, pumpkin, squash, sweet potatoes, etc., that contain beta-carotene, the powerful antioxidant.

Mustard, Broccoli, Cabbage, and Cauliflower

Sulforaphane in these vegetables is the most powerful plant chemical that fights cancer.

Broccoli and cabbage stimulate excretion of oestrogen, linked to breast cancer risk.

Researchers at Rosewell Park Center Institute at Buffalo found that just three servings a month of raw broccoli/cabbage can reduce the risk of bladder cancer by as much as 40 per cent.

Beets

The purple crimson pigment betacyanin in beets is a proven cancer fighter.

Garlic and Onions

As mentioned before, allicin and germanium in garlic and onions enhance immune function. According to researches of Carlotta Galeone and others of Instituto di Ricerche Farmacologiche in Milan, people whose diets are rich in onions, garlic, and other alliums have a lower risk of several cancers like that of mouth, larynx, oesophagus, colon, breast, ovary, and kidney.

Celery

Coumarins in celery also prevent cells from becoming cancerous. Acetylenics, another set of compounds in celery, stop the growth of tumour cells.

Tomatoes

Eating tomatoes (lycopene) is linked to less risk of cancer.

Olive Oil

There is evidence that antioxidants rich omega-9 olive oil fights cancer.

Researchers at Harvard and University of Athens found that women who had olive oil in more than one meal a day cut the risk of breast cancer by 25 per cent. Breast cancer rates in Mediterranean countries are 50 per cent lower than in USA. Olive oil can reduce oxidative damage to body cells that can initiate cancer development.

Almonds

Apart from olive oil, get your omega-9 from almonds. Vitamin E, a powerful antioxidant in almonds, gives them the reputation of an anti-cancer food.

Flaxseeds and Mustard

Researchers at Duke University Medical Center, North Carolina, evaluated the role of omega-3 on men who were scheduled to undergo surgery for prostate cancer. They found that the cancer growth diminished in those who ate flaxseeds. Mustard also has omega-3.

Tea

Green tea has anti-cancer properties. Black tea also has some but in a lesser extent. The effect may, however, be nullified if milk and sugar are added to tea.

Red grapes/wine, dark chocolates, blueberries, garlic, soy, and teas are foods that starve cancer cells. Angiogenesis Foundation head William Li says that what we eat is really our chemotherapy three times a day.

Wheat Grass

Wheat grass has preventive and curative properties against cancers. You can plant wheat in seven pots. Then you can use the new grass from one pot every day of the week.

Sada-Bahar (Periwinkle)

These pink and white perennial flowers are strongly believed to be a cure for cancer. They contain several chemical compounds some of which are similar to drugs used for treating cancer.

21.5 PREVENTIVE MEASURES

- **Do not smoke.** Smoking is the single most cancer-causing factor. About 87 per cent of lung cancer deaths are linked to smoking. It also contributes to cancers of bladder, pancreas, liver, colon and others.
- **Dietary factors** account for almost 30 per cent of cancers. Especially detrimental to cancer patients are meat, saturated

fats and inflammation causing omega-6 fats found in corn, vegetable oils and margarines. Junk, processed and refined foods should be avoided.

- **Limit consumption of alcohol.** A little red wine may cut prostate cancer risk to half. But a large glass of wine a day increases the risk of liver and bowel cancer by a fifth.
- **Do not take iron supplements** as excess iron levels in blood only increases the risk of developing cancer cells. Excess iron suppresses the ability of WBCs to kill cancer cells.
- **Do not take cold water after meals.** It forms sludge with oily food. The breakdown products promote cancer. It is best to take hot soup or liquids with meals.

21.6 OTHER RECOMMENDATIONS

Detoxify

Follow a fasting program to detoxify, and decrease the load on the digestive system. Taking fruits on empty stomach helps in detoxifying the system.

Use enemas for cleansing the colon with lemon and water, or garlic and water.

Beware of High Oestrogen Levels

Female hormone oestrogen stimulates cells in breasts and female reproductive system to divide faster which may lead to cancer of gall-bladder, cervical, uterine, breast, etc.

Other Measures

Use only glass and wooden cookware to avoid carcinogenic elements in metallic wares. Avoid microwave ovens. They may have radiation leakage.

Even cell phones are harmful. They emit radiation even when switched off. Sit at least 8 feet away from television screens. Also avoid X-rays.

Avoid use of chemicals, hair sprays, pesticides, aerosols, cosmetics, etc. Chemicals form free radicals, damage healthy cells, and lead to formation of cancerous cells.

Pesticide residues are ranked as a high cancer risk factor.

21.7 COMBATING CANCER BY HAVING AN IMMUNE SYSTEM THAT IS STRONG AND NOT OVERACTIVE

Sleep

Prolonged exposure to light dampens the brain's ability to produce melatonin, a hormone that triggers sleep by producing serotonin and plays a key role in the production of powerful cancer-fighting immune cells.

Women who produce the most melatonin at night not only get restful sleep, but they also have 32 per cent lower risk of breast, uterine, and ovarian cancer.

Darkness is your brain signal to start producing melatonin. The less light you have in your bedroom; the better it is for sleep. Hence draw curtains, turn off every light, shut down the computer, and turn the clock away from your face.

Exercise

Exercise promotes general well being, and helps overcoming depression. Cancer is much less common in physically active people. Physical fitness brings protection against cancer.

In a long term study of some 6000 US women, researchers led by James McClain at National Cancer Institute found that those who exercised the most had 25 per cent lower chance of developing cancer.

Avoid Stress

Stress is the greatest culprit in many chronic and degenerative diseases, and in weakening of the immune system. As much as possible, avoid it or learn to de-stress with relaxation.

Shun away from people and situations that cause you tension.

Massage Therapy

New research demonstrates that regular massages stimulate the production of natural killer cells, a key component in immune health.

Spirituality

Be a spiritual person. Know that cause of suffering is not outside. It is inside you. Practise meditation, mindfulness, awareness, development of virtues, compassion, etc. Have hope and faith. Keep your mind calm and positive.

21.8 OVARIAN, BREAST AND UTERINE CANCER

Ovarian cancer is a silent killer. It is very hard to detect as there are no early symptoms. Women who choose not to have a baby have normal menstrual cycles. But ovulation occurs all the time. This hyper-ovulation in some cases leads to ovarian cancer.

Since these women do not breast-feed, there arises a greater risk of breast cancer as well. The American Cancer Society has published a report which says that a woman who has had children has a lower risk of ovarian cancer.

Female hormone oestrogen is considered to be the most likely cause of breast cancer. Oestrogen promotes cellular growth in breast tissues and female reproductive organs. Some risk factors are early menses, late menopause, having childbirth after the age of forty, having no children, or too many child births. Obese women have higher levels of oestrogen.

Obesity and use of hormonal replacement therapy (HRT) increase risk of uterine cancer.

Fibre as in wheat bran can reduce oestrogen levels.

Breast Milk and Breast Feeding

Breast feeding cuts breast cancer risk. Researchers at Lund University and University of Gothenburg Sweden found that breast milk contains a protein and a fatty acid which together can kill 40 types of cancer cells.

It has been found recently that getting enough of choline in your diet (egg yolk, soybeans, legumes, fatty foods, lecithin) cuts risk of breast cancer.

Ashwagandha and *Shatavari* herbs together help to increase milk in breasts.

Mediterranian Diet

Scientists of North Western University School of Medicine, Chicago, discovered why diet rich in fruits and vegetables, and olive oil (which is rich in oleic acid) can help protect women from breast cancer by blocking action of cancer causing oncogene.

Karela/Bitter Gourd

Ratna Ray along with other scientists from Saint Louis University, USA, found that *karela* extract killed breast cancer cells and prevented them from multiplying.

21.9 ORAL AND LUNG CANCER AND CANCERS OF COLON/ RECTUM

More than 85 per cent of oral cancers are linked to tobacco use, and lung cancer is linked to smoking. Those who are addicted to both tobacco and alcohol are at greater risk than people who have only one addiction.

How to Prevent Oral Cancer?

Avoid smoking, chewing tobacco and consumption of alcohol. Maintain good oral and dental hygiene.

Tomatoes – According to an Italian study, those who ate seven or more servings of raw tomatoes a week had a 60 per cent less chance of developing colon, rectal and stomach cancer.

Mangoes – Study by Texas AgriLife shows that polyphenols in mangoes are selectively effective against breast and colon cancer cells, and they do not harm normal cells.

21.10 SKIN CANCER

The most common skin cancer occurs over the skin as ulcerous growth. It is more common among fair-skinned people. The other kind occurs under the skin. The third, a much more serious one, develops as a malignant tumor in the deeper layers of the skin.

The cause usually is over-exposure to UV rays of the sun damage causing to the tissues, and harm to the normal repair mechanism of the skin.

Drink upto four cups of tea (preferably green) daily. Tea drinkers have lower skin cancer risk. Antioxidants in tea may limit the skin damage by UV radiation.

A diet rich in vitamin E, such as asparagus (*Shatavari*), green leafy vegetables, nuts, wheat germ, etc., protects skin from UV rays' damage. Most importantly protect your skin from the sun. Stay in shade.

21.11 PROSTATE AND BLADDER CANCER

Prostate Cancer

Mayo Clinic research has revealed that quercetin may prevent or stop the growth of prostate cancer by blocking the hormones that encourage the growth of cancer cells.

Quercetin is present in concentrated amounts in tea, apples, strawberries, other berries, onions, and red wine, and in relatively high amounts in broccoli and spinach.

In a study in Japan, men who drank 5-6 cups of green tea daily had their prostate cancer risk cut by half compared to those who drank less than a cup per day.

How to Prevent Prostrate Cancer?

Pomegranates: According to Dr Allan Pantuck of University of California, the effect of pomegranate is so marked that men can live out a full lifespan without the need for treatment of prostate cancer. The juice destroys prostate cancer cells.

Fruits, as mentioned before, are recommended as possible protection against prostate cancer. Lycopene and active substances in tomatoes and water melon not only reduce prostate enlargement but also cut prostate cancer risk.

Whole Milk/vitamin D: Researchers at University of Hawaii claim that whole milk may help prevent prostate cancer. Vitamin D is fat soluble. Drinking full-cream milk increases vitamin D absorption.

21.12 LEUKEMIA

It is often called blood cancer. Leukemia, in fact, is a cancer of tissues.

In leukemia, millions of abnormal and immature WBCs called leucocytes are released into the bloodstream and the lymph system. These immature cells cannot fight infection.

The uncontrolled multiplication of abnormal cancer cells results in crowding out of the WBCs, RBCs and platelets so that WBCs cannot fight infections, RBCs cannot prevent anaemia, and platelets cannot control haemorrhaging.

Chemotherapy is by far the current method of treating leukemia. Powerful antioxidant EGCG in tea prompted leukemia cells to die in 80 per cent samples tested at Mayo College.

21.13 HUMAN IMMUNO-DEFICIENCY VIRUS (HIV), HUMAN PAPILLOMA VIRUS (HPV) AND ACQUIRED IMMUNO-DEFICIENCY SYNDROME (AIDS)

The best advice that can be given to avoid these diseases is to practise discretion and precaution in physical relationship and to follow a regimen of strict cleanliness.

HIV

Anti-retroviral therapy (ART) is being used to arrest its progression. The best advice is to eat nutritious food, and to follow a healthy living style. Eating well is the key to treating HIV-positive patients as malnutrition weakens the immune system, lowering resistance to secondary effects.

Lemon/Lime Juice – Australian researcher Roger Short of the University of Melbourne has suggested that lemon or lime juice used vaginally can prove to be a sperm-killing contraceptive.

Bananas – BanLec the lectin found in bananas is as potent as anti-HIV drugs, says David Marvovitz, professor of internal medicine at University of Michigan.

Yoghurt – Probiotics found in yoghurt have been genetically modified by researchers in the US to produce a drug that blocks HIV infection.

Cow's First Milk – It is well known that mother's first milk develops the immune system of the baby.

Amul India has now developed a product from the cow's first milk to be used as a spray in mouth from where it travels to the heart and there onwards it is pumped around the body. This oral spray helps the human immune system combat viruses including HIV and H1N1.

AIDS

HIV is a precursor to AIDS. The same line of treatment is to be followed as for HIV.

Ayurveda, however, treats this problem as lack of '*oj*', the vital energy in the body, and excess of '*aam*', the toxins. It aims at developing a strong but quieter immune system by leading a disciplined and balanced sex life.

St. Johns Wort is a natural blood purifier. It fights AIDS virus. Alpha Lipoic Acid, an antioxidant, may prevent and treat HIV and AIDS.

21.14 MIRACLE OF PRANAYAM AND MEDITATION

Ramneek Wig narrates in his book *The Miracles of Pranayam* how he was diagnosed with cancer, and told by doctors that he had only a year to live. Chemotherapy and bone marrow transplant cured his disease but it soon relapsed.

He then began practising pranayam regularly, and has been healthy ever since.

Meditation slows progression of AIDS in just a few weeks of practice by strengthening the immune system. Researchers at University of California, Los Angeles, led by David Creswell found that the more often the volunteers meditated, the higher their counts of T-cells, a measure of the ability of the immune system in fighting the AIDS virus.

22
Endocrine System: Thyroidism and Diabetes

There are two types of glands secreting hormones and other essential substances in the body:

1. Exocrine glands
2. Endocrine glands

Exocrine glands secrete substances through a duct or tube, usually leading to an outside surface. Examples are salivary glands, sweat glands, and prostate gland.

The endocrine system comprises glands that secrete substances directly into the bloodstream, which carries it to tissues, or organs where it stimulates the required action.

Endocrine glands work together in monitoring the body's various functions. The substances synthesised are hormones, antibodies, and prostaglandins.

22.1 ENDOCRINE GLANDS

Some of the important glands and their functions are as follows:

Pituitary Gland

The pituitary gland regulates and controls other glands, and that is why it is known as the master gland. For example, it secretes thyroid-stimulating hormone (TSH), and hormones namely growth hormone

(GH), oxytocin and gonadotrophic hormone (GnH) to stimulate adrenal and reproductive glands respectively.

GH stimulates the growth of bones, and other tissues.

TSH stimulates secretion of thyroxin from thyroid gland while GnH boosts production of sperms and testosterone hormone in men, and egg and oestrogen hormone in women.

Oxytocin stimulates the uterus to contract and maintain labour during childbirth. It causes production of milk in breast glands. It is referred to as the 'cuddle hormone'.

It is seen that a healthy pituitary gland is essential not only for healthy metabolism and functioning of the body, but also for body's gender physiology. Needless to say that good nutrition is very important to keep the pituitary healthy. Magnesium and potassium are important to the functioning of the pituitary.

Thyroid Gland

It secretes thyroxin hormones T3 and T4. They are synthesised in the gland from trace mineral iodine. Thyroxin controls body's metabolism.

Diseases of the thyroid gland result in either production of too much or too little thyroxin. Too little thyroxin can cause excessive fat to accumulate which results in weight gain, sluggishness, low energy level, low BP, lowered basal body temperature making one feel colder, and lethargic. This is called under active thyroid, or hypothyroidism.

Too much thyroxin can cause body's fat to be burnt faster which results in opposite symptoms such as weight loss, excessive sensitivity to heat, feeling hot all the time, and so on. This is called over active thyroid or hyperthyroidism.

Parathyroid Gland

The hormones produced by it control calcium and phosphorous levels in the body.

If we do not get enough calcium from diet, parathyroid secretes hormones that take calcium from bones to make it available in blood for the important functions of nerve conduction and muscle contraction.

Thymus Gland

Located in the center of the chest, it helps in strengthening the immune system. After puberty, thymus starts shrinking, and may even atrophy with age.

Vitamins C, E, and B6 are important for thymus, as are antioxidants, and minerals zinc and selenium to maintain it's functioning, and to prevent it from atrophy.

22.2 HYPERTHYROIDISM

When thyroid gland becomes overactive, it produces more thyroxin hormones. It is called hyperthyroidism. There is an increase in the metabolic rate in cells and is followed by weight loss. Diarrhoea and tremors may also occur.

Treatment involves use of drugs that reduce the amount of thyroxin produced by the gland. But these drugs often have serious reactions.

The other treatment is to knock down the gland by administering radioactive iodine or by surgery, and then handling a sluggish gland by a more easily amenable treatment that is for hypothyroidism.

Preventive cures:

- **De-stress and Relax**
- **Pranayam and Meditation**
  Simple, slow deep breathing is recommended. Vigourous Pranayams should be avoided. Thyroid glands need calming down. Meditation on breath is the best remedy.
- **Water Cure**
  Accumulation of toxins is another cause. Water cure and fresh fruit juices are the best way to cleanse the system.
- **No iodised salt**
  Iodine may be playing havoc with your glands. It is best to stop using iodised salt and instead, use natural rock salt. The

table below lists the iodine content of some foods.

Food	Iodine Content, mcg/100 g
Iodised salt	3000
Seafood	66
Meat, eggs	26
Dairy	13
Bread, cereals	10
Fruits	4

Fruits and cereals are best. Avoid foods and supplements containing iodine.

- **Improve diet**
  Since the thyroid hormone production is at a high level, one needs more food to be metabolised. Hence, one should increase the volume of one's diet. Add more proteins to your diet.
  Minerals such as calcium and phosphorous should be increased to twice the normal requirement.
  It is also necessary to consume extra fats, otherwise the hormone will consume body's stored fat. That is how one goes on losing weight.
  Foods that supress thyroid activity are cabbage, cauliflower, broccoli, Brussels sprouts, kale, spinach, turnips, soy, beans, mustard green (*Sarson ka Saag*), peaches, and pears.
  Stay away from refined foods, sugar, and all stimulants including coffee.

22.3 HYPOTHYROIDISM

This results from under-activity of the gland. Thyroxin production falls below normal leading to fatigue, sluggishness, depression, constipation, and weight gain.

The cause is usually poor nutrition. Going on dieting can permanently inhibit thyroid function. A condition like goitre (*jheenga*) may develop.

Iodine deficiency is also a common cause. Use iodised salt.

22.4 DIABETES

Diabetes occurs when blood sugar levels are higher than normal. Table below shows desirable, borderline, and high-risk levels of blood sugar:

Blood Sugar	Desirable	Borderline	High Risk
Fasting	80-100	100-120	>120
PP	140-150	150-200	>200

Insulin, which helps the body convert sugar (glucose) from foods into energy, is a key factor in diabetes. The high sugar levels occur:

1. When pancreas does not secrete enough insulin.
2. When body cells become resistant to insulin. It is referred to as insulin resistance.

Accordingly, there are two types of diabetes: Type-1 and Type-2. Type-1 diabetes is associated with juvenile onset, while Type-2 has adult onset.

Type-1 Diabetes

Type-1 diabetes, also referred to as insulin-dependent diabetes, is characterised by destruction of beta cells of the pancreas resulting in insulin deficiency. It is thus caused due to body's inability to produce enough insulin.

Type-2 Diabetes

Type-2 diabetes is referred to as non-insulin dependent diabetes. It is the most common form of diabetes in which there is resistance to the action of insulin (insulin resistance), and later on decreased insulin release from pancreas to metabolise glucose produced from food. To maintain a normal blood glucose level, pancreas has to secrete additional insulin. In some cases, body cells resist or do not respond to even high levels of insulin resulting in the build-up of glucose in the blood.

What is Impaired Glucose Tolerance (IGT)?

Impaired glucose tolerance or glucose intolerance is a state associated with insulin resistance. It means one has increased glucose levels following a meal.

Eventually glucose toxicity may cause further impairment of insulin secretion by beta cells.

Eating right and exercising can go a long way in stabilising blood sugar levels. During exercise, muscles use the sugar available in the blood reducing blood sugar level.

Eating a diet low in sugars and fat, and high in fibre can prevent blood sugar levels from rising abnormally.

Glycemic Index (GI) of Foods

Glycemic index of a food indicates how it compares with glucose. Glycemic index of glucose is taken for reference, and is assigned a value of 100.

A food, which raises the sugar level as fast as glucose, will have glycemic index of 100. Foods with high amount of sugar and fat and with very little fibre have high GI. White sugars, white flour, white rice, and potatoes have very high GI. Alcohol with empty calories is the worst. Other examples are sweets, fats, and fruits like grapes, banana, *chiku*, and mango.

Diabetics should take low glycemic index foods. Low GI foods do not raise the sugar level abruptly. Foods with fibre, like complex carbohydrates such as whole grain cereals, unpolished rice, etc., have low GI. Other foods in the low GI diet include vegetables, most fruits except a few, whole grains, beans, legumes, quinoa, etc.

Milling and polishing brown rice removes most of its fibre, vitamins and minerals like zinc and chromium.

David J A Jenkins, lead author of a study by University of Toronto says that foods like beans and nuts provide better control of diabetes than even the whole grain diet.

Symptoms of Diabetes

The symptoms of diabetes include the following:

1. Excessive urination as sugar reaches a limit which the blood cannot hold. This causes kidneys to fail in reabsorbing water.
2. Excessive thirst because of dehydration caused by frequent urination.
3. Excessive hunger and eating, as sugar is not metabolised to produce energy required by the tissue cells, and the patient feels fatigued.

Ill Effects of Diabetes

Glucose is the preferential form of fuel supply in the body. In diabetes, glucose is denied entry into cells due to a problem with insulin supply and resistance.

This simple defect gives rise to many serious complications. When sugar levels rise they can damage the eyes, kidneys, nerves, heart, and arteries.

Primary complication is coma when blood sugar levels go too high. The body then tries to mobilise its fat for fuel. As a result, fat floats freely in the bloodstream causing destruction of blood vessels with atherosclerosis leading to heart attack, and stroke. Alternatively, body tries to utilise protein from its lean tissues.

Most areas in the body are flexible in regard to the fuel they use. But, the eye-lens, nerves, brain, lungs, kidney, and vascular walls are totally dependent on glucose as fuel. These parts of body become vulnerable to damage when diabetes is not controlled.

There are functions of insulin other than metabolising glucose. They include protein synthesis, wound healing, providing resistance against a disease, and production of certain brain chemicals. A diabetic is, therefore, prone to muscle wasting and poor wound healing.

A diabetic has plenty of glucose in the bloodstream. The kidneys have the responsibility of filtering this excess glucose from the bloodstream. For the purpose, body demands excessive water (hence thirst). This causes excessive urination.

It may result in destruction of kidneys often requiring dialysis to save them.

Causes and Treatment

Apart from genetics and heredity, diabetes can be caused by overweight or obesity, wrong food habits, lifestyle, lack of exercise, and stress.

Type-1 diabetes patients require injections of insulin to maintain a normal sugar level. Type 2-diabetes is divided into two subgroups: obese and non-obese.

The most common cause of Type-2 diabetes is obesity as it results in insulin resistance. Obese people have 400 per cent greater chance of developing diabetes. Among overweight people, a loss of only 5 kg in weight can lower diabetes risk by as much as 60 per cent. Remember that it is not just the weight loss but more importantly the thinning of waist line that is required to beat insulin resistance.

There is overwhelming evidence indicting Western diet of fast foods, snacks, fats, sugars, soft drinks, etc., for causing diabetes.

A diet high in complex carbohydrates and fibre (HCF), low in sugars, fat, and animal foods has consistently demonstrated superior therapeutic effect in treatment of diabetes.

The old school diabetic treatment recommended high protein diet. This often accelerated the process towards heart disease. With HCF diet, there is no sudden rise in blood sugar level. Additionally, this diet reduces cholesterol and triglyceride levels, and raises good HDL.

During stress, some hormones are released which work against insulin. Therefore stress can result in onset of diabetes or uncontrolled glucose in old cases.

Can one control Type-2 diabetes with diet, exercise and stress management?

In a study conducted at University of California, Los Angeles, participants ate meals low in fat (12-15 per cent), moderate in protein (15-20 per cent), and high in complex carbohydrates (65-70 per cent). They walked 45-60 minutes everyday, and ate no refined carbohydrates.

In just 3 weeks, 6 out of 13 were diabetes-free. They had normal sugar levels.

Exercise with Precaution

Exercise boosts the utilisation of sugar by tissues. Thus it lowers blood sugar levels. It prevents obesity which could lead to insulin resistance.

One should not however exercise when the blood sugar level is likely to be low.

Always keep a packet of sugar and some carbohydrate-rich snack with you while you exercise so that you can take them at the first warning of symptoms of low blood-sugar level.

Stress Management and Sleep

Avoid stress. But at least manage it if you cannot avoid. Use relaxation techniques. Like pranayam and meditation. Pursue hobbies, and listen to soothing music.

Previous studies have found that several nights of poor sleep can result in impaired use of insulin, but now Esther Donga of Leiden University Medical Centre in Netherlands found that partial sleep restriction of a single night reduced insulin sensitivity by 19-25 per cent.

Recommendations for Diet

- **Chromium and Zinc**
  Zinc plays an important role in the processes involving insulin production. Chromium assists insulin in allowing glucose into cells. Legumes, and certain other foods like melon, garlic, onions, etc., are chromium-rich. White flour, white rice and white sugar are depleted of both chromium and zinc.

- **Magnesium**

  Magnesium regulates blood sugar by influencing the amount of insulin secreted. Magnesium is present in abundant quantities in all types of seeds, particularly sunflower and pumpkin seeds.

- **Cinnamon**

  Cinnamon is an easy non-drug therapy for reducing blood sugar. A powerful phenol compound in cinnamon increases glucose metabolism by as much as 20-fold. Take ¼ tsp of cinnamon in a cup of tea right after lunch and dinner.

  Hlebowicz and researchers at Malmo University Hospital in Sweden found that adding one teaspoon of cinnamon to a bowl of rice pudding helped in lowering blood sugar level.

- **Coffee and Tea**

  Data gathered by researchers at University of Minnesota states that consuming 4-6 cups of regular or decaf coffee daily lowers diabetes risk by 22 per cent. Rachel Huxley of University of Sidney found that every additional cup of coffee consumed each day reduced the risk of diabetes by 7 per cent. And in studies that examined tea drinking, people who drank over 3-4 cups of tea daily were at 18 per cent lower risk of diabetes.

- **Vinegar**

  Vinegar helps controlling blood sugar and insulin levels when taken after/during a meal. However, it should not be taken in excess.

- **Coconut Oil**

  Coconut oil protects against insulin resistance, a major factor leading to Type-2 diabetes.

- *Sadabahar* **(periwinkle)** is supposed to aid in normalising the blood sugar level. Take 5 leaves and flowers of *sadabahar* on empty stomach in the morning.

- *Jamun* (Jamboo) fruit has been shown to bring down blood sugar in 3-4 months. Its seeds can also be powdered and taken with water 3-4 times daily. During its season, dry and grind the seeds, and use them during off-season.

- **Pumpkin and Carrots**

  Study by researchers led by Tao Xia of East China Normal University has found that compounds in pumpkin could drastically reduce daily insulin injections.

  New research suggests that brilliant orange-coloured carotenoid in carrots and pumpkin prevents the progressive destruction of pancreatic beta cells.

- *Kundru*

  A 3-month study conducted by the Institute of Population Health and Clinical Research, Bangalore, shows that *kundru*, a cousin of *parwal* vegetable, can reduce blood sugar. The team found that consuming 50 grams of *kundru* daily by new diabetics decreased their fasting blood sugar level by 16 per cent.

- *Herbs*

  Kari-Pata

  Kari-Pata (curry leaves) is India's traditional diabetic remedy. It slows down the action of a digestive enzyme in the breakdown of dietary starch to glucose. This leads to a more even trickle of glucose into the bloodstream from the intestine.

  Fenugreek/*Methi* seeds and leaves are effective in controlling blood sugar levels. It is claimed that by taking a few leaves of *neem* with cumin seeds/*jeera* and *ajwain* (celery) over a period of 30 days, the blood sugar level will come back to normal.

  Juice of Bitter gourd/*karela* should be taken with a little lemon in the morning. Mixed juice of *karela*, cucumber and tomatoes is even better.

  Neem and turmeric should also be consumed by diabetics every day. *Karela-Jamun* and *Neem-Karela* powders for diabetes are being marketed these days.

  Brinjal/egg plant is anti-diabetic.

  Gurmar Booti/**Gymnema** is found mostly in southern India and Madhya Pradesh. *Gurmar* means sugar-killer. It has been recommended for centuries for reducing blood sugar. Its leaves suppress glucose absorption. Scientists say it increases the effectiveness of insulin rather than causing the body to produce more insulin.

Amla also helps in diabetes.

22.5 HYPOGLYCEMIA

'Hypo' means low, and 'glycemia' means sugar. Hypoglycemia means low blood sugar. It is the opposite of diabetes. Take some sugar, and nutrient-rich foods to recover.

In the case of diabetics, the main cause of hypoglycemia is accidental or mistaken overdose of anti-diabetic medicine, insulin or oral drugs. Stress is a contributory factor for hypoglycemia. It is therefore necessary to take rest.

Since glucose is the primary fuel of the brain, hypoglycemia affects mental function. One may get blurred vision, confusion, convulsions, and depression.

Body tries to compensate for low blood sugar by increasing adrenal secretions. This may give rise to headache, sweating, trembling, heart palpitations.

Faulty diet, malnutrition, fasting, etc., could also cause hypoglycemia.

23
Respiratory System: Asthma

One can live without food for days together, and even without water for a few days, but one cannot survive a moment without air, rather oxygen.

Respiration involves both external as well as internal respiration by lungs. External respiration is the mechanical process of breathing – inhaling and exhaling. It involves exchange between lungs and atmosphere, of air during inhaling, and of carbon dioxide laden breath during exhaling.

Internal respiration is the exchange of gases which takes place in the cells within the tissues and organs of the body. In the process, tissue cells give away their carbon dioxide to the bloodstream and in exchange, absorb oxygen from the bloodstream. The blood carries away the carbon dioxide to the lungs to be exhaled out.

The respiratory system has upper and lower tracts, separated by pharynx.

Upper tract comprises nostrils and sinuses. Sinuses are air-filled expansions in the bones of the skull. Their function is to warm, humidify, and filter the inhaled air.

Pharynx is in the throat. It separates the nasal part of the throat from the oral part. The nasal part has lymphatic tissues called adenoids, and the oral part has lymphatic nodes called tonsils.

Lower tract comprises larynx, trachea, bronchi, and the lungs.

Larynx, also called the 'voice box', contains vocal cords that can vibrate to produce sound. Larynx is guarded by epiglottis that closes when one swallows food or water. Trachea is the windpipe. It bifurcates into two branches leading to each lung.

Bronchi or bronchial tubes are branches of trachea having mucous membrane which can trap foreign matter. Bronchi end in lung chambers.

Lung Chambers contain cavities and air sacs. The walls of the air sacs are moist and surrounded by capillaries. Exchange of carbon dioxide and oxygen between blood and air takes place through these walls.

23.1 ADENOIDITIS, TONSILITIS AND BRONCHITIS

In adenoiditis, the adenoids get inflamed when microorganisms infest the region. Enlarged adenoids obstruct the flow of air, forcing one to breathe through the mouth. This could affect the warming, moistening, and cleaning of the air.

Similar inflammation of tonsils is called tonsillitis. This is very common in children. Inflamed tonsils may cause fever, swollen glands with pus, and difficulty in breathing.

Bronchitis is the inflammation of the bronchi. It may be acute, or chronic. Acute bronchitis is accompanied by persistent cough, wheezing, and fever. Chronic bronchitis is usually caused by inhalation of air laden with dust, smoke, chemicals, etc., over a period of time. There is difficulty in breathing with chronic cough.

23.2 RESPIRATORY TRACT ALLERGIES, INFECTIONS, COLD VIRUS

An allergy is an over-active response by the body's immune system to certain substances identified as allergens that may or may not otherwise be harmful.

Common allergens for respiratory tract allergies are smoke, automobile exhausts, pollen, dust, dust mites, metals like nickel, cosmetics, animal hair, insect venom, moulds, cockroaches, insects, odours, drugs and chemicals.

Moulds are microscopic organisms that thrive inside carpets, sofas, and damp dark places.

Viruses responsible for a variety of respiratory infections are highly contagious. Usually a simple medicine and ample rest is enough to deal with them.

Vitamin A

It has been found that if you take vitamin A (beta-carotene) rich foods like carrots, mangoes, etc., over a long period, you develop immunity against respiratory problems.

Almonds

Chemicals present in the skin of almonds boost ability of WBCs to fight viral infections.

23.3 COLD, COUGH (*KHANSI*), FLU, INFECTION AND PNEUMONIA

Cold and cough can develop into pneumonia if immunity is weak. To treat pneumonia, strong antibiotics are needed. Following recommendations will provide relief and boost immunity:

Vitamins

Vitamin A enables you to develop immunity and keeps the mucus thin and fluid. Vitamin C rich foods boost immunity. Vitamin C helps in early stages of cold, and reduces its intensity. Do not take vitamin C tablet on empty stomach since it is acidic.

Honey

Honey is nature's own expectorant. Put honey on rear of tongue to bring relief in cough.

Ginger and/or tulsi juice mixed with honey retards the progression of cough.

Onions

Onions have antibacterial and antiseptic properties. Keep a few unpeeled onions near you. They will absorb flu virus. You will not contract flu. Even if you do, it will be mild.

Cloves

They soothe the throat and are safer and healthier than sugary cough syrups.

Eucalyptus Oil

Sprinkle a few drops of the oil on a cloth, and inhale frequently if you have a stuffy nose.

Pranayam

Breathe slowly and deeply to strengthen the lungs.

Humidify Your Room

Higher relative humidity results in shorter survival time for bacteria and viruses. Hence, a humidifier can reduce incidence of winter colds.

Homoeopathic Medicines

BC 6 biochemical combination increases resistance from flu virus. Ferrum Phos 6X is for mild fevers.

Aconite is given in early stages of cold. Bryonia is the best medicine for common cold. Euphrasia is for running nose. Kali Mur is for colds with thick white phlegm. Sambucus Nigra is for blocked nose and difficult breathing.

Ipeccac is good in cold with nausea, vomiting, and *khansi*.

Kali Bichrome is for harsh cough and asthma.

Merc Sol is recommended for sore throat accompanied by dysentery. Antimony Tart is for feverishness, chill and *khansi* with little expectoration. Rhus Tox is for feverishness during change of season and humidity.

23.4 ASTHMA

Asthma is an allergic disorder characterised by spasms, constricting and narrowing of airways, and secretion of mucus in lungs causing extreme difficulty in breathing. It may be accompanied by cough, wheezing if there is excessive mucus, and life-threatening inability to breathe. In asthma, the individual tries gasping for breath, reaching for fresh air near a window, or going outside, or running the fan at high speed. A sense of choking is felt in asthma. And the attack is worse when lying down.

Although brain comprises only 5 per cent body weight, it uses up 25 per cent of the oxygen in air we breathe. The brain is, therefore, adversely affected in asthma.

Haemoglobin in RBCs is responsible for carrying oxygen. The effect is, therefore, manifold if one simultaneously suffers from low haemoglobin.

Asthma is either hereditary or caused by environmental factors like humidity and temperature, and due to hypersensitivity to allergens like pollen, pollution from cars, tobacco, dust, chemicals, etc., or due to respiratory infection, or causes such as anxiety, stress, exertion, and so on.

A single gram of dust can hold thousands of dust mites. These microscopic cousins of spider are the worst allergy-causing offenders in dust. The best way to reduce dust mites is to use covers for cushions, mattresses, etc., and frequently wash them in hot water. Note that dust mites survive on the shed human skin.

To avoid cockroaches, make sure you have no standing water, left-over food, etc., for them to survive. Keep your kitchen clean. Pests won't stick around if there is nothing to sustain on. A humid house can have mould growth.

Asthmatic attacks are more common in late summer or early fall when pollen, smog, dust, etc., are at peak, and when temperature and pressure in the air are changing.

It is caused if your system is overfilled with waste matter, and cannot take it anymore.

Meta-bisulfite (MBS) chemical used as a preservative in processed foods may provoke a serious attack in individuals sensitive to asthmatic allergies.

Monosodium Glutamate (MSG) chemical used in Chinese foods causes a range of side effects named Chinese restaurant syndrome.

Those who consume MSG become deficient in vitamin B6. B6 deficiency impairs brain, and weakens breathing muscles.

Preventions and Treatment for Asthma

The following foods should be avoided in asthma as they cause mucus formation.

1. Heavy foods: Sweets, cakes, pastries, fats and fried foods, heavy protein diet, etc.
2. Cold foods: Sherbets, syrups, soft drinks, radishes, more than moderate amount of yoghurt, etc. Sipping warm drinks when under attack, or even otherwise, helps.
3. Sour foods: Raw mango, tamarind, lemon, sour tomatoes, sour yoghurt, etc.
4. Foods with gum (*lehs*): Okra, *arabi*, urad dal, etc.
5. Foods with MBS, MSG, preservatives and chemicals.

The treatment prescribed for asthma includes the use of antihistamines, inhalers, nebulizers and medications to dilate the bronchial tubes to allow more air to be taken in.

An oxygen cylinder must be kept ready for emergency purposes.

Wheezing and fever are indicative of serious infection and bronchitis. A course of antibiotics and sometimes steroids becomes necessary.

Dietary Recommendations for Asthma and Respiratory Problems

Eat light

Overall, it is recommended to eat light. Always keep the stomach soft and a little empty.

Vegetarian diet

A 1-year therapy with fully vegetarian diet provided significant improvement in 92 per cent non-vegetarian patients. The diet excluded even milk and milk products. Chlorinated tap water was prohibited. Coffee, tea, sugar, and salt were excluded.

Vegetables used freely included beets, carrots, celery, lettuce, onions, cabbage family, cucumber, artichokes, all beans except soybeans and green peas. Fruits were used freely. They included all berries, black currants, plums and pears. Berries have anti-asthmatic effects. Citrus fruits are to be avoided.

Beneficial effects of dietary regimen could be attributed to elimination of food allergens, and fatty acids found in animal products that cause allergies and inflammatory reactions.

Ginger Juice and Honey

Ginger dries up mucus. Honey is considered as a proven remedy for coughing spasms. Chew salted ginger at regular intervals to ease out phlegm.

Seetophala plus Honey

Seetophala, an Ayurvedic herb, suppresses and cures cough.

Black Peppers and Cloves

Consume them liberally in preparations. They, like ginger, eliminate cough.

Apple Juice

A study led by Professor Peter Burney of National Heart and Lung Institute, Imperial College, London, says that drinking apple juice could reduce the risk of developing asthma.

Apples suppress histamine production. Apart from flavonoids and various other nutrients, the benefit could also be due to improvement in haemoglobin level as a result of very easily absorbable iron in apples.

Tea with garam masala and tulsi

Tea with either garam masala or with tulsi leaves provides relief.

Turmeric

Ayurvedic practitioners consider turmeric as a wonder food for treating colds, cough and asthma. It works as a preventive as well as a curative remedy. Take turmeric with cow's milk at bedtime.

Garlic

It dissolves mucus in the sinuses, bronchial tubes, and lungs. Chinese and Egyptians have used it as a cure for respiratory problems. Hot soup garnished with garlic is also beneficial.

Figs

Fresh or dried figs are an Ayurvedic treatment for asthma.

Beta-carotene/Vitamin A

Foods rich in beta-carotene provide protection against lung disease/ inflammations. They are found in highest amounts in orange and red vegetables and fruits like carrots, pumpkin, squash, papaya, mangoes, bell peppers, and peaches.

It is very essential for an asthmatic to take foods rich in anti-infection vitamin A and carotenes to develop immunity and resistance against respiratory problems.

Coffee

Coffee contains natural chemicals similar to asthma medications. You may drink 2-3 cups of coffee daily to help control an asthma attack.

Cocoa

Theobromine in cocoa is more effective than codeine in treatment of coughs.

Alum (*Phitkari*)

Powdered alum placed on tongue is said to arrest an asthma attack.

Vitamin C

Vitamin C seems to reduce sensitivity to allergens by reducing histamine production.

Vitamin B6

Vitamin B6 is found to reduce the frequency and severity of asthma attacks. In fact, vitamin B6 protects from respiratory diseases. Consume foods rich in vitamin B6.

Magnesium-rich Foods

Asthma is a violent spasm of throat and chest muscles. Magnesium is involved in relaxation of nerves and muscles. Magnesium-rich foods will provide relief to asthmatics.

Haemoglobin/Iron

Since oxygen is transported to tissues and cells using haemoglobin as carrier, it is important that asthma patients improve their haemoglobin levels. Usually, their haemoglobin is low.

Anti-inflammatory Foods

Take MUFA like in olive oil, almonds and avocados, and omega-3 like in canola oil, mustard seeds, mustard oil, flaxseeds, broccoli, green leafy vegetables, tofu, etc.

Aspidosperma and Passiflora Mother Tinctures

Aspidosperma strengthens lungs, and Passiflora relaxes the respiratory system.

Pranayam

Lungs are exposed to air from outside. The air is most of the time laced with dust, pollutants, infections, and organisms. Over and above, lungs are exposed to a large supply of oxygen in air. Hence, cells in lungs are prone to damage by oxidation. In an asthmatic patient, lungs are already very weak.

It is ironic that the air we desperately need for our survival becomes the cause of our cellular demise.

Breathing exercises, though excellent for supplying oxygen to body, may harm lungs due to cellular oxidation. Slow deep breathing exercises or Pranayams (Chapter 32) is the answer. The best pranayams for an asthma patient are Kapal-Bhati and Anulom-Vilom. Do Anulom-Vilom for 15 minutes daily.

Pranic/Abdominal Breathing

Pranic or abdominal breathing technique of Pranayam is designed to curb over-breathing—the rapid shallow breaths in the top portion of the chest taken under stress.

Inhale deeply through the nose using the abdomen and diaphragm rather than the chest, as practised by singers and yogis, and then breathe out through the mouth.

How Can I Reduce My Dependence on Asthma Inhalers?

Asthma patients did slow breathing exercises. After three months, use of inhaler dropped by 86 per cent.

Pranayam increases the capacity of lungs to hold air (oxygen). It also trains the body to withstand lack of oxygen over longer periods thus helping to avoid asthmatic attack.

A patient on medication, deriphyline, antibiotics and inhalers for years left her daily dose of medication after starting Pranayams.

Meditation and Music

It is known that asthma is partly a psychosomatic disease. It is an example of an overactive immune system. Listening to music, practising meditation, and such other activities help one relax. Nilambri (day), Megh (night), and Bhairavi (any time) Ragas are particularly recommended. They take the mind away from any impending attack, in the process avoiding an attack altogether. Inculcating the habit of listening to soft music in his infant child, a father was able to cure the child of asthma almost for his whole life.

23.5 PROTECTING AND STRENGTHENING LUNGS

Lungs are the mainstay of a healthy respiratory system. Weak lungs not only cause frequent colds, coughs, etc., but may also lead to asthma, and other more serious diseases such as bronchitis, pneumonia, tuberculosis, and even cancer.

Lungs are a vulnerable organ of the body as they are directly exposed to particulate matter and pollutants in atmospheric air that is breathed in.

Risk factors for lung diseases are poor diet, shallow breathing, air pollution, exposure to chemicals, and advancing age. Smoking is the primary cause of serious lung disease COPD (Chronic Obstructive Pulmonary Disease), and cancer. COPD symptoms include bronchitis, shortness of breath, cough and fatigue.

A person who smokes has 20-25 times higher risk of developing lung cancer. Around 87 per cent of lung cancer deaths are linked to smoking. Quit smoking. This is the minimum you can do to protect your lungs. Passive smoking, air pollution, vehicle exhausts, etc., also damage the lungs. Exposure to asbestos is another risk factor for developing cancer of lungs.

And obesity has as much adverse an effect on lungs as on heart. It impairs lung function.

ACE Vitamins

Experts believe that vitamins A, C and E, the so called ACE antioxidants, can combat oxidative damage in lungs. People who take vitamin E supplement regularly for years have much reduced risk of COPD.

Vitamin E, in addition to vitamin C, selenium, and Coenzyme Q10, has the ability to slow down the oxidation of lungs.

Get your vitamin E from dark green leafy vegetables, olive oil, mustard oil, sunflower oil, sesame oil, butter, nuts, almonds, walnuts, whole wheat, wheat germ, soybeans, etc.

Co-enzyme Q10

It is a powerful antioxidant, aids blood circulation and improves oxygenation of cells. A supplement is usually necessary. Take 100mg daily.

Beta-carotene/Vitamin A protects lungs against inflammation. Vitamin K found in green leafy vegetables lowers the risk of lung cancer.

Broccoli

Researchers found that the activity of a healthy gene in lung cells increases because of sulforaphane in broccoli and its family of vegetables.

Apples

Finnish researchers found that those who ate apples were 58 per cent less likely to develop lung cancer.

Pippali (long peppers) are an age-old remedy for rejuvenating the lungs. To strengthen the lungs, take 7 ground *pippalis* with honey and cow's ghee with warm water for a year.

Aspidosperma Mother Tincture

It is a tonic for lungs as Digitalis is for the heart. It stimulates the respiratory centres, decreases carbon dioxide, and increases oxygen in the blood. It is an effective remedy in many cases of asthma. 'Want of breath' during exertion is the guiding symptom for it.

How to Clear Mucus from Lungs?

If you have mucus accumulated in bronchial tract, the process of strengthening lungs becomes difficult. Hence avoid foods that promote mucus such as milk, yoghurt, sweets, cakes, pastries, fats, fried foods, heavy proteins, sherbets, syrups, soft drinks, radishes, tamarind, okra, *arabi*, urad dal, etc.

Include in your diet more foods that are anti-mucus in function such as garlic, onions, fresh ginger, cayenne pepper, freshly ground black pepper, and warm drinks.

Lemon juice, honey and cayenne pepper are also recommended for drinking empty stomach in the morning.

Juices with Ginger and Cinnamon

Drink juices from fruits like apples, berries, pineapples, and vegetables celery, etc., with ginger juice and cinnamon at least once a day.

Antioxidants in grapefruit and pineapple juice help in making the lungs healthy. Take carrot juice that is rich in beta-carotene. Carrot and vegetable juices will alkalise your blood. Cranberry (*Karonda*) juice will help in fighting bacteria present in your lungs.

Tea with ginger/tulsi/black pepper/rose hips, or garam masala will help burn off mucus.

Breathing Exercises/Pranayam/Mindful Breathing

The breathing, the most important thing for our survival, is taken for granted.

Practise breathing exercises, by taking occasional deep breaths. Breathe from the diaphragm squeezing the stomach and internal organs. Develop a rhythm for your breathing. Do mindful-breathing or pranayams to strengthen your lungs. See Chapter 32.

Further, lungs are affected as much by the state of the mind as of the physical body.

It was observed that people had significantly poorer lung function after nurturing a level of long-standing anger or grievance.

23.6 PULMONARY EMBOLISM (PE)

Pulmonary embolism is the blockage of lung's main artery or its branch by a substance that has travelled from elsewhere in the body through bloodstream. Severe cases may lead to rapid breathing and rapid heart rate, very low BP, and sudden death. Usually it is due to blood clot from a vein in legs. The risk of PE is increased in prolonged bed rest/sitting, and cancer.

Asthma and heart patients should avoid long distance non-stop flights.

24

Urinary System

24.1 ANATOMY AND PHYSIOLOGY OF URINARY SYSTEM

The urinary system maintains the water-electrolyte balance by removing the waste products, such as uric acid, which are formed as after-products of metabolism.

The system comprises two kidneys, a pair of ureters connecting each kidney to the urinary bladder, and urethra from the bladder to discharge the urine.

24.2 KIDNEY FUNCTION AND FORMATION OF URINE

Kidneys are the filtration system of body fluids. While they remove the waste products of metabolism from the blood and eject them out of the body in the form of urine, they are said to retain 90 per cent of the nutrients, maintaining a balance of salts in the blood, and subsequently, a reasonably normal blood pressure.

Blood enters each kidney through a renal artery, which is further divided into a network of capillaries. These capillaries are subject to a process of filtration. The walls of these capillaries are thin enough to allow water, salts, sugar, uric acid, etc., to leave the bloodstream, but they do not allow larger molecules like proteins and blood cells to pass through.

Attached to the capillaries is a twisted renal tube. As water, salts, sugar, urea, and other wastes pass through these renal tubes, about 95 per cent of water, all of sugar and salts such as sodium, potassium, calcium, phosphorous, and chloride, are re-absorbed into the bloodstream through capillaries attached to each renal tube.

Thus, water is conserved, and a delicate balance of electrolytes is maintained.

The final urine contains only wastes, some water, salts, acids and toxic substances.

24.3 URINARY TRACT INFECTION (UTI)

Urinary tract infection is the most common type of bodily infection. In small children, use of diapers is a contributory cause. In adults, improper cleaning can be responsible. Long intervals between urinations can often cause UTI.

In women, bacteria may also be transferred from anus to vaginal areas causing infection.

Measures to Prevent UTI

- Too little water intake triggers UTI. Drink plenty of water and fluids to flush out bacteria.
- Women should wipe from vagina towards anus after defecation, and not the opposite way.
- Avoid tight clothing. It may irritate tissues, trap heat, and promote bacterial growth.
- Take foods rich in vitamin C since it reduces bacterial growth.
- Cranberry (*Karonda*) is a remedy. It may not be able to cure, but it can prevent UTI. Cranberry is one of the most powerful antioxidants.
- Homoeopathy recommends a few doses of Cantharis 30.

24.4 KIDNEY FAILURE

Kidney failure refers to the loss of the filtering ability of the kidneys. As a result of kidney failure, dangerous levels of fluid and waste accumulate in the bloodstream.

If one follows a proper diet, lifestyle and exercise, he/she can maintain a healthy kidney system as kidneys are capable of performing their function for the entire lifespan of an individual.

Kidney failure is of two kinds:

1. **Chronic Kidney Failure or Chronic Kidney Disease (CKD)** – CKD or chronic kidney disease occurs gradually when kidneys are overworked. The capillaries in the kidneys get blocked over time due to deposits. It becomes irreversible unless the deterioration of the kidneys is checked in time.
2. **Acute Kidney Failure** – Acute failure occurs when blood flow to kidneys is obstructed. This can happen after serious injury, complicated surgery, infections, etc. Such failure is usually reversible as kidneys can be brought to health once again.

Causes and Risk Factors

- High BP or hypertension, obesity, diabetes, and alcoholism are the most common causes. Hypertension causes the filtration rate to become too fast for effective purification of blood. Diabetes puts excessive load on kidneys.
- The other causes are infections, inflammations, irritable bowels, gastroenteritis, too little potassium content in body, dehydration, acidic diet, and too much phosphorous, sodium, proteins, etc. Smoking too is a cause since it causes stiffening of arteries. The outcomes of chronic kidney failure are often worse. The failure may result in heart attack, stroke, serious infection, and so on.
- Metals in water raise kidney risk. Many metals, especially lead, mercury, cadmium, and aluminum are toxic to kidneys. Avoid consuming water contaminated with such metals. This may become difficult as it depends on the city water supply which may be affected by some polluting industry around. Cadmium is found in excess in automobile exhausts.

  Early diagnosis of biomarkers homocysteine that causes atherosclerosis, aldosterone hormone that affects salt handling by kidneys, and high BP can save kidneys from failure.

Measures for Kidney Health

- Kidney inflammations can be treated with fish oil, and foods containing omega-3 fats.

- Avoid high protein intake, animal foods, excessive legumes, eggs, dairy, etc., containing purine that breaks down into uric acid.
- Drink 10-12 glasses of purified water daily.
- Eat more of garlic, potato, asparagus, watercress, celery, cucumber, papaya, banana, watermelon, pumpkin, sprouts, yoghurt, etc.
- Eat less of sodium and phosphates/phosphorous-containing foods, salt, spinach, etc.
- Strict blood pressure and blood sugar control is crucial to avoid kidney damage.
- Diet high in sodium, sweetened drinks, and sodas causes progressive kidney decline.
- Herbal remedies
  - Dandelion root aids in kidney function of waste excretion.
  - Celery and parsley are diuretic. They decrease uric acid, and keep kidneys clean.
  - Marshmallow tea cleans kidneys.

24.5 KIDNEY STONES

Kidney stones restrict urine flow, thereby often causing severe pain.

CAUSES

Calcium, oxalate, proteins, and sugars, toxic metals, and stone particles from certain foods are instrumental in causing kidney stones. If you eat too much of foods containing calcium and oxalate, stones may form.

Most kidney stones contain calcium as calcium-oxalate, and phosphorous/phosphate.

First, it has to be diagnosed whether the stone is calcium stone or oxalate stone, accordingly, dietary precautions need to be taken.

In case of calcium stones, calcium supplement and calcium foods are to be avoided. Calcium supplements are not advisable even for patients with osteoporosis lest there be risk of developing kidney stones. As is the case, calcium supplements are often responsible for causing kidney stones.

In case of oxalates, it is important to avoid foods containing oxalic acid. Spinach and tomatoes contain oxalic acid. Spinach is rich in both calcium and oxalate.

Proteins

Proteins increase calcium excretion in urine. Increase in urine calcium is the main cause of stone formation in kidneys. Hence, over-consumption of proteins including legumes should be avoided.

Salt

Avoid taking too much salt in your food. A low salt diet lowers BP and simultaneously reduces chances of kidney stone formation. Processed foods, as well as sodas and canned products have the highest sodium content.

Sugar

Sugar also increases the level of calcium in urine. Hence sugars, sweets, refined carbohydrates, etc., should be avoided. Complex carbohydrates such as whole grains, legumes, fruits and vegetables should be eaten instead.

Iced Tea

Urologist John Milner of Loyola University Illinois warns that drinking iced tea could lead to kidney stones. Iced tea contains high concentration of oxalate. Though hot tea also contains oxalate, it isn't consumed in a quantity large enough to lead to stone formation.

Toxic Metals

Many metals such as lead, mercury, aluminum and cadmium are toxic to kidneys, and may also lead to the formation of kidney stones. Avoid aluminum utensils for cooking.

Stone Bearing Foods

Spinach, which is grown in sandy soil, invariably gets infused with sand particles.

Also, fruits like guavas and tomatoes contain seeds. The seeds lead to stone formation. It's better to take these foods after removing the seeds. For example, have tomato soup with seeds filtered out instead of consuming raw tomatoes.

PREVENTION AND TREATMENT

Some Diets Dissolve Certain Kinds of Stones

Magnesium, for example, increases the solubility of calcium oxalate, thus inhibiting formation of stones.

Note that milk lowers magnesium level in addition to contributing stone-forming calcium.

Effect of magnesium is enhanced with vitamin B6. Hence, the consumption of foods high in magnesium and vitamin B6 should be increased. Such foods include barley, bran, oats, brown rice, bananas, avocados, kidney beans, and potatoes.

Drink Water/Eat Diuretic Foods/Increase Urine Flow

Diluting urine by increasing urine flow is preventive to the formation of stones. Hence, drink 3-4 litres of purified water daily. Eat diuretic foods like barley, brown rice, etc.

Limiting salt in diet and drinking plenty of water are the best ways to prevent common types of kidney stones.

Citrus Fruits/Oranges

Citrus fruits like oranges reduce urinary saturation of calcium. These fruits contain citrate that has been shown to inhibit formation of kidney stones by forming complex compounds with calcium and, thus, preventing their growth into stones. Lemons have the highest concentration of citrate. The best way is to squeeze about ¼ of a lemon into your drinking water 4 times a day.

Potassium-rich Foods

Researchers have a tip for people prone to developing kidney stones. Potassium, as against sodium, lowers risk of formation of stones. As such, potassium deficiency may cause kidney stones. Eat potassium-rich fruits like bananas.

Note: If you have a family history of stone formation, cut down on dairy products, antacids, chocolates, sugared tea, and proteins. Eliminate meat altogether from your diet.

Sexual and Reproductive System

Reproduction is brought about by the union of the female sex cell, the ovum, with the male sex cell, the sperm. The sex cells are produced in endocrine glands; in females they are produced in the ovaries, in males they are produced in testicles or simply testes.

25.1 OXYTOCIN AND OTHER SEX HORMONES

Oxytocin, the hormone released by pituitary gland, is considered to be the cuddle hormone, named so because it is believed to induce emotions of human bonding and togetherness. Apparently, women release it more than men.

Researchers found that women who had the highest levels of oxytocin after childbirth remained extremely attached to their child. Oxytocin performs a number of roles, and it is especially important for expecting and nursing mothers because it can help induce labour and stimulate lactation. Scientists claim that the reason why kids bond more with their mothers is because the maternal love is guided by the cuddle hormone.

25.2 FEMALE REPRODUCTIVE SYSTEM

The female reproductive system consists of two ovaries, two fallopian tubes, uterus, vagina, and external genitalia. Breasts are also a part of the female reproductive system.

Ovaries located in the lower abdomen produce ovum or egg. At the time of birth, a female child possesses about one million ova or eggs in a dormant state. By puberty, there are only about 400,000 ova left. By the time a woman is 35, her ovarian reserve is low.

It is important to realise that the best chance of bearing a child is before the age of 32.

Ovaries also produce female hormones, oestrogen and progesterone. Ovaries have follicles where an ovum is matured for release into uterus at the end of menstruation.

Fallopian tubes collect ovum from ovaries when it is mature, and lead it to the uterus. In the uterus, if ovum combines with sperm to form an embryo, it is called fertilisation. After fertilisation, the uterus performs the supremely wondrous task of transforming this fertilised egg into a baby, a new human being.

Functions of Oestrogen and Progesterone

Oestrogen promotes development of female secondary characteristics such as development of breasts, thickening of uterus lining and other aspects of menstrual cycle, deceleration of height, vaginal lubrication, maintenance of skin, etc.

Oestrogen also increases HDL and decreases LDL. That is the reason why women have less heart problems. But there is also a risk factor associated with it; oestrogen may become the cause of breast cancer in women.

To support pregnancy, progesterone becomes the main hormone produced after conception. Low levels of progesterone can lead to a miscarriage. This hormone is responsible for growth and maintenance of uterus lining. It suppresses further maturation of eggs. By relaxing uterine muscles, it prevents early contractions and birth. It also prevents lactation until the child is delivered.

In today's world, girls are reaching puberty before the age of ten. A meat-rich diet, chemicals such as Bisphenol A used in plastic containers, unhealthy eating habits, and obesity, are responsible for leading girls to earlier puberty and preparing the body for pregnancy.

Oestrogen Dominance

Oestrogen dominance means that oestrogen levels are too high in relation to progesterone levels. Both the hormones are needed to work together in a complementary fashion to keep the body operating at optimum level. For example, oestrogen increases body fat, while progesterone helps burn fat. And while oestrogen elevates mood, progesterone acts as a sedative, and so on.

Oestrogen dominance is experienced during the 7-10 years before menopause, when oestrogen levels start fluctuating, and progesterone levels start declining steadily.

Dietary Changes For Balancing Excessive Oestrogen

- Eat a low-fat, high-fibre diet to help your intestines eliminate oestrogens from the body. Include plenty of fresh fruits, vegetables, whole grains and legumes.
- Eat citrus fruits and flaxseeds to help reduce oestrogen production. Flaxseed oil or ground flaxseed not only helps balance oestrogen levels, it also promotes more progesterone production.
- Eat a vegetarian diet. Meat increases oestrogen production, and contains fats that cause menstrual cramps, inflammations, etc.
- Take omega-3 fats as they reduce cramps and inflammations.
- Avoid potato chips, caffeine, alcohol, chocolate, sugar, soft drinks, fried or fatty foods and salt. All these hamper the process that metabolises oestrogens and eliminates them from the body.
- Also avoid dairy products. They have an effect similar to that of meat.

Natural Contraceptive

Defense Institute of Physiology and Allied Sciences, Delhi, says that 5-10 drops of neem oil in vagina is surprisingly very effective in killing sperms, and preventing conception. However, too much of neem can cause infertility.

25.3 MENSTRUAL CYCLE

Duration of each menstrual cycle is about 28 days, almost equal to the lunar month. Menstrual cramps is the most common problem women face during menses. While the intensity of pain varies from person to person depending on the genetic makeup and biological health, it can be controlled by leading an active lifestyle.

Dealing with Menstrual Cramps

- Consume the magic mineral magnesium present in foods like beans, nuts and seeds. Magnesium regulates female hormones.
- Take vitamin E. It inhibits prostaglandins which cause contractions in uterus leading to cramps. It also increases blood circulation. So, more blood and oxygen are supplied to uterus.
- Exercise. Those who exercise, experience less cramps. And because exercise makes us breathe deeply, it brings more oxygen in blood which helps alleviate depression. It massages the pelvic area, and prevents cramps.
- Heating pad can soothe the pain by relaxing muscles.
- Taking hot herbal tea, soaking in warm tub, or a massage can work wonders.
- According to Ayurveda, menstrual pain is caused by excess of *vaata* (gas). To avoid *vaata*, do not take foods like urad dal, rajma, cauliflower, okra, etc. that produce gas. Also, do not take foods such as yoghurt, rice, radishes and cold drinks.
- Take some good quality fats, and warm drinks like vegetable soups.
- Do a massage with warm *til* oil over lower abdomen and lower back.

25.4 PREMENSTRUAL SYNDROME (PMS)

The onset of menses is often preceded by uneasiness, heaviness in abdomen, irritability, and tenderness of breasts. PMS starts affecting most women about a week before menstruation cycle begins.

The main cause is hormonal imbalance: rise in oestrogen level and fall in progesterone level, which usually occurs about a week before menses. This affects blood circulation, thereby, reducing the amount of oxygen reaching brain, uterus, and ovaries.

What Aggravates PMS?

Salt, sugar, refined flour, caffeine, alcohol, soft drinks, fried foods, and dairy products aggravate PMS symptoms. Some PMS sufferers are found to be consuming too much salt, or sodium-containing foods, like pickles, processed and canned foods. Keep salt consumption to a minimum.

Why Not Salt?

Salt results in fluid retention. Excessive salt causes the water to accumulate in tissues.

Avoid Chinese food. It contains sodium, viz., monosodium glutamate (MSG). Meat and dairy products may aggravate the hormone imbalance greatly.

Because of certain bacteria, non-vegetarian food is associated with greater absorption of oestrogen in intestines, and hence increased oestrogen to progesterone ratio.

High sugar intake may also increase this imbalance. Those consuming more of sweets, refined sugar and refined carbohydrates are found to suffer more cramps. Alcohol and sugar cause electrolytes, particularly magnesium, to be lost through urine.

PMS is also linked to allergenic foods like chocolates. Caffeine is a nervous system stimulant. The more caffeine is consumed, the more severe is the effect of PMS symptoms.

What is Best to Prevent PMS?

- Fasting on fresh fruit juices for days before the onset of menses gives relief. But one should not starve oneself.
- Vegetarian food is associated with a more desirable ratio of oestrogen to progesterone. Plant foods have phyto-oestrogens. These neutralise effects of oestrogen.
- Take omega-3 fats, flaxseed oil, primrose oil, and black currant oil to supply gamma-linolenic acid (GLA), an EFA effective in relieving inflammatory symptoms.
- Take magnesium-rich foods. Magnesium relaxes nerves.

- Take vitamins B6 and B12 in your diet. Premenstrual tension among young women is often due to the deficiency of vitamin B6. The increase in oestrogen at the onset of menstruation is believed to be due to B6 deficiency caused by a malfunctioning liver.

  B6 supplement alone is often able to benefit most women. It also helps to synthesise serotonin. It reduces water retention, and increases oxygen flow to organs. Foods rich in B6 are bananas, green peas, beans, etc.

  B12 reduces stress. It is needed for all nerve functions. A tablet of Neurobion, a combination of vitamins B6 and B12, and a nerve remedy can help.

  A diet rich in plant foods, particularly whole grains and legumes, increases magnesium and B6 levels.

  B-vitamins are essential for healthy liver. Liver plays a key role in neutralising excessive amounts of oestrogen produced by ovaries during this time.

  Vitamin E can help block prostaglandin production and relieve PMS symptoms. It should be taken two days before and three days during menstruation, twice a day, to ease cramps.
- Drink lots of water.
- Exercise increases oxygen level, aids nutrient absorption and elimination of toxins.

  Take warm water baths. Use heating pad or hot water bottle. Warmth increases blood flow to muscles and organs in the pelvic region.
- Herbs

  Shatavari can be called the best friend of women. It can be taken for most female problems. It balances hormones, regulates periods, and strengthens the reproductive system.

  Saffron is believed to relieve depression symptoms via brain chemical serotonin.

  Blessed thistle too balances hormones.

25.5 FRIGIDITY AND INFERTILITY

Frigidity means lack of desire and/or inability of a woman to experience pleasure in sex.

It is usually of psychological nature arising out of fear, guilt, disdain or conflict with mate, depression, inferiority complex, unpleasant memories, etc. Chronic stress may lead to frigidity since stress decreases production of nitric oxide that relaxes blood vessels and muscles, thereby, reducing the flow of blood to the pelvic area.

Faulty diet can also cause oestrogen deficiency leading to frigidity. Oestrogen deficiency will also result in lack of lubrication. It will further irritation and depression.

Female Libido/Fertility

Exercise is the best aphrodisiac for both the sexes. But exercise leading to exhaustion is very detrimental. Heavy exercise may cause women to lose their feminine characteristics since exercise can reduce the oestrogen levels. Their menstrual cycle can be affected, or the menses may stop altogether. Researchers from the Norwegian University of Science and Technology found that a quarter of those who exercised most, could not conceive during their first year compared to the national average of 7 per cent.

Obesity could be the biggest threat to female fertility. It affects ovary function and production of hormones. Many women in fertility clinics are found to be overweight.

Tips to Improve Sexual Health:

Cocoa/Dark Chocolate causes body's endorphin levels to rise.

Banana is rich in potassium and B-vitamins. Both potassium and B-vitamins are needed for production of sex hormones.

Vitamin E, the scientific name for which is tocopherol coming from the Greek word 'tokos' meaning 'to give birth', plays a role in fertility.

Zinc is a precursor to testosterone. Testosterone also helps women.

Testes and ovaries contain selenium. So consuming selenium-rich foods like wheat germ, garlic, whole grains, oats, Brazil nuts, sesame, and sunflower seeds is beneficial for the sex organs.

Niacin helps increase blood flow to genital parts.

Asparagus. Experts recommend you should eat only the tender shoots of asparagus to achieve the aphrodisiacal effect. The tougher older ones are likely to have the opposite effect.

Shatavari is the first and foremost among herbs in Ayurvedic treatment for frigidity. It improves hormonal balance. It is a cure for many problems related to female reproductive system.

Damiana is the herb that improves blood flow to the genitals. The herb contains testosterone-like substances. Accordingly, it can also be used by men.

Ashoka tree's bark, leaf, and fruit are used in the treatment of excessive uterine bleeding, menstrual cramps, and menstrual disorders.

Soybeans and soy products contain natural chemicals that mimic the effect of oestrogen. Soy contains genistein, which is known to act like oestrogen.

Asafoetida is used as a sexual stimulant in Ayurvedic medicine.

Celery (*ajwain*). Many women consider celery and ajwain as having an aphrodisiac effect. It is believed that it stimulates the gland in the brain that controls sex hormones.

Nutmeg or *jaiphal* is known as Chinese women's aphrodisiac because of its aphrodisiacal properties.

Kava is popular in Fiji as a fertility drink made from herbs damiana and ginseng.

Methi seeds have a warming effect. They promote lactation in nursing mothers.

Avoid stress by all means. Stress is a killer of passion.

25.6 FIBROCYSTIC BREAST DISEASE (FBD)

FBD is a benign but painful cystic swelling of the breasts. It is considered a risk factor for breast cancer.

Causes

Some of the causes could be specified as high fat and low fibre diet, chronic constipation, accumulation of toxins in the body, and environmental factors including pollution, pesticides, etc., that promote oestrogen dominance and alter hormonal balance.

Women on a vegetarian diet excrete 2-3 times more oestrogen than women on non-vegetarian diet. The latter have 50 per cent higher levels of oestrogen than the former.

Recommendations:

Vitamin E not only relieves PMS symptoms but also those of FBD. Eating foods such as garlic and onions that are high in germanium is very beneficial since germanium helps to improve oxygenation of tissues.

25.7 UTERINE FIBROIDS

Uterine fibroids are benign growths on the inner and exterior wall of the uterus. It may involve the cervix also. These growths tend to form during the early forties. Usually they shrink after menopause. This suggests that oestrogen is involved in their growth.

In about 50 per cent of cases, these fibroids cause no symptoms at all. In the remaining cases, they may cause heavy and frequent menses, bleeding, vaginal discharge, and anaemia.

Recommendations:

Fibroids are almost never malignant. As long as they are small and harmless, treatment is not required. Do not take birth control pills as they contain oestrogen, and may stimulate growth. Since the fibroids usually shrink with onset of menopause, surgery may not be necessary.

Turmeric (Haldi)

Fibroids can be prevented and treated by consuming haldi.

Kachnar

Kachnar flowers and the bark of the plant can dissolve uterine fibroids.

25.8 MENOPAUSE

On an average, at the age of 52, all women go through a phase which begins with progressive stoppage of menstrual cycle. It happens simultaneously with reduction in the production of oestrogen hormone. Oestrogen is required for the normal female functions of reproduction: pregnancy, child birth, and nursing of baby. The production of hormone reduces as these functions are not required any more at this age.

But the sudden changes in hormone level in blood cause some unpleasant symptoms such as hot flashes, depression, irritability, etc. Women who enter menopause often develop HBP, Type-2 diabetes, heart problems, loss of calcium, osteoporosis, etc.

To counteract the undesirable effects of menopause, women should take proper diet and care, right from the time of adolescence. For example, they should take adequate calcium and vitamin D in their diet. The best source of calcium, vitamin D and phosphorous is milk.

Significance of Practising Relaxation

Long working hours and stressful situations can affect levels of hormones, key to a woman's reproductive cycle, and hasten the onset of menopause by a year or even more.

Women who are suffering from depression are twice as likely to go through menopause before they have reached 52.

Deep breathing cuts the frequency of hot flashes by about half.

Soham Pranayam

Sit in a comfortable position in a chair. Take a deep breath through your nose mentally saying *So* taking the head backwards. Then exhale through your mouth bringing your head forward till chin touches the chest making the sound *ham*.

Do this a number of times, first slow, then medium and finally at a fast speed. This pranayam is also good for alleviating depression and HBP.

Abdominal breathing is the best way to relax. Your abdomen, not the chest, should rise and fall as you breathe. Follow the breathing rhythm with *aan-apaan* meditation. This can be practised in sitting position as well as while lying on your back in Shavasana.

Earlier it was thought that oestrogen hormone replacement therapy (HRT) was the answer. But now it has been realised that, in some cases, it could have harmful side-effects. According to a research published in *Unleash the Inner Healing Power of Foods* by FC&A Medical Publishing, HRT initiated a 26 per cent rise in cases of breast cancer, 22 per cent in instances of cardiovascular disease, 29 percent increase in heart attacks, 41 percent jump in strokes, and twice the rate of cases of blood clots. As a result, the FDA now advises doctors to prescribe HRT only when its benefits clearly outweigh health risks. So researchers have started looking for plant oestrogens as alternatives.

New research by Dr J. Michael Wyss, a physiologist at the University of Alabama at Birmingham suggests that polyphenols, found in grapes, soy, and kudzu, may blunt some of the effects of menopause. Soybeans and soy products contain natural chemicals like genistein that mimic the effects of oestrogen. They may, therefore, be good for menopausal women.

Kudzu is a vine native to Southern Japan, South-Eastern China, and Eastern Asia. It has oestrogen-like elements. Kudzu root helps in reducing BP, blood sugar levels, and the fat hormone 'leptin'. It is a remedy for lack of sexual interest/frigidity.

Black Cohosh herb is an established reducer of hot flashes. It is used for providing relief from discomfort of menopause. It is also helpful in setting right delayed periods.

Flaxseeds were also found to reduce frequency of hot flashes by 60 per cent.

25.9 MALE REPRODUCTIVE SYSTEM

The primary male reproductive system comprises testes, vas deferens, prostate gland, penile urethra, and penis.

Scrotum is the sack that encloses the testes outside the body. Cells in testes manufacture sperms and the male hormone testosterone.

Two glands situated before the ejaculatory duct secrete a thick substance that nourishes the sperms, and forms much of the volume of the ejaculated semen.

Prostate gland secretes a thick fluid that also becomes a part of the semen, and that aids the motility of the sperms.

Testosterone

Testosterone is the male hormone that controls libido in men and also in women.

Researchers found that low levels of testosterone were associated with abdominal obesity, and aspects of metabolic syndrome.

The lower a man's testosterone level, the higher his risk of death from any health cause.

It does not mean that those with low testosterone should start taking hormone pills. It may do more harm. Better work on overall health through nutrition and exercise programme.

What is more, there is no evidence that above average testosterone levels increase longevity.

Pollutants interfere with male sex hormones. Some vertebrate animals affected by pollutants were discovered to be producing no sperms at all.

25.10 ERECTILE DYSFUNCTION (ED) AND MALE LIBIDO/ FERTILITY

Factors necessary for normal erection are:

1. Brain stimulation with healthy nerve function.
2. A stress-free mind.
3. Healthy blood vessels and blood circulation.
4. Adequate hormone level.

The most common factor leading to erectile dysfunction (ED) is stress.

Stress decreases the production of nitric oxide that relaxes muscles and blood vessels. Nerve impulses constrict blood vessels, thereby, reducing the flow of blood to the genitals.

But there can be some physical causes also. Blocked blood vessels, and cardiovascular problems that impair blood circulation are the most common physical cause. Smoking and eating fatty foods lead to formation of plaques that may clog the arteries serving the genitals.

Use of alcohol, tobacco, drugs, and some medicines inhibit hormone production. The more the cigarettes smoked, the greater the risk of ED. Further, chronic illnesses such as HBP and diabetes can cause ED.

Soybeans/soy products contain genistein that mimics the effects of female sex hormone oestrogen. Ren-Shan of Wenzhou Medical College in China found that genistein could adversely interfere with the production of enzymes involved in production of sperms in men.

Exercise

It is said that the best aphrodisiac is exercise.

According to a study reported by WebMD, walking on a daily basis reduces the risk of ED or even reverses current impotence. Lead researcher Katherine Esposito of Naples, Italy, says that sedentary men may reduce the risk of ED by adopting regular activity equal to burning at least 200 calories per day. That corresponds to walking briskly for 3 km.

Kegel Exercises

A study showed that 75 per cent of men suffering from ED improved or regained normal erectile function as a result of Kegel exercises. It involves exhaling while simultaneously contracting the muscles as if to hold urine, and holding out your breath for a while, followed by slow inhaling. Repeat a number of times.

No Heavy Workout

A study shows that men who exercise to the level of exhaustion experience a significant fall in their hormone levels, a drop in sperm counts and even in the ejaculation volume. Exercise to exhaustion could disrupt the interactions of the brain, the pituitary gland and the testes.

ED Drug Viagra

Viagra (generic name *Sildenafil citrate*) is now known as the ED drug. The drug works by enhancing the effects of nitric oxide which makes blood vessels expand, and causes more blood to flow in the body. It increases blood flow to the genitals on arousal. It does not cause arousal by itself. Note that Viagra is not an aphrodisiac. It does not increase sexual potency. It just helps in getting over inhibition, fears, physical causes of obstruction to blood flow, etc.

Viagra may cause symptoms of headache, hearing loss and blurred vision. In some rare cases, men taking Viagra developed blindness.

Do not take it without consulting your doctor, particularly if you are undergoing treatment for heart disease and HBP.

Essential Nutrients for Maintaining a Healthy Sexual System

Vitamin A is necessary for cell growth. Along with zinc, it is very essential for sperm production and sperm quality. Professor Debra Wolgemuth of Columbia University says that men whose bodies are deficient in vitamin A may lose their fertility.

Raymond Mcilvenna in *The Pleasure Quest: The Search for Aphrodisiacs* advises eating foods rich in beta-carotene like carrots, sweet potatoes and spinach.

Vitamin D – Researchers at Medical University of Graz in Austria have found that the levels of the male sex hormone, testosterone, in blood rise with vitamin D. An hour of exposure to sunshine can boost a man's testosterone level by as much as 69 per cent.

Vitamin E increases blood circulation. Considered a sex vitamin, it is involved in the production of testosterone and other hormonal activity. Its deficiency results in low sperm count in men, and frigidity in women.

A study by Kinsley Institute of Indiana, US, showed that testicles and ovaries of rats deprived of vitamin E began to atrophy. And when vitamin E was included in their diet they returned to normal. Eat plenty of lettuce to get your dose of vitamin E.

Zinc is important for sperm production, sperm health, prostate gland function, etc.

Folic Acid – A study showed that those with the lowest levels of folic acid had the lowest sperm counts and the poorest quality sperms. Folate sources include beans, spinach, and orange juice.

Zinc plus Folic Acid – A new study conducted in The Netherlands has found that when men with low sperm count took combination of zinc and folic acid, their sperm count increased significantly.

Arginine/Nitrate, an amino-acid, is absorbed in the body and converted to nitric oxide. Nitric oxide dilates the blood vessels to allow more blood to flow to the genitals.

Take more of foods rich in arginine/nitrate such as beetroots, cabbage, celery/ajwain, spinach/greens, garlic, oatmeal, peanuts, cashews, walnuts, dairy and legumes.

Fruits and Vegetables Improve Fertility

A new research reported in American Society of Reproductive Medicine found that the more fruits and vegetables a man consumed, the more potent are his sperms. Results showed that 83 per cent of infertile men had a low intake of fruits and vegetables.

Beetroots

Beetroots are rich in nitrates which, as mentioned before, increase the supply of blood to organs. Get nitrate in a natural form from beets instead of from a chemical drug.

Pomegranates

According to Dr Christopher Forest of University of California, pomegranate juice being extremely rich in antioxidants increases blood supply to the heart and also to the genitals.

Watermelon

Higher levels of lycopene are associated with increased fertility, and watermelon is rich in lycopene. Bhimanagouda Patil and researchers at Fruit and Vegetable Improvement Center of Texas A & M University in College Station have found a new phyto-nutrient, citrulline, in watermelon, which indirectly promotes sexual potency. Citrulline is converted to arginine through certain enzymes in the body which boost the production of nitric oxide in the blood. Nitric oxide has the same effect as Viagra.

Aphrodisiacal Properties of Ordinary Vegetables

- Onions were considered so potent that celibate priests in Egypt were prohibited from consuming them.
- According to pharmaceutical chemist Matts Bergmark of Sweden, garlic contains compounds related to both male and female sex hormones.
- Potatoes, excellent for skin, are considered aphrodisiacal.
- Tomatoes are good because of being rich in lycopene and vitamin C.
- Radishes and watercress are also helpful in keeping sex organs healthy.
- Cauliflower, cabbage, broccoli, with their high sulforaphane content are said to be preservers of youth.
- Pickled cabbage consumed over time is said to improve blood circulation.
- Pumpkin seeds are known to cure zinc deficiency which affects production of hormones, healthy sperms and healthy prostate.

Herbs and Spices

Charak rishi has said in *Charak Samhita* that the best aphrodisiac is a sexually excited good-looking partner. All objects of senses/beauty – *roopa, rasa, gandha, sparsha, and shabda* – are assembled in a woman.

However, there are also various herbs and spices for stimulation. They are as follows:

Sarasparilla, an Ayurvedic herb, contains testosterone-like substance.

Ashwagandha increases vigour in general.

Ajwain/Celery has been known to boost virility, sex hormones both in men and women. Asafoetida/*hing* is aphrodisiacal when used liberally in cooking.

Elaichi/cardamom is supposed to be a remedy against impotence.

Lavang(laung)/clove was considered an aphrodisiac in China.

Adrak/ginger is recognised for its health benefits throughout Asia.

Black pepper was used by Greeks, Romans, and Egyptians as an aphrodisiac.

Saffron/*kesar* is a key ingredient in many exotic dishes known for their aphrodisiacal effects. Cinnamon, nutmeg, mustard, etc., help stimulation.

Rose and Vanilla help to arouse passion.

Gold mineral, in Ayurvedic preparations, boosts sexual vigour. In addition, it improves digestion, enhances memory, and rejuvenates the body.

Saw Palmetto helps to normalise prostate function.

Avena Sativa (Oats), available as homeopathic mother tincture, helps cure sexual debility. An extract of oats does wonders, say officials at San Francisco Sex Institute.

Lycopodium 30 – a dose of 5 pills daily of this homoeopathic drug, helps in age-related ED. Note that licorice herb reduces testosterone levels.

Factors Affecting Male Libido/Fertility

Low sex drive with advancing age among men is akin to male menopause.

Exposure to excessive heat has an adverse effect on sperms and subsequently, on fertility. Working with the laptop placed on one's lap for long hours may reduce the sperm count.

Keeping mobile phones in pockets and belts also harms male fertility. The radiation from phones generates more free radicals, decreases antioxidants, and affects sperm count and sperm mobility.

Long, hot tub/Jacuzzi baths hit male fertility. It may take 4-6 months to undo the damage done to sperm count by one hot tub session. Men who give up long hot water baths were found to increase sperm production almost by five times.

Men who turn to alcohol should be aware that it interferes with testosterone production.

Sperms need cool surroundings to survive, which is the reason why the testes are built outside the body in the scrotum. Because of this, men are also advised not to wear tight underwear and pants which cause much heat to build up.

The drop in sperm count is also due to many more reasons including obesity, smoking, stress, pollution, excessive coffee intake, and chemicals which disrupt the hormone system.

Sleep

Sleep deprivation damages male libido, and triggers ED problems. The male libido is highest in the early hours of the morning, towards the end of a deep sleep.

According to Professor Monica Anderson of Federal University of São Paulo in Brazil, there is increasing evidence showing that those who do not sleep enough suffer from lower libidos and, in many cases, from ED. This is the sad outcome of the fast-paced life people are living these days.

Other Recommendations:

- Lead a stress-free life.
- Eat a healthy and balanced diet that is rich in antioxidants, vitamins and minerals.
- Ditch sugar. Canadian scientists found that maintaining a diet high in sugar can temporarily lower your testosterone levels.
- Include pumpkin seeds in your diet for healthy prostate functioning.
- Do not drink. Do not smoke. Smoking and drinking interfere with potency. Smoking not only effects fertility and potency,

it also damages the DNA of the sperm. Women who smoke during pregnancy will cause considerable harm to their foetuses. Even passive smoking will cause damage, though less in intensity.

• Do not eat animal fats, junk food and fried foods.

25.11 PROSTATE ENLARGEMENT

Prostate enlargement causes reduced force in urination, intermittency of urge resulting in frequent visits to bathroom, and so on. When serious, it results in urine retention in bladder, and then in the blood, which in turn may cause urinary tract infection (UTI).

Prostate gland invariably enlarges with age.

Recommendations:

Zinc, EFAs, Selenium and Vitamin E

Zinc reduces the size of enlarged prostate gland. The best way to get zinc and EFAs together is to consume ¼ to ½ cup of pumpkin seeds daily. Pumpkin seeds are also packed with antioxidants selenium and vitamin E.

Lower Cholesterol

Breakdown products of cholesterol collect in prostate. Hence, maintaining a low cholesterol level would be advised.

Diet should be free of pesticides and toxic chemicals. They lead to enlargement of prostate. Avoid animal foods. Synthetic hormones given to animals for growth before slaughtering them have been shown to lead to prostate growth.

The diet should comprise natural whole foods, full of fibre, minerals, vitamins, carotenes, flavonoids and poly-phenols, that fight free radicals.

Lycopene

It has been shown to be beneficial to prostate health. You find the highest amount of lycopene in ripe tomatoes, tomato ketchup, water melons, pink guavas, etc. It is best absorbed when tomatoes are cooked with a little fat/oil.

Cucumber taken in the morning is believed to help in preventing prostate enlargement.

Saw Palmetto

Berries of this herb greatly reduce symptoms of enlarged prostate.

Quercetin

Quercetin flavonoid has been shown to be effective in easing prostatitis. Foods rich in quercetin include tea, apples, onions, garlic, broccoli, spinach, red wine and grape juice.

25.12 SEX AND HEALTH

Sex burns up calories. The pulse rate rises from about 70 to 150 beats. Blood circulation increases, thereby, encouraging release of waste products.

After an orgasm, muscle tension reduces and our breathing, pulse rate and BP slow down. Sex causes increased production of oxytocin which surges up to five times the normal. This, in turn, causes release of endorphins, our natural pain-killing hormones. Also, there is a boost in the immune system cells as a result of the endorphins released.

Serotonins produced promote the afterglow which makes men and women look younger.

Best Time For Sex

The answer lies in your hormones which trigger the desire for sex. They reach a peak early in the morning for both the sexes.

One has to understand the divine purpose of sex as well. Sex is healthy. Sex is normal. The urge is indeed linked to procreation. The spiritual aspect of it shouldn't be ignored. Nature deems it a divine act when it happens between two people linked with a bond as strong as matrimony or love.

26
Ageing and Longevity

Human beings have the potential to live up to a hundred years and even more. Although death is certain and one who is born must die, however, the duration of your life and its quality depends very much on how you have lived your life. Once you realise this, take charge of the factors governing good health and long life which are:

- Nutrition
- Active lifestyle, exercise, pranayam, yogic principles
- Sleep, since sacrificing sleep is detrimental to health in every way
- A stress-free life, living in equanimity and contentment
- Absence of negative thoughts or *vikaras* like *kama* (lust), *krodha* (anger), *lobha* (greed), *moha* (clinging) and *ahankar* (ego)
- Presence of positive thoughts like wishing well for everyone, love, and compassion
- Protecting oneself from exposure to toxins, pollution, infections, drugs and intoxicants.

26.1 AGEING

Ageing is not a disease. But the process of ageing gives rise to many minor, major, and degenerative diseases. Instead of suffering from diseases in old age, we should live our life in a way that we age gracefully, remain free from diseases, and live healthier and longer.

There is only one magic formula to look young and healthy (and stay away from disease). This can happen if you give your body, mind, and soul the correct nutrition meant for each.

What is Ageing?

Ageing happens when some of the cells in the body die, and new cells are not formed to replace them.

Two things happen with age. One, the process of formation of new cells becomes slower. Two, some cells die prematurely.

When the number of new cells being formed becomes less than the number of old cells dying, the process of ageing begins. This transition takes place around the age of 45.

Is Ageing a Genetic Process?

In some people, genetics may play a significant role in bringing early or late ageing.

Contrary to popular belief, the regeneration of brain cells has been observed in adults as old as 72 years. The key is to remain mentally active to activate this process.

Longevity is not entirely governed by genetics. About 25 per cent of it is related to genes, and the remaining 75 per cent can be controlled by nutrition and lifestyle.

Causes of Ageing

Free Radicals (FR) Damage

The natural cause of ageing is the damage done to cells by free radicals (FRs). Many of the degenerative diseases are not simply the result of passage of time but of damage by free radicals. Avoid saturated and trans-fats altogether. They are breeding ground for FRs. Take foods with lots of antioxidants.

Malabsorption of Nutrients

As we age, nutrients in food are not properly absorbed in the gastro-intestinal tract. This can result in nutrient deficiency.

Low Nutrient Intake

Because of the malabsorption tendency in advancing age, it is very important to always take the right food in the right amount. Older people are found to be deficient in vitamins and minerals, particularly zinc, calcium and iron. Post-menopausal women have a deficiency of magnesium in their body. Magnesium is needed to balance calcium levels in the body.

If your diet lacks essential nutrients over a long period of time, it becomes a cause for several degenerative diseases. Generally, old people have vitamin B12 deficiency, which causes nervous and neurological symptoms.

Normal Wear and Tear

This applies to all organs and parts of the body.

Four Bad Habits

Researcher Elisabeth Kvaavik of the University of Oslo states that smoking, drinking, inactivity and poor diet can make you biologically older by 12 years.

26.2 CHANGES WITH AGEING

As the organs of the body start ageing, their functioning gets improper. Also, if the use of certain organs is reduced, they tend to become dysfunctional. For example, if mental work is lessened, the brain may become sluggish in action. It may also lead to dementia. The rule that applies is: 'Use it or lose it'. Many problems arise not only from misuse but also from the disuse of body.

Still, there are changes that take place as we age, and which cannot be prevented, only delayed. Important ones may be listed as follows:

1. Ejection fraction (pumping capacity) of heart reduces by around 30 per cent.
2. Ability of lungs to draw oxygen and supply it to tissues decreases by 50-70 per cent.

3. With age, we start losing our brain cells. Nerve transmission also decreases.

4. Basal metabolism decreases by about 20 per cent. Calorie requirement decreases. We lose around one-third of our body weight by the age of 90.

5. Because the body's energy requirement also decreases with age, energy intake must decrease; otherwise weight gain occurs resulting in indigestion.

6. Digestion and absorption are less efficient. Lactose tolerance may decrease. Production of digestive enzymes and stomach acids slows down.

7. With age, filtering capacity of kidneys decreases by about 50 per cent. It is advisable to lessen the intake of protein and drink lot of water. The nutritional need of proteins is much reduced with age.

8. Loss of height. Minerals start leaving the bones. By the age of 80, we lose as much as 2 inches in height. Loss of teeth is also a well-known ageing phenomenon.

9. Bones begin to lose density at the age of 50 exposing us to higher risk of osteoporosis and fractures. Normal movement puts pressure on our joints. The wear and tear may lead to joint pain/osteoarthritis.

10. The number of cells in spinal cord begins to drop, leading to a decrease in sensation.

11. Without exercise, muscle mass declines by about 20 per cent by the age of 70.

12. Macular degeneration of eyes is common to all. Some may even develop cataract.

13. Hearing loss occurs in 70-80 per cent of those above the age of 75-80.

14. The size of prostate gland almost doubles between the ages of 20 and 90 leading to problems in urination in men.

15. Cholesterol and triglyceride levels become elevated.

16. As you age, the body loses capacity to tolerate sugar. Hence, avoid refined carbohydrates, and minimise on sugars. Use complex carbohydrates.

Age Gracefully

Ageing is a natural process. Accept this and make the best of it. Prepare for it from a young age. Here are a few suggestions to age gracefully:

1. Cultivate the habit of walking or some form of regular exercise. It is never too late.
2. Eat in moderation. Take wholesome meals, avoiding junk foods.
3. Be humble. Do your chores yourself without demanding or commanding.
4. Make use of your talent and wisdom. Offer services as a volunteer for any social organisation.
5. Develop a hobby. Do something you have always wanted to but could not.
6. Allow your children to use their discretion and choice. Do not interfere.
7. Be generous; believe in giving, and forgiving.
8. Do not hold grudges against people. It only harms us by affecting our peace of mind and our health.
9. Never grumble. Be grateful for all the good and positive things in life.
10. Talk a little less than you have been used to, and smile a little more.
11. Spend some time doing yoga, pranayam, meditation, reading, etc.

26.3 AVOID SUGAR

We all know that sugar adds to our waistline. Dermatologist Fredric Brandt writes in his book *10 Minutes/10 Years: Your Definitive Guide to a Beautiful and Youthful Appearance* that sugar is the biggest enemy of our health. You may have observed that when sugar is burnt, it leaves a very dark sticky residue. The same thing happens after sugar is metabolised in our system. It leads to the formation of wrinkles on our faces. Sugar hastens the degradation of skin proteins. In other words, it makes us age faster.

Brandt believes that simply by reducing our sugar intake, we can turn back the clock by ten years, and improve the texture, tone, and radiance of our skin.

Brandt saw a remarkable change in his own skin when he eliminated sugar from his diet.

Not only did he lose about 9 kg, he also noticed, within 10 days, a glow and increased elasticity in his facial skin. At 40, he felt as healthy as a teenager.

Sugar is the main cause of diabetes. Brandt's father who owned a sweet shop died at the age of just 47 from kidney failure. Because of the increased intolerance of glucose with age, people above 40 should avoid sugar as much as possible.

Sugar is bad for the heart. It will immediately raise the triglyceride level in the body.

Sugars, colas, etc., glycate on metabolising. The process creates inflammation in the arteries, ultimately leading to their scarring and plaque formation, and thereby, faster ageing.

26.4 BOTH OBESITY AND UNDERWEIGHT NEED TO BE CHECKED

While slightly overweight people are not at risk, excessively overweight/obese people are at higher risk of dying from heart disease and diabetes.

People with larger waistlines are 40 per cent more likely to suffer a heart attack. Women should have a waistline of less than 32 inches and men less than 37 inches.

In advanced age, it is difficult to reduce the size of the waistline. Hence, people should become conscious of this from a younger age.

Fitness Pays

Fitness is more important than body weight. Exercise expert Steven Blair of the University of South Carolina tracked 2,600 people of age 60 and above. He found that men who were fit, as judged by a treadmill test, but were overweight or even obese had a lower mortality risk than those of normal weight but low fitness. The study showed that even a modest effort to improve physical activity can provide quite a few health benefits.

26.5 NUTRIENT NEEDS OF OLDER ADULTS

The older adults are most deficient in calcium, vitamins D, B12 and folic acid.

Calcium

Calcium is needed for healthy bones, and normal heart function. It lowers BP. Calcium absorption is impaired with age. Milk and milk products are the best source of calcium.

Magnesium

Magnesium is needed to maintain balance with calcium. You get magnesium from oats, almonds, cashew, soybeans, spinach, peas, bananas, potatoes, green vegetables, etc.

Vitamin D

Vitamin D deficiency may intensify calcium loss. Its presence is essential to prevent osteoporosis. The body synthesises vitamin D from exposure to sun and also gets it from some foods such as butter, eggs, full-fat dairy products, etc.

Vitamin D is linked to lower risk of some cancers. A study in the American Journal of Clinical Nutrition found that high levels of vitamin D can slow the ageing process by up to 5 years.

B-Vitamins

Dementia and mental disarray are often the result of vitamin B1 (thiamine) deficiency.

Get your thiamine from peas, beans, whole grains and nuts.

Vitamin B2 (riboflavin) deficiencies can lead to cataract. Get riboflavin from broccoli, asparagus, leafy greens, milk, yoghurt, cheese, almonds, etc.

Vitamin B3 (niacin) keeps cholesterol under control while increasing good cholesterol (HDL). Get niacin from whole grains, brown rice, milk, legumes, and high quality protein foods. Diets low in proteins are at great risk of B3 deficiency.

Vitamin B12 improves RBC count. Its deficiency can cause anaemia. Many ailments of the brain are the result of B12 and folic acid deficiency. B12 absorption in intestines is hindered in elderly people.

You get B12 from milk, fermented soybeans and moong dal. And you get your folate from whole wheat, beans, asparagus and sweet potatoes.

Vitamin B5 (pantothenic acid) is necessary for formation of certain proteins for nervous system, wound healing, and arthritis. It can be obtained from beans, nuts, cheese, and sweet potatoes.

Omega-3 Fats

They are important for cell formation. Hence, they are anti-ageing. They are anti-inflammatory and prevent development of plaque in artery walls.

Potassium

Potassium plays a role in cell health, water balance, and blood pressure control. It is found in abundance in fruits.

Zinc

Zinc is part of an enzyme that protects cells against free radical damage. It is also present in large amounts in prostate gland, which stores zinc.

It is needed for cell formation, cell metabolism, hormone production, sexual health, wound healing, healthy skin, and enhanced immune function.

Zinc deficiency may be partly responsible for bruising of skin that is permanently seen on the facial skin of elderly people. Heavy drinkers (of alcohol) are prone to the loss of zinc from their bodies. Get your zinc from pumpkin seeds, sunflower seeds, nuts, milk, cheese, beans, legumes, peas and lentils.

Selenium

Selenium boosts immunity, protects against cancer, and promotes prostate health. It helps produce an enzyme that breaks down toxic substances.

Get your selenium from whole grains, wheat germ, kidney beans and soybeans. Do not take supplements for selenium. They may cause toxicity. You get wheat germ from whole wheat bread.

Vitamin A/Beta-carotene

Important antioxidant beta-carotene works as a trap for free radicals. It protects lungs. It is needed for growth and repair of body tissues, eye health and smooth skin.

It is derived from yellow/orange vegetables like carrots, sweet potatoes, squash, pumpkin, and fruits like papaya, peaches, cherries, cantaloupe, and dairy products like milk, yoghurt, butter and cheese.

Vitamin C

Vitamin C, as powerful antioxidant, soaks up free radicals. It keeps WBCs healthy enough to fight diseases, enhances immune system and reduces allergies.

All fruits and vegetables provide vitamin C.

Vitamin E

As a potent antioxidant, it fights cellular ageing by protecting cellular membranes. It improves blood circulation, and prolongs the life of RBCs.

The combination of vitamin E and selenium is an antidote to prostate enlargement and cancer.

Because the lungs are directly exposed to oxygen from air, they are the most vulnerable organs of the body to be affected by oxidation. Vitamin E, in addition to vitamin C, selenium, and Coenzyme Q10, has the ability to slow down the oxidation in lungs.

Get your vitamin E from dark green leafy vegetables, olive oil, mustard oil, sunflower oil, sesame oil, butter, nuts, almonds, walnuts, whole wheat, wheat germ, soybeans, etc.

Co-enzyme Q10

It is a powerful antioxidant, aids blood circulation and improves oxygenation of cells. It is the only nutrient which can help in regeneration of damaged heart muscles and protect them. A supplement of 100mg daily is usually necessary.

Sulphur

A sulphur-bearing amino acid is considered to be a great life extender. Get your sulphur from asparagus, broccoli, garlic, onions, beans, and high protein foods. Asparagus contains vitamins C, B2, folate and sulphur.

Apricots (*Khubani*)

Hunzas, a tribe living in northwest part of Pakistan, is believed to have an exceptionally long span of life. They eat a lot of apricots, the fruit grown locally.

Bioflavonoids as Antioxidants

Those who eat foods rich in bioflavonoids (such as apples, tea, cocoa, onions, strawberries, citrus fruits and grapes) cut the risk of degenerative diseases and have longer and healthier lives.

Strawberries for Heart

Research by Harvard University scholars found that strawberries may help reduce inflammation linked to clogging and hardening of arteries.

Tea

Tea may be the key to a long and healthy life. According to Gary Williamson of University of Leeds, tea is one of the most beneficial polyphenol-rich food. Green or black tea is especially helpful.

Probiotics and Enzymes

Enzymes and probiotics are essential as digestive aids. They strengthen the immune system. As we age, their production is reduced.

Hence, it may be necessary to take a supplement. Yoghurt is one of the best sources of probiotics.

Olive Oil for Longevity

Long life expectancy is possible with olive oil because of its high amounts of antioxidants, polyphenols, vitamin E and MUFA that protect against brain cell damage. For women on a Mediterranean diet rich in olive oil, the rate of death by a disease is less by 20 per cent.

TV celebrity Helen Udy consumes olive oil, and uses it on her skin and hair on a regular basis. Presence of antioxidant substances in olive oil wards off skin problems.

Famous actress Sophia Loren looked young even in her late sixties. Part of her secret was olive oil. She applied it on her face and body, and snacked on olives to fight ageing.

Old age brings with it reduced digestive capacity and poor absorption of nutrients. Olive oil has properties best for improving digestibility and nutrient-absorption.

Melatonin

Melatonin is the principal hormone produced by pineal gland which regulates hormonal balance, and the effectiveness of the immune system. It induces sleep.

It is also obtained naturally from grapes, red wine, bananas, cherries, onions and rice.

Melatonin is said to reverse the ageing process, prevent depression, and bolster immune system to ward off cancer, Alzheimer's disease, AIDS, and many degenerative diseases.

Mostly, melatonin is secreted at night by the pineal gland. Its levels peak a couple of hours after midnight. As we age, there is a substantial drop in melatonin levels effecting our sleep-wake cycle, and diminishing cognitive ability.

But melatonin is also an over the counter (OTC) available drug.

Herbs and Memory Enhancers

- *Ashwagandha*
  This Indian ginseng relieves stress, and aids in maintaining ideal body weight.
- Rosemary
  Rosemary herb is anti-inflammatory and contains a compound that defends against free radical damage in brain.
- Garlic strengthens immune system, and protects the heart.
- Saw Palmetto arrests prostate gland enlargement and enhances sexual vitality.
- Milk Thistle promotes good liver function.
- Sanjivani Booti
  Dr Khare of Botanical Research Institute, Lucknow, is collecting samples of this plant from Mirzapur forests in UP. Tribal people are already using it as a cure for treating burning sensation during urination, venereal diseases, and dysentery.
- Ayurvedic medicines like Brahmi and Shankh Pushpi, Kali Phos 6X, a biochemical remedy, Gingko Biloba, another well-known herb are recommended for enhancing deteriorating memory with age.

26.6 CUT CALORIE INTAKE, LIVE LONGER

Fasting

Researchers at Intermountain Medical Center found that Mormons a member of the Church of Jesus Christ of Latter-Day Saints and others who fast for 24 hours once a week reduce their risk of heart disease by 39 per cent.

Our ancient sages laid a great emphasis on fasting (*upvaas*). It meant sitting in meditation in a temple or near an idol of a deity in close proximity to a divine presence and immersing oneself in prayer without partaking food. Fasting could comprise taking just one meal a day or going without food for one whole day. This led to a thorough cleansing of the body, mind, and soul.

How Does Cutting Calories Increase Lifespan?

We already know that whatever we eat will produce free radicals. FRs damage the cells. A restriction on intake of calories lowers the production of free radicals that translates into less oxidative damage in cells, and helps one live longer.

Modern day scientists have discovered that the way to live longer is by living in a constant state of feeling a little hungry and eating only nutritious food. Limiting calorie intake without risking malnutrition can significantly extend lifespan.

It is not the calories you eat, it is the calories you do not burn that increase the risk of many chronic and degenerative diseases. Professor Tim Nagy of University of Alabama, Birmingham, says that when you eat more food than you burn off, you store the extra calories as fat. These extra fat cells, rather than the extra calories, affect cancer risk. Toxins are stored in fat cells, not in the liver. Fat cells emit many kinds of chemicals that have an adverse effect on the body. One of these chemicals is leptin. Leptin promotes some cancers. It is now well known that restricted-calorie diet cuts the risk of getting cancer.

J. N. Zugich at Oregon Health & Science University found that limiting consumption of calories seems to boost infection-fighting T-cells in the immune system. That explains how a low calorie diet can extend lifespan.

Eating in a balanced way and in small quantities is one of the many secrets of a long life.

However, crash dieting is a strict no-no. Regardless of the failure or success in losing weight, studies at California University San Francisco and Minnesota University show that dieting increases stress and levels of stress hormone cortisol. Chronic stress is linked to heart disease, HBP, diabetes and cancer.

26.7 RESVERATROL

David Sinclair, a professor of pathology at Harvard Medical School, Director of Glenn Laboratories for the Biological Mechanisms of

Ageing discovered in 2003 that resveratrol, found in high amounts in red grapes, red wine and some other plant products, extends the lifespan of mice by as much as 24 per cent. It is considered as the 'longevity molecule'.

Sinclair believes that resveratrol works by activating a gene protein called SIRT-1 which is thought to combat ageing. His mentor Professor Leonard Guarente, at MIT proposed that SIRT-1 is activated by calorie restriction. Biologists have known for years that mice will live much longer when they are fed a nutritious diet with 30-40 per cent fewer calories.

Resveratrol may be mimicking calorie restriction without an arduous diet control. People who drink a glass of red wine a day tend to live longer than teetotallers.

But beware of consuming alcohol in large quantities. Researchers at Milan University (Italy) found that drinking alcohol damages cells by causing stress and inflammation to telomeres, the DNA strands in cells. It accelerates the process of ageing and increases the risk of cancer. People who drink habitually look older than their biological age. Apart from red grapes and wine, you find plenty of resveratrol in apples and tea.

26.8 TELOMERASE ENZYME, SECRET TO ETERNAL YOUTH

Telomeres are DNA strands at the end of chromosomes. They protect chromosomes from deterioration. However, telomeres get shortened and are slowly consumed during the process of cell division. An anti-ageing enzyme telomerase – said to be the secret to eternal youth (*The Times of India*, 1 December 2010) – helps in elongating telomeres and replenishing them. But telomerase is like a time clock. As we age, this enzyme goes on depleting leading to further ageing and many age-related illnesses including cancers. The only way this enzyme can be increased is by reducing unnecessary intake of calories, adding important nutrients to our diet by way of whole grains, fruits and vegetables, foods with less fat, and a healthy living style, doing moderate exercises, pranayam, relaxation, and managing stress.

Healthy Living Style

A healthy living style means:

1. A diet rich in fruits, vegetables, whole grains, legumes and soy products.
2. Moderate exercise such as walking for 45 minutes a day.
3. An hour daily devoted to pranayam, meditation, music, relaxation, etc.

A small study on 30 people led by Dr Dean Ornish, Head of Preventive Medicine Research Institute in Sausalito California, revealed that drastic changes brought about in lifestyle as per the above listing raised the levels of telomerase in the blood by 29 per cent after 3 months. Telomerase controls longevity. It is vital for maintenance of immune system cells.

How many years can a healthy living style add to our life?

Experts say that if you eat lots of fruits and vegetables, do not smoke, exercise regularly, and drink only in moderation, you can add 14 years to your lifespan.

26.9 MANTRAS FOR LONGEVITY

High HDL Level and Diabetes-Free

This follows the discovery of three genes, found in a group of people with an average age of 100, all of which significantly increase chances of living past 100. Two of the genes increase production of good cholesterol HDL, reducing the risk of heart disease, stroke, and Alzheimer's disease, and the third helps in prevention of diabetes.

Role of Inflammation

Undetected or unresolved inflammation, particularly chronic inflammation, can impact a person's ageing process. It can eat away years from your life.

While our body continuously tries to fight off foreign invaders, in that very process of fighting, it can inflict collateral damage to our organs and tissues. If this becomes the case, our body can actually become our own enemy. Taking concerted and continuous steps to avoid and control inflammation can go a long way toward decelerating the ageing process.

Strong Immune System

The immune system has to be strong, but it should not be overactive. An over-sensitive immune system can give rise to allergies and auto-immune diseases.

Its condition depends very much on what you eat, how you breathe, how active you are, how positive your attitude is, your state of mind, your nature – whether it is benevolent or self-centred, whether you love yourself and others, and so on. It means to live in moderation, and in harmony.

Happiness Adds Years to Your Life

Dutch professor Ruut Veenhoven of Erasmus University, Rotterdam, says that the effects of happiness on longevity are comparable to that of 'not smoking'. It can add 7-10 years to your life.

Happiness may help to heel. But, more importantly, it protects you from illnesses.

Dan Buettner, a writer and adventurer, bicycled round the world. Following are some observations he noted:

- In the mountainous Italian island of Sardinia, where farmers work hard in the fields, drink red wine, eat the fruits and vegetables they grow themselves, and are taught to respect their elders, people live for 100 years or more.
- In the Japanese island of Okinawa, there is no word as 'retirement'. But there is another word, *ikigai,* which means 'purpose' or 'that which makes one's life worth living'. The male population in Okinawa has one-fifth of the cancer cases as in America, and one-fourth of the cases of heart disease. He noted that the people of Okinawa were active throughout

their lives. They ate a lot of fruits and vegetables, but little meat – the habit responsible for keeping them lean and rarely accumulating fat. Also, they put a premium on family, friends, and religion for emotional support.

Note that happiness does not lie outside of you. It is within. You do not need any reason to be happy. If you need a reason, you will probably never be happy.

Physical Activity

Maintaining physical activity as you age, whether taking a stroll, or dancing, or working in a garden, adds years to your life. It uplifts mood, promotes sense of self-efficacy, and reverses loss of brain tissue that occurs with age.

Exercise

Exercise three times a week; it is claimed it can extend your life by 2.1 years.

A Harvard Alumni Study found that those who regularly burned 8400 kJ of energy a week by exercising lived two years longer on an average as compared to their sedentary counterparts.

Even in the case of the elderly, a little physical activity goes a long way in extending life by at least a few years. It is never too late to start. Israeli researchers found that exercise reaps benefits even for previously sedentary 85-year olds.

Doing regular pelvic exercises, such as Kegel's exercises, improves bladder control and sexual vitality. It may also help in urinary incontinence as you grow old.

Maintaining a healthy weight through diet and exercise can add 1.5 years to your lifespan.

Pranayam

Even if you do not exercise, practising slow and deep breathing can keep your lungs robust.

Inhale and exhale all the air you can (exhaling is longer than inhaling in pranayam), and hold for a while after every inhalation and exhalation. Repeat this several times. If you do this every morning and evening, and if you do not smoke, by the age of 70 your lungs will be similar in health to that of a 45-year old.

High Altitude Regions

High altitude is good for health even if you have high blood pressure. Thinner air actually lowers one's blood pressure. Also, more exposure to the sun means more vitamin D. Adaptation to high altitudes helps you cope with lower levels of oxygen, and walking uphill on a regular basis aids the heart. Frequenting mountainous regions every now and then is a good idea, therefore.

Pollution-free Environment

Scientists have long known that the grit in polluted air or particulates can lodge deep in lungs and raise the risk of lung disease, heart attacks and strokes. The grit is made of dust, soot, toxic metals and chemicals coming from factories, power plants and engine exhausts. They have now found that lifespan is increased by a clean and pollution-free environment.

No Smoking

It is common knowledge that smoking constricts the arteries, causes atherosclerosis, heart and lung disease, skin pigmentation, and also many cancers.

Smoking can accelerate the ageing process and shorten the lifespan by as much as 10 years, says Toru Nyunoya a pulmonologist with University of Iowa Hospitals.

Value Life: Live a Life of Piety

Live an innocent and pious life. Enjoy the simple things of life.

A woman named Makhbuba Fatullayeva living in Peshtatuk, Azerbaijan in Iran, was found to have the flexibility of a 12-year-old. There are many people in Azerbaijan past the age of 100. The woman revealed the secret of her longevity. She said, 'I have prayed to God all my life. I am a kind person. I have never envied anyone. I have always been with nature. I knew the value of life ... and I was relaxed. The rhythm and tone of life in this region is set by work ... Sometimes, I eat milk, yoghurt, and honey, [basically] anything that comes my way.'

Qian, a Chinese woman active at the age of 103, maintains a cheerful disposition, and never quarrels with anyone. She enjoys needlework, spinning her own yarn, etc., besides keeping herself and her surroundings neat and tidy.

Chingiz Kasumov, Director, Institute of Physiology, Baku, Azerbaijan gives the following advice for a long life:

Eat yoghurt along with garlic and mint. Eat cilantro and chives, saffron and tarragon, and sumakh – a red spice made from dried berries. This prevents accumulation of cholesterol.

Be Multilingual

Lifelong use of two languages promotes longevity by delaying the onset of dementia by 4 years. Bilingualism enhances brain functioning. Studies have shown that speaking two languages increases attention and cognitive control.

Keep Learning

Learn more about anything you like. It is never too late. If you wanted to learn music but you could not due to preoccupations, never mind, this is the time for it, or anything else whatsoever. An idle brain is similar to the one in Alzheimer's disease.

Food Tips

Following are five dietary recommendations which are believed to enhance longevity:

1. **Sunflower seeds:** They have the highest content of natural vitamin E. Vitamin E is one of the most important nutrients responsible for preserving youth and vitality.

2. **Cheese:** Cheese is a good source of calcium – the most important nutrient for bones and teeth.
3. **Sweet potatoes:** Beta-carotene-rich foods like sweet potatoes and carrots can build up in your skin, and give you many benefits described earlier.
4. **Spinach and beans:** They are excellent sources of various nutrients, particularly iron, folic acid, etc.
5. **Be Vegetarian:** Eat a vegetarian diet, and live longer.

In a study, it was found that Seventh-day Adventist men who were vegetarians lived 9.5 years longer and women 6.1 years longer than meat-eaters.

Cutting back on meat protein, that is methionine foods, may be a key to long life. Methionine is abundant in foods such as fish and meats. Researchers from the Institute of Healthy Ageing at University College London concluded that by reducing such foods people should live longer without the need to cut down on calories.

Maintain Oral Hygiene and Wash Your Hands

Recent studies have linked teeth flossing and washing hands with longevity. People, who do not maintain oral hygiene, put themselves at risk of developing diseases like cancer and heart ailments.

One of the reasons for the benefit is because of the elimination of infections travelling to blood vessels and heart.

A new study published in the American Journal of Infection Control shows that nothing is better in getting rid of germs than soap and water. It washed away 99 per cent of bacteria and viruses in just 10 seconds of lathering.

Dr Trisha Macnair in her book *The Long Life Equation* suggests that good dental hygiene can add 6 years to your life, and washing hands adds 2 years.

Sleep and Lifespan

Sleep is a great natural restorative process. It is a major factor in rejuvenating the body and activating the immune system. In a study, it was found that people who reach the age of 100 are three times more likely to spend at least 10 hours a night in bed.

Rising early in the morning may be bad for your heart and blood pressure. A study led by Diane Lauderdale of the University of Chicago Medical Center found that people who on an average slept longer were at reduced risk of developing new coronary artery calcifications.

According to Japanese physician Mayuko Kadono, subjects who woke up before 5 a.m. were 1.7 times more prone to suffering from HBP/hypertension, and 2 times more prone to developing hardened arteries.

A study by University of Warwick found that people who sleep less than 6 hours each night were 12 per cent more likely to die prematurely.

A relaxed mind is the key to good health and long life. The less worries and concerns a person has, the longer he lives. There is less stress.

Singing

Singing keeps you and your voice young. The voice starts breaking during old age. Continuous training and singing can help reduce this effect. The 103-year-old Dutch actor and singer Johannes Heesters said that he trained his voice daily, first the deep notes, and then moved up to higher tones.

Quoting ENT specialists the German Medical Journal NAJ says that singing is one of the best ways of keeping your voice sounding young when you get older.

Singing also helps increase happiness levels. A study by Don Stuart of Griffith University in Queensland, Australia, based on a survey of 1100 choral singers, found that 98 per cent rated their quality of life as good or even excellent even though some of them were having long-term health problems.

A Supportive Spouse/Unconditional Love

A happy married life and conjugal love helps you stay healthy and thereby, slows down the process of ageing. It boosts immunity.

A 2006 study from UCLA showed that men and women live healthier, wealthier, happier, and longer when they are in a stable relationship. A stable partnership can add 7 years to your life.

Each cell in your body communicates with all the other cells which enable the body to work as one unit. As a result, changes in brain caused by various emotions will have a direct impact on the body. People who feel lonely and depressed are more likely to suffer from illnesses. Close relationships – sexual or just platonic – can boost immune function.

The fundamental human need is to love and be loved. If you want to live longer, learn to love.

Lest you get disappointed, remember that love is not in the object, love is already within you. It is your basic nature. It is not even necessary to get married.

Surround yourself with all that you love. It may be your family, friends, pets, music, plants, hobbies, and books, whatever. Make your home your refuge replete with all the comforts of life.

A Good Life with Family and Friends

Researchers at University College London found that higher levels of DHEA hormones secreted by adrenal glands help boost memory, and also the ability to cope with stress. But the levels of DHEA are found to be higher among those who lead a good and active life, engaging in various hobbies, sports, pastimes, and spending time with friends and family.

The company of our near and dear ones keeps us away from negative thoughts. Our friends and well-wishers nudge us to seek medical help during times of trouble.

But let yourself have cheerful friends. Gloomy pessimistic ones will pull you down.

Is There a Link Between Humour and Long Life?

Laugh often, long and loud until you gasp for breath; you might live longer, a Norwegian researcher reports. Adults who have a jovial attitude towards life outlive those who are more serious by nature and cannot see the humour in life. Sven Svebak of medical school at Norwegian University of Science and Technology found that among adults diagnosed with cancer, those who scored in top 25 per cent for humour appreciation had 70 per cent greater chances of survival.

Reducing Body Temperature Extends Lifespan

Animals involved in the studies involving calorie restriction experienced lower body temperatures as a side effect. Researchers at Scripps Research Institute at La Jolla California reduced body temperature of the mice by focussing on hypothalamus in the brain. They found that mice with reduced body temperature lived 20 per cent longer than those with a normal body temperature.

In any case, if you allow the body to cool down before going to bed, it induces sleep. Decreasing the body temperature can induce a state of hibernation where metabolism slows down and the body needs less oxygen and energy to survive. Living in a cool environment may, therefore, increase the duration of life.

Slow Does It

Your grandparents perhaps lived up to the ripe age of ninety or more. In your hurry to extract the maximum from life, you are, probably, burning the candle of your life at both ends.

But there are people even in the twenty-first century who have realised the futility of a fast-paced life. They are seeking a relaxed life and prefer a natural and holisitic diet. They want to savour every moment of their life. This go-slow, no-rush attitude does not mean they are neglecting their responsibilities.

Habits like chewing your foods slowly, savouring their taste, aroma and colour go a long way in strengthening your digestive system. It also enhances the feeling of satiety.

Even slow breathing helps to de-stress. It is believed that everyone is born with a fixed number of breaths. It depends how quickly you exhaust them, and thus bring your life to an early end.

Our ancient sages established the science of Yoga and meditation and by its practice, they achieved robust health; they used to live for more than a 100 years. We too, by practising yoga, meditation, and by pursuing a relaxed and calm life can obtain greater fulfillment in life.

Take a vacation. Regular vacations mean a 21 per cent lower risk of heart disease.

Cherish Your Health

Your body is your temple. Worship it and protect it by all means.

If your health is good, preserve it. If it is unstable, take steps to improve it. If you have serious health problems, do not despair. Get help. Pray for early recovery. Know that nothing is permanent, whether bad or good. Things will change.

People who just concentrate on diet and exercise are missing three-fourth of the picture. There is much more than this to help you live longer and better.

27

Nervous System

The nervous system is responsible for controlling and regulating all activities of the body.

Its central organ is the brain which functions through a network of nerves, which carry information to various parts of the body. Like any other organ, the brain requires oxygen, which is supplied by blood from the heart. If the oxygen supply is cut even for a few minutes, it results in paralysis, coma, or brain death.

It is a known fact that the right brain controls the emotional aspect of the personality and the left side of the body, and the left-brain controls the logical aspect of the personality and the right side of the body. Any dysfunction of the right brain affects the left side of the body, and vice versa.

Different sections of the brain control different functions of the body such as hearing, smell, taste, vision, etc., as well as higher functions like emotions, learning, memory, and so on.

Since nerves are most sensitive at their terminal ends most of which lie in the foot area, foot and head massages may help in better development of the brain.

27.1 HYPOTHALAMUS AND THE SPINAL CORD

Hypothalamus gland regulates the functions of other endocrine glands.

All secretions of pituitary gland are controlled by signals from hypothalamus. Pituitary controls thyroid, adrenal and sex/reproductive glands. Hypothalamus, therefore, indirectly controls these functions.

Hypothalamus stimulates sweat glands. Thus, it also helps in regulation of body temperature.

It is involved in cardiovascular response, regulation of BP, centres of hunger and loss of appetite, control of fluid volume in the body through urges of thirst and urination, sleep and wakefulness, positive and negative emotions, sexual urge, etc.

Sensory information from parts of body is transmitted to the brain via the spinal cord and peripheral nervous system. Any damage to spinal cord results in serious consequences including paralysis, and loss of sensory and motor functions.

Neuron is the brain cell, the unit of the nervous system on which the system depends.

27.2 NEURO-CHEMICAL TRANSMITTERS

A neurotransmitter is a chemical substance that bridges the gap between nerve cells and enables the transmission of messages from the brain to a receptor.

These neuro-transmitters are synthesised from raw materials found in diet. They are converted into their active brain chemicals with the assistance of vitamin B6.

Thus, B6 is a crucial nutrient for brain.

The core chemicals include dopamine, serotonin, endorphins, GABA, etc. GABA can be likened to a natural built-in tranquilliser.

27.3.1 Dopamine

Dopamine plays a role in regulating behaviour, cognition, muscle control, motivation, sleep, mood, attention and learning.

It is thus associated with the pleasure system in brain responsible for providing the feeling of enjoyment. It is released when we undergo naturally rewarding experiences such as good food, love and sex with a loving and interested partner, etc. Deficiency in dopamine can cause Parkinson's disease and autism apart from chronic stress and depression.

Poly-phenols in bananas and cheese are natural substrates for dopamine. Co-enzyme Q10 is like a precursor to dopamine.

27.3.2 Endorphins

Endorphins activate sites of pleasure in brain, and provide relief from pain. They boost appetite and immune function.

Endorphins were discovered while investigating the pleasure effect seen with drugs like heroine, cocaine and morphine. But drugs activate too much. In the process, they may, in fact, deaden these sites altogether.

Pleasurable experiences such as foods, meditation, exercise, etc., trigger the release of endorphins to give a euphoric experience. Regular physical exercise thirty minutes daily is necessary to maintain a favourable endorphin level.

Placenta contains endorphins. This may be nature's way to reduce pain of childbirth.

Copper is involved in the production of endorphins. That was probably one reason why drinking water in copper jugs was common in India.

One of the most well-known and popular pleasure-boosters is cocoa/chocolate which releases endorphins.

27.3.3 Serotonin and Tryptophan

Serotonin is the neurotransmitter that regulates and induces sleep, and reduces pain. The more serotonin one has in the brain the less likely is one to feel depressed and/or anxious.

Serotonin is found extensively in the gastro-intestinal tract. About 80-90 per cent is located in the gut where it is used to regulate intestinal movements. The remaining is synthesised in the central nervous system where it has various functions.

This shows that there is an extremely close relationship between the digestive and the nervous system via the neuro-transmitter serotonin. So, an imbalance in one would likewise affect the other.

Low levels of serotonin in the body results in insomnia, loss of appetite and depression.

Tryptophan, derived from diet, functions as a precursor to serotonin production.

Food Sources That Help Raise Serotonin Production

A diet high in tryptophan, calcium and magnesium, EFAs like omega-3 (present in walnuts, flaxseeds), GLA and vitamin C boosts the level of serotonin in your body.

Most whole foods contain tryptophan. It is abundantly found in complex carbohydrates such as sweets and cereals, whole grains, brown rice, oat bran, almonds, nuts, sesame and sunflower seeds, soybeans, tofu, milk, cheese, yoghurt, kidney beans, moong dal, spinach, lettuce, turnip, mustard greens, watercress, mushrooms, pumpkin, asparagus, broccoli, and fruits, particularly banana. Mother's milk is high in tryptophan.

Carbohydrates enhance the absorption of tryptophan and its conversion into serotonin in the brain. Within 30 minutes of eating a carbohydrate meal, you feel calmer, relaxed and sleepy. However, the effect would last for only 2-3 hours. Hence, take your cereal and sweets in supper at bedtime to promote sleep.

Pure carbohydrates like chocolate, sugary sweets, ice creams, etc., instantly raise the level of serotonin in the brain. They act as mood elevators and can be considered as feel-good foods. However, too much sugar may have the opposite effect. Prefer dark chocolates.

But if you want to remain at ease and healthy at the same time, then eat complex carbohydrates – foods that are both sweet and high in fibre – such as brown rice, whole grain cereals, pasta, bread, potatoes, legumes, peas, etc. A bowl of mixed fruit with honey and yoghurt works well.

Refined sugar is a 'feel-bad' food. It has empty calories, is acidic, and causes weight gain.

Long-term Stress Depletes Serotonin

When you are stressed to the extent that you get burnt out, it becomes difficult for the body to produce serotonin.

You must reduce stress in your life. It can be as simple as taking up an exercise programme or meditation, or choosing to leave a stressful job and surroundings.

Stimulants, caffeine, alcohol, drugs, diet pills and tobacco work the same way as stress, and deplete the levels of serotonin.

27.3.4 Melatonin

Serotonin gets converted to melatonin in the pineal gland. It is an anti-ageing hormone.

Your body synthesises this hormone as night falls. It helps to induce sleep and is, thus, also known as the 'sleep hormone'.

Melatonin production may be obstructed if lights or sources of UV radiation like laptop screens or iPods are on, making it difficult for the person to get sound sleep.

The body reduces the production of melatonin as we grow older. Accordingly, older people find it difficult to fall asleep easily. If you want to fall asleep faster, taking a melatonin supplement may help. Begin with the 1mg dose.

Red cherries contain melatonin. Cow's milk also promotes its production.

27.3.5 Oxytocin

Oxytocin, also known as 'cuddle hormone' or the hormone of love and bonding, is released by the pituitary gland under direction from the hypothalamus. It is elicited automatically during sexual relationship, and is involved in sexual attraction, and in maintaining close bonds. The hormone is used clinically to help initiate or to continue labour, to control bleeding after delivery, and to stimulate the secretion of breast milk.

Apparently, women release more oxytocin than men. As a result, sex for them is more for bonding than for pleasure. Mother-child bonding is also promoted by oxytocin. It spurs mothers to protect their offspring. Women who breast-feed their child experience a stronger mother-child bond.

Scientists from Barbara Institute in Cambridge and University of Bonn found that men who were administered a nasal spray of oxytocin showed higher empathy levels like women.

This hormone also promises the possibility of cure for serious conditions like autism.

27.4 NUTRITION FOR BRAIN: LOTS OF VEGETABLES, HEALTHY FATS AND PROTEIN, SLEEP AND ACTIVITY

Our brain is the most crucial organ to our existence as human beings. Any hampering in its functioning can lead to serious, sometimes fatal, consequences. We should thereby keep our brain in good health by taking the following measures:

- Have a good breakfast daily.
- Eat regularly-paced meals throughout the day.
- Stay hydrated by drinking plenty of water. Water is not only good for the body, but also for the brain. Researchers at King's College London found that failing to drink enough water can cause the brain to shrink making it difficult for people to think quickly.

Fat is Food For Brain

You always believed that fat is bad for health. But that is not true for every type of fat.

DHA, an omega-3 fat, is one such fat that is vital for nerve cells. It helps you develop better vision and growth. DHA and EPA are active ingredients of fish oil, and also of liquid soy oil.

Incorporate good fats like MUFA and omega-3 in your diet. Omega-3 fats help maintain brain and nerve health. Fats from healthy oils help keep cholesterol low and arteries clear, both of which contribute to brain health.

Eat Lots of Vegetables

Eating lots of vegetables boosts the production of dopamine, thus keeping the brain young and making one look younger.

Vegetables generally have a higher content of vitamin E (a powerful antioxidant) than that found in fruits.

A diet rich in vitamins especially vitamins B6, B12, and folate, which are brain vitamins, greatly helps in keeping the brain healthy.

Add vitamin A, amino acids (proteins) and magnesium to your diet. It is necessary for maintenance and functioning of nerve cells. Vitamin B6 participates in neurotransmitter formation. Vitamin B12 is needed for cell division. B6 works together with magnesium while B12 works together with folic acid.

Vegetarians are at a high risk of developing vitamin B12 deficiency as this vitamin is not obtained from any vegetarian source except from milk, yoghurt, cheese, sprouted and fermented foods, and that too, in small amounts.

Vitamin C is necessary for manufacture of nerve transmitting substances.

Tyrosine is an amino-acid used by cells to synthesise protein. By producing dopamine and epinephrine, tyrosine reduces stress hormone levels. In addition, it leads to improvement in cognitive and physical performance. The deficiency of this protein may affect brain function to the extent of causing autism. Human body synthesises it from amino-acids derived from foods such as cheese.

Sleep, Exercise and Study

Sleep is the diet of the mind. Repair and healing take place during sleep.

Exercise to improve blood circulation in the brain and spinal cord. Just walking can boost connectivity between brain cells.

Mental activity is the best way to keep your brain young and active. While you sweat doing physical exercises, keep learning new things for mental exercise.

Study a language, take up a college course, read a classic or scripture and memorise shlokas or solve some puzzles like Sudoku, and so on.

27.5 AUTISM

Scientists at Cambridge University discovered that high levels of testosterone in amniotic fluid of pregnant mothers were responsible for autistic traits in children.

The older the age of the mother, the higher the risk of autism in the child. Babies left to cry are at risk of brain damage, and can even develop autism.

The traits shown were lack of verbal skills and sociability. Autism is a spectrum of problems ranging from severe inability to communicate to mental retardation. Autism is often linked to talent. It is a different kind of condition. People with autism include those with extraordinary abilities in mathematics and music.

Autistic kids have an extraordinary grasp of facts, but they have no concept of interpretation. With this incapacity comes an inability to form lasting relationships.

Professor Simon Baron-Cohen of Autism Research Center at Cambridge says that autistic males often turn out to be skilled at mathematics and engineering. Some nearly reach levels of brilliance. He says that Newton and Einstein were almost autistics who found relationships difficult. Artists too have suffered from autism, including the blind pianist Derek Paravichini, and reportedly the famous film director Steven Spielberg.

So consider an autistic child as a potential genius. There is no need to be disappointed. However, try to give love and support to the child and help him or her in cognitive skills and the art of making relationships.

Give the child foods, such as cheese, which contain tyrosine to aid in improvement in cognitive skills, and other foods like bananas and omega-3 fats that raise dopamine level.

Horse riding is believed to be helpful in autism.

27.6 HEADACHE/MIGRAINE

Migraine/headache is common among young men and women. It usually starts on one side of the head, but may migrate to the other side.

Women often suffer from this headache during menstrual period. Some common causes of headache are fatigue, emotional stress, exposure to sun and heat, prolonged fasting, food allergies, etc. One must take steps to steer clear of precipitating factors.

Aspartame, an artificial sweetener, used in diet drinks increases the frequency and duration of migraine attacks.

In case of frequent headaches, be careful about what you eat. The most common suspects of allergenic trigger foods for migraine are eggs, milk, wheat, dairy, sugar, chocolates, artificial food preservatives and chemical additives, MSG, meats, peanuts, tomatoes and fish. Cheese, beer, wine, etc., may also cause headache because they contain certain amines that can constrict or dilate blood vessels in the brain. Magnesium deficiency is often the root cause of headaches.

Vitamin B2 reduces the frequency and intensity of migraine attacks. Drinking lots of water can help cure migraine.

Grape Juice

Drinking a glass of fresh grape juice empty stomach in the morning provides immense relief.

Melatonin

In a study, 32 people took 3mg of melatonin daily. After 3 months, 8 had no migraine at all. The remaining 24 cut the frequency and intensity of pain by half.

Melatonin is a remedy for sleeplessness also. It shows that adequate sleep is very essential to ward off any headache, including migraine.

Almond Oil and Sesame Oil

Ask someone to give you a head massage with sesame (*til*) or almond oil.

Herbs

Feverfew is considered as nature's Aspirin.

Peppermint oil/*Amritanjan*, rose oil and lavender oil are known for their calming properties. Sniffing these oils helps provide a relief in headache. Rubbing peppermint oil on forehead, and also on neck if the pain is in the back-head is the popular remedy in Germany, and in India, preparations like *Amritanjan* are used to cure a headache.

Drinking chamomile tea can give relief from headaches.

Left Nostril Breathing – Keep the right nostril closed. Exhale and inhale slowly through left nostril (*Chandra Nadi*) for ten minutes. This will cool the nervous system. Continue practice over a period.

Rotate your arms clockwise and then anti-clockwise for some time. The Chinese way of treatment is head swinging, or swinging both the arms. Both ways you reduce the flow of blood through swollen blood vessels in the head. For the same reason, an elastic head-band or an ice pack also provides partial relief.

27.7 STRESS

When we are faced with an alarming situation, like when we see a snake approaching, stress is the legitimate response of the body to protect us by preparing to fight or take necessary action.

Stress hormones, adrenaline and cortisone, are released at periods of high stress during nervous reaction from the endocrine system. Our pupils dilate to see danger more clearly, liver produces more blood sugar to give energy, pulse and heart rate speed up to direct nutrients and oxygen to muscles, and so on. But such a situation rarely comes in our life. However, we usually get addicted to stressful response in even very ordinary situations simply because of the conditioning of our minds.

Stress hormones remain high for as long as 72 hours. After this they return to their normal level. Adrenaline tends to drop quickly. But cortisone is the last one to come to normal.

And if there is prolonged or chronic stress, cortisone circulates in the body all the time leading to serious physical, mental and emotional problems. Cortisol may remain indefinitely in your bloodstream leading to a state of constant stress. This will affect metabolism, disrupt the production of feel-good hormones like serotonin, may manifest in the form of digestive problems and headaches, worsen acne and skin problems, cause insomnia, low WBC count and weakened immune system, repeated infections and illnesses, asthma, BP, heart disease, and diabetes – the list is endless.

Stress suppresses production of fertility hormones, and of nitric oxide that relaxes muscles and blood vessels and maintains a normal blood flow to vital organs. All this may lead to frigidity and ED.

Sleep, Deep Breathing and *So-ham* Pranayam

Proper sleep, deep abdominal breathing and *So-ham* pranayam are the best stress-busters. The yogasanas recommended for relieving stress are:

Makarasana – Lie down on your left side. Turn a little towards your stomach. Bend your right leg and bring the knee close to your chest. Keep the left leg straight. Bend the right arm keeping the elbow on the right leg. Rest your head on the left arm. Breathe normally. Maintain the posture. Do it with reverse positions of legs and arms.

Shavasana is practised lying on your back on a flat hard surface, and instructing parts of the body from head to toe and toe to head to relax one by one, and then observing the flow of the breath. It can be combined with Yog-Nidra. See Chapter 32.

Music

In many clinical studies, music ranks as the number one stress buster. Whether it is listening, learning or performing, music has the capacity to make people calm. Soft music can work like a 'sound bath'. It can help you wash away all your worries.

Nux Vomica, the homoeopathic remedy, is extremely useful for people living a stressful life comprising fast foods, alcohol, and excessive medications.

Chamomile Tea, Passion Flower, and Valerian are used to reduce anxiety, and to calm hysteria, and give you restful sleep.

Celery Seeds (Ajwain)

Pthalide compound in celery seeds lowers stress hormone levels and muscle tension even inducing one to fall asleep.

Cold Spinal Bath

Lying down in a tub is an excellent way to de-stress, and a tonic for nervous system.

Aromatherapy

Aromas trigger the secretion of neuro-transmitters such as serotonin. Rose and jasmine oils are excellent for stress management. Citrus oils such as bergamot, mandarin and lemon uplift the spirits. You can even have aromatherapy massage.

27.8 STRESS BUSTING FOODS

Eating when you are stressed can be a good thing. However, that depends a lot on what you are eating. The following foods counteract stress and its effects:

Bananas

Tryptophan-rich foods and foods that raise serotonin level are stress busters.

Bananas are rich in tryptophan, potassium and carbohydrates.

Bananas taken with green cardamom or *elaichi* are even better. It becomes a recipe for digestion.

Carbohydrates

Carbohydrates are best as they produce serotonin which gives out a sense of calm.

Have complex carbohydrates like potatoes, whole grain cereals, rice, spaghetti, pasta, etc. Consuming a little sugar or sweets can curb aggression for some time, and relax you.

Almonds

Take almond *thandai* to de-stress, and apply almond oil on scalp.

Apples

Apples contain flavonoid quercetin that is very helpful in beating stress. They also contain phosphorous that helps in reducing stress.

Yoghurt/*dahi*/Buttermilk/Processed Cheese/Paneer

You feel relaxed with these because they are high in tryptophan and calcium. Yoghurt is also rich in lactic acid which prevents intestinal putrefaction of foods and bloating - a frequent symptom of stress.

Tyrosine in processed cheese gets converted to dopamine, the hormone that possesses mood-lifting properties. All these milk products are rich in calcium too.

Calcium/Magnesium/Potassium Foods

Calcium, magnesium and potassium relax nerves. Milk is best for calcium. It relaxes the brain and promotes sleep.

Fruits and vegetables are loaded with potassium and magnesium and have a calming effect on mood.

Vitamin C/Fruit Juices

We need fruits also for vitamin C. During stress, urinary secretion of vitamin C increases. Vitamin C is also involved in serotonin production. Constriction of the blood vessels is the first effect of stress. Vitamin C keeps the walls of the blood vessels flexible.

Vitamin B5 is a certified stress-buster. It is found in abundance in milk, yoghurt, oatmeal, whole grains, brown rice, beans, legumes, mushrooms, soybeans, broccoli, cauliflower, oranges and strawberries.

27.9 DEPRESSION

Clinical depression is a state of intense sadness, melancholia, or despair.

Depression often leads to constant negative thinking. Conversely, negative thinking may lead to depression.

One suffering from depression wants to be left alone, shuns light, and either eats too little, thus losing weight, or eats too much for gratification through food, thus gaining weight.

WHO study led by Somnath Chatterji says that depression impairs health to substantially greater degree than chronic diseases such as angina, arthritis, asthma, and diabetes.

Causes of Depression

These may be physiological such as genetic, low levels of certain neurotransmitters namely serotonin, medical due to illnesses, injury, or due to the effect of certain drugs, nutritional deficiencies of B-vitamins, vitamin D, omega-3, magnesium, etc., poor sleep, seasonal disorders, socio-psychological factors like low self esteem, not being able to cope with external pressures, stress, job loss, financial difficulties, loss of spouse, divorce, lack of partner or friends, sexual disorders, traumatic events, and lifestyle.

Winter depression is very common. The days are short, while the nights are long. The sun sets early, and rises late. The whole rhythm of life is disrupted.

How to Tackle Depression?

Here are some tips to tackle depression in general.

1. Get up at nearly the same time seven days a week.
2. Go outdoors as much as possible. Walk in sun. Sunlight generate vitamin D which lifts your mood. Continue your morning walks. Open your windows. Get bright lights into your room. Bring in more sunlight. Do not stay in dark.
3. Exercise helps beat the depression. Do gardening. Plan a trekking trip.
4. Do not try to beat depression with alcohol/caffeine. It will only worsen situation.
5. Meet positive people, and take part in social activities. Make a conscious effort to forgive. Refuse to think/talk negatively about anybody.

6. Watch your diet. Sugar is a known depressant. It may give you a momentary high, but soon bogs you down. Eat lots of fruits and salads. Drink plenty of water. Depression can get enhanced by dehydration.
7. Wear bright colours. Get a body massage. Take warm water baths. Keep your surroundings clean. Change your linen. Dress yourself well.
8. Listen to spiritual music. Read humour. Indulge in a hobby. Learn some new activity like, singing, dancing, musical instrument, game, aerobics, Yoga, and Pranayam. Above all, learn to love yourself. Give yourself credit for many good things.

Treatment

There are only two lines of treatment: medication/diet and psychotherapy.

Diet/Nutrition

Low vitamin D causes depression. Get your vitamin D by going outside in sun.

Most depressed people have low levels of neuro-transmitter serotonin. Vitamin C is vital in making serotonin. Anti-depressant drugs tend to uptake neurotransmitters. Fortunately nutritional therapies to raise levels of serotonin and dopamine to regulate mood and prevent depression can be very helpful. The therapy requires diets of:

Tryptophan, like in apples, bananas, carbohydrates

Tyrosine as in cheese

Phenylalanine as in soybeans and legumes, almonds, pumpkin and sesame seeds, which get converted to serotonin.

Comfort Foods

A survey claims that onions bring the most pleasure followed by carrots, baked beans, bananas and potatoes.

All carbohydrates are great comfort foods. Omega-3 fats may calm your nerves. According to Psychosomatic Medicine magazine, researchers found that men with lowest levels of omega-3, EPA and DHA, were more likely to have risk of falling into depression. EPA and DHA are key brain components. Higher levels of omega-3 can bolster serotonin and dopamine, potent mood enhancers.

Increase the intake of omega-3 by eating walnuts, flaxseeds, broccoli, and mustard and canola oils.

Take foods containing magnesium, zinc, biotin, and vitamin B12. Chocolate contains plenty of magnesium. It relaxes and gives comfort. As it releases serotonin, it reduces physical and mental fatigue.

Vitamin B deficiency, more specifically B12, B6, folate and thiamin, is frequently connected to mood swings and depression. Even a mild B12 deficiency can produce depression.

The best way to check depression is to eat whole grain cereals, foods rich in B-vitamins. A baked potato provides half your daily need of B6. Folate affects how your brain uses dopamine and serotonin. You get your folate from beans, greens, etc.

Iron Deficiency/Anaemia

Anaemic people are most likely to suffer from depression. No wonder since it is the haemoglobin that carries oxygen to cells and brain. Hence, raise haemoglobin level by eating iron-rich foods and vitamin C which helps your body absorb iron.

Herbs and Supplements

St John's Wort (and not Prozac) is the number one drug of choice for common depression in Germany and in Europe. It is considered as the Prozac of Plants.

SAMe (S-demosyl methane) is a natural compound your body makes and uses to produce dopamine and serotonin. Supplement helps produce these feel-good chemicals.

Saffron is used in Ayurveda to treat depression. It works by aiding to increase serotonin.

Thianine in tea relaxes the brain.

Cannabis. The active ingredients in marijuana have mood-elevating properties which can be harnessed to treat depression.

Kali Phos 6X may help taper off dosage of allopathic drugs.

Psychotherapy involves expressing and releasing your deeper emotions. There are two types of methods:

1. Cathartic release methods.
2. Expressive release methods.

Cathartic release frees your mind of suppressed negative emotions. You can do it in three ways. One way is to vent your feelings aloud. Second way is to do vigorous exercise/s. Third is to open up to a sympathetic listener.

All these can be combined in a group meditation, or even alone in a secluded place, that involves rhythmic exercise, loud music and shouting out all your feelings of fear, anger, abuse, betrayal, losses, etc., ending it with slow movements and soft music, followed by complete silence and meditation.

Emotions are like energy. Physical exercise releases pent-up negative emotions. Exercise also generates endorphins.

Expressive release methods involve curing yourself by creative expression through writing, painting, music, dance, drama, social work, etc. Such activities lead to a deeper resolution of your long-standing problems, clearer understanding of life, self-knowledge, and self-healing.

Artistic pursuits and pursuits for a universal cause shift your mind from negative to positive thinking, that is, from stress to deeper relaxation.

In the ultimate analysis, take the following three most important measures:

1. Exercise or physical activity. Go for walks. Now doctors recommend working outdoors in a garden or on a farm than just sitting at home on medication.
2. Satsang. Keep company of pious people. Talk out your problems. Seek emotional support from a close friend.
3. Positive Attitude. Uphold a positive attitude and keep no room for negative thoughts.

The above-mentioned points are explained in details:

Exercise/Physical Activity

According to Samuel Harvey of Kings College London, people who take part in regular exercises, during leisure time and for fun, could almost halve their risk of depression.

In one study, participants who exercised showed the same reduction in symptoms of depression as those who received Prozac medication. Medications have side effects but exercise has none. It is an easy remedy for self administeration.

People with mild to moderate depression when engaged in 30-minutes of aerobic activity 3-5 times a week reduced the severity of their symptoms by 50 per cent.

Note that in depression, brain is starved of oxygen. Any activity, like exercise, which increases oxygen supply to the brain, is beneficial.

Satsang

Depression is always about something, which you desire, and which is missing in life.

Did you ever think that the best things in life are for free?

Recent studies show that spending time relaxing with family/noble friends/*satsang*, helps in making people happy from within.

Learning from the lives of happy people, activities such as listening to music (soft, melodious, spiritual, and classical), reading a book, taking a walk in the garden/woods, just the very act of deep breathing with awareness can make one happy in the real sense.

Basically, you do not need any reason to be happy. If you need a reason to be happy, probably you will never be happy. This is the Mantra of Happy Life that has no place for depression.

Positive Attitude: Banish Negative Thoughts

Probably the most significant factor in depression is the feeling that you do not have control over what is happening in your life. You feel powerless. The solution lies in two steps:

1. First is to be aware of the fact that you have the power to change your life, may be not much, but at least a little bit.

2. Second is to realise that action is essential. You have to do something. You can not achieve anything simply by sitting in gloom.

Do something about your problem. It will automatically make you feel happier. It will start a snowballing effect. You will be doing more and more and feeling better and better.

27.10 SLEEPLESSNES/INSOMNIA

Sleep is the diet of the mind. Repair and healing take place during sleep. Lack of sleep causes great harm to your body and nervous system. It weakens your immune system. You may even develop inflammations of various kinds.

About 7-8 hours of sleep is essential for everybody. According to new research by University of California, Berkley, taking a mid-day nap can also dramatically improve brain's learning capacity (*The Times of India*, 1 March 2010).

If you do not get sleep, there is no escape from resorting to sleep-aids. But you must sleep adequately under all circumstances.

The cause of insomnia could be the simple apprehension that you may not fall asleep. There could be other causes such as anxiety, grief, depression, use of anti-depressants, stress, HBP, pain, breathing problem, alcohol or caffeine consumption, etc. Sedentary lifestyle is also responsible for sleeplessness.

Vaata controls all movements in the body, whether of bowels or of thoughts. It is usually the *vaata* types who are more prone to insomnia. It is therefore important to pacify *vaata-dosha*. Take diet which pacifies *vaata*.

Take a warm water bath 1-2 hours before bedtime to lower body temperature. Lightly massage forehead, temples and head with sesame (*til*) oil for 5-10 minutes. Then drink a glass of warm milk, preferably with an Ayurvedic rasayana (herbal potion).

Next turn off the lights, sit quietly and meditate. Listen to soothing music until you feel drowsy. Most people fall asleep without any difficulty by following this routine.

Body Temperature

One important factor for inducing sleep is body temperature. It must come down before the body can enter the sleep phase. The natural mechanism for cooling down the body becomes weak with age. For elderly people, it is recommended that they go for a walk 5 hours before bed time, thereby, allowing time to cool down for sleep.

Switching on air conditioner while going to sleep may help.

Suggested Nutrients/Supplements

Lack of calcium and magnesium could disturb sleep. Calcium can sleep. It has calming effect on nerves and relaxes the brain. A glass of warm milk just before going to bed works like a sleep aid. In addition to calcium, milk contains tryptophan that promotes sleep.

Magnesium-rich foods relax the muscles and the brain.

Melatonin lowers BP and body temperature. Start with 1mg supplement if necessary.

Taking cow's milk, carbohydrates like rice, desserts and cereals, bananas, cherries, etc., at bedtime trigger production of melatonin by the pineal gland. Having a glass of unsweetened cherry juice twice a day helps in providing sound sleep.

Tryptophan converts to serotonin, and serotonin converts into melatonin. Carbohydrates like sweet fruits, pasta, oatmeal, and brown rice, as they have tryptophan, help produce sleep-inducing hormone serotonin.

You may have a bowl of cereals with milk at bedtime. Carbohydrates (cereals) contain tryptophan, and milk contains calcium and magnesium. Both help in inducing sleep.

Note that it takes about 1 hour for tryptophan in food to reach the brain. Banana contains a lot of tryptophan.

Aroma of balsam flowers and fragrance of lavender induce sleep.

Reflexology

Apply pressure on both big toes for a restful sleep. The point on the outside of big toe just below the tip corresponds to the pineal gland which regulates sleep hormone melatonin.

Herbs and Mother Tinctures for Refreshing Sleep

Avena Sativa promotes tranquility and sleep. It is also a treatment for male impotency.

Passiflora Incarnata is a treatment for insomnia in addition to asthma and diarrhoea.

Being a tonic for lungs, Aspidosperma induces sleep simultaneously and helps in coughs.

Valerian herb and chamomile tea promote sleep by relaxing nerves. Hops flowers, used in making of beer, are also good. That is why, small quantity of beer helps in inducing sleep. But too much beer, because of its alcohol content, may disturb sleep.

Aniseed (*Saunf*)

Tea prepared by boiling *saunf* in water taken at bedtime is found to be beneficial.

Kali Phos 6X, a biochemical medicine helps soothe brain and promote sleep. Nux Vomica 30 or 200, a homoeopathic medicine, is a general remedy for anxiety, constipation, sleeplessness, and for reducing side-effects of alcohol and other drugs.

Recommendations

There should be no light in the bedroom. Using a laptop or an iPod just before going to bed can turn you into an insomniac. Bright light after darkness causes the brain to stop secreting the hormone melatonin that makes us sleepy.

Sprinkle sheets and pillowcases with lavender to promote relaxation, leading to sleep. Use cool thin pillows that are filled with cotton, not synthetic fibres.

Sesame (*til*) or almond oil massage on head will greatly help induce sleep. Sunbath for 20-30 minutes enables the body to make its own melatonin.

Regular exercise reduces insomnia. But no exercise should be done within 3-4 hours of bedtime. Exercise raises your body temperature, which falls 5-6 hours later, causing drowsiness and enhancing sleep.

Increase your intake of vitamin B. But do not take vitamin supplements in the evening. Caffeine and other stimulants help keeping you awake. Avoid drinks containing caffeine after lunch including coffee, colas, etc. Even tea should not be taken after 4 p.m. Avoid alcohol. It invariably disturbs sleep. Tobacco is a strict no-no.

If you cannot fall asleep, then do the opposite. Try to stay awake. For some, this works.

Other Recommendations

Good sleeping habits help in curing insomnia.

Always go to bed at a fixed time and get up at a fixed time.

10 p.m., according to nature's biological clock, is the time to go to bed. One should sleep 7-8 hours daily. 5-6 a.m. is the natural time to wake up.

Eat a light carbohydrate snack before bedtime. Do ritualistic jobs, which do not require any mental activity, to get to winding down slowly.

Use bedroom only for sleep and relaxing, not for studying, working, eating, or watching TV. Keep your bedroom quiet, clean, comfortable, and with a soothing ambience.

If too much quietness is the problem, then play some soothing music, if it helps.

Concentrate on pleasant thoughts at bedtime. Start your night with a prayer. Go to sleep chanting softly *om shanti shanti, om shanti shanti,* or any other chant you prefer.

Insomnia is usually a problem of hyper-arousal during the day. The solution is to permit yourself deep relaxation.

Relax by breathing deeply 15 minutes before bedtime. Deep breathing helps to relax muscles and regulate the activity of parasympathetic nerves that slows the heart rate, dilates blood vessels and lowers blood pressure.

Another common method is to play a tape on 'Yog-nidra' by some authentic Yoga teacher. You can practise Yog-nidra on your own.

Massaging of feet, calves, neck, head and shoulders, helps to relax the body. Massaging the whole body followed by a warm water bath enables a good sleep.

Reiki helps you regain energy as well as sleep. Doing Reiki, particularly on the crown, forehead, eyes, back of head, temples, neck, chest and abdomen is helpful.

Turn over on to your tummy to sleep if you still have trouble falling asleep.

Balakasan Posture for Sleeping

This is the best posture to sleep.

Lie on your stomach with head turned to the right side. Let the left arm be kept along the body. Bend the right arm and place forearm near the face on the bed with palm facing downwards near the head. Keep right elbow close to the body. Fold your right leg. Bring the knee side-wise. Now relax yourself fully. Breathe deeply till the breath becomes calm and slow.

Relax in this pose as long as it takes to sleep. If you feel uneasy, turn to the other side in exactly opposite positions for left and right legs and hands. You may alternate in these positions if it takes more time to get sleep.

Yog-Nidra

Lie on your back in Shavasana pose. Breathe from the abdomen and allow the breath to become natural. Now just remain aware of the breath. Take your attention to vital centres in your body. Relax them one by one. Start from forehead. Move progressively to Ajna Chakra, the area between the eyebrows, eyes, face, nostrils, lips, throat and neck, shoulders, arms, elbows, wrists, fingers, finger tips and palms. Stay at palms for a while.

Now begin with throat, chest and heart, abdomen, pelvic area, thighs, knees, calf muscles, ankles, feet, toes, and soles of feet. Stay at the soles for a while.

You may stay at various energy centers such as heart, navel, pubic area, etc., for longer intervals to promote sleep.

Stay, with breath awareness, on various Chakras (energy/nerve centres) along the spine.

Start with Mooladhar at the base of spine. Move to Swadhishthan (sex chakra), then Manipur (navel), Anhad (heart), Vishuddhi (throat), Ajna (the eye centre), and finally to Sahasrar (crown). Drop all thoughts. Just feel surrendered to the Divine/God.

27.11 DEMENTIA/ALZHEIMER'S DISEASE (AD)

Dementia

Dementia is gradual loss of memory with age. It happens to elderly people above the age of 65. Incidence of dementia is much lower in India as compared to Western countries.

Study shows that consumption of turmeric in India helps preventing the disease.

A study demonstrated that those who consumed about 3 servings of green and cruciferous vegetables a day showed 40 per cent slower rate of cognitive decline.

Alzheimer's disease (AD)

Alzheimer's disease is like a heightened state of dementia. It is a degenerative disorder of nerve fibres in the memory centres of the brain due to plaque build-up that gradually destroys a person's memory.

By age of 80, 40 per cent of Americans are likely to be diagnosed with dementia and often Alzheimer's disease. Its precise cause is not known. Insulin deficiency in diabetics may cause AD.

1. **Brain damaging plaque has been seen in AD patients.**
   Studies have shown that if you keep your cholesterol under 198 while in your forties, you are 50 per cent less likely to develop AD. Managing cholesterol could, therefore, play a key role in preventing and treating AD.
2. **High levels of inflammation-causing homocysteine are associated with AD.**
   Folic acid together with B12 is known to reduce homocysteine levels in blood. In addition, a clean and healthy lifestyle avoiding frequent inflammations and infections is needed.

3. **High levels of CRP are also linked to inflammation which can lead to AD.**

   Just 30 minutes of walking, 5 days a week, has been shown to lower CRP levels. Many illnesses, including AD, result from a weak immune system.

General Recommendations and Nutrients

There are no cures for AD. Prevention is the key. Yian Gu at Columbia University, New York, found that fatty acids in meats and butter need to be avoided. People who consume olive oil, omega-3 fats, vitamins E, B6, B12 and folate foods, tomatoes, fruits and leafy greens have 40 per cent lower risk of developing dementia and AD.

A balanced diet of natural foods, pure water, plenty of fibre, using oats and rice with bran is recommended.

Strictly avoiding alcohol, tobacco, processed or canned foods, and environmental toxins specially metals like aluminum and mercury prevents and treats dementia and AD. Signs of alcohol abuse and AD are similar.

The line of treatment is to first try vitamin B12 or Neurobion injections. If that works, it means there is no AD.

Nitrate

Nitrate expands arteries increasing blood flow to brain, thus, preventing dementia and AD. Eat foods like beetroots, cabbage, spinach and Ajwain/celery for nitrate requirement.

Coenzyme Q10, in general, increases oxygenation of cells, including heart and brain.

B-Vitamins

Researchers at Oxford University have found that high doses of B-vitamins reduced memory decline to the extent of 70 per cent. It also halved the rate of brain shrinkage.

Vitamin B1 is needed for neuro-transmitters. It protects against dementia and AD. B5 is needed for memory; deficiency of B6 causes depression. B12 is important for brain function.

Vitamin B12 is found in milk and milk products, eggs, and fermented moong.

Folic Acid and Vitamin B12

British researchers found that AD progressed twice as fast in those with high levels of homocysteine. Folic acid, vitamin B12 and B6 decrease blood levels of homocysteine.

Good folic acid sources are orange juice, fruits and vegetables, and wheat germ.

Zinc: Plaque formation and damage to nerve cells is associated with zinc deficiency. Alcohol and many medications deplete elderly people of vitamins and minerals like zinc.

Antioxidants

Dr Garry Small, in his book *The Memory Bible,* points out that free radicals can do serious harm to brain cells. Fortunately vitamins C, E and flavonoids can help combat this damage.

Whole grains, fruits, vegetables and nuts are flavonoid-and fibre-rich. They prevent plaque formation in brain, thus, preventing dementia and AD.

Vegetables and fruits based diet provides enough vitamin C. A study showed that those who drank fruit or vegetable juice 3 times a week were 76 per cent less likely to develop AD.

In a study, 633 disease-free but suspected 65-year olds were given large amounts of either vitamin C or vitamin E. None of them developed the disease until 5 years later. Extra fibre imparts more protection to brain by lowering cholesterol and BP, both linked to AD.

Dr Abha Chauhan of New York State Institute found that vitamin E and flavonoids in walnuts help in destroying free radicals that cause dementia. They can keep mental skills sharp. Vitamin E has been shown to protect neurons.

Pomegranate Juice

According to FDA, Alzheimer's could be kept at bay by pomegranate juice.

In a 10-year study at University of South Florida, people who drank juice 3-times a week had 75 per cent lower risk of dementia. It is attributed to high concentrations of polyphenols.

Brain Minerals

Calcium, potassium, selenium, zinc and boron are the key minerals important for brain health.

Calcium helps brain and nerve cells work together. Milk is the best source of calcium. But you get it from white seasame (*til*), orange juice, leafy greens, etc. also. At the time of birth, the first and immediate nutrients needed for the development of the body and the brain are calcium and protein which are obtained from mother's milk.

Potassium is needed for electrolyte balance, nerve cell function and nerve transmission.

Selenium, an antioxidant, protects brain cells. Zinc retards plaque formation and damage to nerve cells. Alcohol depletes zinc.

Boron is an amazing mineral that prevents mental degeneration.

Omega-3 Fats and Olive Oil

Those who eat anti-inflammatory omega-3 fats are less likely to suffer from memory loss.

Add omega-3 fats to your diet through nuts and flaxseeds, canola and mustard oils. Extra-virgin olive oil can prevent AD.

Catechin/Tea

Catechin in green tea and cocoa has been shown to arrest cognitive decline by 50 per cent.

A recent study published in the American Journal of Neuroscience shows that the compound may boost memory by improving blood flow in the brain. A Japanese study on people over 70 years of age, revealed that those who drank 2-3 cups of green tea daily scored better on cognitive tests. This may explain why dementia and AD rates are lower in Japan.

Turmeric

Recent studies indicate that turmeric is effective in preventing AD, arthritis, heart disease and cancer. Potent antioxidant and anti-inflammatory properties of turmeric are attributed to curcumin present in turmeric. Indians take 100-200mg of curcumin by way of turmeric. Incidence of AD in India is 4 times less common than in USA.

According to a study conducted by Milan Fiala of University of California, LA, curcumin boosts the immune system to destroy peptide, a brain-clogging protein.

A new study reported that curcumin in turmeric inhibited the formation of destructive plaque deposits in the brain, broke up existing plaques, and reduced AD related tissues.

Herbs
Gingko Biloba

It is considered to increase blood flow through brain, and to enhance memory in the elderly.

Marijuana

New research at Scripps Research Institute in California shows that the active ingredients in marijuana may prevent progression of AD by preserving important neurotransmitters.

Chronic inflammation in the brain is believed to impair memory. According to Gary Wenk at OSU, certain substances in marijuana may help the ageing brain by reducing inflammation and even stimulating formation of new brain cells.

Brahmi, Shankh Pushpi and Kali Phos 6X are memory enhancers.

Rosemary

Rich in antioxidants, it is said to reduce inflammations, and to help improve concentration and long-term memory.

Five Great Memory Aids

1. **Sleep:** Research has shown that a nap as short as 6 minutes can improve memory. Adequate sleep should be considered necessary to maintain good memory.

2. **Sports/Walking:** Blood glucose levels rise as we age. This is linked to memory lapse. Try sports/games to regulate blood sugar level. Scientists at University of Pittsburg have found that walking, at least 8 km per week, may protect brain from growing smaller and thus slow down and even prevent the progression of dementia and AD.

3. **Reading:** According to research at Mayo Clinic in USA, reading reduces risk of developing mild memory loss by 30-50 per cent.

4. **Coffee:** According to a study in Journal of AD, three cups of caffeinated coffee daily could lower risk of developing dementia by 70 per cent.

5. **Eating less:** Eating less can help older adults improve their memory, and prevent or delay the onset of memory loss and AD.

6. **Chewing food:** Chewing stimulates the production of insulin which may affect the area of the brain responsible for memory. Chewing also increases heart rate that tends to raise blood flow and oxygen to brain.

High Protein Diet Can Shrink Your Brain

A research team from USA, UK and Canada led by Sam Gandy of The Mount Sinai School of Medicine, New York, has found that the body uses proteins to generate plaques typical to AD. Mice fed with high protein/low carbohydrate diet had 5 per cent lighter brains.

Low Carbohydrate Diet Causes Memory Loss

The body breaks down carbohydrates into glucose, which it uses to produce energy. Proteins, on the other hand, break down into glycogen, which can also be used as fuel to produce energy. However, glycogen cannot be used by the brain as efficiently as glucose.

A study on women aged 22 to 55 years conducted by psychology professor Holly Taylor of Tuft's University Massachusetts showed that those on low carbohydrate meals suffered impaired memory function after just one week. But when carbohydrates were re-introduced, the women's mental function returned to normal.

Alzheimer's disease and Aluminum Connection

There is a link between AD and high concentration of aluminum in brain. Aluminum may come from aluminum cookware, antacids, painkillers, coated aspirin, aluminum coated containers for juices, food additives and anti-dandruff shampoos.

Plastic Bottles/Cookware Deadly for Brain

Canadian researchers at the University of Guelph have found that Bisphenol A (BPA), a chemical used in the making of plastic containers, disrupts communication between brain neurons. The chemical might be percolating into the human system through leakage into the solid and liquid foods kept in plastic containers.

Use It or Lose It

'Use it or lose it' applies to brain as well as for other organs.

Just like our muscles need physical exercise, our brain too needs mental exercise. University of California, Irvine, neuro-biologists have provided evidence that learning promotes brain health. New learning builds new brain cells.

The best way is to keep learning, say, an art or a new language or a new subject. It is found that those who know more languages never or rarely develop dementia. MRI studies show that introducing brain to new experiences leads to growth of newer brain cells even at an advanced age.

Both under-use and over-use of the body and body organs are to be avoided. Under-use may result in loss of functioning of the organs. Over-use may impair the body and the organs.

Rest is, therefore, essential for the body and the organs including the brain. The brain rarely gets rest. Even during sleep when the body and other body parts are resting, the brain keeps on working processing the data and repair of the body.

Meditation and *Trataka* for Brain

Meditation is one way when brain goes into a state of rest.

Trataka **involves simply gazing at an object.** The brain gets bored and goes to sleep. The rest rejuvenates the brain and helps prevent degeneration. Meditation on breath is a kind of *trataka*.

Lead a righteous and purposeful life.

Robert Wilson of Rush University Medical Center Chicago found that people, who are conscientious, self-disciplined, and scrupulous, appear to be less likely to develop AD.

Patricia A Boyle of the same Center has shown that individuals who have greater purpose in their lives are less likely to develop AD or its precursor, cognitive impairment.

27.12 PARKINSON'S DISEASE (PD)

PD is a degenerative disorder of central nervous system (CNS). It impairs the person's motor skills and speech, characterised by muscle rigidity.

Its symptoms are tremors, slowness in activities and stiffness of the entire body. Parkinson's disease is caused by insufficient formation and action of dopamine, or due to damage to the area substantia nigra in the brain which produces dopamine.

It is generally clear that lack of pleasurable experiences in one's life, or one's own stiff, uncompromising, and egoistic attitude may lead to PD.

At present, there is no cure for PD. Treatment primarily involves only controlling symptoms of the disorder with medication. First, one must learn to adopt a relaxed attitude and let go.

It requires management of the disease and the patient with careful knowledge, support, general wellness maintenance, exercise, and nutrition.

In order to partially treat or slow down deterioration, substances/ foods, which promote dopamine production, may be used. Coenzyme Q10 is involved as a precursor to dopamine. Banana helps in the natural production of dopamine.

Vitamins C and E, in large doses, can lessen cell damage.

27.13 EPILEPSY (*MIRGI*)

Epilepsy is the disease of the central nervous system beginning in hypothalamus.

To understand epilepsy one has to imagine two types of nerve cells or neurons, viz., those that are exciting, and those that are calming.

In a normal person, both types of neurons are present in a balanced state. But electric charges produced by exciting cells in an epilepsy patient can cause a sudden explosion, resulting in seizure and sudden failure of all mental and muscular motor actions. Such an explosion may be triggered by an injury to the nerves, some other ailment, or by certain chemical imbalances.

In the triggering of seizures, the electrolytes calcium, potassium, and sodium play roles.

EEG test is necessary for treatment. Medical treatment is a must in epilepsy. As a precaution, the patient should avoid being in hot, humid and crowded places. The patient should never be left alone. S/he should live among sympathetic people, and should take up a profession with no stress or tension.

J. Helen Cross, professor of pediatric neurology at University College London and Great Ormond Street Hospital found in a study that a high fat diet proved very effective in reducing seizers in children whose epilepsy does not respond to medications.

A fat diet appears to work by forcing the body to burn fat instead of sugar for energy.

Onion juice, two tsp in a glass of water, taken daily in the morning for 40 days, is believed to alleviate epileptic attacks.

27.14 MULTIPLE SCLEROSIS (MS)

MS is a progressive degeneration of the central nervous system (CNS), including spinal cord. The onset of MS occurs in early youth between 20-40 years age.

In the beginning, the person may experience fatigue, and difficulty in walking. As the disease progresses, extreme fatigue may set in, and the movements become more spasmodic. Paralysis may occur. This disease has periods of flare-ups.

Causes

Cause of MS is not known, but it is believed to be an auto-immune disease, which occurs as a result of an overactive immune system. In an auto-immune disease, the immune system becomes an enemy instead of being a friend. In MS, WBCs start attacking their own nerves' sheaths as if they were foreign invaders.

Stress could also be the factor of a weakened or overactive immune system.

Chemical and Environmental Poisoning

Chemical poisoning of nervous system by pesticides, other chemicals, and heavy metals, and damage to nerves' sheaths by environmental toxins play a part in causing MS.

Cure and Nutrients

There is no cure for MS. But taking care of diet, environment, living style, relaxation, etc., soon after symptoms are detected, may slow, or even stop the progress of disease.

There is evidence that a diet low in saturated fats maintained over a number of years prevents the disease. The beneficial effect is believed to be due to decrease in platelet aggregation, and decrease in auto-immune response.

An abundance of vitamin D in form of sunshine seems to help prevent MS. Coenzyme Q10 improves blood circulation and tissue oxygenation, and strengthens immune system. Omega-3 fats inhibit inflammations and prevent MS from worsening.

Garlic is an excellent source of sulphur. It protects against chemical/environmental toxins.

Vitamin B6 promotes RBC count, aids nervous system, and strengthens immune function. Its deficiency may cause MS in people prone to the disease. Extra vitamin B12 aids longevity of cells, prevents nervous damage by maintaining protective nerve sheaths.

Calcium, magnesium and potassium deficiency causes predisposition to MS. Potassium is needed even for normal muscle function.

Natural antioxidants/flavonoids must be consumed in large quantities. Selenium and vitamin C are powerful antioxidants and immune system stimulants. Beta-carotenes/Carotenoids are other important antioxidants.

Vitamin E promotes circulation, destroys free radicals, and protects nervous system.

Bromelain in pineapples is found effective in treating immune system diseases like MS. Manganese is a mineral often found deficient in MS patients.

Recommendations

- Eat organically grown foods. Avoid pesticides, all sorts of chemicals or additives.
- Develop a strong immune system. Take only fresh foods.
- Eat plenty of sprouts, dark leafy greens for vitamin K, and wheat grass for chlorophyll.
- Drink plenty of water to prevent build-up of toxins in muscles.
- Stay away from meat, alcohol, tobacco, coffee, fried/refined/processed/canned foods, excessive salt, sugar, etc.
- Take a fibre supplement like isabgul to avoid constipation.
- A clean colon is important for keeping toxic wastes from accumulating. Short duration fasts are helpful. Take warm water with fresh lemon in the morning.
- Take EFAs. Never take saturated fats, or oils subjected to heating or that are rancid.
- Check possible food allergies. They are a major factor in MS. Gluten intolerance from wheat makes one susceptible to MS.
- Avoid stress and anxiety. MS attacks are often preceded by trauma and emotional stress.
- Avoid exposure to heat, sunbathing, exhaustion, viral infections, etc. All these, that increase body temperature, may worsen the condition.

- Get massage, physiotherapy; do regular light exercises, Yoga, *Pranayam*, meditation, etc. A study of people with MS showed that lifting weights increased endurance, and decreased inflammation.
- Take rest for atleast two days if symptoms occur.
- Keep company of people who give you emotional support. A positive input is a cure.

28

Skeletal System

28.1 BONES, JOINTS, CARTILAGE, TENDONS AND LIGAMENTS

Bones are composed of 75 per cent inorganic material like calcium, magnesium, phosphorous, carbonates and sodium, and 25 per cent organic material like collagen and fibrous tissue.

The hollow inside the bones is filled with bone marrow. Within bones, there is a system of small canals that contain blood vessels that bring nutrients and oxygen to the bone, and remove waste products such as carbon dioxide.

Joints are provided where two or more bones meet, and movement is needed. Some joints are immovable such as those in the skull bones. Others are partially movable as between the vertebrae. Most joints allow considerable movement.

Cartilage allows friction-free movements of the joints, and reduces wear and tear. The bones themselves do not touch each other. Wherever there is a joint between two bones, they are separated by cartilage. The cartilage of one bone comes in contact with the cartilage of the other bone. It cushions the joint, and allows it to move smoothly.

Tendons are connective tissues that connect muscles to bones. Ligaments are connective tissues that bind bone to a bone.

Bursae are little sacks, which secrete a very thick fluid that acts as a water cushion. Some common locations of bursae are at the elbow, knee, and shoulder joints.

There are two main disorders of the skeletal system – arthritis and osteoporosis.

Arthritis is concerned more with damage to the cartilage, while osteoporosis means weak and porous bones.

28.2 NUTRIENTS FOR HEALTHY SKELETAL SYSTEM

Vaata people particularly suffer from stiff joints and Rheumatoid Arthritis (RA). Certain dietary sources can alleviate the ailments related to the skeletal system.

Omega-3 fats prevent inflammations. Consume plenty of omega-3 to avoid joint pains. Calcium, magnesium, phosphorous and silicon foods are needed for healthy bones.

Silicon: Cucumber and beetroot are rich in silicon. Beer from barley has been claimed to be an important source of silicon. Consume whole grains to obtain silicon from diet.

Vitamins C and D, and sulphur improve calcium absorption while vitamin K holds calcium in bones. It is necessary for bone health.

Boron and phyto-oestrogens reduce urinary excretion of calcium, thus preventing calcium loss. Just as it is important to absorb the calcium that we intake, it is equally important to prevent calcium loss through urinary excretion.

28.3 BAD BACK

As in osteoarthritis, in the case of back pain it is plausible that the lower back joints may have suffered cartilage damage. Bad back may also be due to wrong postures while sitting, standing, or even lying down.

The following suggestions may help:

- Do not slouch while standing. Always stand straight.
- While standing, ease the pressure on the back by resting one foot preferably elevated in front of you on anything above floor level.
- Wear flat sole shoes. They do not require arching of your back as high-heeled shoes do.

- Sagging stomach muscles exert weight on the back. Exercise to strengthen abdominal muscles.
- While sitting, raise your knees an inch higher than your hips by resting feet on a support. While sitting in your car, do not slide car seat back. It is better to slide it forward so that your knees are above your hips, and your back remains straight.
- Use car-seat with lumbar support.
- Always sit with your back straight and supported.
- Do not stand or sit in one position for too long.
- Avoid sudden and jerky movements of the body.
- Use hard bed for sleeping with just a thin pillow under your head.
- Further, it is very important that when you are going to lie down, you do not just lie down straight on your back. First lie down on the side, and then you may turn over to lie on your back. Similarly, when you are trying to get up, turn on your side first, bend the hips and knees and take support of the upper arm to get up.
- If you sleep on your back, sleep with your knees raised. If you sleep on your stomach, put a pillow below pelvis. If you sleep on your sides, curl your legs in foetus position.
- Another very important tip is to never bend forward. And do only those exercises which involve bending backward. In this connection, if you have to pick up anything from the floor, then don't just bend down to pick up while remaining standing. You may first bend your knees, and sit down on your haunches keeping the back straight, pick up the thing, and then slowly stand up.

Yogasanas for Bad Back

The following asanas will strengthen your spine, ankles, knees, thighs, shoulders and arms. They help lessen backaches and even sciatica pain.

Tadasana

Stand erect. Keep your hands near your chest with fingers inter-locked. Stretch out your arms in front of chest. Breathing in, slowly raise your arms upwards. Simultaneously raise your body standing on tips of the toes.

Stretch your body upwards breathing normally. Stay in this position as long as you can. Slowly unlock your fingers, bring your arms down on sides while exhaling and relax.

Tanasana

It is like Tadasana, but it is done while lying down. Inhale and pull the hands and legs in opposite directions. Feel the stretch in your spine. Hold the posture for some time. Exhale and then relax. Repeat a few times.

Backache may also be caused by an upset stomach and mucus formation in GI Tract.

28.4 ARTHRITIS

In all forms of arthritis – osteoarthritis (OA), rheumatoid arthritis (RA), and gout – there is progressive destruction of cartilage that acts as a cushion between bones. Whereas strenuous exercise may increase the chances of developing it, light exercise can help in preventing arthritis or delay its onset, claims a new research at the University of California.

A team at Greek Island Labs Company has produced a 'joint mud' cream which claims to reduce arthritis pain in just 18 minutes. This cream prominently contains cherry oil, sage oil and pomegranate oil among some 25 of its ingredients.

In arthritis, the first step should be to shed extra body weight if you have any.

28.4.1 OSTEOARTHRITIS (OA)

Osteoarthritis is a condition in which the cartilage begins to physically wear out, thereby causing inflammation and pain.

CAUSES OF OSTEOARTHRITIS

Some primary causes of osteoarthritis are:

1. Age-related wear and tear, cartilage destruction and fusion of bones.
2. High uric acid in body, when uric acid crystals get deposited between joints.
3. Obesity is a major factor of OA of knee. By treating obesity, OA can be cured.

Cartilage doesn't have nerve endings. This is both, advantageous and disadvantageous.

The advantage is in the sense that you are not incapacitated of movements even if OA damage has begun in the cartilage.

The disadvantage is that it is possible to have substantial cartilage damage without even your realising it. You do not see cartilage even in an X-ray. The disease may have started 10-20 years before you get the first symptoms.

NUTRIENTS AND CURES

Reduce Body Weight

The more the weight, the more is the load on joints and the more is the damage. Studies have demonstrated that every 1/2 kg lost is equivalent to 2kg less of pressure on the knees. Dropping 5 kg could spare each knee 20 kg of pressure.

Take Water

Cartilage is made up mostly of water. In addition, water in joints acts like oil in a car engine. Drinking plenty of water enables you to maintain a steady flow of nutrients to the joints.

Sulphur

Sulphur is a building block of the body's cells including cartilage. SAMe contains sulphur. Take folate-rich MSM (methyl-sulphonyl methane) which is a sulphur compound present in foods such as milk, fruits, vegetables, tea and coffee.

Sulphur is needed for repair of bone cartilage and connective tissues, and aids in absorption of calcium. Take garlic, onions, asparagus, and cabbage-family vegetables.

Aloe Vera (*Guar-Patha*)

Aloe Vera, as pulp and juice, is the traditional remedy for arthritis. Aloe Vera pulp *saunth* and sautéd wheat flour can be mixed and made into laddoos.

Minerals

Selenium: Those who consume a lot of selenium in their diet are 46 per cent less likely to have OA.

Manganese: It helps the body build strong joints. Whole grains and legumes provide manganese.

Boron: It could help prevent arthritis and ease joint pain. Apples, peas, raisins and pears have high amounts of boron.

Zinc: Body becomes deficient in zinc in advanced age. Take whole grains to fulfil selenium and zinc requirement.

Treatment with MUFA and Omega-3 Fats

A group of products of metabolism called leukotrienes cause arthritic inflammations. The omega-6 fats found in vegetable oils of corn, sesame, soybean, sunflower, safflower, and saturated fats as in margarines, generate these inflammatory chemicals. There is reduction in production of inflammatory chemicals with MUFA and omega-3 fats.

Vitamins

Vitamins C, E, B5 and B6 are required for synthesis of collagen. Vitamin E, plentiful in almonds and sunflower seeds, is essential for maintaining healthy cartilage, for lubrication between joints and analgesic effect. Take a supplement.

Vitamin C protects against inflammations in joints. Fruits have the most vitamin C. Without vitamin C, joints can weaken three times faster.

Vitamin D protects cartilage and bones, and helps body absorb calcium. As mentioned before, vitamin D is synthesised in the body in the presence of sunlight.

The specific arthritis-fighting nutrients like folate and B6 are present in high amounts in bananas.

Natural Antioxidants

Apples, avocados and grapes/wine contain antioxidants which reduce the rate at which cartilage breaks down, and thus help to slow the process of OA.

Green Tea

Poly-phenols in green tea inhibit inflammation causing chemicals.

WAYS TO EASE ARTHRITIS PAIN

Bromelain in pineapples breaks down proteins in blood. This explains its ability to curb pain-causing inflammations. Ginger extract or *saunth* taken daily gives significant reduction in knee pain.

Curcumin in turmeric is a powerful anti-inflammatory compound.

Fenugreek (*methi*) prevents inflammations, relieves arthritic pain and improves mobility. Consume green *methi* as vegetable and *methi dana* (seeds) soaked in water.

Capsaicin in capsicum, the compound in all peppers, is an effective pain reliever. It neutralises the neuro-transmitter of pain, says Theodosakis, author of the book *Arthritis Cure.*

Celery (*ajwain*) is another spice recommended for OA, RA, and gout.

Arnica : an ointment made from arnica plant reduces inflammation. Arnica 200, a homoepathic medicine, is used to reduce pain.

Rosehip Powder

Research presented at World Congress of OA in Rome says that rosehip powder can be used to ease joint pain. It has the ability to protect and stimulate regeneration of cartilage.

Cloves

High in omega-3 fats and flavonoids, cloves can cure and relieve arthritic pain.

Foods That Worsen Arthritis

Meat, saturated fats and vegetable oils produce inflammatory chemicals and worsen arthritis pain. Stop taking the standard fast food acidic diet of meat, eggs, dairy, white flour, sugars, caffeine, alcohol, processed foods, and soft drinks.

Instead, choose a more alkaline high-fibre diet of vegetables, complex carbohydrates, legumes and fruits.

Do not drink cold fluids, especially with meals. Cold fluids change the surface tension of fats in intestines, and also affect fluidity of bone cartilage. Instead drink only warm and hot fluids. Note that our bone cartilage needs lubrication, not solidification (cooling). One should not eat curd, cucumber, radishes, etc., in joint pains.

Eliminate nightshade family foods like tomatoes, potatoes, brinjal, and tobacco. The alkaloids in them inhibit normal collagen repair in joints. Individuals might develop arthritis from consumption of alkaloids found in them.

Avoid gas-causing foods like black urad dal, cabbage, etc.

Treatment

RICE implying rest, ice, compression with a bandage or support, and elevation is the immediate treatment for most joint problems including injuries.

Massage with *Mahanarayan Tel* (Ayurvedic oil with some 50 herbs), or with a gel containing methyl salicylate and linseed oil, an omega-3 fat, followed by heat therapy.

Glucosamine sulphate supplement helps produce mucous shield, critical to joint movement. Glucosamine is found in small amounts in some foods, and is made by cartilage cells. It produces certain long chain sugars necessary to rebuild the cartilage.

Exercise

Physiotherapy exercises, diathermy, and ultrasound, are therapeutic.

Remember that in arthritis both overdoing exercise and not doing anything is bad. Those who over-exercise may unwittingly damage their knees increasing chances of OA.

Knee Exercise

Just lie down, straighten the feet, and tense the knee muscles. Then hold for a while, and release. This way you can prevent development of arthritis in your knees.

In any case, keep walking long distances albeit slowly. In case of emergency, use crape bandage or knee cap.

28.4.2 SPINAL OSTEOARTHRITIS (SPONDYLITIS) AND BACK PAIN

Between two consecutive vertebrae in spine, there is a cushion or disc or cartilage. The spinal osteoarthritis affects the function of cervical (neck), chest, and lumbar (lower back) areas. The discs are weakened and shrink in height by loss of fluid content.

In an effort to repair itself, the body forms bone spurs, and the joints enlarge. Symptoms are pain, tenderness, and stiffness in the neck, shoulders, arms, or lower back. There is difficulty in bending and walking, and occurrences of headaches in the back of head, vertigo, etc.

Diet in spinal osteoarthritis should be same as in any other type of osteoarthritis. Do not take vegetables of nightshade family, sour foods, cold drinks, etc.

Keep your weight close to the ideal weight according to your height.

Massage followed by hot fomentation is recommended for relieving pain. Avoid violent massages, cold exposures, and cold bath.

Correct postures while sitting, standing, or sleeping are advised. Do not remain in one position for a very long time.

One should not lie down all at once. One should first lie down on side, and then change to any position. Similarly, one should not get up straight but first turn on a side and also get up on the side.

Do gentle neck, waist and stretching exercises. Never do forward bending. Bend backward as far as comfortable. Hold for a few seconds, and relax. Repeat it 5-10 times.

Avoid weight lifting, and activities that might cause damage and worsen pain.

28.4.3 RHEUMATOID ARTHRITIS (RA)

Rheumatoid arthritis causes the lining of the joints to become inflamed. The joints become quite warm, tender and swollen.

Whereas osteoarthritis develops over many years, rheumatoid arthritis usually begins in young age.

Osteoarthritis affects mainly the weight-bearing joints like knees and hip joints. Affects of rheumatoid arthritis first appear in the fingers.

Diet is both the cause as well as the cure for arthritis. A diet rich in whole grains, vegetables and fibre, and low in sugar, refined carbohydrates and saturated fats is necessary.

Avoid allergenic foods such as wheat, corn, milk and dairy products, meats, and nightshade family foods (tomato, potato, egg plant, peppers, and tobacco).

One is benefitted from fasting. Fasting decreases the absorption of allergenic foods. One should take anti-inflammatory foods only.

A regimen of vegetarian diet results in substantial reduction of rheumatoid arthritis. Vegetarian diets decrease the availability of certain acids that convert into inflammatory compounds.

Oil Up Your Joints

Just as oil keeps the engine running smooth, natural oils in food can keep your joints moving smoothly. Olives and olive oil could ward off rheumatoid arthritis. MUFA in olive oil could relieve inflammation while its antioxidants could destroy free radicals.

Mustard oil, flaxseed oil, canola oil and pumpkin seeds are rich sources of omega-3 that inhibit production of inflammatory prostaglandins and leukotrienes. Omega-6 fats as in vegetable oils produce inflammation causing prostaglandins.

Recommended nutrients for osteoarthritis are good for rheumatoid arthritis as well.

People consuming vitamin C are three times less likely to develop rheumatoid arthritis. Both copper and manganese are involved in antioxidant activity. They reduce symptoms of RA by neutralising free radicals.

Fresh pineapple juice with its anti-inflammatory bromelain with fresh ginger helps greatly during flaring up of inflammation. Other common anti-inflammatory foods such as ginger, turmeric, olive oil, broccoli, red grapes, and green tea need to be included in diet. Pomegranate juice is consumed by many people as a treatment for inflammatory conditions that arise in those suffering from arthritis in general.

Turmeric packs and turmeric in food preparations is recommended. *Nirgundi,* in addition to turmeric, is useful in the treatment of arthritis.

Concentrate on alkaline diet by eating more vegetables. Coffee and other acidic foods can increase joint pain. Switch to tea instead which contains a number of protective antioxidants and anti-inflammatory agents.

Exercise in Rheumatoid Arthritis

Whether you have osteo- or rheumatoid arthritis, it is important to keep moving otherwise your muscles will lose strength and flexibility. Walking, biking, Yogasanas, Pilates, and Tai Chi are good.

Swimming is healthy because of the weightlessness offered by water. With this you can almost eliminate the total pressure on the joints. You take 90 per cent of your body weight off.

In osteoarthritis, the pain increases with movements, and reduces with rest. Hence, one should never overdo on exercise or movement.

But in rheumatoid arthritis, the pain will increase with rest. One should do regular exercise; otherwise, the pain will worsen.

28.4.4 GOUT (*GATHIYA*)

Gout, a painful type of arthritis, occurs due to being overweight and increased concentration of uric acid in blood. Uric acid crystals get deposited in joints, tendons, kidneys, and other tissues where they cause inflammation and damage. More than half of the gout attacks strike the big toes in the feet. Gravity is to be blamed for uric acid crystals settling in the toes.

Gout is usually considered as a rich man's arthritis. It is associated with affluence.

Uric acid is the breakdown product of purines which is found in ample amounts in meats, poultry, yeast, protein-rich foods, etc., which are thus, considered uric acid producing foods.

Those who consume meat and alcohol are more prone to develop gout. That is why, even at the age of 30, many young people suffer from gout. Drinking alcohol puts you at greater risk of developing gout. It can also make gout attacks more severe.

Arthritis may further trigger the deposition of uric acid crystals in joints. There is, thus, a strong association between gout and arthritis.

Recommendations

Eliminate alcohol. Be a vegetarian. As a matter of fact, on the whole, keep protein intake low. Proteins produce uric acid. Take milk, yoghurt, etc., for protein. Have liberal consumption of complex carbohydrates. Avoid refined carbohydrates since they increase uric acid production. Consume only healthy fats.

Eliminate saturated fats. Saturated fats decrease excretion of uric acid. People with gout are usually obese, and prone to high BP and diabetes. Hence, follow a weight reduction programme. Avoid over consumption of calories.

Take plenty of water. Have a liberal fluid intake. Fluids keep the urine diluted, and promote elimination of uric acid. Dilution of urine also diminishes the risk of developing kidney stones.

Nature Cures

If you have gout, try the remedies celery (ajwain) and cherries. In an article in Texas Reports on Biology and Medicine 1950, Ludwig Blau described how he had cured his crippling gout by eating cherries every day.

Flavonoid-rich foods like cherries, berries, etc., lower uric acid levels and prevent gout. The secret of cherries lies in their anthocyanins. Do not take aspirin for relieving pain. It can affect excretion of uric acid by your kidneys.

Vitamin C appears to reduce uric acid in the blood. New research reveals that those who get more vitamin C in their diet lower their chances of developing gout.

28.5 SCIATICA

Sciatica pain is a problem of the nerve that extends from lower back to the foot. Due to pressure in the region, the nerve gets compressed. The recommendation is to practise massage, particularly in the lower back region.

Tanasana and Tadasana offer relief from sciatica pain. The ayurvedic remedy suggested is to consume petals of pink and white *Sadabahar* (periwinkle) flowers, or orange stems of sweet smelling *Haar-Singar* flowers. Lycopodium 200 is the best homoeopathic remedy.

28.6 OSTEOPOROSIS

Osteoporosis literally means porous bones. After the age of 35-50, the number of new bone cells formed becomes less than the numbers of old bone cells that die. Hence, anyone can get osteoporosis with age.

Osteoporosis is more common among women because their requirement of calcium and magnesium is high due to pregnancy, childbirth, nursing, and stress. In women, incorporation of calcium in bones depends on oestrogen. They are at risk because after menopause their oestrogen levels start dipping rapidly.

Thinning of bones in osteoporosis often causes fractures of wrist, hip and spine. Such fractures can also cause staggering in 1 of every 3 women, and in 1 in every 12 men.

Osteoporosis is largely preventable by:

1. Increasing intake and absorption of calcium, phosphorus, magnesium, silicon and vitamin D.
2. Exercising daily for 30 minutes.

How to Maintain Calcium and Minerals Level Adequate For Healthy Bones?

Milk and milk products are the best source of calcium. Ideally women should take 2-3 glasses of milk daily or its products such as paneer and curd.

Besides milk, yoghurt, paneer and tofu, other food items like green leafy vegetables (like kale, spinach, lettuce), oranges, almonds, and soybeans are also rich in calcium.

Grind white *til* seeds previously soaked in water. Add water and boil. You get calcium from this *til* milk. Phosphorus binds with calcium to make bones strong. Cheese, legumes and seeds have high phosphorus content. Magnesium, present in fruits, makes the bones stronger. Get magnesium from fruits.

Silicon increases bone mineral density and plays a major role in formation of bones. The high level of silicon in cucumber, beer, etc., actually slows down the thinning of bones. A moderate consumption of beer may help fight osteoporosis.

Vitamin K helps retain calcium in bones. It is necessary for bone health.

How to Increase Calcium Absorption?

It is not enough to increase calcium intake but it is also necessary to ensure absorption of calcium.

Calcium absorption is improved with vitamins C and D. Vitamin C can be obtained from *amla*, oranges, pineapple, etc., and most other fruits and vegetables like lemon, bell peppers, etc. Orange juice is one food that contains high amount of calcium along with high amounts of vitamin C that enables the body to absorb it.

One can get vitamin D by exposure to 15-30 minutes of morning sun. Getting calcium from milk has the added advantage of simultaneously getting the required vitamin D.

Sulphur aids in calcium absorption. It is also needed in repair of cartilage and bone tissues. Cabbage, onion, garlic, asparagus, etc. are rich sources of sulphur.

How to Prevent Loss of Calcium?

Osteoporosis, however, is more often about the loss of calcium, particularly in women, following hormonal changes, and not the lack of calcium in diet. The aim should be to prevent the calcium from dissolving into urine.

Vegetarian diet is associated with lower incidence of osteoporosis mainly because of decreased bone loss.

Sodium or salt can sweep away calcium out of your body. On the other hand, says Deborah Sellmeyer of University of California, San Francisco, even if you eat more salt than you should, adding high potassium foods can help save bone loss. Baked potatoes, beans, bananas, fruits have high potassium.

Steer clear of smoking, alcohol, coffee, diets high in proteins, refined sugars, phosphorous, and excessive sodas. They enhance calcium loss.

It is a myth that eating lot of meat can improve calcium reserve. In fact, too much protein in meat comes in way of calcium absorption. Further, meat brings with it a lot of unhealthy fat, and toxins. They increase calcium loss. A high protein diet or a diet high in phosphorous, and saturated fats leads to increased calcium excretion from urine.

With sugars, refined carbohydrates, caffeine, excessive sodas, highly acidic foods, etc., the level of calcium in urine rises. Hence, they should be avoided.

Citrus juices (vitamin C) reduce urinary saturation of calcium.

Olive Oil

Phenols in olive oil prevent bone loss that causes osteoporosis.

Tea

Tea is also rich in phenols. As a matter of fact, tea is found to increase bone density. Researchers at National Cheng Kung University in Tainan Taiwan claimed that high fluoride content and flavonoids in tea, taken over a period, may help preserve bone density.

Drinking tea over a number of years is more important than the quantity of tea you take in a day.

Boron

It was found not only to reduce urinary calcium secretion by 44 per cent but also to raise oestrogen levels dramatically among post-menopausal women. Fruits and vegetables, particularly cauliflower, broccoli, etc., are the main dietary sources of boron.

Phyto-oestrogens

Soy and beer are rich in phyto-oestrogens which keep bones healthy for women.

28.7 TAKING CARE OF TEETH AND BREATH

Calcium is very important for teeth. It can be consumed in the form of fibre foods, fresh fruits and vegetables. Avoid sugars, sticky foods like white bread, chips, and acidic drinks that damage the teeth.

Always rinse your mouth after eating sugars and sticky foods. Drink your fruit juices through a straw, this way, the acidic juice wouldn't damage your teeth.

Black tea contains enough chemicals to prevent tooth decay. It is also rich in polyphenol antioxidants. Sugar damages the teeth.

For healthy teeth, you must have healthy gums. Vitamin C is necessary for healthy gums.

Cloves keep the mouth and gums free of harmful bacteria. Take a clove at bedtime.

Brushing of teeth is best done twice, once just after breakfast, and second at bedtime. Note that it is not necessary to brush your teeth the first thing in the morning, especially if you brush at night. Clean the tongue also to remove white/yellow coating of decaying food particles leading to bad breath.

One of the reasons for bad breath, apart from poor oral hygiene, is the gas or intestinal putrefaction or decomposition. So, avoid gas-producing foods or take them in small quantities, and after cooking sufficiently well.

Another cause is one that nobody seems to care or know about. This is the accumulation of phlegm with toxins in the throat pit and sinuses. This, over a period of time, results in a stink. Put your fingers inside throat every morning for clearing.

Anulom-vilom and Kapal-bhati pranayam also help in bringing out excess mucus and phlegm from the oral cavity.

29

Skin, Hair And Nails

29.1 SKIN

Skin is the largest organ of the body by weight as well as by surface area. And it is also the one most exposed to environmental pollution and UV radiation from sun. The skin performs various important functions such as providing sensation (of temperature and touch), acting as a barrier against friction, infection, etc., protecting us from the harm caused by UV radiations, synthesising Vitamin D induced by UV radiation, and preventing excessive water loss or absorption.

Hair and nails are actually modified extensions of the skin. Much of skin, hair, and nails is made of protein.

The skin is not uniformly thick. It has maximum thickness at the soles and palms. It is thinnest in eyelids and sexual organs. It has two layers – outer and inner. The outer, in turn, has 5 layers, the top one being a dead layer. The inner layer contains collagen that stores water. Below the skin there are tissues, which connect it to the entire network of the body.

Human skin has two principal proteins – collagen and elastin. Consider collagen as the rope, and elastin as the rubber band firmly pulling these ropes.

A diet which produces the least number of free radicals (FRs), and is high in antioxidants provides the best defense against FRs which cause premature ageing of cells.

Fill up on fruits, vegetables, and whole grains, and stay away from sugars, white bread, soft drinks, alcohol, caffeine, tobacco, exposure to sun, pollutants and stress. Yale researchers say polyphenol antioxidants in blackberries, blue berries, pineapple, and pomegranate reduce skin-ageing FRs by 80 per cent, and block UV radiation by 26 per cent. Research from Monash University, Australia, reveals that the more fruits and vegetables you eat, the fewer the wrinkles you will have.

Note: Many nutrient deficiencies and ailments first show up on the skin since the skin functions as the largest organ of elimination in the body. If there is a malfunction in any of our biological processes, the skin takes up the role of providing a backup function. The state of the skin is indicative of the general health of the body.

Most of our skin cells are replaced almost every month. So, for any measures you take to improve your skin, you should at least wait for a month or two to see the effect.

Skin of *Vaata* and *Pitta* Types

Vaata people have rough and dry skin. They should eat a wholesome diet, including a good amount of fats. They should not eat dry, hot and pungent things, steering clear of cold foods and coffee.

Pitta people have oily skin. They may get pimples/acne. They should not take alcohol, hot and sour foods, and also foods that are acidic and heavy.

Sunlight

Avoid direct and prolonged exposure to UV radiations of sun. But then, it should also be kept in mind that the exposure of our bare arms and legs to 15-30 minutes of morning sun is essential for the synthesis of vitamin D.

Studies show that black tea may undo skin cell damage from UV radiation. Also, MUFA in olive oil resists oxidation and protects skin from sun damage.

Facials/Face Packs

Facials and face packs are used to remove dead skin, dirt, grime, pollutants, oils, etc. from the surface of the skin.

Ubtans are used to preserve the softness of the skin and also to rejuvenate it. Use oils like olive oil with flour or *besan*. You can add sandalwood, saffron and other herbs to it.

Papaya Scrub (dried papaya powder in some base) is popular as a scrub for face. Mashed papaya adds lustre and makes the skin smooth.

Potato and Cucumber: Boiled potato-peal dressings are used for the treatment of skin wounds, to reduce bacterial contamination, and to offer faster healing. Cucumber slices can be used on face and eyes.

Milk Cream: Use fresh milk and its cream or *malai* on face. The fresh cream is better than processed moisturisers whose formulations contain chemicals. Dried orange peels, almonds and cream of fresh milk make for a very good face mask.

Besan with lime juice or dahi, honey and turmeric can also be used to apply on face.

Body Odour

Poor hygiene, obesity, diet containing garlic, meat, fish, and heavy foods are some of the causes of body odour.

Take bath twice daily, and once a week with neem water. Apply baking soda, rose water, apple cider vinegar, talcum powder, tea tree oil, turnip juice, etc., over arm-pits or other areas where sweating is heavy.

Keep colon clean by eating plenty of fruits, vegetables, fibres and whole grain cereals.

NUTRIENTS THAT EFFECT THE SKIN

Have a diet which produces the least number of free radicals, and is highest in antioxidants. Pumpkin, sunflower seeds, apple, pomegranate, pineapple, green leafy vegetables, etc., are helpful for achieving a glowing complexion.

Vitamin A/ Beta-carotene

Vitamin A is essential for maintaining and healing skin tissues. Many skin disorders are treated with vitamin A. It is abundantly present in milk.

Vitamin A supplements can be toxic. But it can be synthesised in the body from beta-carotene and other plant carotenes found in yellow and orange vegetables and fruits, and green leafy vegetables like spinach.

Pumpkin, particularly the deep orange variety, is one of the best things you can eat to get more vitamin A, thanks to its rich supply of beta-carotene, vitamin C, and its pH value that keeps the skin slightly on the acidic side to keep the bacteria at bay. Beta-carotene can also be obtained from carrot, sweet potato, papaya, mango, broccoli, and spinach.

Vitamin E

Skin disorders are treated with vitamins A and E. Vitamin E imparts lubrication to skin and fights inflammations. It slows the ageing process by reducing the production of an enzyme which breaks down collagen. It is known for its emollient properties that maintain beautiful and soft skin. Applied topically, it soothes damaged skin. Apply vitamin E from capsule on spots that develop around eyes in women after childbirth.

Oils

Wheat germ oil, olive oil, almonds and other nuts, avocados, sunflower oil, legumes and green leafy vegetables are the best sources of vitamin E. Doctors, however, recommend 400 IU of vitamin E supplement and rosehip oil for those above the age of 40.

Vitamin C

Vitamin C is needed for the formation and maintenance of collagen. As such, vitamin C helps fight wrinkles. It plays a role in the healing of skin.

Include *amla*, guavas, citrus fruits like orange, kiwi, sweet lime, grape fruit, lemon, etc., strawberries, black currants, and sweet peppers, in your diet. You can use peels of citrus fruits as face packs. Being rich in vitamin C, they help in brightening the skin.

Biotin and Vitamin B2

Biotin plays a role in the manufacture and utilisation of amino acids (proteins) and fats. This is the skin vitamin that helps to maintain healthy skin, hair and nails. Its deficiency impairs protein metabolism resulting in dry scaly skin, dermatitis, premature greying and alopecia (hair loss).

A vegetarian diet alters the intestinal flora to support production of biotin. Good sources of biotin are unpolished rice, rice bran, walnuts, almonds, oats, black peas/urad dal, peas, cauliflower, whole wheat, pulses, legumes and egg yolk. White of eggs prevents absorption of biotin.

Vitamin B2, often referred to as the beauty vitamin, is found in papaya, custard apples (*sharifa*), eggs and milk. Raw papaya juice is used to cure skin disorders.

Olive Oil/Essential Fatty Acids

Adequate intake of healthy fats, MUFAs in olive oil, almonds and avocados, and omega-3 in flaxseeds, canola and mustard oils, and walnuts, serve as internal moisturisers.

Olive oil is best for intake as well as external application. It nourishes and protects the skin's underlying collagen. Inhabitants of Mediterranean countries consume a lot of olive oil, and hence, usually have a great skin. Do not avoid fats altogether. Researchers from Monash University found that adding two tablespoons of olive oil into your daily diet prevents dry and flaky skin.

Coconut Oil

Apply coconut oil on bruises and acne to speed up the healing process. It is used in cooking and also as hair oil. It gives a smooth texture and shine to hair, and prevents them from greying.

Zinc

Zinc helps to maintain collagen and elastin to give skin its firmness, thus, preventing sagging and wrinkles. Zinc is also needed for healing since it works by linking together amino acids for formation of collagen. Its deficiency results in skin infections and disorders. At puberty, requirement of zinc increases since it is required for hormone production. Low levels of zinc are responsible for acne during puberty.

Maximum zinc is found in pumpkin seeds, ginger, mushrooms, low fat milk, whole wheat, whole grams (chana), split peas, pulses, black beans/urad dal, oats and nuts.

Silicon

Silicon is known as a beauty mineral. It is essential for the growth of healthy bones, skin, hair, nails and teeth. Silica contributes to the strength of collagen.

Cucumber, rich in silica, is beneficial for the skin. Take one whole cucumber in the morning after removing its bitter part. Cucumber slices are also used on face to improve skin texture. Beets, oats, and barley are rich in silica. It is also found in pumpkin, cabbage, and carrots.

Potassium

Potassium helps in inter-cellular transfer of nutrients. Its deficiency may lead to acne, and other skin-related problems including dryness.

Lycopene/Tomatoes and Watermelons

Ripe tomatoes and watermelon are packed with high levels of antioxidant lycopene which reduces collagen damage that promotes wrinkles.

Berries

Berries are a great source of polyphenols. Recent studies revealed that blueberries contain 3 times the amount of antioxidants as compared to that in oranges. Other berries are *jamuns*, strawberries, *amla*, etc. They contain high amounts of vitamin C too.

Apple Cider Vinegar

Apple cider vinegar brings a healthy and rosy glow to one's complexion.

Fibre

Include a lot of fibre. In fact, replace a part of meal with fibre to keep your gut clean. The effect of a clean GI tract can be immediately seen on your face.

Drink Water

Many people have dry and rough skin because they do not drink enough water. Not only does water keep your skin hydrated, it delivers nutrients and oxygen to cells, and carries away waste products. It acts as a great detoxifier. It flushes out your toxins.

Drink 12-14 glasses of water, fresh fruit juices, and vegetable juices/soups daily.

Natural Care for Glowing Skin

Start by cutting off all fried foods, excessive fats, sweets, rich salad dressings, meats, sodas, coffee and other stimulants, and processed foods from your daily diet. Replace these with curds, salads, fruits, vegetables, and at least eight glasses of water daily.

Keep your bowels clear. Take Isabgul with water/curd daily. Miss a meal once a week.

Keep your skin clear and oil-free. Wash your face alternately with warm and cold water. Make a thick paste of *besan*, yoghurt, turmeric powder, rose water and honey, and use it as a face pack. Regularly cleanse your skin with rose water-dipped ice cubes at night.

Never compromise on your sleep. After food, sleep is the most important thing for good health. Follow a regular exercise regime. It will improve blood circulation.

For eyelids and face, and for sunburn relief, soak the area in cold water and apply aloe or put cold cucumber slices for about 10 minutes or more. Almond is good for dry skin while aloe vera suits oily acne-prone skin.Taking a dose of rosehip oil every night helps to keep your skin soft.

Sleep and Relaxation

Taking 7 to 8 hours of sound sleep is necessary for restoring skin to normal health. Getting up early at 6 or 6:30 a.m. is best for the body, skin included.

The glands in the brain secrete hormones early in the morning. So if we sleep till late, the glands under-secrete, and our metabolism becomes slower, which may affect our skin.

Decrease Stress

Stress triggers inflammatory skin diseases. Researchers at University of Medicine, Berlin, and McMaster University, Canada, found that stress may over-activate immune cells in the skin leading to inflammatory skin diseases. It is an example of overactive immune system. Even skin is affected by stress.

Meditation

Meditation is very effective for keeping your skin de-stressed. It makes the skin glow due to peace and contentment.

29.1.1 WRINKLES

While the body continuously produces collagen, it stops producing elastin with advancing age. That is the cause of wrinkles. Some foods may strengthen elastin. Coenzyme Q10 boosts elastin naturally and, energises and protects skin cells.

A study appearing in *Aesthetic Surgery Journal* says that women are more prone to wrinkling around their mouth and nose. This is due to the presence of fewer sweat glands. Women must avoid direct exposure to sun, and drastic weight loss methods.

Apply a mixture of honey and lemon everyday on face and use only cold water to wash it off the face. Here are some tips to avoid wrinkle formation and premature ageing:

Take 7 to 8 hours of sleep, drink plenty of water, eat lots of fruits and vegetables, and protect your skin from damage from sun, heat, dust, and pollutants. Exposure to sunlight could give you wrinkles, say Trevor McMillan and Sarah Allinson of Lancaster University. Natural ingredients like lemon, lime juice, rose water, honey, yoghurt, milk, papaya, lentils powder, *besan*, cucumber, and olive oil, might help you avoid wrinkles. Mix and match, and find out what works best for you.

Sweat More

Sweating is a must as it flushes out the toxins, and opens the skin pores. So, do not forget to indulge in some exercise till you start sweating. Secretions from sweat and oil glands reduce wrinkling of skin.

29.1.2 AGE SPOTS/WARTS

With age, people experience the occurrence of round or oval, flat, brownish or blackish skin spots. They are harmless though, but they look ugly. They are caused by free radicals.

Eat foods high in beta-carotene which scavenges the free radicals. Such foods include spinach, pumpkin, mangoes, sweet potatoes, and carrots. Antioxidant vitamins C and E, when taken in high doses, also help. For vitamin E, it is desirable to take a supplement in addition to whole grains, etc. Vitamin E is useful in the treatment of a wide variety of skin problems.

An emollient base cream with benzoic acid or equivalent acid lightens the age spots. Apply slightly dampened aspirin tablet on the wart. Salicylic acid in aspirin will make the wart degenerate and fall in a few days after overnight application.

29.2 ACNE/PIMPLES (*MUHANSE*)

Acne happens mainly during puberty. It is caused by overactive oil-producing glands which are triggered by hormonal changes. It may also be caused by heat, stress and overuse of cosmetics.

One possible way to stay pimple-free is to avoid refined foods. These foods increase the production of the androgen hormone that increases oil production. Eliminate trans-fats, margarine, fried foods, aerated drinks, sodas, and sweets. Keep your stomach clean. Avoid constipation.

Bacteria on the skin break down the excess oils which triggers break-out of acne. Lauric acid in coconut oil, when applied onto pores, can fight bacteria, and may cure acne.

Mixture of lemon juice and rose water, in equal amounts, applied on face is another remedy for acne.

Avoid exposure to oils and greases, and use of creams and cosmetics on face. Thoroughly cleanse face with sulphur-containing soap, or Calendula soap. Many people have got rid of acne by using milk of magnesia. Aloe vera is also effective for treating oily skin.

Mint (*Podina*), Cucumber and Aloe Vera

One of the factors that causes acne is an increase in the *pitta* element in the body. To reduce *pitta*, drink mint and cucumber juice. Apply cucumber slices on face. Aloe vera also suits acne-prone skin.

Fruits and Vegetables

Eat three to four apples daily to clear your acne. Increase your intake of fruits and vegetables to obtain potassium and fibre.

Face Packs for Acne

Make a paste of roots of neem with water and apply on affected areas. Make a face pack by mixing 2 tsp fuller's earth, 4 drops clove oil, 2 tsp neem leaf paste, pinch of camphor, and rose water.

If the damage due to acne has already happened, apply the following face pack as scrub:

2 tsp red masoor dal powder, 2 tsp sandalwood powder, 1 tsp *rakt chandan* (red sandalwood), 2 tsp orange peel powder, 2 tsp fuller's earth, pinch of camphor, and rose water.

Red Light

Italian researchers have shown that red light can cure moderate acne. Among those who were given red light treatment twice a week, the complexion improved by 50 per cent in just a month. According to Piergiacomo Calzavara-Pinton, author of this study, the wavelength of red light annihilates bacteria that breed in closed pores.

Zinc

Zinc is vital for healthy skin. But zinc levels drop at puberty, as the mineral is needed in larger quantities for the production of hormones. So consuming foods – such as nuts, whole grains, and legumes – that are rich in zinc is beneficial.

Beta-carotene and chromium are also effective in dealing with acne. Do not use refined foods as they are stripped of their chromium and zinc content.

Berberis Aquifolium mother tincture treats acne/pimples.

29.3 ECZEMA/DERMATITIS AND PSORIASIS

Eczema is inflammation of skin from the inside, leading to scaling and intense itching.

Psoriasis, in contrast, appears on skin surface in the form of skin plaques, inflammation, etc., appearing over elbows, knees, ankles, scalp or genitals.

Eczema may be the result of intestinal or immune disorders, or allergies caused by certain foods, or contact with lotions, cosmetics, creams, metals in shaving razors, etc. Psoriasis is an auto-immune disease. The immune system sends faulty signals that cause the growth of faulty skin cells.

Chronic stress can also cause psoriasis and other skin problems. Skin problems may also be triggered by consumption of allergenic foods, or gluten. Simply eliminating allergenic foods like meat, eggs, milk, peanuts, corn, wheat, gluten, tomatoes, artificial colours, and food preservatives helps reduce skin exacerbations.

Avoid refined and processed foods, saturated fats, soft drinks, sodas, sugars, etc. Consume anti-inflammatory olive oil. Apply it externally too. Increase dietary intake of omega-3 by consuming nuts, seeds, flaxseeds, mustard and canola oils, broccoli, etc., to increase synthesis of anti-inflammatory prostaglandins.

Foods rich in carotenes, vitamin E, and zinc are critical for skin health. Zinc aids healing, and enhances immune function. Vitamin E relieves itching and dryness.

Biotin, the vitamin for skin, hair and nails, helps in all skin disorders. For biotin, add brown rice to your diet. Do not eat eggs as they contain a protein that binds biotin, and prevents its absorption.

Have a diet rich in fibre. Consume isabgul (psyllium husk) to keep the colon clean.

Any skin problem is a manifestation of an internal problem. So, topical applications are not enough. Stress is often the cause, so de-stress yourself and sleep well. Exercising regularly and taking short mild exposures to sun's UV radiation helps. Regular fasting, and low-calorie vegetarian diets improve symptoms. Live in a cool temperate climate.

Oregon-grape, Goldenseal, and Berberis Aquifolium mother tincture are effective for treating psoriasis. Graphite 30, a homeo-medicine, can be used to make facial skin smooth.

Shaving Allergy

It is a kind of allergy to shaving creams, after-shave lotions, soaps and razors. The first line of treatment is to stop using aftershave lotions altogether. The second step is to change your shaving cream. Use one designed for sensitive skin and that which contains no perfume. The third step is to use fine razors. Never use blunt or electric razors. If this does not help, then the best strategy is to shave on alternate days.

Use warm water for shaving. Splash chilled water or rub ice on face after shaving. If the problem persists then use a mild steroid cream as prescribed by your skin specialist.

Know that this cream will not treat the problem, but it will keep it under control. Too much use of the cream may aggravate the problem. Hence, apply it sparingly.

29.4 LEUCODERMA (VITILIGO)

Vitiligo, commonly called leucoderma, is a pigmentation disorder in which melanocytes in the skin are destroyed. As a result, white patches appear on the skin in different parts of the body. It is considered to be a genetic disorder.

Practitioners of Unani medicine in India have been using melon extract to cure it. Psoralens is prescribed for treatment to be applied topically, and used orally also.

UV light therapy can also be used .

29.5 CORN

Some people are genetically prone to developing corns in the soles of their feet. Surgical methods of removal are not a permanent solution. They may also lead to infection. The best way is to soak the corn in warm water and then gently file it down with a pumice stone.

29.6 HAIR AND NAILS

Hairs

Hairs are almost 98 per cent protein. Thinning of hair is the result of protein deficiency.

At their roots are follicles, and glands that supply oil, nutrients and hair pigment. The follicle or root gives rise to the hair. Hence, the roots must be kept in good condition. To ensure healthy hair, a balanced diet of proteins and sufficient iodine is a must. In addition, fresh fruits, vegetables, water, rest and exercise are necessary.

Dry hair is indicative of *vaata*, fatless food and lack-lustre lifestyle of the person. Oily hair is indicative of *pitta* and passionate aggressive personality of the person.

The commonest reason for hair-fall among women is iron deficiency. Iron-rich foods may clear up the problem. Maintain a normal haemoglobin level for healthy hair. Avoid the use of any chemical on hair. Massage of scalp with an oil, preferably almond, Brahmi Amla, coconut or olive oil is necessary. Lauric acid in coconut oil protects your scalp from bacterial infections. Use oil enriched with vitamin E.

Nutrients for healthy hair are about the same as for healthy skin.

Proteins: Hair is made of keratin protein. For strong hair, eat protein-rich foods like nuts.

Biotin: It helps in metabolising amino acids (protein) and fats, and thus, stimulates hair growth. Biotin supplement 1,000-3,000mg is recommended in case of hair-fall and skin disorders.

In case of dandruff, treat the hair with castor oil at night, and shampoo it off in morning.

An excellent conditioner for hair can be prepared by mixing curd, tea water, coffee powder, *amla* powder, and *henna*. Leave it in an iron vessel for a couple of hours. Then apply on hair, leaving it on for a few hours, before washing your hair.

Male Baldness

Male hormone testosterone is responsible for the loss of hair in men. An enzyme converts testosterone into hair-unfriendly dihydro-testosterone (DHT).

Avoid meat. It is a DHT activator. Catechins in green tea inhibit DHT. So drinking green tea is good for hair growth. Soya is also a natural DHT inhibitor that helps reducing hair loss. Zinc interferes with the conversion of testosterone into DHT, thereby retarding hair loss and prompting hair growth.

Common deficiencies responsible for hair loss are that of zinc and biotin. Increase your intake of nuts and seeds, whole grains, beans, etc.

Home Remedies for Hair Loss/Dull Hair

- Rub lemon juice mixed with olive oil on scalp. Keep it overnight, or for a few hours, and wash.
- Boil rosemary leaves in water. Use the water to wash hair everyday.
- Control dandruff using a mixture of lemon juice, camphor, and coconut oil on the scalp.
- Massage with vitamin E oil to stimulate hair growth or almond oil if hair feels dull.
- *Amla, Brahmi, til* oils are commonly used to maintain healthy hair and for calming the brain. Use *amla* plus *shikakai* herbal shampoo.
- Apple cider vinegar is a clarifier. It ensures shine by wiping out mineral deposits and chlorine. Hence, rinse your hair with it after bath.
- Sarvangasana prevents hair from falling and greying. But do it slowly and carefully.

Nails

Nutrients necessary to maintain healthy nails are the same as for healthy skin and hair. A healthy protein intake and omega-3 fats will do as much good to nails as to the skin.

Vitamin B6, zinc, GLA, and copper are other nutrients that assist in forming nails. GLA increases the absorption of zinc. It is the best supplement for brittle nails. The best sources of GLA are evening primrose and black currant oils.

30
Eye and Ear

30.1 EYE

The human eye is one of the most important organs of the body yet it is most often neglected. To learn how to maintain eye health, it is essential to understand its anatomy first.

The eye is made up of three layers of tissues. The innermost light-sensitive layer is called retina. The cornea is a fibrous transparent tissue that extends over the coloured portion of the eye.

Light rays enter the dark centre of the eye called pupil. The pupils control the amount of light entering the eye. The conjunctiva is a mucous membrane in the eyelids. It coats the anterior portion of the eyeball over the white of the eye. Muscles of the pigment are responsible for constriction of pupils in response to light. The tiny muscles that hold the lens are responsible for focussing light rays on the retina.

Behind the pupil is the lens. The lens is a transparent bi-convex structure. The shape of the lens can be altered by contraction and relaxation of muscles. When the muscles contract, the lens focusses objects at a long distance. When the muscles relax, the lens focusses nearby objects.

Retina consists of light-sensitive cones and rod cells. These impulses on retina are transmitted to the brain through optic nerve.

Sugar the Enemy

White sugar is stripped of chromium and zinc. An absence of chromium has a role to play in the development of myopia i.e. short-sightedness.

Excessive sugar in the body is eliminated partially through the eyes. Sweets cause sleepiness, enabling the eyes to excrete it in the form of crystals found in the eyes in the morning.

30.2 FAULTY VISION

If the eye ball is at too long a distance from pupil to retina, it is a case of myopia. The image is formed short of the retina. The distance sight becomes faulty. You may have blurred vision of distant objects but a clear vision of close objects. Hence, those with myopia generally do not need glasses for reading. Myopia is often inherited genetically.

If the eye ball is too short, it is the case of hypermetropia or long-sightedness. Blurring occurs when viewing close objects. People develop hyperopia with age which is when glasses are required for reading.

Causes of Faulty Vision

There are many causes but the following are the main ones:

1. **Lack of Nutrition.** If exact nutrients are missing or if toxic and harmful substances are entering the body, vision can be affected. Not only the eyes but the nerves and brain cells transmitting and processing information need proper nutrition. Those suffering from myopia are often found to be consuming lot of meat and sugars. White sugar lacks chromium and zinc, important for blood pressure and muscular function.
2. **Lack of Self Love.** Children who lack self love tend to contract their body organs including eyes. They try to win praise by showing academic and social performance. They win medals but lose on eyesight. Such children can be helped by simple emotional support.
3. **Stress.** Stress causes the eye balls to alter in shape. They lose their round shape.
4. **Genetic disposition:** It is also a factor for eyes as in many other health problems.

30.3 AGE-RELATED MACULAR DEGENERATION

Breakdown of the macule, the central portion of the retina, due to ageing is referred to as age-related macular degeneration (AMD). AMD can be arrested.

Antioxidants for Eyes

You can drop AMD risk to half by consuming carotenoids lutein, zeaxanthin and beta-carotene. Red grapes, orange and red bell peppers, eggs and corn are packed with both lutein and zeaxanthein.

Carrots, pumpkin, papaya, mangoes, etc., are full of beta-carotene. Fill your diet with various other antioxidants to provide your eyes with extra protection.

Spinach contains lutein, a substance known to increase the pigment on the macula in the eye. In one study, macular pigment levels in the eyes increased by 19 per cent in people who had a daily helping of spinach. In addition to lutein, spinach also contains zeaxanthin, another antioxidant pigment compound needed for eye health. Accordingly, spinach is highly recommended for keeping eyes healthy.

High blood sugar level is the most common cause of vision loss in older adults. AMD appears to share risk factors with diabetes and cardiovascular-related diseases. Researchers led by Dr Allen Taylor of Tufts University Boston found that regular consumption of diet with high glycemic index foods (refined sugar, white bread, white rice, etc.) significantly increases risk of AMD as compared to a diet with low glycemic index. They found among people of 55 years of age and older that those who ate above average amounts of white bread, white rice, white sugar and other foods with high GI were 17 per cent more likely to develop AMD. To protect your eyes, stick to whole grains; avoid sugars, sodas, sweets.

High blood pressure is another risk factor for macular degeneration. Add fruits and vegetables to your diet to obtain potassium and to reduce sodium to maintain a normal BP. In any case, maintain healthy blood pressure with or without medication.

Omega-3 Fats: Studies show that those who avoid unhealthy fats and eat omega-3 fats instead, as in flaxseeds, mustard seeds and oil, canola oil, walnuts and broccoli, have less than half the risk of macular degeneration. Omega-3 oils help reduce inflammations. They lower the risk of cataracts.

A prominent study found that those AMD patients who took 500mg of vitamin C, 400 IU of vitamin E, and 80mg of zinc daily significantly slowed the progression of degeneration.

30.4 EYE CARE AND NUTRITION

Read or watch television in a well-lit room. Protect your eyes from direct sun rays. Use 100 per cent UV protective sun glasses. After a tiring work session or visit outside, splash your eyes with cold water.

Factors Necessary for Healthy Eyes:

1. **Blinking.** Blinking briefly turns off the light entering the eyes giving retina cells a short rest. It works as a constant vibration of eyes providing them opportunity to exercise. Hence, it is beneficial if you blink often and avoid staring for long. Those who have a tendency to stare are found to have myopia. Blink whenever you can.

   Blink the eyes 10 times. Close and relax. This cleans the eyes. The natural cleanser of the eyes is a tear film that spreads across the cornea.

   Cultivate the habit of blinking regularly. This is very important for those who constantly work on computers. So, if you are working on a computer, take regular breaks after 10-15 minutes, look away from the computer screen every now and then, and blink.

2. **Sunshine.** Eyes need plenty of sunshine. However, never look at the sun directly. Always see at 90 degrees to the sun. Take the sun in your eyes moving your hand around them for a few minutes. You get your daily dose of UV light, eye muscles get

relaxation, and retina cells are stimulated. Protect your eyes from UV radiation.

Most Important Nutrition

Human retina is made up of compounds comprising vitamin A. Its deficiency may cause night blindness, and even total blindness. Eat a diet comprising vitamin A or beta-carotene.

Vitamin A/beta-carotene as in carrots, leafy greens, spinach, papaya and mango, is the health vitamin for eyes. Carotenoid antioxidants lutein and zeaxanthin (pigment) are vision-saving.

Eggs, spinach, carrots, corn and kiwi fruit have plenty of lutein and zeaxanthin. Eggs have more carotenoids than carrots. And they are also more easily absorbed.

Yellow, orange and greens like green peas, pumpkin, honeydew melons, and pomegranate and sweet red peppers have high amounts of both lutein and zeaxanthin.

Avocados contain MUFA fats. Nutrients in vegetables are better absorbed when eaten with healthy fats as in avocados. A study showed that those who ate avocados with their salad had five times more lutein and fifteen times more beta-carotene in their blood.

Reverse Myopia with Exercises

Close your eyes and gently tense the eye muscles. This relaxes the eyes. Eyes love movement. Exercise your eyes by moving eyeballs up and down, side to side, and in circulatory movements clockwise and anti-clockwise.

All these exercises should be done slowly with attention on movement, and not with a jerk.

There are other eye exercises also that you may do. For example, stretch your hand with the tip of the forefinger or thumb in front as far away from you as possible. Fix your gaze on the nail. Slowly move the tip closer to your eyes. Then slowly move the tip away maintaining the level and the gaze. Repeat this a few times.

Fix your gaze at the nails of both forefingers or thumbs. Move the nail tips apart as far wide as possible and move them close to each other maintaining the level and the gaze.

Palming Technique

Warm your palms by rubbing them against each other. Cup your eyes with the palms. Open your eyes slowly. This exercise will help relax and strengthen the eye muscles.

Sleep

Perfect and adequate sleep gives the eyes a break. It replenishes the tear film, a thin layer of mucous, oil and water in the eye responsible for providing moisture and protection.

Reflex Points for Eyes

Nerve channel blockages are removed by applying pressure on reflex points. These points for eyes are:

1. Peace point/Crown centre. Say 'I am at peace' while the pressure is being applied.
2. Love points at the base of skull in the form of two indentations. Feel love.
3. Angle wing points at corners of shoulder blades. Feel energy entering eyes.
4. Finger points at the tips of the fore and middle fingers. Feel you are cared about.
5. Toe points at the tips of the two toes next to the big toes. Massage and hold.
6. Duckling point at the base of the spine. Feel your eyes are beautiful.

'Itone' Eye Drops and Rose Water

'Itone' Eye Drops is a preparation formulated from a number of ayurvedic herbs made by Dey's Medical Stores. You can put a few drops in your eyes at the time of going to bed every night. In addition, if you put rose water regularly, it slows down macular degeneration. Rose water can be an effective preventive against cataracts.

Herbs

Saffron: Research has established that saffron rejuvenates the eye's key vision cells. Not only does it protect cells from damage, it also slows and reverses AMD. Patients' vision saw improvement after taking the saffron pill, says Silvia Bisti of University of Sydney.

Camphor: Camphor too is known to improve eyesight.

30.5 CATARACT

Cataract usually occurs in people at an advanced age. It refers to misting or clouding of the lens due to damage from free radicals to sulphur-containing proteins in the lens. Some of the causes are decreased nourishment and blood supply to the lens, HBP and diabetes. Damage may also be caused by UV rays from the sun.

In the event of a cataract, the lens fibres become denatured. With time these proteins coagulate to form opaque areas. The condition is usually corrected by surgical removal of the lens, and its replacement by an artificial lens implanted inside the eye. Even after the cataract operation, the vision may remain cloudy and the distant vision foggy.

Recommendations:

Those who wish to avoid cataracts should take the following measures:

- Vitamin B2 deficiencies can lead to cataracts: Get B2 from milk, cheese, yoghurt, etc.
- Sulphur-containing proteins: Increase the intake of sulphur proteins present in foods like legumes.
- Beta-carotene in foods like carrots, etc., provides protection against AMD and development of cataract. There is truth in the saying: 'munching carrots improves eyes.'
- It was found that those who eat plenty of fruits and vegetables are less likely to develop cataracts. Vitamin C in fruits and vegetables is a very potent antioxidant. Consuming 500mg

of vitamin C lowers cataract risk by 50-60 cent. Consume fresh fruits and vegetables because of their high content of glutathione that is one of the major constituent elements of the eye-lens. Antioxidant glutathione prevents cell damage from free radicals and UV radiation. Get extra glutathione from asparagus, avocados, potatoes and spinach.

- Lutein and Zeaxanthin: You may be better off consuming spinach, kale (karam-kalla), green leafy vegetables, eggs, corn, pumpkin and pumpkin seeds which contain antioxidants lutein, and zeaxanthin known to prevent cataracts. Sweet red peppers also supply lutein and zeaxanthin. Vitamin C and beta-carotene in bell peppers have protective effect against cataracts. These can reduce the need for cataract operations.
- Omega-3: Consuming lots of anti-inflammatory omega-3 lowers the risk of cataract by 12 per cent.
- Avoid a high-glycemic-index diet, exposure to direct sunlight and any other bright light, and wear UV protection glasses when going outdoors in hot sun.
- In a study, it was found that those who ate the most sweets were 20 per cent more likely to have cataracts. And in another study, those who ate lots of sweets raised their risk of AMD by 170 per cent.
- Reduce salt intake. Too much salt can raise your blood pressure and interfere with the state of blood vessels in your eyes. People who eat the most salt, have a higher cataract risk.

30.6 NIGHT BLINDNESS

It is primarily a sign of vitamin A deficiency. Vitamin A helps maintain the optimum level of the light-sensitive pigment present in eyes. Eating lots of carrots can help prevent and rectify the problem. The body also needs zinc to convert vitamin A into a form usable in the retina. We already know that good sources of zinc are black-eyed peas (urad dal), rajma, etc., whole grains and unrefined foods.

30.7 GLAUCOMA (*KALA-MOTIA*)

Glaucoma occurs when the eye is not able to drain fluid properly causing a build-up of eye pressure (tension), which eventually damages the optic nerve that transmits visual messages to the brain.

Glaucoma can either be painful or painless. Painless is more dangerous, and is difficult to diagnose. There are often no obvious symptoms in the early stages. Hence, it is advisable to see your doctor every year after the age of 40. People with diabetes, HBP, and a family history of the ailment are at a higher risk.

The symptoms are blurring of vision, difficulty in adjusting to dark, seeing coloured halos around bright lights, etc. Be warned that acute glaucoma develops rapidly and can lead to drastic loss of sight.

Glaucoma is the leading cause of blindness in the elderly. Early diagnosis is, therefore, necessary. The treatment is simple and involves drugs. Majority of patients are advised to use regular eye drops throughout their lives. Some require laser surgery to reduce pressure in the eye if the drugs are not effective. Chances of suffering from glaucoma are higher in diabetics.

30.8 EAR

The human ear is designed to hear sounds with frequencies between 20 hertz and 20 kilo-hertz. This is known as the audio range. The ear also works to give the body its sense of balance.

The ear is divided into 3 segments – outer, middle and inner. The outer part collects and directs sound waves to the ear-drum. The vibrations caused on the ear-drum are carried into the inner ear. The hollow channels of the inner ear, or spiral-shaped cochlea, are filled with liquid. These fluid canals contain thousands of sensory cells or stereocilia. The vibration of these cells stimulates the auditory nerve connected to the brain. This is how we are able to hear.

A whisper is about 10 decibels, while a thunder is 100 decibels. Listening to loud sounds with intensity above 85 decibels may damage your hearing. Repeated exposure can cause irreversible damage to sensory cells and hearing.

One of the most common problems is loss of hearing due to ageing, and of course, due to damage caused by loud noises. Chronic sore throats also affect the ears.

A diet rich in minerals like selenium and magnesium, and vitamins A (beta-carotene), C, and E has been shown to prevent hearing loss.

The ear is protected by the production of ear wax. Inexpert attempt to cleanse the ear of this wax may either push the wax in, or may cause damage to the ear drum.

Kaan-Rog Nashak Pranayam

The name of the pranayam implies the killer of ear diseases. It involves the following steps:

Fill your mouth with air. Bring your attention to the ear drums. And apply pressure on the drums using the mouth as bellows. Repeat it for a few times for better results.

Do this pranayam regularly. It will protect you from loss of hearing even in old age.

Ear Infection

Throat infection often travels to the ear, causing an ear infection. The best way to clear up a child's ear infection is to take the child off milk, and remove dairy products from the diet. Milk and milk products cause an immune response that results in mucous formation which can cause ear infections.

Putting three to five drops of sesame oil sautéed with cloves cures ear pain.

Section 3
Mind

31

Science Of Body, Mind And Soul

If you follow a regimen of proper diet, exercise and living style as described in the previous chapters, it is most likely that you will never fall ill. And if at all you do fall ill, you will find that you will be able to tackle most of the illnesses without any medication. But still there is no guarantee of not falling ill.

To understand the reasons of falling ill and to be completely free from disease, we have to know ourselves more deeply.

We are well aware that stress and inflammation are the two most common causes of all diseases. We all have reasons for stress in our lives. But more often than not, we ourselves create stressful situations by our negative thoughts and deeds. Spirituality helps us avoid stress, and to cope with it successfully.

31.1 WHO IS HEALTHY?

One is considered healthy if the following conditions are met:

- The three humours of the body, *vaata*, *pitta* and *kapha*, are in balance.
- *Jathragni* (appetite, digestive power and body heat) is adequate.
- Seven *rasas* of the body (digestive juices, blood, flesh, *meda*, bones, muscles, and *virya* for men and *raja* for women) are in right proportions.
- Excretory functions are in proper shape.
- *Indriyas* (senses) and *mana* (mind) are all healthy and working in harmony.

The three pillars of achieving such a state of health are:

1. *Ahaar* (food)
2. *Nidra* (sleep)
3. *Brahmacharya* (virtuous conduct/celibate life)

The other pillars are *vyqyam* (exercise), *snaan* (bath, hygiene, etc.) and dhyana (meditation). Such a healthful way of life increases *oj* or vital energy. An unhealthful lifestyle causes *aam* or toxins and depletes you of your vital energy.

31.2 YOUR DAILY ROUTINE/*DINCHARYA*

To enhance your *oj*, and minimise *aam* follow a programme as follows:

- Adjust your waking time to around 6 a.m.
- To get up, first tilt yourself on one side. Do not get up with a jerk. This is very important for protecting your back.
- After getting up, take 1-2 glasses of warm water without rinsing your mouth. The saliva in the mouth is like an antibiotic for the stomach.
- Then do some brisk breathing, neck exercises, backward bending for the lower back, stretching exercises, etc.
- After this, drink more water at room temperature to help detoxify the system.
- Thereafter, go for either a brisk or a slow morning walk for 45 minutes.
- Follow the walking with, say, 15-20 minutes of pranayam, yogasana and meditation. Meditation follows pranayam almost automatically.
- Now you are ready to take a bath. Once a week, massage your body with sesame or olive oil.
- Wear comfortable clothes so as to allow your skin to breathe. Avoid tight clothes.
- Never skip your breakfast. Your body needs it after 12 hours of night-fast. Your breakfast should be the most wholesome of all the meals.

Start with fruits to obtain minerals, vitamins, natural antioxidants and sugars. Almonds soaked in water are the best food for strengthening your brain and memory. Have a healthy bowl of cereal such as oats boiled in water or milk with honey. You may add to your cereal a variety of health foods like saffron, amaranth (*Ramdana*), cocoa, herbs like *Ashwagandha* and/or *Shatavari*, resins, nuts and ground flaxseeds.

- After breakfast, it is time to brush your teeth the first time of the day.
- Your evening snack and tea should also include some fruit/s.
- Your lunch and dinner may include a bowl of vegetable soup, salads of various kinds, baked/boiled vegetables, chapattis made from whole wheat flour, brown rice and dal/legumes, curds, etc., and a sweet or fruit like orange, water melon, etc.

A glass of red wine with dinner is fine if you are used to taking alcohol. Avoid drinking water at meal times. Take water an hour after a meal.

Your cooking mediums should preferably be mustard or canola oils. Use olive oil in its raw form.

- After a meal, you may sit in *Vajra-Asana*. The posture involves sitting on your feet folded under you and with spine erect. This aids the digestion process.
- After dinner, it is time to brush your teeth the second time of the day.

An hour before going to bed, if you take a warm water bath enriched with lavender oil, it is very soothing to the nerves and promotes sound sleep.

- Sit for a while in prayer and meditation before going to sleep.
- Once you are in bed, put a few drops of rose-water or any other herbal drops in your eyes to cleanse and rejuvenate them.
- Go to bed and get up from the bed at the same time everyday. Reserve 10 p.m. to 6 a.m. only for sleep. About 7-8 hours of sleep is necessary for a healthy immune system and longer life.

During the day ignore anything that isn't useful, beautiful and joyful. Note that balance is the rule of the game of life. Do everything in moderation.

31.3 *ROG* (DISEASE) AND *SHOK* (SUFFERING)

What Causes Disease and Suffering?

It is the violation of the basic laws of nature. If you violate the laws of nature, you receive punishment in the form of diseases and ill-health. But if you lead a pious life, you are rewarded with gifts of good health and happiness.

The first and the foremost *sukh* (happiness) is a healthy, clean body and a peaceful mind. And the first and foremost *dukh* (suffering) is a diseased body.

You may possess all the things in the world, but if even one part of the body is diseased, it could mean unbearable suffering.

Indriyas and *Rog*

God/Nature has bestowed on us five *gyan-indriyas* (organs of senses) and five karm-*indriyas* (organs of karma or action).

The five organs of senses are eyes, tongue, nose, ears, and skin. Their respective sense objects are *roop* (sight), *rasa* (taste), *gandha* (smell), *shabda* (sound), and *sparsh* (touch).

The five organs of karma are organs of excretion, reproductive organs, hands, feet and speech. Our *mana* or mind is the sixth *gyan-indriya*, and the master-indriya as all the sense organs and organs of karma are controlled by it.

We should make the right and balanced use of our *indriyas*. Excessive use, or no use at all, or improper use of our *indriyas* will invariably result in an imbalance leading to ill health and suffering.

31.4 YOUR REAL SELF AND TRUE NATURE

We rarely see the real 'I', the real 'self'', the soul or *atma*. We only see the apparent individual 'I' with the body and the mind. Whatever we call as 'I' or 'Me' or 'I am this' and 'I am that' is formed by the union of *chetan,* the conscious self, and *jada,* the unconscious body. This individual 'I' is not the real self. It is the ego self.

You are neither the body, nor the mind, nor the emotions nor the thought. You are the soul. The controller is you, the *chetan*, not your body, the *jada*.

But remember that the body is the temple in which the soul resides. Serve the body as your temple till the last breath.

The moment you realise this, and learn to separate the self from the body, most of your suffering will be mitigated.

Your True Nature/Your Dharma

Vastu-Swabhava, meaning basic nature of a being, is the dharma of that being. For example, the nature of a scorpion is to bite. Hence, the dharma of a scorpion is biting. If a scorpion bites, it is not committing any sin.

The basic nature of a human being is to love. Hence, your true dharma is love, kindness, compassion, non-injury, benevolence, and so on.

Remain aware of your true nature. If you act against your true nature/dharma, it will be adharma, invitation to disease and suffering.

31.5 SHARIR TRAYI, ANTAH-KARAN AND PANCH-KOSH (FIVE SHEATHS)

To experience our real/true self, we have to transcend the body and the mind. This body-mind fort or temple in which the self resides has three layers comprising five *koshas* or sheaths. These are:

1. Sthool Sharir or gross body.
2. Sukshma Sharir or subtle body.
3. Karan Sharir or causative body.

We are a trustee of our body. It is our bounden duty to purify our three *shariras*.

Sthool Sharir/Gross Body

The Sthool Sharir or the gross body is further made of two *koshas/* sheaths.

(a) Annamaya Kosh, the visible physical body.
(b) Pranamaya Kosh, the invisible pranic or vital energy body.

Annamaya Kosh is the physical body formed by the food we eat. *Anna* means food.

The food is first converted into *rasas* (juices) and *rakta* (blood). Juices and blood may be *sattvic, rajasic* and *tamasic* depending on the nature of food. *Sattvic* food generates feelings of piousness, *rajasic* food generates feelings of arousal, *and tamasic* food generates evil desires. What you eat plays an important part in determining your state of mind.

Pranamaya Kosh is the energy body – an aura, all around the physical body. Prana pervades throughout the body in the form of *pranvayu*, the breath. It is primarily absorbed by lungs through respiration. It is also absorbed from food and water. Fresh food contains more prana than preserved, processed, or stale food.

You also get pranic energy from sunlight and natural surroundings with trees, flowers, hills, mountains, rivers and lakes, witnessing good deeds, meeting pious and calm people, and so on. Look for sources with positive pranic energy.

On the other hand, you can feel depleted of energy by indulging in grief, witnessing evil deeds or human suffering, living in polluted environments depleted of trees, and so on.

It is necessary to insulate yourself from such sources of negative pranic energy.

Sukshma Sharir/Subtle Body

Now, the working of the gross body is governed by the Sukshama Sharir, the subtle body formed by *mana* and *buddhi* components of *antahkaran.*

Mana, Buddhi, Chitta and *Ahankar* are the four wings of our *mana/* mind, which the Self uses to interact with the rest of the creation.

The self uses *mana* wing, with the help of *indriyas*, to sense objects of senses. *Buddhi* wing analyses these sensations whether good or bad, favourable or unfavourable, based on its past memory, that is, conditioning of mind as one may say. *Chitta* wing experiences these sensations, *sukha* and *dukha* of life, as they come.

But, *ahankar*/the ego is the part which clings. It is that which insists on 'me' and 'mine', and 'you' and 'yours'. It wants to cling to favourable and avoid unfavourable sensations. It leaves deep imprints on *chitta* in the form of delusions/*vikaras*, that is, craving/*raag* for the pleasant and aversion/*dwesh* for the unpleasant.

Craving and aversion are two sides of the same coin, the root cause of suffering.

How Do We Respond Then?

We must go through the experiences and just remain aware. We should maintain perfect *samta*/equanimity without clinging to things and emotions. Clinging to them will result in *sanskars* of 'I want it' or 'I hate it'. There is no harm done by *mana, buddhi* and *chitta*. But as soon as *ahankar*/ego enters, the *vikaras*/delusions start tormenting the Self.

All the *koshas* of the body-mind are *jada* i.e., unconscious, and changeable. *Koshas* emerge, sustain and disappear, i.e. they arise, stay and die.

Only the Self that resides in the body is *chetan* i.e., conscious, and unchangeable. Self has no birth and no death. All *koshas* become dead when the Conscious Self leaves the body.

31.6 NADIS AND CHAKRAS (ENERGY CENTRES)

Spine/*merudand* is the central column of the body with nerves leading to and from all parts of the body and the brain.

Nadis

Corresponding to the nerves in the physical body, there are *nadis* in the energy body. *Nadis* are channels for the flow of prana or breath and vital energy. There are 72,000 *nadis* in total but the primary ones are ida, pingla and sushumna.

Ida Nadi, also named Chandra-Nadi, runs through left nostril and left side of spine. Pingla Nadi, also named Surya-Nadi, runs through right nostril and right side of spine. And Sushumna-Nadi runs through central cord/channel of the spine.

All 72,000 *nadis* meet at the *ajna*, referred to as the third eye, and then at the navel. After *ajna*, the left-side ida goes to the right brain, and the right-side *pingla* goes to the left brain, and *sushumna* goes to the brain centre.

Ida or Chandra (Moon) Nadi is the essence of peace and emotions, the right side of the brain. If you have a headache, exhale and inhale through left nostril to cool the nervous system.

Pingla or Surya (Sun) Nadi is the essence of energy and intellect/logic, the left side of the brain. If low in energy, exhale and inhale through right nostril to energise the nervous system.

Face Reflexology – which involves working over *nadis* on forehead/back of the head/face with fingertips – is a way to allow adequate blood to flow to nerves, release muscle tension, de-stress and induce sleep.

Chakras

Corresponding to organs in the physical body, there are chakras in the energy body. These chakras are energy centres whirling like lotuses in a healthy body. The health of chakras affects the aura of a person.

The centres of these chakras, as seen by the *yogis*, are located all along the spine. There are seven main chakras in Yogic tradition as described in the table below:

No.	Chakra	Location	Function & Organs	Diseases
1	Muladhar or Basic	Base of spine	Centre of vitality, bones	Low vitality, lack of courage

2	Swadhisthan or Sex	Pubic area in front of spine	Sexual organs, pelvic area	Urinary, HBP, kidney, sexual
3	Manipur or Navel	Navel region	Stomach, liver, intestines, pancreas	Indigestion, constipation, diabetes
4	Anahat or Heart	Heart Centre Chest	Heart, lungs, thymus gland	Heart disease, asthma
5	Vishuddhi or Throat	Centre of the throat	Throat, thyroid, lymph system	Tonsils, thyroid, asthma
6	Aggya or Ajna	Eyebrows Centre	Pineal gland, Will power	Glands, nerves
7	Sahasrar or Crown	Crown of the head	Brain, pituitary, God connection	Confusion

In Pranic Healing, the healer transfers energy to the chakras of the patient through his own palm chakras.

Solar plexus, the hollow area below the ribs, is considered as a separate chakra.

Spleen Chakra is considered as a separate chakra corresponding to spleen, while at the back of the navel, adrenal glands are felt through a separate Meng Mein Chakra.

The Muladhar or Basic Chakra is predominantly of *prithvi-tattva* or earth element. It represents solids in the body and the survival instinct or courage in the person.

Swadhishthan or Sex Chakra is predominantly *jala-tattva* or water element. It represents blood, water, and sexual vigour, *virya*/seminal fluid in men and *raja*/egg in women.

The centre of the human body is at the navel. All the 72,000 *nadis* meet at navel also. This centre is predominantly *agni-tattva* or fire element. It represents *jathragni*, the fire that burns incessantly in the stomach till the very end of life. By far, life itself depends on the health of the navel energy centre.

The soul is considered to reside in Anahat or Heart Chakra. This chakra is predominantly *vąyu tattva* or air element. It represents human affection.

Vishuddhi or Throat chakra is predominantly *akash tattva* or ether element. It is connected with the Sex chakra. It represents creativity.

All the 72,000 *nadis* meet at the *ajna* at the centre of the eyebrows, behind which pineal, the master gland is located. *Ajna* as the third eye (Shiva-Netra) is beyond all five *tattvas*.

You can look within by meditating on the *ajna* with tongue touching the palate. One can attain will power and other powers/*siddhis* by meditating on *ajna*. *Tratak Vidhi* (concentrating on *ajna*) is a method of developing *ajna*/will power.

Sahasrar or Crown Chakra or Brahma-Randhra is the *dasham dwar*, the tenth door of the body. By meditating on Crown Chakra we can develop a connection with the divine aspect.

Energy flows wherever the attention goes. Sensing the ill health of a chakra, just bring your full attention on that area and breathe on to it, and feel that it is being cleansed and energised with Divine Energy.

Doing pranayam by holding the breath is the best way to open up your chakras.

31.7 SELF HEALING

Law of Self Recovery

Even if you do not undertake any medication, in most cases, Nature will take care of your health and ensure recovery from illness. The body is capable of healing itself at a certain rate depending on the state of your health and age. For example, if you have a wound, it will heal even without the use of antibiotics. Same is the case with any viral infection. But you can speed up the recovery process by taking self measures and some medication.

Law of Life Energy/Prana-Shakti

Life exists in the body only if *prana-shakti*, the life force, is there. A strong life force will not only prevent disease but it will also heal the body faster. For healing, it is very necessary for you to love yourself, not just your body but your real Self, the Being that resides in the body. Do not do anything that will hurt your Being.

If you create anger or bitterness inside you, how will you be at peace with your inner self? Rule of the game of life is equanimity, i.e., maintaining emotional or mental balance under all situations.

Discard Negative Attitude and Invite Positivity

Turmoil in life happens due to our desire to have that which we do not have. If we adopt a negative attitude we blame this on external factors. Thus we further aggravate and perpetuate our suffering. With a positive attitude, we direct our body organs towards heal and greater well-being.

Art Mathias (*The Times of India*, 20 September 2010) was allergic to hundreds of food items including fibre. One day he listened to a teaching on forgiveness and simply decided to adopt a forgiving attitude and bless those who hurt him, instead of harbouring bitterness. He suddenly realised that from that day he could eat many foods which he was otherwise allergic to. Even his skin allergies disappeared.

American journalist Norman Cousins on whom doctors had given up and said he would be gone in a few days, was convinced that positive emotions would help him recover. He simply rented the most humourous movies and began watching them regularly. He could then eventually sleep without taking sleeping pills, was less dependent on pain killers, and so on. He wrote about his experiences and the lessons he learnt from them in the *British Medical Journal*.

- Discard the negative attitude and let positive thoughts fill you with energy.
- Realise that you yourself are solely responsible for whatever happens to you. Nobody in this creation has the capacity to do any harm or even good to you.

- Everything in this world, whatsoever, is ordained by god or by a higher power called Nature. Enjoy whatever is allotted to you.
- Never aspire for anybody else's wealth or possessions.

Depression

Depression is always about something, which you desire, and which is missing in life.

Spending time relaxing with family, and in *satsang*, contributes to your cheerful state, while the company of negative people adds to stress and unhappiness.

Activities such as listening to soft and melodious music, indulging in spiritual activities, reading a book, enjoying a glass of wine with some nutritious snack, having a walk in the garden or woods, or just the very act of deep breathing with awareness can make you happy.

Researchers at Temple University, USA, found that those who had high levels of existential well-being were 70 per cent less likely to have depression.

The Four Immeasurables and Their Enemies

In Buddhist teachings, The Four Immeasurables are:

Mitta or Loving Kindness – Practise loving kindness to overcome anger.

Karuna or Compassion – Practise compassion to overcome violence.

Mudita or Sympathetic Joy – Practise sympathetic joy to overcome hatred.

Samta or Equanimity – Practise equanimity to overcome bias, strong likes and dislikes (craving and aversion).

Practise these states, and you will become a sea of health and happiness. And beware of fake emotions. Do not misunderstand clinging for loving kindness, pity for compassion, being judgmental for sympathetic joy, and indifference for equanimity.

Law of Karma

One can never aspire to be happy and healthy without love. And one can never hope to have love and happiness by letting ego come in the way. You never know when ego appears and in what form. You may be trying to display an ostentatious image of yours, or appearing boastful or underestimating the qualities and accomplishments of others, and so on.

So start living a simple and an honest life giving no room to ego. You can follow these ways to live a mentally and physically healthy life:

- Learn new things. Learning makes us humble. The more you learn, the more you realise that you know very little. You become unassuming.
- Clean your house including your washroom, without the support of any helper/servant. You are an ordinary person like anyone else. Why should you not yourself clean the area made dirty by you?
- Do not order people around, including your spouse, for personal things.
- Donate generously and anonymously. Do not make it look like a favour done.
- Life is about giving and taking. We cannot survive without taking anything from anybody, the food we eat, the clothes we wear, the comforts of home, etc. Every moment of our existence depends on the benevolence of innumerable people. Learn to make this process of 'giving and taking' divine by taking with gratitude, and giving with humility.
- Tone down your voice. Always talk less. Speak correctly and sweetly whenever you have to.
- Lying down grounds the ego. It also de-stresses and lowers BP.

Where is Your *Mana*/mind Actually Located?

Our thoughts and emotions comprise our mind. When our mind is at peace, our body and face appear relaxed. The body and face reflect what we are thinking in our mind.

That means our mind pervades through our entire body. Brain works for the mind as its processor unit.

The gut has a mind of its own. In fact, every cell in our body has its own mind, its own intelligence. It is capable of feeling and expressing thoughts and emotions.

Mind-Body Interaction

Once it is realised that thoughts and emotions are felt in the entire body, it is easy to understand how repressed or stored emotions can create blockages that interfere with the synchronised functioning of organs, nerves, and various systems in the body, ultimately manifesting into physical diseases.

Reiki masters believe that lack of trust and self-acceptance may result in heart problems. Rigidity of attitude makes the body stiff. It may cause joint pains, Parkinson's disease, etc. The real problem is that this 'intelligence', spread all over the body, cannot tell the difference between an actual situation and a perceived thought situation. Thoughts are treated by the mind-body as real. They bring about the same changes as real events. No wonder many diseases root from the mind.

Healing Power of Thoughts/The Law of Attraction

Like things attract like things. In fact, you will become just what you think and feel. Negative thoughts will invite ill-health, while positive thoughts will attract health and happiness.

Visualisation Techniques for Self Healing

When we visualise ourselves to be healthy, calm and joyous, neurons carrying those positive thoughts and emotions begin to flow through our entire body triggering the secretion of healthy hormones, juices and fluids strengthening our immune system.

For example, try this visualisation technique:

Imagine the grace of god falling on your head as brilliant white liquid light. Imagine this light is cleansing your brain and then energising it. Let this light flow into your eyes, all over your face, throat, back-head, neck, shoulders, hands and fingers one by one cleansing and energising them. Follow this process to cleanse and energise your chest, lungs, heart, liver, stomach, intestines, kidneys, bladder, genitals, thighs, legs and feet up to the toes. In the end say: Every cell in my body is happy and healthy.

31.8 RAJA YOGA: EIGHT-FOLD PATH OF PATANJALI YOG

You are two selves – the True Self, free and floating like an iceberg in the ocean of cosmic existence, and the Individual Self, which is not free, and sees only a small portion of present life, becomes frustrated, disappointed and depressed with mundane existence. Raja Yoga gives us the tools to bridge the gulf between the outer world of day-to-day life and the inner world of the Soul. This is the path of Balance/Equanimity.

'Yog' means union, implying union with the Divine. Following are the eight components of Raja Yoga, the eight-fold path of Yog propounded by Maharshi Patanjali: Yama, Niyama, Asana, Pranayam, Pratyahar, Dharna, Dhyana, and Samadhi.

Yama

Yama requires five precepts to follow:

1. *Ahimsa* that is non-violence or non-injury to anyone by body, speech or even mind.
2. *Satya* or truthfulness.
3. *Asteya* meaning non-stealing, not even coveting that which belongs to others.
4. *Brahmacharya* meaning to abide in Brahma, the Creator and the Creation as one. It requires moderation in sense activity, and self control following the path of non-arousal.
5. *Aparigraha*, means non-possessiveness of things.

As every action has an equal and opposite reaction so if you follow *ahimsa*, everyone will be kind and loving to you. Likewise, *Brahmacharya* will bestow on you *oj*, *virya*, glow on face, and good health.

Aparigraha leads to detachment. If you are free from attachment, you are free from sorrow.

Niyama

Niyama involves following five precepts:

1. *Shauch* or cleanliness that is purification of the body and the mind.
2. *Santosh* or contentment.
3. *Tapa* or ability to bear pleasure-pain, profit-loss, respect-insult, victory-defeat, etc., with equanimity.
4. *Swadhyaya* means study of scriptures or holy texts that leads us to the divine.
5. *Ishwar-Pranidhan* or faith in God, the highest truth.

Shauch purifies your body and mind. *Santosh* is your spiritual wealth in comparison to which all worldly wealth is meaningless like dust. With the life of *tapa*, you never feel any *dukha* or suffering. *Swadhyaya*, the teachings of great ones, are your anchor.

By way of Ishwar-*pranidhan,* when you dedicate all your activity in the service of the divine, you become free of all responsibility.

The fulfillment of your needs, thereafter, becomes the responsibility of the Divine.

Yogasanas

Most people practise only asanas, and consider them as Yoga. Without Yama and Niyama, it can only be deemed as a fitness programme and not yoga.

Pranayam

Pranayam is conscious breathing to purify, energise, and harmonise your body and mind.

Pratyahar

Once *mana* becomes *antarmukh*, i.e drawn inward, the *indriyas* become quiet.

Dharna

Dharna, transcendental meditation, involves concentration on an object. *Mana* can be directed on the internal as on one's breath, or on the external as on a mantra, or image.

Dhyana/Meditation

When object of dharna disappears, one reaches the state of dhyana or meditation.

Samadhi

When the meditator just lets go and loses awareness of existence, it is the state of Samadhi.

Scientists have found that the very genes that are turned on by stress are turned the other way by yoga, meditation, and prayer. The mind can turn genes on and off.

In the mind-body game, attend to the mind before you attend to the body.

32

Yogasanas and Pranayam

32.1 YOGASANAS

One is advised to refer to an authoritative text or manual on Yoga and Yogasanas. Refer to the bibliography section for details.

Always end your Yogasana session with Shavasana or Yog-Nidra.

Shavasana or Yog-Nidra

Yog-Nidra is Shavasana with a *sankalp* (resolve) to surrender to the divine. *Shava* means a dead body. For Shavasana, you lie down on your back on a flat hard surface like a dead body. Keep your hands apart a few inches away from the body and palms facing the sky above, and your feet spread out about a foot from each other. Then close your eyes and relax. Relieve your body and mind free of stress. Slowly take a few deep breaths. Make a *sankalp* (resolve) to relax each part of the body one by one. Remember, whatever you suggest to your mind, it will make it happen. Start from feet and move upwards. With the inner eyes of your *mana*, look towards your toes. Instruct them to be completely stressfree and relaxed. Follow this resolve one by one to relax your ankles, calf muscles, legs, knees and thighs.

Slowly move on to relax the upper part of the body starting with Muladhar Chakra lower back, spine, and upper back.

Bring your attention to the navel. Be aware of the breath in the abdomen. Take a few abdominal breaths. Instruct your Manipur or Navel Chakra, the whole abdominal area, to relax.

Say 'My digestive system is healthy and functioning well. There is no tension in the gut'.

Focus likewise on the Heart centre.

Just forget everything, take refuge in your beloved god, and leave yourself completely in divine hands.

Then relax your shoulders, upper arms, elbows, forearms, wrists, hands, fingers and palms one by one in that order. Feel the palms and soles. Feel that all the ills of the body and mind leaving you from palms and soles.

Relax your forehead, *ajna*, eyebrows, eyes, nose, temples, ears, gums, cheeks, and lips. Glance towards your face as a witness and feel it radiating with peace and joy.

Now bring complete silence to the *mana* also. Just let the mind observe your breath, and do nothing else.

Then we reach out to our true 'Self', the soul. Know that your true Self is neither the mind nor the body. You are beyond the senses, beyond *paap* and *punya*, *sukha* and *dukha*. Now allow the soul to be free of the body and mind.

Imagine that you have come out of the body. The body is now lying on the ground as *shava*/dead body. You are observing the body from a distance. You are completely free from the bondage of the body, from the bondage of the world.

Realise that you are an *ansha*/part of the Divine. Your true Self wants to unite with the Divine. Just surrender yourself to the Divine and try to see the vastness of this Creation as part of the Divine.

After a while, slowly return to feel your body. Feel that you are now rid of any health problem you had. Turn your body to left-side. Then slowly sit up.

Yog-Nidra is the best treatment for many health problems. It will bring down your blood pressure and induce sound sleep. Many audios are available on Yog-Nidra. Choose the one from an authentic healer/practitioner.

32.2 PRANAYAM

Pranayam is a method of conscious breathing.

Why We Call It Pranayam?

Because it is not simply air that we are breathing, it is *prana*, the vital life force itself that we are breathing along with air. Prana is present in every cell of the body.

Moreover, breath is the *vaata* element, one of the three humours in our body. *Vaata* provides movement and motive power to all our internal processes.

We can survive without food for days or even months, but cannot survive even for a few moments without prana or breathing.

Breathing correctly will help in overcoming many health problems, particularly linked to stress. Breath is the link between the body and the mind. Further if the body is not well, or if the mind is restless, the breath gets disturbed.

Usually we do not breathe properly. Under stress we tend to have suppressed breathing.

Pranayam is the remedy for many diseases. It ensures adequate supply of oxygen to the heart, brain and other organs. It opens up the channels of flow for breath, pranic energy, blood, nerves, food-digestion, absorption, excretion, and so on.

Pranayam increases lung capacity. Singers and asthma sufferers can greatly benefit from it.

Simple Pranayam

This is the most basic pranayam suitable for everyone.

Research has shown that just by making breathing slower and deeper, more oxygen is taken into the lungs and into the muscles surrounding blood vessels.

Sit in a comfortable position with eyes half-closed and spine erect. An incorrect posture prevents free flow of prana.

The Pranayam involves the following four steps:

1. Inhaling deeply: Breathing in a slow deep manner.
2. Holding the breath for a while.
3. Exhaling completely: Breathing out just as slowly.
4. Holding the breath out for a while.

Note that duration of exhalation should be longer than duration of inhalation as it is more important to breathe out the carbon dioxide and toxins before breathing in oxygen.

Aan-Apan Pranayam

Aan-Apan Pranayam is a simple pranayam which is done without holding the breath. One inhales and exhales slowly and deeply, and remains aware of the silence in the gap after inhalation and exhalation.

Bhastrika Pranayam

This pranayam involves breathing rapidly in and out through lungs without stopping. It is good for cleansing the respiratory, circulatory, lymphatic, nervous and all other systems. It removes toxins from both the body and the mind.

However, those suffering from heart disease and high blood pressure should not do this or any other vigourous pranayam or activity.

Kapal-Bhati Pranayam

'Kapal' means head and forehead, and 'Bhati' means brightness and shine. In this pranayam, all effort is directed towards exhaling and simultaneously pulling the abdomen back. No effort is made to inhale or to push the abdomen forward. The latter processes happen automatically.

Each inhalation and exhalation should not take less than one second. Thus the speed at which Kapal-Bhati should be done is about 60 per minute.

Start this pranayam with five minutes in the beginning and then increase the duration.

This pranayam brings glow on your face. It strengthens the organs at the base of spine, the pubic area and the abdominal region. Thus, it is good for reproductive organs, kidneys, pancreas, intestines, stomach, liver, gall bladder, spleen, and so on. It is an anti-dote to constipation and depression. Many people have reduced their abdominal fat by practising Kapal-Bhati.

Anulom-Vilom Pranayam

Anulom-Vilom Pranayam is done by alternately opening and closing the two nostrils.

Use the right thumb to close/open the right nostril, and the little and ring fingers to close/open the left nostril. Put the middle and forefingers on the *ajna*. Then do the following steps:

Close the right nostril. Inhale deeply from the left nostril.

Close the left nostril and open the right nostril, exhale from it. After exhaling, inhale deeply from the right nostril. Close the right nostril, open the left nostril, and exhale from it.

Continue repeating the cycle as above. In the beginning, do it for a minute. You may slowly increase the duration to five minutes.

This pranayam purifies the nerve channels, balances the right and left brain, opens blockages of coronary arteries, and effects cholesterol and triglyceride levels favourably.

Nadi-Shodhan Pranayam

Shodhan means cleansing. *Nadi-Shodhan* means cleansing of the *nadis*. Nadi-Shodhan Pranayam is similar to Anulom-Vilom Pranayam but with the following modifications:

1. Both inhalation and exhalation are done very slowly, and so softly that the sound of breathing is not heard even by your own self.
2. Hold the breath in after inhalation, and out after exhalation for a while.
3. During pranayam, centre your *mana* behind the *ajna*, in the centre of the head.

The benefits of this pranayam are similar to those of Anulom-Vilom. But in addition, it strengthens the nervous system. It also balances the emotional (right) and logical (left) sides of the brain.

Do Nadi-Shodhan very slowly – at the most two cycles a minute.

Bhramri Pranayam

Bhramar means the large black humming bee. The exhalation sound in this pranayam is similar to that of the bee.

Put your forefingers on the forehead. Close your eyes with the other three fingers. And close your ears with the thumbs. Take a full breath.

Bring the attention/mind to the centre of the brain, the area behind the *ajna*. Now exhale slowly producing the divine sound of '*om*', with '*o*' very short and '*m*' extended making it sound like the humming bee. Do this 5-6 times or more.

This pranayam nourishes and calms brain cells, soothes the nerves, and lowers hypertension/HBP and heart rate. It is very helpful if done just before meditation. It also increase concentration, and is thus, beneficial for students.

Omkar Pranayam/*Om* Chant

Close your eyes and be aware of your breath. Centre your *mana* behind the eyebrows centre. Invoke god with love, prayer and gratefulness. Take a deep breath. Then recite a long chant of OM. Take full one minute or so while exhaling slowly. Observe the movement of your breath in the whole body. Be aware of the stillness, peace and divine bliss in the gap between the chants.

This *omkar* chant is a remedy to all *rog, shok* – diseases and sufferings.

33

Healing and Meditations (Dhyana)

After pranayams, one gets naturally prepared for dhyana or meditation. Dhyana establishes you in your true Divine Self with awareness and equanimity. When you are in harmony with your environment, and also with your own self, there is no room for depression, hypertension and other ailments.

For dhyana or any other pranayam, never sit on a chair with legs crossed. When you sit on a chair with legs crossed, you are your ego self. You block the receptivity of the mind. In addition, you block the circulation of the blood to the heart.

33.1 AAN-APAN MEDITATION OR MEDITATION ON BREATH

The simplest meditation – basis of all meditations – is Aan-Apan Meditation or Meditation on breath. It involves just sitting and watching the breath as a witness (*Sakshi Bhava*). Note that it is not a pranayam. Watching the breath brings awareness.

Sit in a comfortable posture with spine erect, eyes gently closed, tongue touching the palate, hands resting on the knees or in the lap, chest open as if to embrace, and head slightly tilted forward. Let the body be still. If the body is not still, the mind can't be still.

Now just be aware of your breath. Focus entire attention on the area above the upper lip and below the nostrils observing the flow of respiration, the incoming breath and the outgoing breath. Do not try to alter the breath. Just remain aware of the natural breath.

As a result of concentrating, the mind becomes sharp and sensitive. Hence, you may start feeling some sensations here and there in the body. Thoughts may also appear and go. You cannot stop these sensations and thoughts. Just ignore them. As soon as you realise this, bring back the mind to watching the breath.

As meditation proceeds, the breath becomes softer and shorter, so much so that you may not be able to feel it. Nevertheless, maintain awareness of the breath, howsoever subtle it may be.

You may find that sometimes you cannot maintain awareness. Your mind wanders away. As soon as you find that your mind wanders away, take a few conscious deep breaths and bring the mind back to the breath without in any way reacting to it.

Do not be angry with your mind. Accept this as the natural pattern of the mind. In this meditation you become aware of the nature of the mind.

Do not be disappointed with yourself either, since you are not the mind. By simply remaining aware of this, you find that the nature of the mind changes.

33.2 ABDOMINAL AND PRANIC BREATHING

Abdominal Breathing or Sukha Pranayam

When you have a hard task to do or when you have a stressful situation to meet, you generally take a deep breath in the upper chest and then deal with the situation. But when you breathe slowly in the abdomen, you feel relaxed completely.

So whenever you are tense or disturbed or when you are tired, just sit erect or lie down. Put your palm on the navel and do abdominal breathing. Concentrate on the breath, feel the rise and fall of the abdomen with your palm, and relax until you feel fine.

Pranic/Yogic Breathing

Pranic or Yogic breathing is essentially abdominal breathing that enables you to draw lot of pranic energy (*prana-shakti*) from the surroundings.

For the purpose, you either sit with your spine erect as in meditation or lie down on your back on a flat surface. Then do abdominal breathing.

Inhale slowly and retain the breath. Holding the breath after inhalation is called full retention. Exhale slowly and retain your breath out before next inhaling. Holding the breath after exhalation is called empty retention. There is a tremendous amount of prana flowing into the body when inhalation is done after empty retention.

Keep the mind set on drawing *prana-shakti* from the whole cosmos. You also feel energy flowing from the palms of your hands and the soles of your feet. Feel the breath at the navel and in the whole body. Feel each breath is energising you during inhalation and relaxing you during exhalation.

Pranic breathing is the treatment for depression, anger, high BP, heart disease, and so on.

33.3 BREATH HEALING AND SOHAM MEDITATION

Breath Healing

For breath healing, you lie down in Shavasana and bring your body and mind to rest. Then be aware of your breath near the nostrils. Slowly feel the breath in the entire body. It is not just the lungs that are breathing; you find that your whole body is breathing. Remain aware of the breath in your whole 'being'. Now direct the attention to the effected part or organ of the body.

For example, breathe deep into your heart and exhale from there in case of palpitations in the heart or heart problem.

Similarly breathe into your abdomen for abdominal or digestion problem, pubic area for sex problems, base of spine for orthopedic, blood deficiencies or general weakness, knees for arthritis, calve muscles, feet and up to the toes for problems in leg, and so on.

Feel intense love for that part of the body. Feel every inhalation and exhalation in that part. Feel the divine energy flowing in that part/organ with every inhalation and energising it. Feel the disorders exiting, cleansing and relaxing it with every exhalation.

Know that God loves you. Be grateful to the divine for all the good things of life. Be grateful to the divine for the healing.

Soham Meditation

Inhale mentally saying *So---*, taking your head backwards. Then exhale producing the sound *ham*, and bring the head forward till the chin touches the chest. Do it several times.

When you stop, just be aware of your whole body, and the flow of energy in the body. Then be aware of the physical breath, inner peace, inner stillness and divine bliss.

This meditation will take you to deep-sleep theta-state of complete tranquility. For relieving emotional stresses, you can do *so-ham* breathing at fast speed also, but not if you have HBP or any heart problem.

33.4 PANCH-KOSH DHYANA AND SHARANAGATI (SURRENDER)

Sit in a comfortable posture with eyes gently closed, spine erect and head slightly tilted forward. Invoke the divine grace. Following are the five techniques of dhyana:

Anna-Maya Kosha, In Harmony with the Body

Concentrate on the physical body and be aware of each part, each organ. Relax the mind.

Feel in complete harmony with your physical body.

Prana-Maya Kosha, In Harmony with Your Self and Surroundings

Take a few deep breaths. Be aware of the breath near the nostrils.

Be aware of the breath in your brain. Be aware of the breath in your lungs, breasts, and heart. As you breathe your chest expands with immense love and compassion for everyone. Be aware of the breath in your body, hands and feet.

Be aware of your environment. Be aware of the whole universe. You are in harmony with your breath/self and the surroundings.

Mano-Maya Kosha, In Harmony with the Emotions

Bring your attention to the centre of your eyebrows. Feel your *mana*. Be aware of your emotions. Feel yourself in harmony with your emotions.

Say to yourself, 'I surrender my *mana* to the Divine'.

Vigyan-Maya Kosha, In Harmony with Thoughts and Intellect

Feel your *buddhi*, the intellect, in the forehead. Be aware of your thoughts. Feel yourself in harmony with your thoughts.

'I surrender my thoughts to the divine. Let God's will prevail, and not my urges.'

Anand-Maya Kosha, Experiencing the Self, the Bliss

Be aware of your *chitta*, and the Heart Chakra.

Let your heart expand and say that 'I am in harmony with all. I surrender my *chitta* to the divine.'

Be aware of your *ahankar*, the ego, which robs you of your happiness.

Say, 'I am not the Ego Self. I am the True Self.

I am the Soul. I am one with God. I am one with all.

I am pure *ananda*, pure bliss. I surrender my ego to the Divine.'

Sharanagati (Surrender)

Now be aware of the Supreme Self which resides alongside the Self in the heart region.

The self only wants to become one with the Supreme Self.

Say, 'O Beloved One, I seek only your love and joy.'

Feel the love within you. Feel the joy within you. Surrender your whole being to the Supreme Self.

Slowly return to the body. Take deep breaths. Chant OM three times.

End your meditation with *mangal-kaamna*: Let all beings be happy. Let all beings be free from suffering.

33.5 TWIN HEART MEDITATION

Twin Heart Meditation devised by Master Chao Kok Sui founder of Pranic Healing Foundation is based on the following prayer of St. Francis of Assisi:

> Lord, make me an instrument of Thy Peace.
> Where there is hatred, let me sow Love.
> Where there is injury, Pardon.
> Where there is doubt, Faith.
> Where there is darkness, Light.
> Where there is sadness, Joy.
> O Divine Master, grant me that I may not so much seek
>   to be consoled as to console;
>   to be understood as to understand;
>   to be loved as to love;
>   for it is in giving that we receive,
>   it is in pardoning that we are pardoned,
>   and it is in dying that we are born to Eternal Life.

Before starting meditation, join hands near your heart to invoke the Divine. Silently say:

'To the Supreme God, our Father, Mother, Friend and Beloved,

To all saints and great ones, I humbly invoke for divine guidance, divine love, for illumination, divine bliss, help and protection.'

To activate the heart centre, recall a happy event of your life. Re-experience the feeling of sweetness, tenderness and love of this happy event. You are filled with love and happiness. Your heart centre is a centre of love.

Now be aware of your heart centre, and silently say, 'God! Make me an instrument of Thy Peace.' Feel the peace within you.

Raise your hands to chest level with palms facing outwards.

Let the peace within you flow through your arms to your palms. Gently and lovingly, share this peace with the whole earth.

Allow yourself to be a channel of divine love. Feel this love within you. Feel the love flowing from your heart through your arms to your palms. Bless the earth with peace and love.

Where there is hatred, let me sow love. Where there is injury, pardon. Allow yourself to be a channel of divine forgiveness.

Where there is despair, hope. Where there is doubt, faith. Allow yourself to be a channel of divine hope and divine faith.

Where there is darkness, light. Where there is sadness, joy. Allow yourself to be a channel of divine light and divine joy, especially for people who are sad, people who are in pain, people who are depressed. Fill them with light and joy.

'O! My Beloved God! Grant that I may not so much seek to be consoled as to console; To be understood as to understand; To be loved as to love; To be given as to give.

Let every person, every being on earth be blessed with divine sweetness, divine joy, divine love, with inner healing, inner beauty, with divine bliss, divine oneness with all.'

Gently put hands down.

Take a deep breath and chant OM several times. In between two *om*s, be aware of the stillness.

After a few chants, just relax and let go. Continue your meditation. After a few minutes, very gently return to your body.

33.6 DIVINE HEALING

Spiritual Remedies for Divine Healing

We take care of the body and mind with diet, exercise, living style, pranayam, yogasanas and meditation. In spite of this, we fall sick. Doctors are there to treat us.

Sometimes, it is beyond the doctors to help. We may be suffering from very serious problems or incurable diseases. When the suffering becomes so great that one is unable to bear it, then one invokes the Divine. How does one do that?

The only way is that of intense prayer for help and protection, for physical healing, inner healing, surrendering the ego and letting go, and waiting for divine grace.

The primary principle to deserve divine grace is that of giving rather than that of always hankering for receiving. Whatever you want to have for yourself in life, you start giving the same.

If you want to be loved, start giving love to one and all. If you want to be healthy and happy, start wishing that all beings be free from suffering. Cause no harm to anybody either by your body or speech or mind.

We know that it is only by circulation of blood in the body that one can live. Any attempt to stop the circulation by blocking the flow will result in illness and eventual death. It implies from this that one has to maintain circulation of divine energy.

Here are some ways of maintaining this circulation, some spiritual remedies to alleviate suffering and to enhance happiness:

- Sacred vows/resolves (*sankalpa*)
- Austere penance (*tapa*)
- Sacrifices (*tyaga*)
- Recitation of prayers or chanting of names of God (*japa*) or healing mantras
- Charity (*dana*)
- Virtuous deeds (*punya*)
- Compassion (*karuna*) and service (*sewa*)

All these have the effect of either exhausting past negative evil karmas by sacrifices or neutralising them by new positive good Karmas of the present birth.

Reiki Healing

KI is the life force. Reiki is a Japanese word meaning 'Universal Life Force Energy'. The healer taps the healing energies of higher spiritual planes and channels them into the patient. Keeping your fingers together, the hands are placed gently in different positions over the diseased centres in the body, with the intention of healing, beginning at the crown. There are 24 positions in the entire body. For 21 days, first heal yourself giving full body treatment at all 24 points. Reiki on heart has been shown to reduce stress and improve circulation. Consult a professional therapist.

PRANIC Healing

Prana (breath of life) is the life energy which keeps one alive and healthy. In Pranic healing, the healer cleanses the aura and projects prana to the patient.

The healer first scans the chakras or energy centres feeling the aura with palms to know if there is congestion or depletion of energy. Then the healer cleanses the chakra by sweeping the aura with palms at the chakra or organ where there is congestion. The healer then energises the particular chakra by first invoking divine energy to flow through his/her palms and then projecting it on the chakra or organ of the patient where there is depletion.

Generally, the healer should do Twin Heart Meditation first, and invoke the divine help to make himself/herself an instrument of God before doing the healing.

Theta Healing

The healer in Theta healing, relying upon unconditional love of the Creator, does the healing by transfer of energy by touch, and through focussed thoughts to reprogram beliefs held in our conscious and subconscious minds, and through making connection with the Divine.

Note: In Reiki, Pranic and Theta healing, the healer must be a pious soul, and one who has the intention of healing others acting only as an instrument of the Supreme Soul.

Mantra Healing

Mantra means that which can take you out of the flow of life's miseries by awakening the Self. It has great healing power.

The subtlest matter is the sound, the vibration, the energy.

Mantra is usually a word/*naam* or syllable/s by which thought can be fixed on God. Repetitive chanting of mantra, God's name alone or in the form of syllables aloud, silently or mentally with feeling and understanding the meaning, produces vibrations of immense spiritual potency that purify and harmonise the body, mind and the soul. Mantras bring the suffering individual in direct communication with God in prayer, love and surrender.

The prime mantra is the primordial sound OM or any one name out of the innumerable names of God. All bring immediate solace to the suffering soul.

When faced with emotional turmoil and dilemmas, recite Gayatri Maha Mantra:

Om Bhur Bhuvah Swaha
Om Tat Savitur Varenyam
Bhargo Devasya Dhimahi
Dhiyo Yo Nah Prachodayat

(O! The Supreme God!
The protector of life, the eliminator of suffering, the abode of bliss,
The source of all light and energy, the giver of happiness.
The destroyer of all evil, we take refuge in you.
Awaken our wisdom (*dhi*), the sense of discrimination, to show us the way.)

When life becomes unbearable, when one is suffering from life-threatening disease with no remedy whatsoever in sight, the best thing to do is to have faith – in God, in whatever religion you practise.

In Hinduism, the Maha Mrityunjaya Mantra is considered to be an immensely powerful mantra. One can recite one rosary of this mantra, viz., 108 times, to attain peace and health. The mantra, addressed to Lord Shiva, the Three-Eyed One, is as follows:

Om Trayambikam Yajamahe
Sugandhim Pushti Vardhanam
Urvarukamiv Bandhanat
Mrityor Mukshiya Mamritat.

(O! The three-eyed one, the Supreme God, I worship you.
O! The fragrant one, our nourisher.
The way the cucumber is severed from the bondage of the creeper,
The same way, liberate me from death for the sake of immortality!)

To conclude, I would say that the key to a healthy and happy life lies in eating right, breathing mindfully, staying active through exercise, and adopting a positive and compassionate attitude towards life.

Bibliography

Balch, PA and Balch, JF. *Prescription for Nutritional Healing.* Garden City Park, NY: Avery Publishing, 1997

Boericke, Willia and Oscar E. Boericke. *Homeopathic Materia Medica.* US: Kessinger Publishing, 2004

Brandt, Fredric. *10 Minutes/10 Years: Your Definitive Guide to a Beautiful and Youthful Appearance.* Free Press, 2007

Johnson, Richard J; Gower, Timothy; Gollub, Elizabeth. *The Sugar Fix: The High-Fructose Fallout That Is Making You Fat and Sick.* Simon & Schuster, 2009

McIlvenna, Raymond L. *The Pleasure Quest: The Search for Aphrodisiac.* San Francisco, California: Specific Press for the Institute for Advanced Study of Human Sexuality, 1988

Murray, M T. *The Healing Power of Herbs.* Roseville, CA: Prima Publications, 1995

Quillin, Patrick. *Healing Nutrients.* UK: Vintage Books, 1989

Ramneek Wig, *The Miracles of Pranayama.* Delhi: Yoga Enjoyment, 2009

Small, Garry. *The Memory Bible.* Hyperion, 2003

Theodosakis, Jason; Adderly, Brenda; Buff, Sheila; Fox, Barry. *Arthritis Cure.* US: St. Martin's Press, 2004

'Lemon juice may kill AIDS virus: research – AFP'. Available online at http://www.abc.net.au/news/2004-07-12/lemon-juice-may-kill-aids-virus-research/2008356

'Cow's first milk oral spray tackle HIV and H1N1 viruses'. Available online at http://www.techtipspro.com/2009/09/cows-first-milk-oral-spray-tackle-hiv.html

Gray, Richard (science correspondent). 'Eating almonds can help to fight off viruses'. Available online at http://www.telegraph.co.uk/science/science-news/8098656/Eating-almonds-can-help-to-fight-off-viruses.html

'Spoonful of sugar makes infections go down'. Available online at http://www.pakobserver.net/201109/08/detailnews.asp?id=112979

Collins, Nick. 'Sweet drinks reduce stress and aggression'. Available online at http://www.telegraph.co.uk/foodanddrink/foodanddrinknews/7876248/Sweet-drinks-reduce-stress-and-aggression.html

www.ingramcontent.com/pod-product-compliance
Lightning Source LLC
Chambersburg PA
CBHW021957050726
47498CB00001BB/150